RUNAWAY SANTA

THE FESTIVE AND THE FURIOUS
BOOK 2

HEIDE GOODY

IAIN GRANT

1

CHARLOTTE

Charlotte Mitchell was a snowman. A big jolly round snowman.

She gazed down at herself – at her spindly twig hands, her coal buttons, and the tassel ends of her stripey scarf fluttering in an unfelt wind – and wondered if she should really be a snow*woman*. Would that require some snowboobs? She checked herself. Why should the default be snowman and the snowwoman thing require extra attachments? The classic two-blob snowman shape was quite feminine already; almost an hourglass figure.

She was a snowwoman. Let the snowmen make changes to assert their masculinity if they must!

"You okay in there?"

"Huh?"

"Is it all okay?"

Charlotte lifted the VR visor and she was no longer Charlotte the body-and-gender-questioning snowwoman, but Charlotte the regular woman at a stand at the Xmas Expo in the city of Hull.

As Christmas sales manager for a large garden centre, the Xmas Expo was a cornerstone of her working year. Each December, buyers and retailers would flock to this exhibition hall in the waterfront city to pick up next year's hot trends in decorations, celebrations, festivities and food. Tinsel merchants vied with tree manufacturers, with Santa supply agencies, and with a whole avenue of purveyors of puddings, pies, stollen, gingerbread, chocolates and cakes.

Charlotte wasn't sure if she was all that interested in bringing a VR wonderland to life at Hedgelord Garden Centre, but she was here for the full three days, with a room in the hotel across the street, so she felt she might as well sample all the products and sales pitches on offer.

"As long as you're comfortable," said the sales rep from 'Festive Visualisations' (the slogan *Let's make magic a reality* was printed across his polo shirt). "Let's get you back in there. We've got some other customers lined up. We'll put it in Snowball Mode."

"Snowball Mode?" she said and lowered her goggles.

The wintry scene surrounded her once again. This was augmented reality. The VR goggles didn't block out the entirety of the real world but painted over it with cartoonish scenery. The floor was icy white. Nearby tables became snowbanks. Giant candy canes and Christmas trees dotted the landscape. And every person was transformed into a snowman or elf or nutcracker soldier.

There was another snowman in the small fenced off VR arena, wobbling to and fro.

"Snowball Mode," repeated the sales rep. "Pat your hands together."

Charlotte clapped her twig hands but nothing happened. Then she saw the other snowman was making far more airy gestures and a snowball was appearing between its hands. Ah, she thought, pretending to pat down a snowball between her hands. That worked.

The other snowman unleashed their virtual snowball and missed Charlotte by a good distance.

"Ha! Got it!" she said.

She finished her snowball and hurled it. It hit the snowman square in the face and exploded into sprinkles. The customer laughed. It was a man's laugh. He was already fashioning fresh snowballs. Charlotte skipped sideways, circling like a boxer in the ring. The other snowman hurled again and missed again. She lobbed her second one and hit home once more.

"Where does it keep the score?" she called out.

"Fun is the winner!" said the sales rep.

"Fuck that," she muttered. On her wrist, her smartwatch buzzed. She had an app which buzzed each time she swore. Her profanity and her temper were personal problems and she was working on both with the aid of technology. It was definitely a work in progress.

She and her snowman foe bobbed and wove and hurled balls. She spluttered when one struck her in the eye. In retaliation, she knocked the corncob pipe out of her opponent's mouth.

"Uh-oh, here comes Santa!" said the rep in a sing-song voice.

A big cartoon Father Christmas came lumbering from the distance, snowballs piled up in his mittened hands.

"Wait," said the other customer. "We're supposed to fight Santa?"

"All part of the fun!" said the rep.

"Santa's going down!" Charlotte growled.

But Santa was a mean snowball thrower. His arms were a windmill of attacks – Snowball! Snowball! Snowball! Charlotte lost her top hat in the first salvo. She had to be constantly on the move to avoid being demolished by this festive flinger.

The other snowman got in a couple of good shots, but he wasn't moving fast enough. He seemed to be savouring the whole experience too much.

"Shield me," she said and hung close to him while she made her own snowballs and chucked them with considerable accuracy.

The snowman was laughing, even as Santa took him apart, coal button by coal button. But Charlotte, who found she was having a monstrously fun time, kept her focus on making balls and hitting her target.

And then, for no discernible reason, Santa spread his arms and declared "Merry Christmas!" in a huge jolly voice and wandered off.

"Did we win?" said Charlotte, discovering she was panting with the exertion. "Did we win?"

"Fun is the winner!" sang the snowman at her side in a silly voice that matched the reps own.

Charlotte laughed along with him. "Okay," she admitted. "That was fun." She took off her VR goggles and blinked, then had to take a step back. "Jack Hartigan," she said, all humour drained from her voice and her soul.

The other customer whipped off his goggles. There were pink rings from the goggles around his bright and surprised eyes. "Charlotte Mitchell!" he grinned. "What are the chances of bumping into you here?"

"We're both Christmas sales managers and this is the UK's biggest Christmas expo—"

"The Festive Retail Show in Cardiff is getting bigger and bigger each year," put in the sales rep. "We're going to be exhibiting there in January."

Charlotte ignored him. She took another step back from Jack. "I'd say it was a sad and unfortunate certainty that we would bump into each other."

Jack Hartigan. He was Charlotte's opposite number at Bloomers, a garden centre less than a mile away from Hedgelord. If Charlotte had to have a nemesis, Jack Hartigan would be it. He looked at her with that goofy, happy, carefree expression he often employed. Superficially charming, that was Jack Hartigan.

"I thought you were meant to be in Paris," she said. "A romantic Christmas break with your girlfriend, what's-her-face – Methalene."

"Kathryn."

"That's her."

"What's Methalene?"

"No idea."

"We flew back in yesterday morning. I came straight here from the airport."

"Wow. Dedicated. Going to try to get ahead of us with the top buys for next Christmas?"

"I believe we did it this year. No reason we're not going to do it next."

Xmas Expo took place before Christmas and was the premier place for showcasing the must-buy items for the following year. And Jack was right. Their LumaGrid light system, which had lit up a whole street of houses in recent weeks had given Bloomers the march on Hedgelord's frankly paltry selection.

"Well, our VR units are going to be hot properties next Christmas," said the sales rep. "Guaranteed."

Charlotte slapped the goggles into the rep's hand but kept her steely gaze on Jack fucking Hartigan. "No thanks, mate," she said. "I prefer something with a bit more substance."

She backed away like she'd delivered a savage on-stage mic-drop and stalked off.

CHARLOTTE LOVED CHRISTMAS. It was a rare person who didn't. Her love of the season was wrapped up in her own Christian faith, but the joy of the season went deeper than that. The child-like wonder at the songs, the celebrations, the cosy comforts and the anticipation of the big day had never dimmed in her heart over the years. Nonetheless, it was hard to be cheered by hand-crafted wreaths, kitsch ornaments and scrumptious looking treats when one has a surprise encounter with one's chief competitor.

She had been enjoying herself at the Expo so much, but now it was immediately coloured in by the stress and worry of what Jack Hartigan might be buying while he was here. Bloomers had trounced Hedgelord with their lighting displays and there was no reason why they might not do it again. Charlotte was a hundred percent attuned to Christmas, but maybe, just maybe, she was the kind of person to play it cautious.

She moved on.

"Charlotte?" called a voice. "Charlotte? Is that you?"

"Fuck," she said before she'd even seen who it was. If this was a day for unpleasant reunions, who could it possibly be? Maybe one of the many clergy who'd banished her from their congregations for her occasional furious and foul-mouthed – and *totally* understandable – outbursts?

The elf sitting at the high stool by the pop-up mulled wine stall waved at her. For a moment, Charlotte didn't recognise him, which was perhaps forgivable considering the man's face was squashed between a high collared and garish elf jacket (which gave off some serious Elvis vibes) and a towering, fur-trimmed elf hat, and that his cheeks were dotted with big red circles of rouge. But it was the jutting spikes of dark hair and the tight cutesy smile he wore which forced the connection in her mind.

"Alejandro?" she said.

"I know!" he said, giggling. "It's me!"

He held his arms for her to embrace him, as though he couldn't possibly come down from the stool to meet her. And she did go and embrace him.

Alejandro Aramburuzabala had been an elf at the

Hedgelord grotto for several years, right up until the beginning of this December, when he'd been forced to quit when his international work visa had run out. And he'd been a bloody fine elf too! Always cheerful, always welcoming and always on the move. He could caper with the best of them.

"It is so nice to see you!" she said.

"I know!" he said, grinning. "Oh, I love your nails. What is that colour?"

She glanced at her fingernails. It was so rare for a man to notice when you'd had your nails done. "It's plum pudding. I think it's festive."

"I could gobble them up!" he giggled.

She pulled back to admire his get up, far more luxurious than any Hedgelord elf outfit. "This looks wonderful. But you can't work, can you?"

He gave a glorious shrug. "I am not technically working here. I am just passing through. I'm elfing for Irakli Egadze these days."

"Egadze! He's like the number three Santa in the world, isn't he?" she said.

"Number two! I know! He is the best!" said Alejandro. "I'm part of his official elf entourage. He's doing a courtesy visit here tonight, then we're off to Rotterdam. Fucking jet-setting, baby!"

"Oh, Daffyd and the elf team will be so pleased to hear you're doing well," she said. "Can I?"

She already had her phone out and he gladly consented to a photo, adopting a cross-armed rapper pose for her to snap.

"That is the best," she said.

"Come on," he said, tapping the table. "Join me!" He raised his plastic cup of mulled wine. "This stuff is *meada*, er, piss-water, but my company more than makes up for it."

It was a tempting offer and one she could find no reason to refuse. Charlotte hopped up onto a stool and Alejandro waved to the stallholder for two more mulled wines.

2

CHARLOTTE

Charlotte was on her third mulled wine. Her tongue and lips were furred with the sweet tipple and it felt like her insides were now at least fifty percent herbs and spices. But that was fine. Alejandro, young and vivacious and always so attentive, was the easiest of company.

"Do you have time for one more?" she said, waggling their empty glasses.

"One more but no more!" he said. "Don't want me throwing up over the North Sea! And you must tell me about how you managed to get Mr Mickey Bubbles to perform at that charity concert last week!"

She laughed. How had they even got onto that topic? It was a brilliant story though. Having caused considerable upset and no small amount of physical harm to a valued customer while squabbling over lighting displays with Jack Hartigan, Charlotte (with minimal help from Jack) had won the customer back with an impromptu outdoor concert from celebrated Christmas crooner, Mickey Bubbles.

As they waited for their fourth round of drinks to appear, Alejandro opened a little tobacco tin and offered it to her. Inside were little square packages, like small teabags. "It's *snus*. Swedish chewing tobacco," he said. "It's the best."

"No, thanks," she said. "I'll stick to one vice at a time if it's all the same."

He shrugged, pushed a little bag into his upper gum and then, when their mulled wines arrived, Charlotte slapped Alejandro with the details of how they'd got Mickey Bubbles to perform for them. "We blackmailed him," she said, simply.

"You did what?"

"We..." She paused. She wouldn't normally tell anyone this. "We happened to be in Mickey's house and we discovered his secret room of – what can I say? – pornographic Christmas ornaments."

Alejandro shrieked in delight. "Oh, I knew it! I knew it! I had heard about his holly-whipping fetish thing—"

"Also true," she nodded.

"—I fucking knew it!"

"The things people are interested in," she said with a disbelieving shake of her head.

"Oh!" he said, grasping her hand. "Christmas is very popular in all sorts of ways." He gave her a sly, sidelong look. "I have something I want to show you."

"Is it your penis?" she asked, having experienced the things men sometimes felt inclined to show women after several drinks more than once.

"It is not. It is literally better than my penis, and that is saying something, *mi muñeca.*" He produced a phone from his pocket and woke it. "An SD card full of delights. But take a look at this..." He scrolled through what appeared to be many images and videos. "You will like it," he assured her. "It will tickle you."

Alejandro found the video and began playing it. It was a high quality piece, not just a phone selfie. A Santa with a full beard beckoned the camera into his workshop and grotto.

"A promo video?" Charlotte said.

"Not quite, but you like the production values, yes?"

The décor of the grotto seemed familiar. There was a sort of airport arrivals theme to the outer area and Charlotte recognised it. "That's Bloomers. Oh, and that's Seamus, um thingy, their top Santa this year."

"A great actor," said Alejandro.

Santa Seamus pushed through an inner door, and inside was a large fibreglass and fur-covered model of a reindeer. The sound on the video was down low so Charlotte didn't hear what Santa Seamus was saying, but there was a close up of his narrowed eyes, a shot of him licking his lips and then he slapped the model reindeer on its rump.

"Er, what's happening here?" she said.

Santa Seamus stroked the reindeer's fabric tail and then lifted it up. There was a cut to Santa's wide and delighted eyes.

"Oh," said Charlotte, which really was an understatement at the direction in which the video was going. "Oh—! Oh, my!"

"I know!" giggled Alejandro.

"What? He's not going to—?" She stared in horror as Santa Seamus, with his trousers round his ankles, did exactly what she'd feared he'd do.

"Christmas is so very popular," said Alejandro. "A big market for this stuff."

"Really? Fuck."

"Really fuck," he agreed.

"But why would..." She pointed at the video, unable to take her eyes off it. "You are going to share this?"

"Premium porn site stuff, for sure," he said.

"But if this goes public... Why would Seamus do it?"

"For money," said Alejandro simply. "He is an actor. Hard to turn down paying jobs."

"I mean not everyone will recognise that is Bloomers, but that's their Santa. He's a recognisable face. If it became public knowledge that Bloomers' Santa was engaged in—" Her mouth flapped.

"Anal intercourse with plastic Rudolf?"

"Yes. That!" Charlotte's mind boggled, and not just because it was swimming with multiple mulled wines. She was shocked, and more than a little horrified; yet more distracted wondering if she was horrified at the existence of Santa porn or horrified by seeing an old man's old man vigorously pounding an artificial animal butt, and if her horror was a mark of her prudishness or a perfectly ordinary and moral response to this bizarro piece. But above all she was filled with a rushing excitement at the thought of something horribly damaging to Bloomers' reputation existing in the world.

She jumped down from the stool. "Don't go anywhere. You're not going anywhere, are you?"

"Why?" grinned Alejandro.

"I simply have to show this to Jack Hartigan," she said.

Alejandro's laughter rang in her ears as she ran off to find Jack.

3

CHARLOTTE

Finding Jack Hartigan in a huge exhibition hall full of people and all manner of stimulatory excitement was not that easy. Charlotte shut her ears to the charming sleigh-bell infused tunes and ignored every appealing aisle of porcelain Christmas figurines, focussing on the task in hand. In the end, she found him chatting to a purveyor of Christmas cookie cutters. She grabbed him by the elbow.

"I need you," she said and pulled.

"I'm just talking to the—" he began, but her mulled-wine-energised tugging was insistent. "I'll be right back," he smiled at the cookie cutter saleswoman and allowed himself to be dragged away. "What's this all about?"

"I've just got to show you this thing," Charlotte said. "It's going to blow your mind."

"Er, right. Is this like the time when you said reindeer

antler ring toss was going to be the must-have present of the year?"

"Shut up. Walk faster."

Alejandro was still at the mulled wine bar, looking as happy and as self-satisfied as ever.

"Alejandro, this is Jack Hartigan. Jack, this is Alejandro Aramburuzabala." Charlotte had spent two grotto seasons trying to wrap her tongue around his surname and now felt obliged to utter it at every opportunity.

"Er, hi," said Jack.

"Oh! He is a handsome one!" said Alejandro. "He your boyfriend?"

"Absolutely not. He's got a sickeningly beautiful girlfriend of his own."

"I wouldn't call her sickening," began Jack. "I mean, actually—"

"Show him the thing," Charlotte demanded of Alejandro. "Show it to him."

"Show me what?" said Jack.

Alejandro was highly amused. "Charlotte here is a big fan of independent film making."

"Wait till you see this," she said and tried to hide the delight in her voice. But she was desperate to see the look on Jack's face when he was shown a pornographic movie of Bloomers' Santa debasing himself with a toy reindeer in Bloomers' own grotto. Oh, it would wipe the smug look right off his face!

"She likes my movies," shrugged Alejandro. "Let me show you one, but I've got to go soon. I must be on an eight o'clock to Rotterdam with Irakli Egadze."

"Elfing with the top Santas," said Jack, nodding appreciatively.

Charlotte fumed. He should be fearful at this point, worried about what he was about to be shown, not chit-chatting and exchanging compliments.

"Show him!" she snapped.

"Sure!" said Alejandro. "Here is a lovely one. I know you will like it."

He opened a video on his phone. It took Charlotte several seconds to realise it was not the same one. It was another grotto, another fake Christmassy scene.

"What's this?" said Charlotte.

"It's called Turkey and Stuffing," said Alejandro.

The imagery cut to the interior of a grotto kitchen, the usual domain of Mrs Claus, except in this shot the kitchen was empty but for a Father Christmas and a just-roasted turkey sitting on a table. With a horrid jolt, Charlotte recognised the Santa and then the setting.

"Isn't that Raymond, your Santa?" said Jack. "That's the Hedgelord grotto too?"

Charlotte felt that all the blood in her body had drained to her feet and that she would die of shock at any moment. "No, no, no..."

"Yeah, look," said Jack. "You've got the signage on the wall. *Hedgelord*. Never miss up an opportunity to promote yourselves, even once the customers are inside."

"This isn't the video I wanted," she whispered.

On the screen Santa Raymond eyed up the cooked turkey with predatory eyes.

"Such a master actor," said Alejandro. "He did King Lear in a National Trust open air production."

Turkey stuffing, thought Charlotte. "Oh, no. He's not going to—" she struggled to find breath "—penetrate that turkey, is he?"

"Good cinema is about subverting expectations," said Alejandro.

Santa Raymond dropped his elasticated trousers to expose his round hairy bum and then ripped off a large turkey drumstick from the cooked bird.

"He's not going to...?" murmured Jack. "Oh...! *Oh!*" He turned away, shocked, but Charlotte was unable to tear her eyes from the screen.

"Why?" she said, her voice trembling. "Why would anyone do that? Oh, God! Is he actually enjoying that?"

Jack couldn't resist looking back as Santa Raymond ripped off the other turkey leg with greasy fingers.

"No," he said. "He can't put both of them— Oh, flipping heck. Oh, my."

On the screen, Raymond continued his lewd act with the Hedgelord name on the grotto wall directly behind him.

"Who would want to see this?" she demanded of the universe.

"Christmas is very popular," said Alejandro and, with a happy shrug, turned it off.

"Why would you want me to see that?" Jack asked Charlotte, his voice constrained to a squeak.

"I wanted you to see the other one! Fuck!"

"What other one?"

"Santa Seamus doing ... doing things in the Bloomers grotto."

Jack paled in horror. Finally he looked as she had hoped he would, but there was no joy in it now. The Hedgelord video was just as bad as the Bloomers one, if not worse.

They both stared at the happy elf perched on his stool.

"What is that?" said Jack.

"Premium entertainment. World wide web."

Jack shook his head. "But why did you show it to us?"

Alejandro's fur-trimmed hat jiggled as he shrugged. "Charlotte and I were talking kinky things. I had time to kill..."

"This is blackmail?" said Jack.

"No," said Alejandro. "I don't want anything from you. This is my business model. Making movies, *mi tesoro*. Me and my little camera. A world of Yuletide wonders on my little SD card to be released globally in time for Christmas."

"You can't..." breathed Charlotte.

"Of course I can." He giggled.

Jack reached suddenly for the phone but Alejandro leaned out of reach. "Uh, uh, uh. *Muy macho*, Jack, but do not get violent. The security here will not approve."

"We can't allow this," Jack said to Charlotte.

"It could ruin us," she agreed.

"No," said Alejandro. "You might have to lay off the Christmas stuff for a year or two, but garden centres will always survive. Where else will the British people get their little plants and their little lawnmowers?"

Lay off the Christmas stuff? A year or two? Charlotte was reeling.

"No fucking way," she said. "We can't allow it. That card? Your SD card. It's the only one?"

"Maybe," said Alejandro, which was as close to a 'yes' as Charlotte could hope for.

"I'll buy it off you. I'll pay you to delete the video."

Alejandro frowned, but with a coy and playful expression. "Each of these videos represents a night's filming. Hours of work. Lighting. Sound. True filming costs money."

"I'll pay," said Jack, firmly.

"A thousand pounds," said Alejandro. "Each," he added, in case there was any doubt. "Bring me a thousand pounds cash and I will delete your videos."

"Videos?" said Charlotte. "Santa Raymond did more than one?"

"The man is a powerhouse. He does this thing with a Christmas pudding and the custard. It's pure artistry, I tell you."

"Cash?" said Charlotte, wondering where on earth there might be an ATM nearby. "Now?"

"Tick-tock," said Alejandro. "I can't wait here forever."

Charlotte didn't want to go. She didn't want to leave Alejandro with the power to destroy Hedgelord in the palm of his hand. But she needed to. And a thousand pounds, even if she had to get it out of her personal account, was a small price to pay to save her beloved garden centre.

With one final look at Jack, she ran off.

4

CHARLOTTE

Exhibition centres were stupid, thought Charlotte.

This place literally spent half its year hosting events where people gave money to vendors and exhibitors. For half the year it was effectively a great big shop. It should be geared up for people who wanted easy access to money. Yes, everything was cashless and digital now, but still, there should be at least one functioning cash machine in the place.

She'd done a frantic circuit of the hall and found two standalone cash machines, the kind that charged an extra fee for the privilege of getting your own money out. One declared itself to be out of order, the other wasn't even plugged in.

"Fuck!" she fumed and her smartwatch buzzed at her in response.

She found an event steward in a hi-vis tabard and asked him if he knew where there was a working cash machine. He thought about it lazily, then suggested she might find one on the Prince's Quay shopping centre up the road.

Charlotte ran out into the lobby and outside. Night had fallen hours ago, and a cold wind swept through the streets. The expo was winding down and there was a growing queue of people at the taxi rank outside, cluttering the pavement. She looked at her watch. It had gone seven o'clock. That bastard Alejandro had said something about being somewhere at eight. She had no time.

She ran up to the big indoor shopping centre along the road. The doors were shut, the interior dark.

"Fuck!"

Maybe there was another entrance. Maybe there was a bustling high street round the other side with a handy bank – an actual bank with proper ATMs. She ran on. There was no bank in the street round the corner, only nail salons, hairdressers and a gaudily-lit little corner shop. The shop did however have a little cash machine inside, a clunking chuntering thing that would only give out three hundred quid at a time and charged her two pounds for the pleasure on each occasion. Charlotte had to draw it from separate accounts but, ten minutes later, she had a thousand pounds in her hands and was running back towards the exhibition centre.

She was sweating and had a stitch in her side when she got back to the Xmas Expo hall.

"We're closing soon," said a steward as she tried to go in. It was the same one she'd asked about cash machines.

"I'm just going back in for a minute," she said and waved her bundle of money in his face.

He relented with a shrug. He didn't really seem to care.

It took her a moment to orientate herself and head towards the mulled wine bar. She slowed as she neared. The little high table on which Alejandro had sat was empty. He'd gone. The owner was collecting plastic cups and packing away. The only evidence that he'd been there was the remnants of the soggy tobacco pouch he'd been sucking on.

"The elf..." Charlotte panted. "The elf that was here..."

The owner nodded. "Went off with some Santa five minutes ago."

"Irakli Egadze?"

"I don't know what that means," said the owner.

"No. No, no, no. He was here. He said he was going to be here."

The owner gave her a helpless look.

Charlotte thought. What had he said? Alejandro had mentioned not wanting to throw up over the North Sea. Something about catching the eight o'clock to Rotterdam. Hull was a port city. Ferries ran out from here.

"Where's the ferry terminal from here?" she asked the mulled-wine woman.

"Dunno. Sorry. I'm from Leicester."

Exasperated and wishing she had more physical stamina, Charlotte ran outside again in search of a taxi. The queue for taxis was still there but her need was greater than anyone else's because her garden centre, her career, everything that she cared about depended upon it.

"Fuck," she muttered. Her smartwatch buzzed at the profanity.

A taxi pulled away and another slid forward.

"Excuse me!" she yelled. "Medical emergency! I need a taxi to take me to the hospital. My, er, dad's just been taken off life support."

The crowd sagged back, murmurs of sympathy drifting over.

She climbed in the back and sighed with relief. "Ferry terminal, please."

"P&O Ferries?"

"Yeah, whatever. Fast as you can, I need to catch someone before they leave."

The driver turned and frowned. "You don't want the hospital then?"

She felt briefly awkward that he'd heard that. "I'll go there later. Dad won't mind."

The taxi drove through the city, the Humber River always just behind buildings on her right. What should have been a quick taxi ride seemed to be punctuated by more temporary traffic lights than any one city had a right to.

Panic and fury and a desire to scream and shout coursed through her. She tried to remember the techniques she'd used over the years to control her temper, but even just thinking about taking long slow breaths caused her to huff with irritation. Sometimes it was better to wallow in the anger.

As they drove she tried her best to look at the situation practically. She would either get to Alejandro at the ferry terminal or she would ... well, she would buy a bloody ticket to Rotterdam and then search the ferry high and low for the bastard.

Alejandro might have been a former employee but she

didn't keep his contact details in her phone. She sent a quick message to Daffyd. If anyone was going to have details for Alejandro it would be Hedgelord's chief elf-wrangler.

She then searched the internet. Alejandro had no presence she could find, but then she looked up Irakli Egadze. The champion Santa from Georgia had a significant social media following and within minutes she had an inkling regarding Irakli's future plans. It seemed that Irakli Egadze (and possibly his elfing retinue) was booked for one of the most coveted of the Santa gigs: a week in Rovaniemi, the capital of Lapland.

So, it was Hull to Rotterdam, then on to Lapland. Irakli and Alejandro would probably be travelling first class all the way.

It was seven forty. "Fuck," she growled. The taxi driver looked at her in the mirror.

She needed to get to the terminal before boarding, then somehow persuade Alejandro to hand over or delete the video footage. Her mind veered away from the question of how she was actually going to do that. She had to remain confident in her ability to say the right thing when she caught up with Alejandro.

The taxi was now approaching the ferry port. They passed under a road tunnel and came up to an unbeautiful but well-lit building with *Port of Hull* across its side. Charlotte leaned forward, trying to glean clues from the signs which directed cars towards the ferry. Alejandro would be a foot passenger, as far as she knew, so he would be inside the terminal building. High up, a covered walkway connected the top of the building with a waiting North Sea ferry. The taxi driver pulled up and Charlotte got out her card to pay him.

"Want me to wait?" he asked. "You will go to the hospital?"

Charlotte was too wound up with stress to continue with the lie. "No. Thank you."

She hurried into the building and looked around. There was nobody to be seen in the first open space, but what did that mean? Did ferries work like airports where they would shunt you through into different areas as they processed you like sheep?

She approached the reception counter. "How can I find out about whether a passenger has boarded the ferry?"

The woman smiled. "Have you tried calling them?"

"I don't have their number."

"I'm afraid that data protection prevents us from sharing personal information. Is there anything else I can help you with today?"

Charlotte glared at her. The phrase 'anything else I can help you with' implied that she'd already received help, and that was definitely not the case. "Where is everyone? Can I go and look for this person?"

"Do you have a ticket for this sailing?" asked the woman. "I can check you in if you like?"

Charlotte clenched her teeth. Actually getting on the ferry wasn't an option because she wouldn't be able to get through passport control. Who brought their passport with them when they were just attending an industry conference in Hull. However, if she had a ticket she could move further through the building, that was the deal.

"Can I please buy a ticket?" she asked.

"Yes, of course. You are very lucky, there are only two left."

There was a clattering of footsteps behind her. She looked round and saw a slightly out of breath Jack Hartigan hurrying to the counter. He was attempting to get to Alejandro for the same reasons she was.

"Jack fucking Hartigan!" she muttered.

"What was that name again?" asked the woman at the counter.

Charlotte's thoughts came quickly as she spun back round. "I'll need both of those tickets please."

He appeared at her side at the counter. "Hello Charlotte," he puffed. "Fancy seeing you here!"

She gave him a brittle smile and focused on completing the purchase of the tickets. She tried to pretend that his annoying, smiling face wasn't there at all, but she could see the woman on reception found him charming, as so many people did. Yes, on paper, his face had that superficial appeal, with a nice smile and soft eyes, but it was all part of that smug male big dick energy he had.

"Are you paying with a card?"

Charlotte presented her Hedgelord credit card. There might be questions about the nature of her spending but she would tackle that later.

As soon as the payment was confirmed, Charlotte felt confident to address Jack Hartigan. "Sorry to say that I just bought the last ticket."

"What?" he said.

"Last ticket for this ferry so I guess it's goodbye. In the

words of the proverb, I don't have to outrun the bear, I just have to outrun you."

If she'd been hoping for his face to fall, she was disappointed. He continued to smile in that annoying way that he had. "Bear huh? I was hoping for a word with Alejandro, that's all. Same as you."

"Not the same," she said. "I want him to delete one video off that card. One. My video." Charlotte gave a tiny wave of faux apology. "Last tickets though. Sorry."

"Boarding is now taking place," said the receptionist. "Passport control is just up the stairs there."

Charlotte felt her stomach lurch. "But I can pop through here, before I check in, can't I? Just go into the, er, lounge?"

"No. Passport control is before the lounge. Just around the corner and up the stairs."

Charlotte could feel the eyes of the receptionist and Jack Hartigan on her. She needed to maintain a poker face while she came up with a solution to this.

"Excuse me for one moment, I think I left something outside," she said.

She went out through the swooshing automatic doors, walked around the corner of the square brick building, and screamed with frustrated rage into the bushes at the side.

"Fuuuuuck!"

5

CHARLOTTE

One fuck wasn't enough. She kicked the building, scuffing her shoe and making her toe sore. "Fucking bollocks!" It still wasn't enough.

"Hey!"

She turned to see Jack, standing in the cool streetlights. He had come to gloat. It was only to be expected, she would have done the same.

"You're annoyed," he said.

"Go to the top of the fucking class!" she roared at him. "Stop looking at me! Who said you could look at me?"

"I'll stop looking at you if you answer one simple question. Would you like to get onto this ferry?"

"Yes!" she spat. "Well – obviously no. I do not want to go to Holland."

"Do you want help in getting onto the ferry?"

Why was he doing this? "I want what you want – something like what you want – which is to get hold of

Alejandro, and probably beat the living crap out of him at this point, but there are rules and even you cannot somehow charm the security people into letting me through without my passport."

"No, but I do have a suggestion. Do you want to hear it?"

She wanted to kick the wall again, simply because he was being all reasonable and she was compelled to say yes to his reasonable question. How did he get to be so smug? She looked at her watch. It was ten to eight. "Fine. Yes, I want to hear it. Impress me."

"It just so happens that I have two passports in my pocket. It just so happens that you have two tickets. Can you see where I'm going with this?"

"Oh fuck off, Jack. I can see exactly where this ends. You think it would be really funny if I was arrested for trying to travel on someone else's passport, don't you?"

"Not at all. I think it's very possible that you could pass as Kathryn."

"Girlfriend Kathryn? You have said on many occasions how wonderfully face-smooshingly beautiful she is, so no, I don't think I will pass as Kathryn. Because I am a fucking furious and possibly drunken mess, in case you hadn't noticed."

"Not at all," he said, leaning in to examine her face. He lifted his hands until they almost cradled her chin. "May I?"

"Uh huh?" she said, unsure what he planned to do, but too surprised to refuse.

He tucked her hair behind her ears, took a beanie hat out of his three-quarter length coat and put it onto her head, then he stepped back to look. "Do you have a lipstick?"

She rootled in her bag and wordlessly passed him her lipstick. He applied it to her lips with much more expertise than she expected, then added a couple of tiny dabs to her cheekbones, spreading the colour gently with his thumbs. He smiled and snapped a picture with his phone. "Look." He held it up alongside the passport that he'd pulled out of his pocket.

"Fucking hell." Charlotte saw immediately what he'd done. Her own hair was a similar shade to Kathryn's, but by removing it from her face and highlighting her cheekbones, he had made her face a little broader and more like Kathryn's. "You some sort of makeover wizard?"

He gave a small bow as if she hadn't meant it in a mean and sarcastic manner. Maybe she hadn't?

She huffed loudly. "So, we're teaming up, are we?"

"Yay," he suggested in a small but delighted voice.

"Fine!" she said as she slumped forwards towards the terminal building. "Do me a favour though? No more *yay*. You sound like a teenage girl."

Back inside, they followed the signs for *Ferries* and *Security*. They were about to do something illegal. Very illegal. Travelling on false passports. That was like go-to-prison illegal, wasn't it?

"Fuck," she whispered. Jack held her arm and supported her.

Passport control was ahead. It was just a snaking barrier to funnel people past two little booths, only one of which was manned. Charlotte could feel her hands shaking. She needed distraction. She took out her phone and called Tom Eccles at Hedgelord. She needed to call someone at work anyway. Her plan to leave Hull first thing in the morning, drive straight down the A1 and get to work at a reasonable time seemed increasingly unworkable.

As Tom's phone rang she realised her suitcase and all her things were in her hotel room back in the city. If they did get stuck on a ferry to Rotterdam, there was zero chance of her being back before check-out time. What would happen? Would they charge her further days? Would they turf her stuff out of the room? What kind of state had she left the room in?

Jack handed over the passports as Tom's voicemail clicked in. The woman in the passport booth was looking at the passports and then at them. Did they do that? Did they really do that? Or did they only do that when it was obvious that someone was using a false passport?

The voicemail beeped.

"Oh, hi Tom," she said "It's me ... Kathryn. Just needed to let you know that I'm going to be late in tomorrow. Or possibly not in at all. Look, everything should be fine. No special events on. We've got the princess carriage rides thing and the children's tea party on Friday. Oh, and Santa Paws. But tomorrow, everything should be fine. The grotto should tick over by itself."

The woman at passport control held Kathryn's passport in her hand and gave Charlotte a steely glare. Charlotte swallowed hard.

"You shouldn't use phones in this area," said the woman and handed the passports back.

"Thank you," said Jack, taking both of them.

They hurried on, along the walkway. Up here they could

see the twinkling lights on the far side of the mile-wide estuary. There were ferry staff waiting at the airlock-like doorway high up on the side of the big ship.

"Cutting it fine, aren't we, mate?" said one. He briefly inspected their tickets and waved them through.

"Let's split up and look in all the public areas," said Jack. "Whoever finds Alejandro texts the other one."

"Oh no. I'm wise to your game," said Charlotte. "If you find him you won't let me know. You'll do the deal and try to get off the ferry, leaving me sailing off to Rotterdam like a lemon."

He eyed her. "I would not do that. But I take it, now you've voiced the idea, you definitely would. Let's go round together and check the public areas, shall we?"

It didn't take long to establish that Alejandro was not to be found in the lounge or the bar or the restaurant areas. They even looked in the children's playroom and the small cinema. He should have been easy to spot. He was an elf. He was travelling with other elves and a Santa, and even if they had got changed, a big beardy world-class Santa would not be difficult to spot.

"He's in a cabin, getting some sleep," said Charlotte. "Right. So, we start knocking on doors?"

There was a muffled blast of the ship's horn.

"Are we leaving?" said Jack.

Charlotte looked out a window to see if she could spot any movement. "Are we? But we haven't found them."

Jack stared at his phone. "And there's another reason we didn't find him."

Something in his tone made her scoot across to look at his phone. "What?"

He held up the screen to show her. It was an update from Irakli Egadze's official social media feed: a short looping video of the tall, handsome Santa against the night sky, giving a big thumbs-up to the camera before climbing into an orange helicopter.

"Irakli's making a short visit to friends before his onward travel towards Lapland tomorrow evening," read Jack.

Quite visible in the video footage, Alejandro the elf grinned hugely at the camera before climbing aboard.

"That was their eight o'clock," said Jack. "Not a ferry."

6

CHARLOTTE

"A fucking helicopter!" hissed Charlotte, staring at the phone in Jack's hand. "How is that even possible?"

"Er, he's going to visit one of the Dutch oil rigs, meet the workers and spread Christmas cheer. It says."

"He's Santa, not Taylor Swift!" she snapped.

Jack sat down in a lounger. "I think it's nice that someone can enjoy a bit of the rock star lifestyle, especially in their later years."

"For a man, you mean? Absolutely. All you'll need to do is grow yourself a beard, flash your nice smile at the kiddies, and *boom!* you're riding around in helicopters."

"You think my smile is nice?" he said, a twinkle in his eye.

"Fucking *stop* that twinkling," she growled. "I see you! How do you even do that? I bet Kathryn loves it when you twinkle at her. But I'm telling you now that I'm immune, so you needn't bother."

"Well, don't forget you need to practise being Kathryn for when we go through passport control," said Jack.

"I aced it back there," said Charlotte. She had swept through with maximum confidence.

"Nobody cares when you're *leaving* the country," said Jack. "It's the country you're *entering* that will scrutinise you more closely."

Charlotte frowned. He was right. "Yeah. Fine. Here goes then, this is me being Kathryn." She affected a shrill voice. "Oh hi! I just got back from Paris! Yeah, I know my taste in men is highly questionable, but otherwise I'm a regular person."

Jack made a chopping motion with his hand to stop her. "No, no, no. Are you on helium? She has a deep voice, and she would never say 'Oh hi!' She's more like one of those people who is happy to be quiet until she has something to say."

"Eh? What does that even look like?" Charlotte asked. "Quiet and mysterious? Quiet and confident?"

He thought about it. "More like quiet and adorable."

That made no sense, and was more than slightly nauseating, but Charlotte said nothing. "What else then? Do your impression of her."

Jack took a large swig of wine. "Fine. She sounds like this." He drew himself together, exuding feminine charm. "I can't get enough of this pâté, Jack." He finished with a cutesy little wiggle of pleasure.

"And in that sentence 'pâté' is most definitely a euphemism, yes?" Charlotte asked.

"No," said Jack. "Kathryn is a woman who can derive sensual pleasure from actual pâté."

Charlotte blinked and felt briefly envious. "Right, yeah."

"You do it now," said Jack.

"Gonna need more wine than this."

"More wine?" he said.

She looked about and saw the nearby bar. She wondered what ferry bar prices were like. That said, she had a thousand pounds in cash in her purse and they didn't take sterling in the Netherlands. Best spend some of it now. She needed some alcohol to get rid of the mulled wine taste from her mouth and to head off a mulled wine hangover, which she assumed was like a normal hangover but with extra cloves.

"Wine. I need wine," she said.

"And two glasses," said Jack.

An hour later, Charlotte put her glass of wine down on the table between them. "Ready?"

Jack nodded, pointing silently at his phone to indicate he was recording.

Charlotte tried to channel what she thought Jack's girlfriend, Kathryn, might be like. She tried to enhance her cheekbones with a subtle pout, but was afraid she'd overdone it and gone full duckface. She dialled it back a little.

"I can't get enough of this pâté, Jack," she said in a huskier voice than her natural one. She didn't forget the little waggle dance that went with it. She shimmied her shoulders for good measure.

"Great stuff!" said Jack. "Let's take a look. If you really were Kathryn, you'd have grabbed the phone and be running it through favourite Instagram filters by now."

They watched the recording. The bar was much quieter now, as those with cabins had gone to get some sleep. The wine was palatable and flowed easily as they worked through the task in hand.

"The face isn't bad," said Jack pointing. "You need to work on the voice a bit. She doesn't have a Midlands accent."

"Neither do I," said Charlotte with a frown. "My accent is very neutral."

He pulled a face. "If you say so. Practise saying pâté without opening your mouth wide for the last part, I think it will do the trick. Kathryn always says that people who open their mouths too wide are likely to catch flies. She's pretty funny like that."

"You giving me fucking elocution lessons?" Charlotte thought Kathryn sounded like a nightmare.

"Just try it. We'll go again, yeah?" Jack lifted his phone.

Charlotte scowled at the camera. "Pâté. Fucking pataaaaaaay!" She straightened and delivered the Kathryn line again, as suggested.

"Oh. My. God. It's like she's here in the room," said Jack. "I'm sending that to my sister. It'll make her scream."

Charlotte swirled her wine. "Is it weird that I actually really want some pâté now?"

Jack tapped his phone as he sent the message.

"Will Kathryn be mad about me using her passport?" Charlotte asked.

Jack didn't look up.

"I'm taking that as a 'yes'," she said. "I will refrain from altering her picture with a biro, you can tell her it's in safe hands."

"Yeah, about that."

"Yes?"

"It's not like we're actually together anymore." He still wasn't meeting her eye.

"What?"

He looked up. "We're not together anymore."

"But you just went away together."

He nodded. "She broke with me. Split up. Consciously uncoupled."

"She dumped you? Fuck. She at least do it in a nice way?"

"Is there a nice way? We were on the Pont Des Arts. You know – the bridge with all the padlocks that lovers put there to symbolise their eternal love. A crisp December morning in Paris, walking with my love with scarves and warm coats on and maybe thinking of exploring the little book sellers on the left bank before going to get a hot drink. I took out the padlock I'd brought with me, inscribed with our initials. And she put her hand on mine and said, 'Best not, Jack dear.'"

"Ouch. Cold. She tell you why?"

Jack sighed. "She said I just don't sparkle like I used to. She didn't really explain what that meant."

"Fuck." Charlotte thought for a moment, then her head snapped up. "Another video. Come on." She waved an impatient arm at his phone. "Let's see if I've got the hang of Kathryn."

Jack raised his phone, filming her, a questioning look on his face.

Charlotte summoned her Kathryn face and her Kathryn voice, banishing those imaginary longer vowels. "Jack, you twat! Don't you dare be happy, I forbid it. I am gonna make you wish you'd never been born. Sparkles? There will be no sparkles on my watch!"

Her voice almost collapsed with the artificial growl she'd given it, but she made it through to the end.

Jack grinned at her. "I see what you're doing. Trying to make me feel better. Thank you."

"Send that one to your sister," said Charlotte. "I get the impression your sister's not a big Kathryn fan. She might enjoy it."

7

ANIKA

At a quarter to midnight, Anika Chowdhry was sitting with her parents in their lounge. The decorated no-needle-drop Christmas tree in the corner filled the air with its soft pine scent. A box of Dairy Milk chocolates was open on the little coffee table. The film *Die Hard* was on the television.

Die Hard was one of the few Christmas traditions they had developed which everyone seemed to like. Anika's dad liked the violent action (which was quite tame by modern standards). Anika's mum apparently had a soft spot for Alan Rickman's oozily charming villain. Anika liked the bad old-fashioned haircuts.

As usual, her father had command of the seat which sat square on to the television, remote controls arrayed at his side. She sat with her mother on the settee. Now she was an adult, Anika recognised the subtle reinforcement of gender roles, but she would never bring it up directly with her parents as they'd take it as a personal attack on their marriage. She might attempt to gently steer them, though. She'd installed an app on her mum's phone which allowed her to select television programmes. It had shaken up the dynamic a little, but they had absorbed it into their routine with minimum conflict. It simply meant they now watched more cooking programmes than before. Working with their established habits and beliefs had worked well.

Anika's phone buzzed. It was a message from the Hedgelord Grotto WhatsApp group. She frequently muted it, but never for long. She might work at the garden centre Santa's grotto six days a week, sometimes seven, but that didn't mean she had to live, eat and breathe elfing.

A message from Daffyd, her line manager, read: *This is what a truly professional elf looks like!*

Under it was a photo of a skinny man in elf gear throwing some sort of gangsta arm gesture at the camera. Anika wasn't entirely sure what to make of it. Sure, the guy had a big friendly smile, always key for good elfing, but apart from that and the weird arm gestures, which she was certain was some kind of cultural appropriation, the only difference between this fellow and Anika herself was the quality of the elf outfit she had been given.

Sophie, who split her time at Hedgelord between elfing and working in the Pagoda Café, dropped an *Oh, Alejandro!* and a heart emoji into the chat.

Anika put the phone face down on the arm of the chair and returned her attention to her laptop.

Anika's decision to work at Hedgelord and, as far as she was concerned, not go back to uni after Christmas was something her parents still hadn't fully accepted. They had very strong views about the value of education, so Anika had to feed the idea that a fully rounded person should have more than simple academic achievement under their belts.

"I'm composing a summary of the skills I'm picking up in my job," she said to them, with a wave at her laptop. "Want to hear what I have so far?"

They both nodded. Her father paused the television. Mr Takagi was about to get shot by evil Hans Gruber.

"I will get them to build this into the letter of commendation they promised," said Anika, "but the bullet points I have so far are like this." She read through them:

- *Demonstrated excellent skills handling difficult customers*
- *Applied excellent problem-solving skills*
- *Has shown much flexibility and initiative*
- *Confident communicator*

"WHAT DO YOU THINK? Sounds good, huh?"

The two of them nodded.

"They sound very good," said her mum with a smile. "If they put those in a letter then that will stand you in good stead."

"It's not bad," said her father. "Not bad at all."

Anika frowned. "What? Is there something missing?"

Her dad shrugged. "It's a good basic grounding. Of course

you are too young for any kind of leadership. Demonstrating leadership would be a useful thing. Of course it can't all come from a simple job at a garden centre."

Anika bridled. She had moved mountains at Hedgelord! She'd engineered solutions that had saved the day! As she thought about how to counter her dad's comment she realised her work had been very much behind the scenes. She couldn't even tell her parents, because not all of it had been strictly ethical. Or legal. Still, she was stung by the comment.

"Leadership," she said. "Maybe I can do something."

"They might let you work on the front desk perhaps?" offered her mother.

Anika nodded. Her mum meant grotto check-in, which she'd already done on a number of occasions, but leadership to Anika meant something more. She would have to watch out for an opportunity. Maybe a gap in the garden centre leadership would arise.

Her dad unpaused the TV. Alan Rickman's Hans Gruber raised his pistol and shot the CEO of the Nakatomi Corporation. Poor Mr Takagi!

8

CHARLOTTE

Rotterdam. Morning.

Charlotte knew it was unlikely to be true, but it seemed very much the case that Dutch morning sunlight was far brighter and more painful than the greyer British variety.

She tried to ignore the hangover, but it was a monster. It hadn't been the biggest drinking binge of her life, but it combined with the stress and weirdness of the situation, the uncomfortable seats where she'd attempted to sleep, and the fact that she had no access to headache pills, toiletries or a decent cup of coffee.

"Fucking ferry," she moaned as the few foot passengers walked or cycled away from the terminal building.

The actual ferry building appeared to be a direct copy of the unlovely blue terminal in Hull, something which made her feel like she had stepped through a mirror into a looking glass world. She was hundreds of miles from home, already hundreds of pounds poorer, and on an impossible quest to save Hedgelord's reputation from a pornographer elf. Nightmarish didn't even come close to describing the situation.

Her misery was made so much worse by the apparently irrepressible and jaunty spirit of Jack. He had all of the same problems that she did (*and* he'd just been dumped) but he flashed his smile at her as if he was calm and rested.

"Rotterdam then! Here we are," he said, wandering towards a taxi rank. "Well done to us, eh?"

"Any updates on Alejandro?" Charlotte asked.

"Ah yes. Let's find our taxi, shall we and I'll share what I know."

A taxi appeared with suspicious ease. Jack had obviously booked it, like the organised and hangover-free adult Charlotte strived to be.

"Did you spike my drinks last night or something?" she grumbled.

"Yes," he said drolly. "I spiked the wine that you were drinking with more wine. I'm pretty sure that's standard." While Charlotte was strapping in, he held his phone up for the taxi driver to see. "Do you know where this place is?"

The driver gave a small nod. "Okay. That's the canal by the Pinball Museum in Voorhaven." His English was perfect. Charlotte wouldn't have expected anything less from the Dutch. "It's very pretty. You want to go there?"

"Please." Jack sat back.

"Thirty minutes, okay?"

"It sounded just like he just said, 'pinball museum'," said Charlotte, screwing up her face in confusion.

Jack showed her his phone social media feed. Santa Egadze and his elves, including Alejandro, were posing beside a lamppost near a canal. "This photo's in daylight and posted less than half an hour ago. He must have gone there this morning from wherever his helicopter landed, maybe we can catch him dawdling over his breakfast."

She couldn't even see the pinball museum in the picture, how on earth had the taxi driver recognised it? Charlotte smiled politely, but the hangover claimed her, and she closed her eyes. She could smell something bad and sweaty, and she was afraid it might be her. She huffed with frustration and clamped her arms firmly to her sides. At least she'd be able to incapacitate Alejandro with a whiff of her armpits if they did manage to catch up with him.

As she slumped, trying to claim what sleep she could on a thirty minute taxi ride, a thought occurred to her.

"What are we going to do if we get Alejandro?" she said.

"Hmmm?" said Jack.

She opened one eye. They were zipping along a dull dual carriageway with railway lines to one side and what looked like a chemical works or oil refinery on the other.

"What are we going to do with Alejandro? Just go up to him and wave our money in his face?"

"We could do," said Jack. "And it might work. Or maybe that thing about us paying him a thousand quid was just him having fun with us. Who knows what dirty movies of Santa are actually worth."

"Exactly. If he wasn't fussed about hanging around for us in Hull, why would he have time for us in Rotterdam? We need a Plan B."

Jack made a deep throaty sound. "Your Plan B involve jumping him and mugging him for his phone?"

"What? What makes you think that?"

"I can literally hear it in your voice, Charlotte."

"Fucking mind-reader," she muttered. Her smartwatch buzzed. Her first profanity of the day. "Our respective garden centres are going to have to cope without us today."

"How will they survive?" Jack pondered.

The road from the ferry terminal to Rotterdam seemed to be a perfectly straight line. Charlotte closed her eyes and tried to let the hum of taxis tyres on the tarmac surface lull her into some semblance of sleep.

9

ANIKA

The role of garden centre grotto elf was a more rewarding one than Anika had expected. It gave her paid employment and a sense of independence which felt good. It exercised a playful side of her nature that had been put on the back burner along with the intellectual challenges of her university course. What had come as a completely unexpected bonus was the desirability of the uniform. The elf dungarees were awash with pockets. They felt like a garment that had been designed around the idea of fitting the most pockets onto the human form. There were deep side pockets, a waist pack with a zip, a patch pocket over her abdomen, and another across her chest. It meant she could walk to work hands free while carrying everything she needed for the day, which was a great feeling.

The hat was a tacky thing made from the cheapest of fabrics, but it was surprisingly warm. And she was able to wear boots and a warm jumper. Elves had it good, she decided.

It was fun when cars tooted her. At first she had been wary, assuming it was weirdos who liked hassling women, but no, it was people who were delighted to see an elf walking to work, and so she always greeted them with a cheery wave. It was important to stay in character.

Anika had just passed the double roundabout with the supermarket when her phone buzzed. She crossed the road and checked her messages.

It was not another WhatsApp from Daffyd. It was Karen Woodbine who worked on the tills at Hedgelord. Anika supposed she regarded Karen as a work friend, even though Karen was over forty and like seriously old. Anika knew that Karen was always on the go and had to deal with her two kids first thing in the morning, so it seemed strange that she'd be messaging at this time.

Have you seen Sophie's Facebook update?

Anika replied. *No. I don't have Facebook. What is it?*

Anika had first met Sophie serving in the café at Hedgelord, but she had since applied to work in the grotto. Sophie was a woman in maybe her sixties or something, which made her super old. But now that Anika had got to know this geriatric elf woman she had come to regard Sophie as a naive young woman who happened to exist in the body of someone way older.

Why don't you have Facebook? Get it. Have a look.

Anika wasn't going to explain that Facebook was social media for old people and nobody under the age of thirty had it. It was common knowledge that there were more dead users on Facebook than live ones these days.

Send me a screenshot, she messaged.

How do I do that?

"Bloody hell," Anika tutted as she walked along the verge and into the Hedgelord Garden Centre car park. *Hold down the power button and the volume button at the same time.*

It was a guess, but possibly the right one, for thirty seconds later there was picture in the chat.

Sophie's Facebook update had a picture of a candle, with a simple message: *RIP Douglas. Love you always. My heart is broken.*

"Oh crap."

Anika replied to Karen. *Poor Sophie! Was Douglas her husband?*

Karen took a really long time to reply. She was either distracted (very likely) or typing slowly (also very likely).

I think so?? We need to get the Café Crew together and check in on her.

Anika sent a thumbs-up. The café crew was Sophie, Karen and Anika. The older women had tried to look out for Anika, and she was grateful to them for that. She didn't have much experience with bereavement though. She would follow Karen's lead and hope for the best.

Rather than go straight through to the office or the grotto, Anika swerved to go visit the Pagoda Café where, if Sophie was in, she'd be likely to be serving the early breakfasts.

Anika had never personally known death. She'd not lost parents or grandparents, and those great aunts and uncles who had died, either here or in India, were not exactly real or close to her. She didn't know how people in real life reacted to death, but she didn't expect the suddenly bereaved Sophie to be at work. That wouldn't be normal, would it?

And yet, as she entered the café, she saw that Sophie was there at the till, chatting to a customer, a tall man with a grey pointed beard. The man had a take-out coffee in his hands, but although their transaction appeared to be complete, they were still chatting. The man said something and Sophie giggled and touched his arm.

"Oh, stop," she smiled.

Okay, thought Anika. Experienced in death or not, that wasn't normal behaviour for the bereaved, was it?

"No, it's true," the man said. He didn't exactly have a foreign accent but he spoke a clear, crisp English that suggested it wasn't his first language.

"Well, that's very kind," said Sophie and fluttered her eyelids. She literally fluttered her eyelids at him. Anika wasn't aware that anyone actually did that in real life. The woman was actually flirting with this guy. He was old, maybe Sophie's age, but beneath that dark leather coat he looked like he probably kept in shape. He was somewhere between a papa bear and a silver fox, possibly entirely out of Sophie's league. But she was definitely flirting with him.

Anika felt like she was intruding but couldn't just walk off, not while her recently widowed colleague was engaged in car crash flirting with some foreign silver bear.

"Anyway, I must be going," he said. "I wonder if you can help me. I am looking for my friends, Luka and Gallagher. I know they work here."

"Oh, they'll be outside somewhere," said Sophie, then

saw Anika hanging around near the café entrance. "Anika will know."

Anika did know. She had only been working at Hedgelord a few weeks but had come to know the two men who worked in the outdoor garden section very well. The pair of them, Gallagher and Luka, were a pair of lazy individuals and seemed willing to put in a lot of work so they did as little as possible. Anika got to know them especially well when Luka Sibersky – old and lazy and possessing a white, almost Santaesque beard – had embroiled Gallagher – not-so-old but still lazy and plastered up to his neck in tattoos – in some nasty business with a local drug dealer called Sonia Patterson which Anika had helped them claw their way out of.

"Yes," she said and gestured down to the big automatic doors leading to the outdoor section. "You head straight out, past the water features and the big planter tubs until you see signs for sheds. They're usually in one of them." She considered the time of day. "Possibly having their breakfasts."

"Thank you very much, ladies," he said and, with his take-out cup in both hands, gave them both a little head bow.

Sophie called out to him as left. "See you around, Mr...?"

"Snømann," he said. "Call me Snømann."

"Oh, like the..."

"Like the snowman," he said. "Yes. Snømann."

Once he'd left, Anika turned to Sophie, whose eyes were sparkling.

"Um, he seemed nice," said Anika.

"Wasn't he?" said Sophie.

Okay, this didn't seem the right behaviour for someone who'd suffered a huge personal loss. Anika couldn't resist going there.

"Listen, I just popped in to say I'm sorry about ... Douglas?"

If she'd expected Sophie to be confused or brush it off as some sort of inconsequential misunderstanding, she was wrong. Sophie's face crumpled into tears and a sudden sob came welling up.

"Oh. Oh, no," said Anika and rushed forward to hug her. "I'm sorry. I didn't mean to..."

"Oh, he's gone, Anika. He's gone."

"I know. I heard. I'm sorry."

"Fifteen years together."

Anika had already said sorry and was already hugging her. It was surprising how quickly she'd run out of things to say to someone who had lost their husband. She started to make a variety of shushing sounds and comforting hums.

"Oh, it's silly really," Sophie sobbed. "I knew it was coming."

"I know. I know."

Anika didn't know, but had no idea what else to say. A couple of customers had come into the café and were getting their breakfasts from the hot food counter. Anika didn't want them to get round to the tills and find the cashier sobbing into the chest of a bewildered elf.

"Here," said Anika and grabbed her a couple of paper napkins to dab her eyes.

"I don't know how I'm going to go on," said Sophie.

"No," Anika agreed helplessly.

10

GALLAGHER

Gallagher and Luka had a barbecue going under the eaves of one of their tea sheds. This was definitely not permitted, but the weather was bitterly cold and it had been agreed they would claim they were testing equipment for next season if challenged.

Hedgelord had a considerable outdoor section. Few people ventured beyond the wooden tables of outdoor plants and wide selection of tree saplings, particularly at this time of year. The maze of sheds, summer houses and outdoor offices on all year round display were effectively Gallagher's and Luka's private kingdom.

Nonetheless, they had erected a barrier of fencing panels around their tea shed so any foolhardy members of the public who might be looking for a Christmas tree or a bag of compost would not accidentally drive a trolley into their barbecue. Currently, they were using the barbecue to cook some breakfast sausages.

"Smells good," said Gallagher, inhaling deeply. "Something about that smell makes you believe in a higher power."

Gallagher had been thinking about the fact he wasn't dead a lot in the past weeks. This would not normally sound like a positive thing to be occupying a man's thoughts, but Gallagher was absolutely seeing it as a positive. His life generally fell into the category of 'deeply shitty', typified by the shitty, mouldy flat above a takeaway he lived in, and the shitty amount of personal debt he had with nothing to show for it and almost no means of paying it off. But he had been feeling good about it recently. His situation was still shitty, but he was alive and his head hadn't been crushed inside a drug dealer's cider press, which had been very much on the cards for a while.

Luka raised an eyebrow. "This higher power you speak of talks to you through medium of pork products, eh?"

Gallagher nodded. He was riding a wave of whimsy. It was so long since he had felt cheerful about things that he wanted to make the most of it. "Yeah. Think they might be done yet?"

"Is no good to blast them with heat and have them raw inside. Patience is needed. Few more minutes."

Gallagher nodded and reclined in his deckchair. It was nearly the middle of winter, the sky was almost permanently grey, and the sun was up for no more than seven hours of the day, but that didn't mean a man couldn't enjoy a deckchair.

"You hear that there's going to be a Hedgelord staff Christmas party?" he said.

Luka shrugged. Luka Sibersky was originally from some

far-off Eastern European country that quite possibly no longer existed on maps and he somehow managed to infuse even his shrugs with a certain foreign *je ne sais quoi*. "We are going?"

"Free bar, I hear," said Gallagher. "The boss is paying for it."

A shadow fell over them. They both looked up, expecting to see their manager, Tom Eccles. Luka was normally able to ward off Tom, but being caught in such a flagrant act of disobedience might present a challenge even for him.

However it was not Tom. It was a member of the public: a tall stranger with a grey pointed beard. Gallagher thought he looked like a wizard, or maybe a Viking, albeit one in an expensive-looking leather jacket.

"Sorry mate, you can't come in here," called Gallagher.

The stranger grunted, inspecting their set-up.

"What is it you're after?" said Gallagher.

"You are Luka and Gallagher?" asked the stranger. He had an accent, but it was less growly and feral than Luka's. He sounded like someone who had learned to speak English from Mary Poppins but who liked to inflect the vowels just for fun.

"Er, who's asking?" said Gallagher.

The man looked about, as though inspecting the whole shed display area. "I like this. All of this."

"Yeah?"

"Good square footage."

"Oh, yeah?" said Gallagher. "Yeah, I always like to think about the square footage of a place. Listen, what—?"

Gallagher realised the man had a trowel in his hand. It

looked like it had come straight off the display inside the shop. And now he had laid it on the barbecue along with the sausages.

"Er, mate..." said Gallagher.

"Who are you?" said Luka.

"I am Snømann." He stared at them.

"The Snowman?" said Luka.

"Yes. I see which of you is which," said Snømann. He pointed at them in turn. "You are the older one and you are the tattooed neurotic one. Hah! It turns out that Sonia Patterson was better at describing people than she was at running the business."

Gallagher felt a chill at the use of the word 'was'. Sonia Patterson, local drug dealer, had tortured and threatened both him and Luka. Days on, Gallagher still had bruises. Did the past tense mean Sonia was dead?

Luka extended a hand. "You are colleague of Sonia."

Gallagher was in awe of the way that Luka refused to be cowed.

Snømann looked at Luka's offered hand but did not take it. "Colleague? No. That is not the hierarchy of our business. She answered to me and now *you* answer to me."

"Oh, no but—" Gallagher clamped his lips shut. He wanted to say that they'd fucking WON, that neither Sonia nor any other psycho gangster had reason to come after them now, because they had wriggled free of her evil claws. All debts had been paid. All scores had been settled. It was over. Luka and Gallagher should answer to no one now. But he caught Luka's warning look and said none of those things.

"What is it likely to mean, answering to you?" asked Luka, again keeping his calm.

"Very little." Snømann smiled. "You are well-placed men. You work at this delightful garden centre with—" He paused. "You know, we do not have garden centres where I am from. Yes, we can go buy plants and tools and things." He momentarily touched the trowel on the barbecue. It had lost its label and some of its paint due to the heat. "We can do those things, but we do not have these things called garden centres." He spread his arms wide. He was a tall man and had a long arm span. "This place and the one across the road, Bloomers – they are like holy shrines to the hobby of gardening. It is like you have taken the idea of gardens and you have made them sacred. What is it they say? An Englishman's home is his castle."

"Not my home," said Gallagher automatically.

"I am not English," said Luka.

"But you are. This is your home here. And if his home is his castle then an Englishman's garden is the ... what do you call the bit around a castle?"

"The moat?" said Gallagher.

"No. Inside the moat. The bit that is part of the castle but is not the actual castle."

"The wall?" said Luka.

"Inside the wall."

"Courtyard?" guessed Luka wildly.

Something sprang to Gallagher's mind. Maybe it was the sight of that red hot trowel on the barbecue and this sinister man who was somehow like the dangerous drug dealer Sonia Patterson but *even worse*. Maybe all of Gallagher's life was flashing before his eyes, because out of some primary school history lesson that had been forgotten for decades, a word came to him.

"Bailey?"

Snømann clicked his fingers and pointed at him. "Bailley. That is it. An Englishman's garden is his bailey. His fortifications. You love that. The English love their property and they love protecting it. And this is where they come to buy things so that in those summer days they can sit on their patio and have their afternoon teas and look at the flowers and go, 'This is my bailey. This is my fortress. My property is safe here.'" Snømann nodded in deep satisfied understanding. "I want my property to be safe here and that is how you will help."

"Help how?" said Gallagher who really wasn't following.

"Such a small thing. You will barely notice. A trivial storage job." Snømann raised his eyes and stared at them both. At the same time, he lifted the trowel from the barbecue. He spat onto the blade and it hissed. He came forward, and suddenly he had the trowel up against the side of Gallagher's face, millimetres away in a gentle, caressing motion.

Gallagher stayed perfectly still but he could feel the heat radiating onto his face.

"Yeah? Storage?" he said, speaking like a ventriloquist in case any movement brought the hot trowel in contact with his skin.

"A trivial storage job. There will be a delivery of three crates and you will store them. You will ensure that they are kept dry and that nobody opens them until I need to collect them. Nobody. If you attempt to look inside, I will know and I will come here and hurt you very badly. I think you understand."

"Unnerstan," confirmed Gallagher in his ventriloquist voice.

Snømann put down the trowel, stared at the two of them and then left silently.

Gallagher patted the sides of his face, not convinced that he wasn't somehow burnt. "What the fuck was that? How are we still involved with these maniacs?"

Luka gave one of his enormous shrugs. "Is nothing. We store their shit and then it is over."

Gallagher's good mood had evaporated. It would never be over and they both knew it.

11

ANIKA

It had taken five minutes and several apologies to customers who just wanted to pay for their mini all day breakfasts before Anika had Sophie at a stage where she could be left alone to continue with her work. Sophie assured her she was fine to continue – "The distraction will do me good," she had insisted – and Anika, with tear stains on her breast pocket, had left her to it.

Anika went to the office to check the grotto rota, while making a solemn promise not to go sticking her nose into other people's affairs again.

In the office, the general store manager Tom Eccles looked distraught as he clicked his mouse, staring at his computer screen, and sighing unhappily every five seconds. Anika eyed him nervously. She'd often thought that he looked like a slapped puppy, but she never said that out loud. He was a manager after all. Today he wore that same wounded expression, but his eyes told a story all by themselves. He looked as if he'd glimpsed a terrible truth and his soul would never recover.

She went to look at the rota on the whiteboard. It covered the main indoor grotto, the reindeer paddock outside, and various events taking place in and around these areas in the run up to Christmas. As an elf, Anika could be assigned to one of nearly a dozen stations within that whole grotto world.

Tom sighed.

Anika glanced at him. She should just check the rota, find herself and get out.

Tom sighed again, louder. It was performative now, a childish exaggeration of a sigh.

"Um. Everything all right?" she asked.

Tom shook his head deeply. He'd better not have been recently bereaved as well. Anika wasn't sure she had the skillset for that.

"Charlotte won't be in," he whispered.

"Oh, okay," said Anika. That didn't sound so bad. Charlotte was the Christmas sales manager and somehow Anika's boss, with maybe head elf Daffyd somewhere in between. So she wasn't in. People were off all the time, weren't they? It was winter. Illness was to be expected.

"She left me a voicemail," said Tom and held out his phone.

"Oh, you're going to play it, are—"

"*Oh, hi Tom. It's me ... Kathryn. Just needed to let you know that I'm going to be late in tomorrow. Or possibly not in at all. Look, everything should be fine. No special events on. We've got the princess carriage rides thing and the children's tea party on*

*Friday. Oh, and Santa Paws. But tomorrow, everything should be
fine. The grotto should tick over by itself."*

Tom lowered the phone and gave Anika a look.

"We've got some busy days coming up," Anika agreed.
"But she's not here today. That's cool."

"Did it sound like she was going to come back
tomorrow?" said Tom.

"Er, dunno."

"You heard how she said 'soon'. That was doubt. And she
called herself Kathryn. Why would she do that?"

Anika pulled a face. "Because she was drunk?"

"Did she sound drunk?"

"Do drunk people always sound drunk?"

Anika checked the rota and found she was scheduled to
spend the day with Santa Raymond in the marquee-based
grotto. It was a huge marquee, with a carpeted floor, but it
was very much an outside venue. Today was the Festive Farm
children's grotto experience, while on Friday, as Charlotte
had said in the message, there was Santa Paws, where people
brought their dogs to see Santa. Anika thought Santa Paws
was an absolute delight. Taking pictures of adorable pups
with their owners never got old, especially when they all
dressed up in matching sweaters.

"Everything seems to be in order," she said cheerfully
to Tom.

Tom clearly didn't agree. He was staring at his own
version of the rota, or something similar, and looked one
stage away from tearing his hair out.

"Anything I can do?" she said.

He looked up. "The reindeer for stuffing need taking

down to the grotto," he said pointing at a pile of boxes in the corner. "You could make a start on that if you don't mind?"

"Sure!" Anika said.

"Really?" said Tom.

"Yes," she said. "Won't be a problem."

Tom blinked. "I'm really not used to people just doing things I ask."

"Oh." That sounded pathetically tragic.

"I've been asking Luka and Gallagher to move those pallets of compost by the landscaping office since..." He puffed out his cheeks as a thought seemed to occur to him. "Could you ask them to move them?"

"Yeah. Why not?" she shrugged.

12

CHARLOTTE

Charlotte and Jack had spent way too long searching the area around the pinball museum. The picture on the social media feed had shown Alejandro Aramburuzabala and his Santa outside, but he was nowhere to be seen. The Rotterdam pinball museum sat alongside a canal-like marina. The masts of sailing boats clustered along the high banks. Several of them were strung with Christmas lights, like the old-fashioned lampposts and flat-fronted Dutch houses which lined the Voorhaven.

Since Alejandro was not in sight they had paid to go into the museum, in case he was in there, but they were the only visitors.

"Is it me, or are most of these machines the same, bar the decoration?" Charlotte said to Jack, her hand resting on one of the displays.

Jack ran a hand along the side of the enormous Jawsthemed machine that was a star attraction. "I suspect that if we had the time to properly go down the rabbit hole of pinball machines, we would discover there is a rich, nerdy world to explore, and that each machine is very different and special in its own way. But yeah, on the surface they do all seem to be painted-up versions of fairly similar things."

"We don't have the time to immerse ourselves in the world of pinball, and Alejandro's definitely not in here," said Charlotte.

"I hope there's at least a gift shop. I do love to get a pencil from places I visit," said Jack.

Charlotte tried to give him a withering look, but something about the idea of him having umpteen pencils from all the attractions he'd ever visited made her smile.

"Uh oh. Alejandro's on the move," said Jack, looking at his phone. "He's on a train to Stockholm."

"You're fucking kidding me!" said Charlotte. "Show me."

Jack did so. The social media post was plainly of Iraki Egadze and his two elves in a taxi.

"*Next stop, Stockholm. Choo choo,*" Jack read.

"Right." Charlotte stood up straight to properly engage her brain. She could almost pretend her hangover was in the past and she was a competent human without stinking armpits if she focused. "Right. Options. We could get a flight there and probably beat the train. We could get a train ourselves. We could call the police and report a fake crime and get him arrested. That would stall his progress."

"Easy tiger!" said Jack. "No way is Alejandro going to help us out if we get him arrested."

"Unless we hide the fact that we were the ones who dropped him in it, then swoop in like his saviours," said Charlotte, waving her arms like an angel descending from the heavens.

"Swooping saviours who have not changed their clothes or indeed seen any kind of basic hygiene since leaving Hull?" said Jack.

Charlotte slammed her arms firmly against her sides, assuming her body odour had prompted his thought. "How about we get in a taxi to somewhere we can buy, um, paracetamol?" By which she meant deodorant and fresh underwear. "Then we can both search for tickets to Stockholm?"

He gave a small bow. "I like that idea much more than being evil manipulators of the Dutch legal system."

"To be clear, I am not taking evil manipulating off the table just yet," said Charlotte. "But I do need some paracetamol."

"Good."

As they stepped out, Charlotte checked her phone. There had been no messages from anyone at Hedgelord. That seemed odd in itself. It was coming up for mid-morning. Surely someone needed her?

She sent a message to Tom. Perhaps her voicemail of the other night had seemed less than clear. She explained in a text that she was caught up in an important matter relating to personal and professional improvements, and if anyone had questions about anything that needed doing that day at Hedgelord then they should get in touch.

As an afterthought, she sent a separate message to Daffyd

to ask if he had Alejandro's number at all. It was likely that Alejandro's number was in his personnel records at Hedgelord, but Daffyd was the kind of man who kept tabs on all his elves, past and present.

Jack was also on his phone. "Taxi booked," he said. "Let's go."

13

ANIKA

The route to the Festive Farm grotto in the marquee took Anika through the plant area. Pallets of compost from outside the landscaping office, Tom had said. She could ask Luka and Gallagher to move them on her way through. As she walked, she could smell smoke. Wood smoke.

Ahead she saw smoke drifting out from among the sheds in dark black curls. She hurried forward. Out the front of the plantsmen's tea shed, a fence panel had fallen against a barbecue. The sausages on it were nothing but cinders, while the treated wood fence had gone from charring to fully alight.

Luka and Gallagher were nowhere in sight.

"Fire!" she shouted.

She dropped the reindeer stuffing box and ran in search of a fire extinguisher. There was one clipped to a trellis post in the hot tub displays. A moment of fighting unhooked it and she got back to the shed in time to see Luka and Gallagher emerge from it and stare in numb wonder at the fire they'd started.

Anika had never used a fire extinguisher before but she quickly found the safety pin, pointed the nozzle and drowned the small blaze in white foam. Luka and Gallagher continued to stare at her.

"Did you know your sausages are burning?" she said. "And the fence?"

"Yeah," said Gallagher. "Been really busy. We forgot them."

Anika pulled a face. The two of them were completely motionless, like statues.

"Something wrong?"

"A lot on our minds," said Luka. He waved a hand at the ruined barbecue. "Quality sausages too."

"Uh-huh. Tom asked me to ask you to move that compost from outside the whatsit office."

"Top of our list," said Luka.

"Right. Your boss is in a bit of a tizzy. Apparently Charlotte's not in."

At least she got a response to that. Luka gave a small shrug of mirth at the idea of Tom being their boss. Gallagher raised his eyebrows.

"She's not in on one of the busiest days of the year? He'll be wetting his pants."

"As long as he doesn't come down here to hide out," said Luka.

With the fire extinguisher dangling from one hand, Anika picked up her reindeer stuffing box again.

"What's the deal with stuffed reindeer?" said Luka. "Is better pan fried."

Sometimes Anika had trouble recognising when Luka was joking.

"Just on the way to the grotto with them," she said. "Come by later and stuff one for your shed if you like. You can mount it on the wall like a trophy."

"Yes, yes," said Luka, absent-mindedly. They were both definitely distracted by something.

In the marquee, Anika laid out the reindeer stuffing kits, ready for the first group to come through. Just as these flat, hollow fabric reindeers would come to life as the children packed in the stuffing, so too would the reindeer activity stuff this place with a bit of Christmas joy. It was an act of creation, and soon everybody would get a taste of that magic.

She heard a voice of someone entering the marquee. It was way too early for Santa Raymond, so she sprang to attention, ready to sprint round and hide the evidence of what she was doing.

It was Karen Woodbine, coming in with a clipboard.

"Oh, thank God it's you," said Anika.

Karen waggled the clipboard in her hand and gave her a long look. "Said literally nobody ever when the Health and Safety officer comes calling."

"You're the Health and Safety officer?" asked Anika. "Since when?"

"Since my last appraisal. Turns out that Hedgelord don't look at this face and think there's a woman with enough on her plate."

"That's a ... compliment?"

The mother of two looked tired. Karen always looked tired. It seemed to be the theme holding her whole face together.

"What's that?" she said. She was pointing with her clipboard pen at the fire extinguisher by Anika's feet. A trail of drying foam hung from the nozzle like a long white bogey.

"Oh, er, yeah. Small fire over in the garden section."

Karen tossed her pen away in exasperation and it dangled from the clipboard by its coiled plastic tether. "This is what I'm bleeding well talking about. Buggeration. We've got an epidemic of carelessness on this site, did you know that?"

"Really?"

"The stats never lie! You should see them! I mean, obviously I can't let you see them because these records contain sensitive personal information, but they are bad. Bloody awful."

"Accidents happen," said Anika.

"If we get anything else that needs to go in the accident book we'll be in the upper quartile again. Cameron gets all hot under the collar about that."

Anika couldn't quite imagine the owner of Hedgelord getting hot under the collar about anything as uninteresting as staff accidents and safety. Anika imagined Cameron Crisp was generally perfectly happy as long as profits were good and nothing interfered with his golf and socialising plans.

"Does Cameron really care?" said Anika.

"If we do worse than Bloomers he does."

"Ah."

"We *always* do worse than Bloomers."

"Right. Got it. No accidents, we'll all be really careful," said Anika. "I'll go put the extinguisher back."

"No, I'll do it," said Karen. "If it's been used, it needs to go on the fire extinguisher record log." She picked up the red cannister by the handle. "Not that I haven't already got too much to do. Christmas is the worst time to have kids you know. School Christmas fayre. School Christmas play. Presents." She pulled a disgusted face. "I think I'm going to have a heart attack from overwork. And then I'll have to write that in the accident book too."

"But still," said Anika, trying to remain relentlessly upbeat, "Christmas day. The looks on their faces. Knowing that you're all part of a loving family..."

Karen gave her a withering look. "Pray you never have children, Anika."

"Er, wasn't planning to."

"Good. See you in the café at break time, yeah?" said Karen. "We need to have that catch up with Soph." She tapped a round badge on her chest. It read HEDGELORD MENTAL HEALTH CHAMPION. "Oh, yeah. I've got all the roles."

"Actually, she seemed fine when I was talking to her earlier," said Anika. "She was even flirting, like old lady flirting, with one of the customers."

"Grief comes in strange forms," said Karen and, with another tired sigh, wandered out.

14

GALLAGHER

The scary visit from Snømann and the loss of their breakfast sausages whilst discussing what to do about said scary visitor had put a serious dent in Gallaghers mood. So he and Luka cheered themselves up with a little rubbish hurling competition. They had invented the game ages ago, although they could only indulge when the outside area was quiet. The rules were simple: they were allowed one full rotation to build up momentum, like a hammer thrower, then they tried to lob the rubbish into the skip over the fence. There was plenty of jeopardy involved, because there was a great deal of breakable glass in the garden centre. It gave the game an extra frisson.

"Remember that time you threw half a paving slab straight into the house plant area inside the shop?" said Gallagher.

"We replaced the glass before Tom saw," said Luka casually.

"But we forgot to go and get the slab back."

"That throw was small miscalculation," said Luka. "But part of refining technique. Probably why I am now superior thrower."

This morning's game had two purposes. To work off some of the stress the day had already brought, and to clear a space for storing the crates Snømann was apparently bringing to them.

Luka grunted. "We will have to move some more things around. The crates for Snømann will need to be secure and hidden. They cannot go here. Also, we do not know how large they will be."

"What do you think's in them?" asked Gallagher.

Luka shrugged. "Drugs? Stolen goods? This Snømann is known to me. Sonia Patterson was afraid of him."

That didn't sound good. "So we should just call the police then?"

Luka picked up an imaginary phone. "Ah, hello, Mr Policeman. I am ringing to tell you that an international criminal wants to store things at our garden centre. No, there is nothing here yet. No evidence of any crime. Yes, we know him because we previously agreed to transport cannabis for his drug dealer friend. My name? My address?" Luka put down the imaginary phone and gave Gallagher a look. "No. We do this, but we get involved little as possible. We are better off not knowing, believe me."

Throughout the morning, Gallagher and Luka continued their ruthless clearing of space for the mystery delivery. They really didn't achieve much more than tidying though.

"I've got an idea," said Gallagher, as he hefted another

split bag of gravel out of the way. "The shed display doesn't get a lot of attention this time of year. How about we put the existing ones a bit closer together and erect a new one? Put a padlock on it. We could even camouflage it with some trellis or signage."

Luka gave a slow nod. "Is good idea. Secret storage shed. Something like a *Tunbridge Slimline*."

"Yeah, exactly. Good choice."

They walked around the shed display, working out which patch of gravel offered the best possibility.

They stopped at a corner plot. "Here we go," said Gallagher. "I can see it clearly in my mind now. We inch this one to the left and this one to the right, opening up the space in the middle for a *Tunbridge Slimline*. Then we pop a trellis in front of it, all lit up with fairy lights, so it's not obvious there's a new shed behind."

"How we get in and out with a trellis in the way?" Luka said.

Gallagher chopped the air excitedly with his hand. "This is the clever part! We erect it as a lean-to against our tea shed. We cut a doorway between the two, yeah?"

"We cut a doorway? Fucking secret passage?"

"Yes!"

Luka shrugged. "Is cool. Definitely doable. Let's go."

15

ANIKA

Anika returned to the office to collect the second box of stuffed reindeer. Tom and Daffyd were standing by the staff rota, in heated discussion. Daffyd was head of the grotto, and spent all day dressed as an elf, although with his bald head and pudgy face he looked more like a massive baby. Tom's grey managerial attire contrasted with Daffyd's colourful elf suit, making them look like a bizarre stage show – Elf Baby and the Suit.

"How can she not be coming in? It's one of the busiest days of the year!" said Daffyd. His voice was high with indignation, making him sound even more like a huge toddler who'd accidentally been given a management position.

"Her latest text says that it's an important matter relating to personal and professional improvements," said Tom.

"But that's training! Who would book training for a day like today?" Daffyd looked at his own phone. "And now she's asking me if I have a number for Alejandro Aramburuzabala."

"Alejandro who?"

"A former elf of ours. Good chap. Had just the right level of mania." Daffyd stroked his chin thoughtfully. "She sent me a photo of Alejandro yesterday. I wonder if he's on that training too?"

"I have no idea," said Tom. "You can ask her when she returns. In the meantime, tell everyone that I am the point of escalation."

"Wait, what? Point of escalation? Why would that be you? You know nothing about running events?" Daffyd said.

"Because I am the only other manager at Charlotte's level," said Tom. He framed a pyramid with his arms. "Like it or not we have a hierarchy: everyone in the store reports in to either Charlotte or me, and we report to Cameron at the top of the tree. We are not escalating operational matters to Cameron. That would be absurd."

"No," agreed Daffyd. "But what about me? I run the grotto. I can step sideways and take on the other events. It's common sense."

Anika watched Tom's face as the oddball from the grotto stood before him preaching common sense while dressed as a giant elf baby. His expression was an essay in puzzled doubt, but some code of politeness or professionalism stopped him from saying anything out loud. "Assume I am the point of escalation, Daffyd. I will, of course call on your common sense if I feel that I need to."

Daffyd turned on his heel and flounced from the office. Anika was fascinated to watch the process. It was a stunning performance, as if Daffyd had practised it many times. If there was a catwalk show, dedicated to flouncing, then he would definitely have aced it. There was a head toss, as if he was shaking hair from his face, although he had none. He led with his chest, as though pulled up by an invisible string, his unfocused gaze towards the heavens. His mouth was half open in an appalled sneer and he took deliberate, measured steps towards the door, his arms wafting at his sides.

Anika was frozen to the spot, but at least that stopped her clapping in admiration at the performance. Tom turned to her, his face irritated.

"Just taking some more of these," said Anika, waggling the box of reindeer for the grotto.

Tom turned his gaze back to the whiteboard, as if he was trying to make sense of it.

Anika left wondering why these men, both of them nearly twice her age if not older, couldn't take Charlotte's perfectly reasonable plans and simply enact them.

16

GALLAGHER

Gallagher and Luka were working on assembling the *Tunbridge Slimline*. It was a straightforward job to erect the shed from stock, one they'd done many times before, but never in an attempt to keep it secret.

The *bzzt, bzzt* sound of the electric screwdriver wasn't the problem, as they used it all the time. What they needed was stopping people from coming to see what they might be doing.

They'd hit upon the idea of assembling two things at the same time. Gallagher would assemble a large dog kennel in plain sight, right outside their regular tea drinking shed, while Luka assembled the secret shed. Gallagher was primed with all sorts of fake reasons why they might need a large dog kennel, depending on who came calling. He would stop people venturing into the space they had cleared for the new shed, so Luka could work unobserved.

Gallagher put the kettle on to make tea for the two of

them and started to sort out the tools and supplies that they'd need.

"You seen the sixty mil screws?" Gallagher shouted to Luka, who was carrying the wood for the *Tunbridge Slimline* into the space where he planned to put it together. "I thought we had a massive box of them in here."

"Yeah, big box on shelf. Cannot miss it!" shouted Luka. "You can tip some in a mug or a pot for me to use."

Gallagher huffed in mild frustration, because he definitely could miss a box of screws if it wasn't there. Luka must have put them somewhere else. He'd need to go over to one of the storage containers where backup stock was stored. He poured out the boiling water to make the tea first.

"You smell something?" he called. "Burning paint maybe?"

"You have curry last night?" Luka called.

"Ho, ho, fucking ho," said Gallagher. "Tea's ready."

He pushed open the door to the shed, holding out a mug for Luka. As Luka appeared around the corner their eyes met, and Gallagher was struck by how funny it was they both had their noses wrinkled up in the same expression.

"What is that funny sme—?"

They both spotted the barbecue at the same time. It was glowing hot, and a small gas cylinder lay on top. It was the source of the burning paint smell, because the branding and logo were now almost completely burned away. The missing box of screws stood on top.

"Fuck!" said Luka. He charged towards the shed. "Inside! In!"

The two of them fell inside and Luka slammed the door

just as there was a loud bang. It was followed by a fusillade of smaller hammering sounds against the shed's front end, like a hail of bullets.

Gallagher went to open the door, but Luka put a hand on his arm. "Wait a moment, there may be more."

Slowly they ventured outside.

"Holy fuck," said Gallagher when he saw the outside of the shed. Screws were embedded into the wood as though they'd been fired from a shotgun. Screws were everywhere. The charred and foam drenched fencing panel forming part of their barbecue screen was now more hole than fence. There was a shattered window in a nearby shed. And the tarpaulin that formed a tiny porch for their tea shed was utterly shredded.

The gas cylinder on the barbecue had ruptured, but it wasn't the mangled mess he had expected. It was simply split around the middle.

"Is fucking nail bomb," said Luka, pointing.

"You what?" Gallagher said.

"Nail bomb. Shrapnel intended to wound and kill."

"Nah mate, we are just a careless pair of idiots who left the barbecue going. Those are screws, aren't they?" Privately, Gallagher assumed Luka had absent-mindedly put the screws and gas bottle down while he was distracted. He wasn't going to say that out loud, because it would only lead to an argument. "We'll need to watch the wheelbarrow tyre for punctures with these bloody things everywhere."

Screws littered the floor. Gallagher started to pick them up, but soon realised it would take days to get them all.

"You think this is accident?" Luka asked.

Gallagher straightened. "Well yeah. What else could it be?"

"We get visit from Snømann and then nail bomb. There are no coincidences."

"Why the fuck would Snømann blow us up if he wants us to do stuff for him? It makes no sense. Let's just face facts, we messed up while we were dashing back and forth with all these supplies, somehow. At least nobody got hurt."

There came a high pitched squeaking sound and a stomp, stomp, stomp that took Gallagher a moment to recognise as feet on gravel. Anika burst into view, another fire extinguisher in her hand and a look of concerned fury on her face, her elf hat quivering with her passionate energy.

"What the bloody fuck?" she blurted, letting go of the pent up squeal of annoyance within her.

"It's okay," said Gallagher. "We're fine."

She waggled the fire extinguisher at him threateningly. "I put out your barbecue fire, turn my back for five minutes to do some actual work and you manage to—" She looked about at the damage and debris. "Jesus! What the hell happened?"

"Nail bomb," said Luka.

"An accident," said Gallagher.

"No more accidents!" she fumed. "Karen is tearing her hair out over the number of accidents that occur in this place."

"Which one's Karen?" said Gallagher.

"The one who works the tills," said Luka. "Hair up like this. Very attractive woman."

"The one who bangs on about how difficult it is to be a mum all the time?"

"That is her."

"Knackered looking rather than attractive, mate," said Gallagher.

"She looks like she has seen life. I like that."

Anika's face was screwed up in disgust. "When you two have finished judging women on their appearance and shaming them for taking on the burden of childcare—"

"I only say nice things about women," said Luka.

"Do you two judge me alongside other women, huh?" she said.

"You are different," said Luka. "You are just a child."

"I'm nineteen, you senile cretin. So, since Karen is the Health and Safety officer and no one seems to have any control over you can I please suggest that a) you start viewing women as people and not as ... whatever, and b) try not to kill yourself and give Karen a heart attack in the process. Dealing with your corpses is not on my job description."

At that, she whirled on her heel and marched off, the bell at the end of her hat tinkling.

Gallagher looked on thoughtfully for a moment. "Come on," he said. "We've got some shed building to do."

"Fine. I guess we better build fucking sheds." Luka took a large swig of his tea and then roared in disgust as he spat out tea and a mouthful of screws onto the floor.

17

ANIKA

Around eleven, with a half hour break in her elfing schedule, Anika met Karen and Sophie in the café. The three of them had hot chocolate topped with a double dose of whipped cream. Sophie insisted that extra cream was a necessary perk they should exploit as staff members.

"Sorry to hear about Douglas, Sophie love," said Karen, putting out a handout to Sophie.

Sophie acknowledged the kindness with a sorrowful nod and a small smile. "He was everything to me. The house feels so empty."

"Are you okay to be here?"

Sophie reached for a napkin to dab the tears that had come to her eyes.

"You let it out," said Karen.

"Being here is a good distraction," blubbed Sophie. The heavy mascara she wore was running now.

Anika felt like she should add something to the conversation, even though she'd had little experience in talking about death. "How long did you say you and Douglas were together?"

Sophie's smile almost collapsed. "Feels like forever. In reality it was, what, ten years?"

Anika nodded.

"Anyway, I'm just trying to focus on keeping busy," said Sophie.

"Anything that helps," said Karen. "But take it easy on yourself, eh?"

Sophie nodded, then took a deep breath and clamped her mouth into a firm line. "But how are things with you, Karen? I know it's not easy for you this time of year."

Karen gave a cold laugh. "Well, I think your news has put my bin fire of a family into a perspective."

"It's not a bin fire, love."

"No. It's a three-ringed circus. It's my circus and they're definitely my monkeys but the— Oh, you don't want to hear this."

"Tell us," said Sophie. "The distraction will do me good."

Karen gave an exaggerated roll of her eyes. "Urgh. Fine! It does get a bit much in the season of supposed good will. If it wasn't enough that I have to find time to buy and wrap everyone's presents to each other, make cakes for the PTA, go to the carol concert and orchestra recital, help out on the Round Table's Santa run, get the kids to orchestra practice, arrange the Christmas schedule with my ex, plan Christmas dinners— What did I forget?"

"Working full time?" Anika suggested.

"Oh yeah, that. Managing the tills and trying to protect Hedgelord's awful Health and Safety record. If that wasn't enough, I have to put up with my in-laws, who switch into overdrive at this time of year. I can't tell you how awful they are."

Anika waited while Karen took a fierce slurp of her hot chocolate, leaving a creamy semi-circle on her upper lip. She huffed.

"Let me try and paint you a picture of my in-laws. Technically my ex-in-laws, but that's a mouthful. Marcus and Maremba. M&Ms I call them."

"Do they like being called that?" said Anika.

"No. But it works well as a name, cos they are sickly sweet and I can only take them in small doses. See, they talk a lot about peace, love and tolerance, but you know what they are really intolerant of?" Karen looked at the two of them.

"Um, you?" hazarded Anika.

"Yes! Me, exactly. Sometimes I want to slam their smug, pretentious heads together and show them how mean they actually are to the people that ought to matter. They have a problem with how I bring up my kids? Well they can just do one!"

"What's their problem? You're doing a good job," said Sophie.

"Oh! Oh! Don't get me started. I give the kids fish fingers for their tea? I get lectures about depleting cod stocks in the North Sea, and how much fat is in that crispy coating. I let the kids have sweets if they do some household chores? I'm setting unhelpful boundaries and imposing conformity on their young minds."

"Imposing conformity?" asked Anika. "Isn't that in the parenting job description?"

Karen shook her head. "You'd think, yeah? Not for that pair. Both academics with flipping PhDs coming out of their wazoos. He's like this imposing type who seems to think that the whole world, and *my kids* ought to be his own pet science experiment. As for her, she's all about getting in touch with your inner child and letting it run free. Apparently in her case that means rolling your boobs in paint and making art by printing them on the walls."

Sophie looked shocked. "Um. Is that to check for lumps or something?"

"No. Apparently it's because we should nurture our most childish instincts. Both of them have this idea that if you put too many rules in place for *actual* kids then it's gonna stop them from being fully-formed individuals as adults. Hence all their opinions about fishfingers and everything else I can't do right."

Anika tried to imagine explaining these ideas to her own parents, but it was a conversation that definitely wouldn't get far. "We did *Lord of the Flies* at school—"

"—Oh! Oh! Marcus talks about that book *all* of the time. I think he sees it as an instruction book rather than a cautionary tale. I swear to god if he could set up his own version, where kids get to run wild on an island, he'd totally do it. Never mind if they turn into cannibals and sacrifice each other—"

"Not sure that's what happens..." Anika began.

"—he'd say that it's all part of getting in touch with their true inner selves."

"They do sound as if they have very unusual ideas," said Sophie. Anika could tell she was still shaken by the idea of naked breast painting. "Do they see the children very often?"

"Twice a week," said Karen. "Which is nice, because quite honestly I have no idea how I would manage to get the kids to all of their activities if they didn't take them to their Woodland Spiritual Wellness sessions and some of the other stuff, but it worries me. I swear to God those kids are starting to talk like tiny little versions of Marcus and Maremba."

"No, surely not?" said Sophie.

Karen nodded.

"What does that sound like?" asked Anika.

Karen thought for a moment. "The other day I asked them if they'd like to get a takeaway pizza for tea. World's biggest treat for a kid back in the day, right? Have a guess what Hermione said to me?"

Anika looked at Sophie. Neither of them had any clue.

"She looked at her brother and then gave me this kind of pitying look. She said 'I think maybe you're tired and you crave the short term calorie boost. We won't disagree with your choices, but I think you know there are healthier options'."

"Oof!" said Anika. She was still wondering what went on in Woodland Spiritual Wellness sessions.

"What food's appropriate, what presents are appropriate, all of that," said Karen. "Marcus and Maremba would rather die than eat an Asda sausage roll, and they're sure to buy the kids some sort of eco-friendly ethical wooden thing made from gourds."

Anika wanted to point out they couldn't be wooden if

they were made from gourds, but that would be very much against the spirit of the venting, which seemed to be the purpose of this café crowd she was now a part of. She wondered what she had to throw into the pot.

"My parents don't think this job is worthwhile," she said.

The other two turned to her.

"Being an elf?" breathed Sophie. "But you're a natural! You're so very good at it."

"I love doing it too, but it's like that doesn't matter. They're not really interested unless I'm running the place," said Anika.

"Yeah, but you totally could run the place," said Karen.

"One day, if I stuck around for the right vacancy, but they don't see—"

"No, I mean now. Haven't you seen them doing their headless chicken thing today? Tom and Daffyd. And bloody Cameron's nowhere in sight. With Charlotte off Tom's gone into meltdown and rather than doing anything sensible, he's just arguing with Daffyd about who should be in charge."

Anika nodded. She'd seen that for herself, and if everyone else had seen it too then nothing had improved since she was last in the office.

"It looks so straightforward though," said Anika. "The rotas and the organising. It's paperwork, admin and communication."

Karen nodded at her, waiting, eyebrows raised. She even rolled her hands to show there was a conclusion to be drawn.

"Oh what? You think I should just go and do it?" Anika asked.

Karen and Sophie beamed at her and nodded.

"Just go and do it Anika," said Karen.

"Yes, do it! We've got your back. We can probably help," said Sophie.

Anika stood up, her brain already romping away with the things that would need to be done. "On it!"

Fifteen minutes later, Anika was standing in the empty office, whiteboard marker in one hand, Charlotte's weekly printout in the other. She would need to confirm all of the third parties which were booked for the special events on Friday, schedule the elves and other support staff to the grottos and those events, and then make sure everyone knew where they were supposed to be and what they were supposed to be doing.

A quick glance at the schedule on the board confirmed that it definitely needed updating, and that they were short by at least three people. Could she could put the shout out to some of the off-duty elves, and see who might be available? She flicked to the back of the printout and found all the contact details. Yes, she could! This was going to be simple.

She pulled a desk phone towards her and started to adjust the rota as she made phone calls. While she was waiting for the calls to connect she fired off messages. She was the queen of admin and she was loving it.

18

CHARLOTTE

A taxi ride brought Charlotte and Jack to the shops on Koopgoot in the centre of Rotterdam. Golden chains of Christmas lights hung high between shops, sprinkling a Christmassy glow over an otherwise grey city.

"We can get a train in two hours," said Jack, consulting his phone as they walked into the mall. "Any further luck with the planes?"

Charlotte had been distracted by the arrival of a message from Daffyd with Alejandro's phone number attached, but she was indeed looking for planes to Stockholm.

"No," she said. "To fly to Sweden it looks like it'd be quicker getting a train down to Brussels, then flying up. But the first flights we could get on won't get us there until tomorrow night at the earliest."

"Well then, the train would be quicker."

"How much quicker?"

He consulted his phone again. "Twenty hours total. Including an overnight from Hamburg."

Charlotte tried to picture that. She always thought her geographic knowledge was reasonable. From the Netherlands to Germany to – where? Denmark? And then?

"Isn't there like a great big sea between Europe and Sweden?"

"There are bridges," said Jack. "And Sweden is in Europe."

"You know what I mean." She scowled. "Fine. Buy the rail tickets."

He raised his eyebrows.

"What?" she said. "I bought the ferry tickets, didn't I? We've both got some peculiar expenses to get signed off. Maybe each time we need to spend, one of us does it. Take it in turns."

"Peculiar expenses indeed," he said, strolling along, a hand in his pocket. "What did you tell everyone at Hedgelord about where you are, by the way?"

"I used the vague phrase 'important matter relating to personal and professional improvements'," said Charlotte.

He frowned. "What? They think you've suddenly gone on a training course on one of the busiest days of the year?"

"It's more generic than that." She thought for a moment, pulling a face. "No, you're right, it's exactly what they're going to think. What did you say?"

"Just told them I was tied up, unable to get away."

Charlotte sighed. "Yeah. Short and sharp, no arguing with that."

"Now, I know you want to go off in search of

paracetamol," said Andrew. He didn't add air quotes to the word, but she felt they were implied. "I'm going to get toiletries and underwear. Maybe a change of clothes."

"Yeah. Yeah, good idea," she said, as though it had just occurred to her. "Department store over there."

They made their way into the store, and without discussion, Jack picked up a basket. They trailed around the shop, adding toothbrushes, toothpaste and deodorant.

They went through menswear and Jack added a multi pack of boxer shorts and socks, then threw in a couple of t-shirts, a pair of trousers, and a sweater.

They moved up a floor to ladieswear, and Charlotte flushed with embarrassment at the realisation she would have to select some underwear, and that Jack would instantly judge her for it. Did she go for something staid and matronly – to dispel any notion she was seeking to enhance her sexual appeal – or did she buy something more in line with what she'd normally choose? That would definitely look like flirting. Even the thought processes made her uncomfortable and she could see Jack had spotted it.

"Want me to turn away while you find your undies?" he asked.

Now she was furious that he had seen her discomfort and was being so nice about it. "No! I am a strong, independent woman and I assert my right to wear what I like under my clothes."

She pulled a pair of knickers off a rack. They were made from bright red lace, and skimpier than any knickers she owned. She thrust them defiantly into the basket. She then followed up with a multipack of black knickers in the style of boy shorts, which would be much more wearable.

"Good. Point made," said Jack amiably. "You'll want some other clothes. I can find somewhere to sit while you try them on if you like."

"What? Why do you assume I need to try them on?"

"Women's clothes are a trickier fit than men's," he said with a small shrug. "It's just a fact of life. I'm very used to sitting and waiting. In fact, I think I'm pretty good at offering advice if you want."

Charlotte once more found herself unaccountably annoyed at him for being so very reasonable and nice. "Fine, I'll grab a few things and hit the changing room."

She tried to be brisk and businesslike as she collected a few items, but shopping for clothes was just never that simple. She couldn't bear to wear anything as sloppy as jogging bottoms, or elasticated waistbands, so she looked for trousers that might work. Then of course there was the annoyance of length. Charlotte was tall, and there had been a trend for trousers to graze ankles in recent years, meaning she often found them to be ridiculously short. She flicked through racks until she found something that might work.

Blouse or t-shirt? She grabbed a couple of both and went to the changing room.

While she was in there, she added Alejandro to her contacts and sent him a message.

Hey. It's Charlotte from Hedgelord. I thought we were going to do some business. You were going to delete a video for me.

That seemed pleasant, casual and unpanicked. If Alejandro was open to business then he would respond and she might not even need to take a stupid overnight train to cold and frosty Stockholm.

She quickly put on a set of the clothes and stepped out of the changing cubicle to find the better mirror.

Of course, Jack was sitting right next to it.

"Nice! What length are those in the leg, though? You probably want the next one up if you're wearing those shoes. I can fetch them if you like."

She gritted her teeth, because he was completely right. A few seconds later he reappeared with a grin.

"Got you the trousers, and I thought you might like this navy V-neck sweater to go with that blouse. Layering is your friend in this weather, and I think it will look just the ticket, don't you?"

Charlotte took them wordlessly. How was it possible for him to be so very irritating and also completely correct?

He was probably simply using it as a distraction so he didn't have to think about his split with his girlfriend. She was providing a public service. She decided to grin and bear it.

She took the clothes back into the cubicle and tried them on. "Well, bollocks."

She looked so much better in the things he had selected. She couldn't decide if she wanted to laugh at the absurdity of the situation, or kick something in temper. She looked around the cubicle and decided that every part of it was too flimsy for a kicking. She could decide later.

With all their purchases made, their old clothes in a backpack Jack had wisely chosen to buy, they headed out.

In the pedestrianised area between the shops, a Santa

figure was making charity collections. He wore a quality suit and Charlotte couldn't help but notice he had a subtly European air about him. Back in the UK, the British Father Christmas had almost entirely given way to the stereotypical Coca Cola Santa Claus, but here he was a much more pagan figure: his beard long and straight, as much blond as it was white, and his boots – proper riding boots! – were adorned with sprigs of holly.

"Nice Santa," said Jack, seeing her look.

"Sinterklaas," said Charlotte.

"Indeed."

She glanced about. "I wonder if he's got a Zwarte Piet with him."

"A what?"

She gave him a sideways look. "Black Peter. You're a Christmas guy. You must know all about Black Peter."

"Sounds like a pirate from a children's TV show."

"No, it's..." She stopped herself. "How long to our train?"

Jack consulted his phone. "We can walk it. Train is in ... that direction. Less than a kilometre."

"Kilometre, eh?" she said. "We've been in Europe for less than a morning and you've gone native." She nudged him in the ribs and they started walking.

19

ANIKA

"Morning all!"

The hearty shout came from the door as Cameron Clasp backed through, hefting a large bag. He beamed at Anika and Tom. "Busy time of the year, eh?"

Cameron Clasp didn't bat an eyelid at the sight of one of the garden centre elves now occupying one of the desks in the Hedgelord main office next to Tom Eccles. No "What the hell are you doing here?". No "Where's Charlotte Mitchell and why are you at her desk?" The man might be the owner of Hedgelord and present on site almost every day, but he seemed to float above it with a constant obliviousness.

Anika sometimes wondered what it was that kept Cameron busy. She could see visible output from the work most people at Hedgelord did, but Cameron sat at the very top, presumably brokering important, unseen deals. Either that or he spent most of his time playing golf or squash, and having long, boozy lunches with his friends. She suspected that much of his activity fell into the latter category.

Meanwhile she had to decipher some of the coded messages on Charlotte's plan for the following day. It was dotted with more than a few bits that said either "Jill not Gill" or "Gill not Jill", and which Anika feared might be important. She was going through other paperwork for explanatory references. If she couldn't find answers here she was either going to have to ask Daffyd (who was not usually a valid source of information), or message Charlotte on the mobile number Anika had been given when she'd first started at Hedgelord.

Tom clearly felt the need to play along with Cameron's comments. "Busy? Yes. Like you wouldn't believe, Cameron." There was bitterness in his tone, as if he was already exhausted from trying to manage the office in Charlotte's absence.

"Well, you'll be delighted to hear that I'm helping to shoulder some of the Christmas burden," said Cameron.

"Really?" said Tom, looking at him. Maybe he thought Cameron was about to sort out the staff rota.

"Oh yes! I will be helping make sure the staff party is an absolute blast. It's a morale booster for us all to piss it up the wall together, isn't it?"

"There's a staff party?" asked Anika. She wasn't sure if she would want to join in pissing it up the wall, but a party was a party and she definitely wanted in.

"Good lord, yes, Anita! How is it possible that word has not yet reached some of our new recruits? Make sure you tell your grotto colleagues to put on their glad rags for tomorrow night, won't you?"

"I will," said Anika.

"We need to pull together in Charlotte's absence." Cameron pulled an unpleasantly conspiratorial face. "Is it women's problems?"

"Um, no. And, ugh, no!" said Anika.

"It's okay. I'm very attuned to the diverse needs of minorities," said Cameron. "Including women."

Tom gestured at the bag. "Is that what you're taking on, Cameron? Organising the party?"

"What? Good God, no. I'll leave that to my team, obviously. No, I'll be buying a little gift for each and every member of staff."

"Including grotto staff?" asked Anika.

Cameron looked sideways at her. "Yes of course." He tapped his chin thoughtfully. "I will need an up to date list, of course. Who can get that for me?"

Tom looked distraught and confused.

"I will," said Anika, given that nobody else had volunteered.

"Great stuff," said Cameron, as though he'd delivered a successful pep talk. "Now, about those gifts. I'm thinking orchids for the ladies and car shampoo sets for the men. What do you think?"

Tom's face did all his talking, but Cameron wasn't picking up on the look of mild horror, so Anika realised she had to speak up.

"I think you might need to consider things at a slightly more personal level, don't you?"

"What? Why do you say that?"

"Well, for one thing, not every man has a car."

"Nonsense!" said Cameron. Then he paused and looked carefully at her. "You're being serious?"

"Yes," said Anika. "And as for orchids, I'm not totally sure, but I think that's a plant, yeah? Speaking personally I don't want a plant."

Cameron looked aghast. "But ladies love orchids!"

"Not all ladies, clearly. And that's another thing. You can't do gendered presents like that. You have at least one non-binary member of staff. What will you give them?"

Anika had the sinking feeling she'd bitten off more than she could chew as she watched Cameron's face as he tried to process this.

"Really?"

She nodded.

His face ran through a series of expressions. There was disbelief, and definitely some curiosity alongside the indignation of his worldview being challenged. "Huh. Who knew? More personal gifts eh? Leave it with me." He tapped the side of his nose.

Anika got up to leave. It was time to message Charlotte for some staffing answers, but then Cameron summoned her back with a click of his fingers. "Hold on, Anita. I shall need a pad and pen and that list of staff. I might as well start with you two."

Anika scrambled to find what he needed in Charlotte's desk, while Cameron turned to Tom.

"Tell me a few things about yourself," Cameron said. "Let's start with your gender, shall we?"

"Not ok!" called Anika over her shoulder as she left.

20

GALLAGHER

allagher took it nice and slowly as he assembled the dog kennel. It was a quicker job than Luka's shed construction, which he was attempting to conceal. This meant he could take great care, so he lined everything up perfectly, checked every angle, and even applied sandpaper to any slightly rough edges.

He still finished before Luka, so he decided to paint the dog kennel in a distinguished shade of green.

"Why you paint fucking kennel?" Luka said, appearing at his side.

"What? So it looks nice. Doesn't it look nice?" Gallagher said.

"Wood is tanalised. Paint may not adhere."

Gallagher scowled. "*May* not adhere. Well I guess that means that it fucking *may* adhere, right?"

"That's the spirit, buddy. If some paint comes off will have rugged camouflage look."

Gallagher sighed. Rugged and camouflage wasn't quite what he'd had in mind, but it sounded cool.

"Come and see shed," said Luka. He shifted a large screen of trellis so that they could access the space. "Once we have our secret passageway, we screw this onto shed on either side." He slid the trellis back in place behind them. "Will be completely hidden once we decorate with lights and shit. Now come, see what you think."

The new shed was bang up against their tea shed. Luka had removed the overhang from the side of the roof so it would fit flush. The two buildings looked like a pair of friends leaning in against each other after having a bit too much to drink.

"I know what you're thinking," said Luka.

"You do?" Gallagher asked, surprised.

"We have created a valley between two pitched roofs. We will need to put guttering there to prevent leaks, yes?"

"Yep mate. Bang on."

Gallagher opened the door and looked inside. The space ought to be big enough for three crates, even if they were really big crates. They would be secure in here, and hidden away from prying eyes.

"So now, all that remains is to cut out secret passageway door between sheds," said Luka. "You want to do that while I keep lookout?"

Gallagher nodded.

A few minutes later he stood in the tea shed with a drill, a jigsaw, some strap hinges, a hasp and a padlock. He used a piece of chalk to draw an arched doorway on the side of the shed. He drilled a pilot hole then inserted the jigsaw blade. It made a horrific noise as he followed the chalk line, sawing through both shed walls. As he completed the arch, he felt the freshly-cut doorway drop away, and he pushed it into the empty shed.

"Cool!" he said to himself as he walked through from one space into another.

There was no time to lose. He needed to fix the door in place and disguise its existence. He picked up the strap hinges and went through to attach them to the wall-door while it lay on the floor. He spent a few minutes using screws to fix the two pieces of door together, as they kept shifting away from each other. He used a spare piece of timber as a cross brace for the new door and was tempted to fetch Luka to help with the next part, as it involved holding the heavy door in place while attaching the hinges other halves to the sides of the cut-away arch. But Luka was lookout, so he'd be better off doing it himself. He wedged the door in place using their chairs, and once he'd got a couple of screws in place, it became much easier.

He stood back to admire the new door. It looked pretty good. He applied the hasp to the other side so they could secure it with a padlock, and the job was done. Well, it was almost done. Now they had to disguise the fact that there was a new door in the side of their tea shed.

Gallagher looked around. There was nothing in here that was big enough to cover a whole doorway. He went outside to find Luka, pulling the door to the tea shed shut behind him.

"Is all done?" Luka asked. "You made a lot of fucking noise."

Gallagher nodded. "How do we cover up the door?"

Luka shrugged. "I don't care. Cupboard? Poster?"

"Have you got a cupboard or a poster?" Gallagher asked. "Someone might see it if they go in there."

"Relax," said Luka. "People only go in there if we say they can go in there. The elf girl, Anika is the only one with free pass and she is team player."

"We cannot involve her in this," said Gallagher with a firm wag of his finger for emphasis. "I'm going to go look for a poster."

Gallagher realised he needed a massive poster to cover the wall in the tea shed. He knew there was a cupboard used by management to store promotional materials, so he decided to explore it. Charlotte would keep signage for events in there, and Tom would have stands and displays sent to him by the producers of the goods sold in the store.

Sometimes there would be a huge push to sell a particular plant, so they would get a big display with colourful artwork declaring why the plant was so good. He pulled one out from last year and shook his head. If the fancy new colour of hydrangea was so good, why did it need lurid plastic display panels to tell you?

He knew the answer of course. Most people didn't really shop for plants with any plan in mind, or any knowledge of what they were looking for. They wanted their attention to be grabbed by the promise of something lovely, so the marketing people would ensure they were dazzled by the cartoon-coloured displays.

If customers would only talk to Gallagher and Luka (well

mainly Luka) they would find out there was a good deal of expertise on tap, free for the taking.

He needed a poster, and he'd been so certain he'd find one in here. The hydrangea one was a massive frame shape, so that people could see the plants through the centre when it was at the end of an outdoors display.

He saw something rolled up in a corner, an elastic band around it. If it was a poster, it could be big enough. He unspooled it.

"Fuck me."

It was an information poster warning of the threat to native UK insects posed by Asian Hornets. He could see why it hadn't been put up in the shop, because it featured a terrifying and enormous hornet, boggling its enormous insect eyes at anyone who glanced at it.

It was perfect! He rolled it back up and put it under his arm.

Back in the shed he used drawing pins to fasten the poster over the new doorway.

"What the fuck is that?" asked Luka as he came through the other door.

"Asian Hornet," said Gallagher.

Luka gave a slow nod. "Is useful that it is scary. People will not see beyond its fucking face. Who made that poster?"

"Says on the bottom that it was sponsored by an organisation called the Friends of the European Hornet." Gallagher straightened. "That's a regular hornet, right?"

"This sounds like some racist bullshit," said Luka.

"No, it says here that it's all about bees and the ecosystem and crop pollination. I mean, it might also be racist bullshit. Who knows?"

"It doesn't matter. That fucking alien face will keep people out, which is main thing."

21

ANIKA

Anika sent Charlotte a text message, asking about the notes on the rota, as she walked over to the marquee for the setting up for the Festive Farm children's grotto experience. She had already made some changes to the elf rota, calling on several elves, including Gillespie who hadn't been scheduled to work. She turned on the music, so the place reverberated to the sound of Christmas songs.

"You were promoted quickly," Gillespie said to Anika when he entered the marquee. "Yesterday you were just Smartypants the elf. Now you're the events manager."

"I'm just helping out with some scheduling while Charlotte isn't in. Now, we're making a few changes to the format in here," said Anika. "We will be building reindeer, so take a look at the kits we'll be using. They are quite straightforward."

Gillespie went over to check on the reindeer. "Ooh these

are nice. Any sign of Santa Raymond yet?"

Anika sighed. "You know how the Santas are. He will appear at some point, I'm sure. I've messaged him already."

As it turned out, Santa Raymond turned up early. He swaggered in and performed an elaborate twirl. "Check out my new robe!" he said to Anika and Gillespie.

"Oh, it's so good!" said Anika, struggling to see how it differed from the one he'd worn previously.

"Custom made, this is. You can tell the quality when you get one made like this. Those cheap imported ones look so tacky in comparison."

"So what's the real mark of quality, would you say?" Anika asked.

"Colour fastness is one thing," said Raymond. "All of the decent ones are dry clean, but you see amateurs just sticking them in the wash and before you know it, the white trim's all pink, isn't it?"

Anika nodded. "Uh huh." She reasoned that a big part of being a temporary events manager was keeping Santa happy.

"Then there's the thermal qualities. Seasonal work like this, you really value an outfit that can keep you warm. But you knew that already, didn't you?"

Anika and Gillespie both nodded fervently. Being out in the marquee was a chilly experience. Squeezing extra layers of clothing underneath the elf costume was essential.

"See this here?" Raymond said, pointing to his bottom.

"Um, what?" Anika asked.

"Heated seat pad in here. Bloody brilliant design. I came up with it, you know?"

"You? You're an actual inventor?" asked Gillespie, who

was now peering at the back of Santas suit, trying to see where the heated part was.

"I am! I reckon I could go on Dragon's Den with this. If I got the right backing I'd take it to that big Christmas Expo in Hull and everyone would want one."

"How does it work?" asked Gillespie.

Raymond was about to drop his trousers, but he eyed Anika and thought better of it. "There's a double layer in the trousers, right? That makes a pocket in the seat area. I bought a heated seat warmer off the internet and it slots right in there. I plug in and phwoaar! Toasty as you like."

"Incredible!" said Gillespie.

Anika watched as Raymond unspooled the power cable and searched for somewhere to plug in.

"You'll need to fetch me an extension lead," he said.

"On it," said Anika.

As she wandered out through the plant area she came across Gallagher applying the finishing touches to a kennel. "A kennel? What's that for?"

"Customer order," said Gallagher, turning away.

Anika had the strangest notion he was being evasive, but she couldn't imagine why. She stepped outside the plant area and gave an exaggerated grunt of frustration.

Karen happened to be walking by with her Health and Safety clipboard in hand. "What's wrong?"

"Huh?" said Anika. "Oh, just, er, you know. Boyfriend trouble."

"Really?" Karen's eyes were aglow. "You must tell me more."

"Actually," said Anika, "it's Sophie who needs our support at this time."

"We shall be lunchtime bereavement counsellors," said Karen, then turned towards Gallagher's work area and the nail-punctured shed. If Karen wandered inside she'd probably find enough HSE infractions to fill the remainder of her accident book.

"Actually," said Anika hurriedly, grabbing her arm. "I wonder if you can help me. It's a good Health and Safety question."

"Oh?"

"Power extension cable."

"What about it?"

"Have you got one and can we use it?"

Karen started to walk back to the shop. Anika fell in beside her.

"What's it for?" Karen asked.

"Santa Raymond," said Anika.

Karen narrowed her eyes. "Portable electrical devices need to be PAT tested. Do not let him plug anything in that hasn't got a current PAT test label on it."

"Yep," said Anika, wondering how on earth she was going to check a device that was buried in Santa's trousers.

"Okay."

Back at the tills, customers queued with their many purchases. The decoration and tree rush had peaked the previous week and now trolleys were filled with presents and luxuries. Books, condiments, woolly garments and a number of amaryllis and poinsettia plants.

Karen fished around inside an unmanned till cubicle and produced an extension lead. "Unspool all of the wire for fire safety and make sure it doesn't constitute a trip hazard," she said.

"Got it," said Anika, even though those two things sounded as if they would cancel each other out.

"Don't forget, we need to be vigilant when it comes to Health and Safety. I want to know everything about everything. You hear of any accidents, near misses or risks that need to be addressed, you come to me, right?"

Anika thought briefly about the incident that had resulted in hundreds of screws being flung through the air with lethal force. No way was she letting Karen find out about that. She was wound so tight that she was practically vibrating with a weird, tense energy.

"Will do," she said with a smile.

Her phone buzzed as she walked back to the grotto. It was Charlotte.

22

ANIKA

Anika wasn't sure why older people phoned you when there were any number of means by which text messages could be sent, but she answered it nonetheless.

"*Hello, Anika,*" said Charlotte. She sounded slightly out of breath and was possibly walking.

"Hi. Sorry. I didn't mean to bother you. You might have been doing something important. Where are you?"

"*Er. A place called Karel Door-something.*"

"*Karel Doormanstraat,*" said a male voice.

"Okay. Sounds nice."

"*Yes. About the rota thing. That 'Gill not Jill' thing means you can't have Gillespie and Jill working on the same station. Daffyd forgets, but you need to make sure they're not together.*"

"And why is that?"

"*They were a workplace thing. Very briefly.*"

"How briefly?" asked Anika. Jill had literally been with them for less than a week.

"*Remember the night when Gillespie did his Mickey Bubbles tribute performance? He worked his very temporary magic on Jill that night. Twenty-four hours later he was heartbroken, she thought it was hilarious, and yeah, we've got to keep them apart.*"

"Oh, okay. I think that was everything. I—"

"*Listen,*" said Charlotte. "*Is Santa Raymond in today?*"

"He's turned up. He's on the schedule."

"*Right, right.*" Charlotte sounded pensive. "*Look, if I give you the nod, can you send him home?*"

"What? Why?"

"*Just do it. We may need to terminate his contract, like immediately, with extreme prejudice.*"

"But why?"

"*For fuck's sake. You don't want to know. I don't want you to know. I'm just asking, are you capable of it?*"

Anika stood erect, head held high. Firing people. That was a true leadership thing. It would look good on a CV, sort of. "Of course," she said.

"*Good. Await my signal. Speak later.*"

Charlotte ended the call. Anika, puzzled, went back to the grotto. Jill was making her way in as Anika approached.

"Jill," Anika called. "Change of plan. You're on reindeer paddock duties."

"Really?"

"Word from the top."

As Jill turned away, Anika when into the marquee where Raymond was sketching some of his other designs for Gillespie.

"Santa travel grooming kits. Beard oil, nose hair trimmer, eye drops to enhance the twinkling. My own formulation."

Gillespie stroked his chin where there was no hint of a beard forming at any point in the near future. "I wonder what the elf equivalent would be?" he mused.

"Give it some thought," said Raymond. "I always have an open mind for a collaboration."

"Yeah?" said Gillespie, excited.

"Oh very much so. I already have some arrangements with people who are resellers of my specialist items."

Anika paused in the act of unspooling the extension cord. "Specialist items?" She ignored the ping of her phone. It had gone off several times in the past few minutes.

Raymond pursed his lips as if he wasn't sure whether to continue, but he beamed with pride. "Calendars. It's a range I started last year. Made almost as much from those as I did from being Santa over the course of the season. A lot of sales online."

"Calendars?" Gillespie asked. "Specialist calendars?"

Anika started to form a suspicion about where this might be going, but she could see Gillespie wasn't there yet.

"Can I see?" asked Gillespie.

"Er, sure," said Raymond. He leaned over to reach a bag that was stashed at the back of his chair and pulled out a glossy calendar. "Obviously I would not sell these while working at Hedgelord. I might sometimes take orders and serve them from the boot of my car in the car park."

Gillespie had frozen in shock as he looked at the images on the calendar. He held the calendar at arm's length and swivelled it through ninety degrees, trying to understand it. "Santa porn? It's a Santa porn calendar?"

"Erotica, dear Gillespie. It's beautifully done though, isn't it? I went to a studio where they had the best lighting. The artistic direction was all mine, and I have to say I'm pretty proud of how it looks."

Anika couldn't help herself. She leaned in to take a look, but Raymond snatched it away before she could see anything.

"Now then, I can't be corrupting young minds, can I?" he said with a wink.

Anika wanted to protest that Gillespie was no older than she was, but then Raymond obviously meant young *female* minds. She wondered what Raymond's Santa-based erotica customer base looked like. Was this part of the reason why Charlotte might wanted him fired?

Gillespie looked as if he was still processing what he'd seen. He wore a stunned, faraway look.

Anika's phone pinged with another message. She pulled it out and realised she had some catching up to do. There were elves to organise for later in the day, and the special events were looking a little more complex than she had initially thought. In fact, it looked as if some wires had got crossed when the bookings had been made...

"I need to make a few calls," she said to Gillespie. "Can you sort out the fairy lights and organise whoever comes to do check-in? I'll just be over there."

Anika found a chair near to the back of the marquee, which would serve as her own office for a few minutes. She pored over her phone. There were two special events on

Friday, aside from Santa Paws. One was a children's tea party in the café and the other was carriage rides in the paddock (which was part of the overflow car park).

She looked up the poster and bookings for the carriage rides. It was fully booked, but she was having trouble picturing how it was supposed to work. The poster featured the weird bauble coach that had arrived at Hedgelord on the same day that Anika had been recruited as an elf. She'd received the impression it had been ordered on a whim by Cameron the owner, and that nobody else knew what to do with it. One thing was certain, it was not a functional coach, it was decorative only.

She looked again at the poster and at some of the names signed up for the event. It was an event for couples who wanted a cute picture for Instagram or for putting on a Christmas card. They would sit and smile together on an adorable coach, get a picture, then sit under a blanket while going for a short horse-drawn ride somewhere picturesque.

Anika made a note to check on what preparations had been made so far. She hoped it was more than buying a coach that was unable to move.

23

CHARLOTTE

The entrance to Rotterdam central train station was a huge looming triangular shard which stood out against the pedestrianised square and open tramlines around it like a protruding tooth. Charlotte and Jack crossed the road and made their way down the escalators in search of information and platforms.

"Everything okay at work?" said Jack, nodding as Charlotte put her phone away.

"Just some minor details. Seems one of the elves is stepping up into the power vacuum while I'm not there."

Jack smiled. "Oh, is that what it is? A power vacuum?"

She tried to shrug it off. "I'm not claiming to be powerful. I'm just... Anyway, I've not seen you getting in touch with your work. Aren't you worried how things are going?"

He wrinkled his nose happily. "I assume everything's fine. I trust the team. I get people to shadow me all the time, assistant for the day, so that they know what's going on."

The mention of assistants prompted a thought in her head. "So, I didn't tell you about Black Peter."

"The children's pirate."

"He's not a pirate. He's... Oh, he's much *much* worse than that." They wandered across the subterranean concourse towards some departure boards. "You know how in different cultures, Father Christmas or Santa or whatever has different helpers."

"Like the elves."

"Right. So you've got elves and in the Alps they've got the Krampus."

"I love the Krampus," Jack grinned.

"Well, in the Netherlands and probably Belgium and Luxembourg and that, they have Black Peter. He's a man, dressed in kind of clownish, sort of Tudor gear, and he goes round with Sinterklaas and listens at the chimneys of all the children to hear if they've been good or bad."

"Well, a bit Krampus-y but it doesn't sound that bad."

"Ah, well. Black Peter is – he's a person of colour. He's black. That's his name."

"A bit on the nose there, but representation is good."

She pulled back to give him a look. "He's been around for centuries. People dressed up as Black Peter – and I don't mean black people dressed up as him."

Jack's eyes narrowed then widened. "You don't mean..."

"Mmm-hmmm. Black face and bright red lipstick. Oh, yeah. The full thing."

"Oh, man!"

"Quite," she said. "Nothing says Christmas like a racist caricature!"

"People were different in the past though," said Jack. "I mean that doesn't excuse anything, but, you know, the Victorians and that were—"

"I'm talking about in our lifetime. I mean even running into this century."

"Oh, fuck. Really?"

"And the Dutch seem such progressive people."

"Christ. Really?"

She rolled her eyes and waved her hand. "Oh, attitudes have changed, but like really slowly. It's like some of the Morris dancers in England who still black up to dance. Old stupid offensive traditions die hard."

"Wow." He cast about. "Is it terrible that I want to see one now?"

"Er, yes. And perfectly understandable. But yes. That's a terrible thought, Jack Hartigan."

They looked up at the information board. Jack started to point out the platform for their train. It was marked as the train to Osnabrück. Charlotte had no idea where that was. They found the right signs and headed in that direction.

"The thing with Black Peter," she said. "It happened, like in so many places, because the people chose to separate the good bits of Father Christmas from the bad bits."

"Our Father Christmas in England was never bad."

"You mean only giving coal to naughty children or sticks for their parents to beat them with?"

"Apart from that."

"So when the bad bits of Santa needed splitting off, they put them in a new figure. Black Peter listens out for news of naughty children and, if I remember this right, kidnaps them, puts them in a sack, and takes them to Spain to work in his workshop."

"I'm sorry?" said Jack. "Naughty children go to Spain?"

She shrugged. "I guess it's the Dutch equivalent of hell. I don't make this crap up."

"Sounds like you do."

Jack laugh-hummed to himself as he contemplated her small lecture. "And you and I are stuck on a quest to undo the work of two bad Santas who should know better."

"'Should know better' doesn't really quite cover filthy pornographic Santa movies, does it?" she said. "At least neither of them had racist caricatures turn up in their solo porno films."

"Oh, yes," said Jack dubiously. "Thank heavens for small mercies."

Their train was waiting for them on the platform. They waited behind a bunch of boisterous young adults with backpacks and Santa hats before getting on.

"Quest, huh?" said Charlotte.

Jack made a silly face. "It's a quest of sorts. Chasing an elf across Europe. Very quest-like."

"Maybe," she said. "You do have an impish, hobbit-like aspects to you."

"Thanks. And I'm sure you'd make an excellent barbarian warrior."

"Oh, really. You picturing me in a fur bikini and wielding a massive chopper."

His expression became worried and confused. "I mean ... I wasn't. Not until just now."

"Dirty minds, some people," she said and stepped aboard

the train. As she did, her phone buzzed with an incoming text.

24

ANIKA

Lunchtime rolled around and Anika forced herself to take time to meet with Sophie and Karen. She was up to date on her messages, and fairly certain that Hedgelord events staff were now all organised for the next twenty four hours.

Things had gone well in the grotto during the morning shifts and Santa Raymond, despite her weird messages from Charlotte and discovering there were such things as erotic Santa calendars, seemed to be doing a perfectly brilliant job entertaining the children and doling out presents.

Nonetheless, she sent a message to Charlotte about Raymond's unpleasant calendar side-venture before going to the Pagoda Café and joining the two women at their table. Sophie had made a round of cheese sandwiches alongside a plate stacked with a small mountain of mince pies, so Anika happily tucked in.

Sophie was also dressed up in her mop cap and ugly,

many-skirted dress for her role as Mrs Claus in the Festive Farm marquee grotto that afternoon. Just as many of the elves were flitting between jobs, so Sophie was fulfilling multiple roles as both café server, ad hoc elf and occasional Mrs Claus.

"Sophie was just telling us about her thoughts on the funeral," said Karen. Anika could hear her deliberately adopting an overly soft and gentle voice, like she was the narrator on a toilet roll commercial.

Anika wondered if it was a bit soon to be thinking about the funeral. She was a stranger to personal grief, but wasn't there a process to all this? If Douglas had just died, wasn't it appropriate to do a bit of all-out grieving first, a bit of raging at God and shaking your fists and just being a big blubbery mess?

"Okay. Funeral," she said as she took another cheese sandwich.

"I just want it to reflect who Douglas was."

"Of course you do," said Karen. "And what was he like? I'm sorry I never got to know him."

Sophie picked up a tissue, though her eyes were currently dry, and held it in her hand while she cradled the cup of tea in front of her. "I loved him," she said. "He was a big old idiot but I loved him."

"Of course," said Karen.

"But he was always there for me. In the night, when I needed him."

Anika worried this was going to veer off into an old people sex talk, but Sophie continued.

"Just a comforting presence, you know. And I think that's it. He always made me feel safe. That's what it was."

Karen nodded and made overly sympathetic noises.

"Sure," said Sophie, laughing weakly. "He hogged too much of the bed and the ... oh, the noises he would make in the night. But you get used to that, don't you?"

It was Anika's experience that sharing her bed with others was frankly a generally annoying experience, but maybe that changed as you got older. She could only speculate that older people like Karen and Sophie, faced with the spectre of their own approaching deaths, felt the need for some comfort in the night.

"And what about his personality?" said Karen. "What was he like as a person?"

"Oh, yes," said Sophie. "Because he really was. He was with me all the time. Loved me completely. Lost without me. Even when I didn't really want him he was there."

"Yes?"

"But the things he liked... He loved the garden – that was his happy place, I think. Either out there among the flowers and shrubs or just sitting on the patio. Long summer days just at peace and..." She dabbed her eyes. "He loved the outdoors. Well, of course he would."

Karen gripped her hand across the table comfortingly.

"Douglas was a bit of greedy bugger, mind you," said Sophie.

"Oh?"

"Loved a packet of digestives. Really did. Turn your back and the next minute they were all gone. But I assumed that was okay because he was always so active. True, he was a little tubby around the middle, but that didn't seem so bad. Not an altogether unattractive aspect."

"You like the chunkier man," said Karen.

Sophie blinked and looked at her. "Um, I don't know. I guess. I think that's the thing about Douglas. I'd had boyfriends before he came along. All sorts really. But with Douglas around, I suppose I never gave that kind of thing any thought. You know, Douglas really filled that part of my life and, while he was with me, I never really sought out another man."

"That's, er, sweet," said Anika.

"And maybe that's what I'm feeling right now," said Sophie.

"What is?"

She sighed. "Maybe a little realisation. I'm sad about Douglas. Of course, I am. But maybe it's made me realise that for a long time I've been too happy with my own company, and maybe I need... Well, to be honest, maybe I need another man in my life. Someone to share it with."

Karen's lips formed around a word but nothing came. Anika similarly had nothing.

"So, er..."

"You want to find another man?" said Anika.

"You think it's too late?" said Sophie.

"Or maybe too soon?" suggested Karen. "Ah, you haven't even sorted out Douglas yet."

"True, true. You think it's a bit disrespectful?"

Anika blew out her lips. "Um..."

Sophie hummed thoughtfully and slurped down the last of her tea. "I think Douglas, if he could speak to me, would say he just wants me to be happy. Not that he was fond of men himself."

"Well, er, no?" said Karen, frowning.

"And maybe that was part of the problem. He didn't like it when I had gentleman callers."

"No?"

"I don't think he could tell the difference between them and the postman, who he hated with a vengeance." She felt the teapot on the table and then stood up. "I'll get us another pot, shall I?"

Anika watched her walk back to the café counter and the hot water dispenser. "So," she said. "Douglas was a dog, right?"

"Yeah," said Karen. "Absolutely. A bloody dog."

ANIKA WASN'T sure why she was irritated when she hurried back over to the grotto. Was she actually annoyed that Douglas had turned out to be a dog rather than a husband? That didn't make Sophie's personal grief any different, did it?

Well, of course it did, she told herself in annoyance. It was a bloody dog. Anika had prepared herself to help out with husband-sized bereavement, not dog-sized bereavement. She had emotionally invested to the wrong level and now she felt emotionally short-changed. Humans were more important. The death of a human was, no matter how much people loved animals, a bigger deal.

Anika could see the ticketed visitors for the Festive Farm marquee lined up outside, alongside the display of potted perennials. Giving the kids cheeky waves and beaming like any elf should, she capered past Gillespie who was on check-in duty.

"Everything okay in there?" she said.

"Think so."

She went in through the little outer area, where excess supplies and the power cable connectors were hidden behind hay bales, and into the marquee itself, where Santa Raymond sat on his wooden throne, adjusting and smoothing down his felted trousers.

"We all good and ready here?" she said.

"Oh, ho," he said jollily. "My tush is toasty and ready to receive the little tykes."

She knew he was referring to his plug-in seat warmer, but after having glimpsed only a little of his unsavoury calendar, Anika did not want any reminders about his toasty tush.

"Right. Good."

"You know I'm used to slightly more salubrious surroundings than this," said Raymond.

"Uh-huh," said Anika, distracted. The new fairy lights she'd brought in to add some much needed festivity were not switched on. She frowned and went back out to where the power came into the marquee.

"I'm the star of the show," Raymond called after her. "I work best when given a bit of VIP treatment."

"Yeah?" she replied, just to indicate she was listening.

Behind the bale, extension cables met in a multi-socket junction. As far as she could make out, everything was already plugged in.

"I did this amazing piece to camera the other week," Raymond continued. "Great director. Great lighting."

She decided to unplug everything, then plug it all back in. It was the electrical equivalent of turning everything off and on again, but she really didn't have any better ideas.

She had all the things unplugged and was starting to reconnect them all when her phone began to buzz.

25

CHARLOTTE

"C'mon, c'mon," Charlotte muttered, pacing back and forth along the eight foot section of train corridor adjacent to the buffet car.

They had just passed through Utrecht and were now heading through flat, sparsely wooded countryside. Their change at Osnabrück was several hours away, while their ultimate destination, Stockholm, was a whole night and a morning away. The very idea of catching up with Alejandro seemed a far-fetched dream, particularly in the light of the message she'd just received from him.

In response to her light-hearted and pleasant enquiry about the video, Alejandro had replied with: *Lol! A grand not going to cover it. BDE are gonna pay ten times that. Couldn't be bothered to wait around. You snooze you lose.*

She'd felt sick in the pit of her stomach. It was all a big joke to Alejandro. The man had some sordid Santa porn and maybe no amount of money would ever make him delete it.

On top of that, there had been Anika's text about Santa Raymond's 'erotic calendar'. No, it was all too much.

Jack had been away down the train aisle, trying to borrow a cable to charge his phone. Charlotte felt she didn't need to tell him she already had a direct line to Alejandro. They might be on a joint mission – quest indeed! – but ultimately it was each person for themselves. She needed to make this whole problem go away and save Hedgelord's reputation.

And so she'd gone out into the corridor towards the buffet car and called Anika.

Anika picked up at last.

"Ah! Thought you would never answer," said Charlotte.

"*Yeah. Kind of busy,*" said Anika. She sounded a little breathless. "*Need to … get these plugs back in. Lights aren't working.*"

"Yes. Listen, we need to pull the plug."

"*Pull the plug?*"

"On Santa Raymond."

"*As in…?*"

"Terminate his contract. Like now, kaput, with extreme prejudice."

"*Get rid of him? Like now? We're just about to let the kids in!*"

"Gone. ASAP. Seriously, Anika. We have to do this."

"*And what do I tell Raymond?*"

"Tell him anything. Tell him the truth."

"*I don't know what the truth is. You haven't told me.*"

"Right… The calendar thing. Go with the calendar thing."

"*But we can't go on without him. A Santa's grotto needs a Santa.*"

"For fuck's sake, Anika!" Charlotte's watch buzzed at her cursing. "Use some initiative. Call Mudge."

"What's Mudge?"

"He's a Santa we've used before. Very competent. I'll message you his number."

"Oh, okay."

"Do it. Yes? You'll do it now. Get rid of Santa Raymond by whatever means you can. He's a liability."

"Sure. Leave it with me." Anika ended the call.

Charlotte should have felt good about that. There was a problem, she was doing something about it. She was one step ahead of Jack, who was still operating under the assumption that Alejandro was going to delete his filthy porn files in exchange for the agreed thousand pounds. It was all a crap situation, but Charlotte was making the best of it.

But did she feel any relief or comfort because of that? The fuck she did.

Idly she googled BDE to see if she could work out who Alejandro might be selling the videos to.

26

ANIKA

Anika slipped her phone back into her pocket and pushed the last plug back into the bank of extension sockets. The lights in the marquee flickered for an instant, then went out.

"Too many things?" she pondered.

Presumably this set up had worked before. Whatever, it wasn't working now. The only addition she could think of was Santa Raymond's seat warmer.

"Hey, Raymond!" she called. "You still got your seat warmer plugged in?"

She hoped he wouldn't make another comment about his heated tushy. Life was bad enough without mental images of old men's bums parading through her mind.

Raymond didn't reply.

She went through to the marquee proper. "Raymond!"

He was sitting on his throne, chin resting on his chest. The man was asleep. Anika sighed, wondering what kind of hedonistic lifestyle kept Raymond up so late that he was falling asleep on the job. If he was doing mucky calendars and extra work on the side then anything was possible.

"Oi, Raymond!" She reached out to shake his shoulder, and saw the wisps of smoke coming from the seat of the chair.

Smoke, fire. Fire, electricity. Electricity, electrocution. Her brain lurched from one thought to the next so rapidly that she almost reached out to check he was still alive. Then a much cleverer part of her brain interceded and stopped her from grabbing a man who was being electrocuted.

"Christ!" she shouted and ran back to the plug sockets. She unplugged them all in a queasy frenzy and ran back. "Raymond, mate!"

She grabbed him. His head lolled slackly forward in a way that made her heart convulse with horror. "Oh no! Oh crap!"

She felt for a pulse, but now he had started to sag forward in his chair she was more focused on making sure he didn't tumble to the ground.

"Gillespie!" she yelled. "Come here, quick!"

"What?" called Gillespie.

"Come here!" she bellowed.

Gillespie came in, eyebrows raised. "We've got a queue, Anika. I'm going to bring the first lot in now."

"No. God, no. Don't. I need a second to sort something out." Part of Anika's brain laughed at the wording. This was definitely *not* going to take a second. She felt again for a pulse on Raymond's neck. "Listen Gillespie, on a scale of one to ten, how squeamish are you?"

"Squeamish? Oh, quite squeamish. Honestly, I can't even talk about how bad I am at the sight of blood because sometimes I even make myself feel fain— Ooh, I feel a bit funny now, come to mention it. What's up with Raymond? Is he drunk?"

Anika had no answer to that. There was an answer, an honest one, and that was 'No, he wasn't drunk', but in her mind the big follow up to that was explaining what Raymond actually was, and that was 'Dead'.

"He's..." She had nothing. "He's not able to continue."

"He's not ill, is he?"

"No, he's not ill," she said, honestly. Only live people could actually be ill. "He's just had a little accident."

"Accident? Do I need to get Karen? She's the Health and Safety—"

"Christ, no!" If Karen saw this she'd have a heart attack and there'd be two bodies to deal with.

Two bodies. On Anika's first day of trying to show leadership qualities. That would *not* look good on a CV.

Against the mounting horror and chaos, she told herself that she needed to deal with this rationally. She was good at coping. She was a coper. Her parents had brought her up to make sure that things got done. Even in the face of utter catastrophe, she needed to cope and deal with the matter in hand.

"Go out front and tell the people it will be another five minute wait."

"I don't think they want to wait."

"I don't give a flying fudgsicle, Gillespie!" she spat. "Get out there and *tell them!*"

"Power's gone to your head," he tutted but did as he was told.

Anika tried to check Raymond's pulse a third time. Anika was no medical professional, but she was certain there wasn't one to be found. She had a Santa corpse in a marquee in the middle of the garden centre and dozens of children outside who, if she was not careful, might potentially have a truly memorable and traumatising experience.

Anika hurried out of the marquee. "No one goes in!" she snapped at Gillespie as passed him.

She averted her eyes from the queuing customers, they would have to wait. She needed help. She hoped that the plant guys were in their tea shed. She ran in their direction. There was a dog kennel with drying green paint on it on the path outside.

"Gallagher! Luka!" she shouted. "Are you there?"

27

GALLAGHER

Gallagher was cleaning his paint brushes with spirits and Luka was in the process of making them a well-deserved cup of tea when they heard Anika starting to shout outside.

Gallagher called back in a mock robotic tone. "This is a recording. The person you are trying to reach can't come to the phone at the moment."

"Gallagher! It's an emergency. Please come quickly."

There was a terrible urgency in her voice that made Gallagher leap up, wipe his hands hurriedly on his overall and head out. "Are we on fire again?" he asked.

"Follow me," said Anika, which was no answer at all, but that horrible urgency was still there. "Can't talk outside," she said, beckoning them on. "There's a queue waiting for the grotto."

She walked briskly ahead of them to the marquee, giving a small smile to the families who were waiting for the Festive

Farm children's grotto experience. She went straight past the elf outside, with Luka and Gallagher in tow.

Gillespie tried to get her attention. "Can we let the people come—?"

"*Not yet!*" she barked.

She all but dragged Luka and Gallagher into the main area. There was a slumped man on the Santa throne. Gallagher knew Raymond. He'd been doing the Hedgelord gig for a few years.

"You need to help me," said Anika.

"Is he sleeping?" asked Luka.

"Looks dead drunk," said Gallagher.

"Well, you're half right," said Anika. "So here's what I think happened—"

"Is he dead?" said Luka, stepping forward.

She swallowed hard. "Santa Raymond is dead."

Gallagher saw that Luka was possibly right, while the look on Anika's face... "What the fuck?" he said.

"I don't know how, but it might be my fault," she said. "What do I do? Call the emergency services?"

Gallagher was about to point out that, yes, obviously, that was exactly what you did. And then he also saw the look on Luka's face. They had just finished constructing a space for a scary international criminal to hide ... well, they had no idea what the man wanted to hide. Could be drugs? Could be guns? Could be boxes of tightly-packed migrant workers? Whatever it was, it wasn't going to be something they would want the police showing an interest in.

"I don't know," he said. "Let's think about this..."

Anika grimaced. "I was supposed to check that his seat

warmer was PAT tested before he plugged it in, but I got distracted."

"Seat-warmer?"

"Do you think he's been electrocuted? The lights won't work."

"There is that smell," said Luka with a small grimace. "Burning smell. We should unplug everything before touching him."

"I did that," said Anika. "The lights have gone off."

Gallagher went out to check the collection of power sockets near the entrance. Everything was unplugged. Back into the Santa section, where he saw Luka following a cable until it disappeared into Raymond's trousers.

"Fucking hell. His trousers are charred. Electrocuted all right." He put a hand to Raymond's neck to check for a pulse.

"I did that too. Oh, God. Karen's going to explode. I'm going to get fired."

"Or...," said Gallagher. "Or..." He had a thought nudging its way to the forefront of his mind, but it was terrible. "If he's definitely dead, you could just get this first lot of kiddiwinks through the grotto, give ourselves a bit of room to think."

"You're saying we invite the families into the grotto and just work around the corpse of Santa?" Anika said.

"The man is dead," said Luka. "Not going to get any deader."

"I think we could make it work," said Anika. There was a faint note of hysteria in her voice now that had replaced the shocked dread. "Tell the kids that Santa's taking a nap and I'll just do the presents, with a bit of extra capering and horseplay to distract them."

"What's up with Raymond?" asked Gillespie, peering round the entrance.

"Santa Raymond is dead," said Luka.

Gillespie fainted straight to the floor.

"*He* is not dead," Luka reassured Anika. "Just fainted."

"There are going to be families coming through here all day," said Gallagher.

"I... I could try to get another Santa to cover," said Anika. "But we can't tell Karen. She's already flipping her shit about this accident stuff. But we'll have to tell someone at some point."

A reported accident would bring blue lights and cops, and there might be another visit from a crook with a pointy beard wielding a red hot trowel. "Well, again," said Gallagher, "here's a thought..."

"Yes?"

"Raymond died being electrocuted by his own seat warmer, right?"

The others nodded.

"What if... What if we were able to get him back to his house and make it look like it happened there? It definitely could have happened there, couldn't it? Then there would be no repercussions, just a terrible accident that happened to a man at home."

"Is fucking insane," said Luka.

"I mean, I don't want us to have more accidents in the book," said Anika. "But still..."

"And you don't want to get fired," Gallagher added.

"But that would be breaking the law, right?"

Luka twitched. "Is hard to say. The law is a funny thing."

"You said it was an insane idea."

"I said was insane, not that we shouldn't do it," said Luka.

"Yeah?" said Anika.

"It makes a lot of sense," said Gallagher. "Kind of. Who wants to spoil Christmas for a load of kiddies, eh? First things first: we need to secure him in his throne and move him out of the light a bit."

Luka placed the unconscious Gillespie's feet on a chair to elevate them. Then he helped Gallagher wrestle Raymond's throne into a corner. Gallagher used the cable from the seat warmer to tie the back of Raymond's hood to the chair.

"Who's Mrs Claus for this next session?" called Gallagher as he worked.

"It's Sophie," said Anika. "I normally go and grab her from the café just before it starts. We can't tell her about this. For one thing she'll freak out and blab to Karen. For another, she's had enough death in her life recently."

"Really?" said Luka.

"Her Douglas. Died yesterday I think. Very sad. So – I'll go and get her when we're sure we have a plan."

Gillespie sat up with a groan. "Ugh. What am I doing on the floor?"

"You fainted," said Gallagher.

The dozy elf looked at Raymond. "Did you say he was hurt? Has someone called an ambulance?"

Anika gave him what she probably thought was a gentle look. "About that. We need a team huddle because this day is going to need some careful planning. Raymond is dead. Sadly passed away from natural causes. Gallagher? Luka? I'll time the session so this group finishes ten minutes early, see if I can book another Santa. And then, when I give the nod, we'll transfer Raymond to his car." She pointed to Gallagher. "Can you find a trolley and a tarp?"

Gallagher nodded.

"Wait, this is a joke, isn't it?" said Gillespie, the corners of his mouth uncertain which way they wanted to pull. "We're going to call for an ambulance now, aren't we?"

"For the sake of Hedgelord, we're going to manage this ever so slightly differently," said Anika, placing a hand on Gillespie's shoulder. "It's what Raymond would have wanted."

28

ANIKA

nika hurried over to the Pagoda Café, retrieved Sophie, and ushered her past the increasingly irate queue. Gillespie could now start to check them in and the session would begin.

Sophie took her place behind the tables and adjusted her hat.

"Small change of plan, Sophie," said Anika. "The kids won't interact directly with Santa Raymond in this session, I will give out the presents as they leave."

"Oh? That will be a bit strange, won't it?" Sophie said.

"No, it's part of a feminist levelling up that I'm trying out. You know how I'm taking the lead with events? Well I thought it was time that Mrs Claus came out of the shadows and stopped playing second fiddle to her husband."

"Goodness me!" said Sophie. "I'm to step into Santa's boots? Well, it's a huge responsibility, and I feel very proud that you think I'm up to it."

"I believe in you, Mrs Claus," said Anika. "Now, knock 'em dead!"

Anika regretted her phrasing as soon as she'd said it, but Sophie was blissfully unaware. She seemed to grow in stature as she absorbed the importance of taking over the key role.

Children filed in and took their places at the tables. There was an excited buzz.

Sophie trotted over to Anika. "Should we give some of the songs a twist as well? Like Rudolph could be a girl's name instead like ... like— Actually, I don't know."

Anika had no idea if there was a female version of the name. "Let's not confuse them too much," she said to Sophie. "Baby steps! We can definitely mention that Santa's reindeer are all likely to be female. Science says so, because they are always depicted with antlers."

"Of course!" said Sophie, with a clap of her hands. She inhaled deeply and prepared to address the group. "Welcome everybody to this very special session! I hope you like singing because while we work on stuffing our reindeer, we will need to make a lot of noise, what do you say?"

Anika helped to lead the group in the first song, which was *Jingle Bells*, then she sidled over to Gillespie. "When it's time for the presents to be given out, will you go over to Raymond and help him give the kids a wave?"

Gillespie opened his mouth in horror. "You have got to be kidding me! You want me to touch a dead person? I can't even— Urgh..." He sagged.

Anika managed to grab him and steer him to a chair. "Don't start fainting again!" she hissed. "It's fine, I'll do it. You just need to be over here and make sure that when the kids start to walk out they wave to Santa, yeah? Not before."

"Uh huh," said Gillespie, looking a little bit grey.

"Now, it's stuffing time. You up to helping?"

Gillespie nodded and the two of them moved between the tables, helping children to push the stuffing right down into the legs of the reindeer with the wooden spoons provided. It was a pleasant relief from the sticky reindeer food they often made, where everything ended up coated in sugar.

"Now then!" shouted Sophie. "Who here knows a fact about reindeer?"

Anika fetched the antlers from a box at the back and showed them around the children so they could all handle them.

Sophie continued with her chatter and they sang another song.

"We need to get these reindeer all finished and move this group out," Anika whispered to Gillespie. "Three minutes or less, which will buy us a bit of time."

They swooped in and made sure that every child had a more or less complete reindeer toy as Sophie rattled through the *Twelve Days of Christmas*. Anika hoped she hadn't peaked too soon. Daffyd warned that it was a song that took its toll on the voice, and they couldn't afford for Mrs Claus to lose her voice.

Anika swept across the room and whispered to Sophie. "Your big moment now. Pose for pictures with each one on their way out."

She signalled Gillespie that he should hand presents to

the children as they filed past and she went over to Raymond.

She had volunteered to wave his arm, but now she was faced with actually doing it, she was overwhelmed by a sense that it was very, very wrong.

She glanced across at Gillespie, who was starting to steer children towards the exit and getting them to give Santa an excited wave. Anika swallowed down her reservations – she was made of sterner stuff than this. She clasped Raymond's hand, which was now cold, and raised it in hers to gave a cheery wave, pumping Raymond's arm and praying she would not dislodge his corpse. She thought perhaps the two of them looked like a boxer and trainer after a match: making sure to raise their hands to their adoring fans, even though only one of them was really capable.

When they were gone, she saw there was a message on her phone from Charlotte.

Is it done? Is Santa Raymond gone?

Anika didn't know how to answer that question, so opted for the truth.

Yes, she texted. *Raymond is no more.*

29

GALLAGHER

Gallagher and Luka occupied themselves by moving some terracotta pots from one display to another, so they could patrol the path to the marquee. When Anika gave the nod they would spring into action and help move the unfortunate Raymond, but until then they were in a holding pattern.

"We got company," said Luka in a low voice.

Tom and Daffyd were walking towards them. There was something in their body language that spoke of conflict. Tom's efforts to stride purposefully were hampered by Daffyd's erratic scampering. He would scoot in front of Tom to make a point, then fall back so that he walked at his side.

"...And of course we have to be careful with reindeer food, because if the children see the actual live reindeer on their way out they might be tempted to feed them what is actually highly inappropriate ingredients," Daffyd was saying, apparently giving Tom an unwanted crash course on grotto operations.

Tom stopped to address Gallagher and Luka. "What's that you're doing?"

"Frost checks on terracotta," said Luka, hefting a large pot. "Big frost is forecast, so we need to move them, make sure no water is pooling inside. Could save a lot of damage."

Gallagher was impressed with Luka's apparently endless, fluid lies.

"And the pallets of compost outside the landscaping office? I asked Anika to ask you to move them earlier."

"Anika?" said Luka. "Yes, she has been very busy giving instructions to everyone today."

Tom opened and closed his mouth as if he might have something more to say, then decided against it. "Very good. Continue."

Gallagher realised Tom had been looking for a way to assert some authority. Daffyd was getting on his nerves, that much was obvious.

"Come along Tom, let's check in on the Festive Farm children's grotto experience," said Daffyd with a dainty clap of his hands. "They are sure to need our assistance as it's brand new."

"Hold up!" called Gallagher, raising an arm. He had to stop them walking in on whatever Anika might be doing with Raymond's dead body.

"Yes?" said Tom, turning to face him.

Gallagher put down the terracotta pot he was holding, taking his time as he worked out what he might say to Tom. He could see Luka further up the path, gathering the tarpaulin and taking it towards the marquee. "I've been meaning to ask you something."

"Right?" said Tom.

"It's about share options."

"What?"

"Share options. Is that something I might get, do you think?"

"Share options?" Tom asked. "As in...?"

"As in share options."

"Are you asking me to discuss your benefits package with you here and now?"

"Oh? A benefits package? Do I get one of those as well?"

Tom gave a small gasp of exasperation. "No, it's not an extra. It's a phrase we use when we talk about your wages and so on."

"Right, that sounds great," said Gallagher. "Can you tell me what the 'so on' part is? I don't think I realised I ought to be getting that. Like, I thought it was just money I got for working here."

"Well, in your case it is," said Tom.

"But other people get, what, different things as well? What sort of things do they get?"

Tom glanced at his wrist. Gallagher could see he wasn't even wearing a watch. "Perhaps you could schedule some time with me in the office and we can discuss this properly. It might not be an appropriate conversation for a public place."

"Yeah, I can see that," said Gallagher, nodding. "So what time shall I pop over?"

"Um, no. Today won't be convenient at all. I have lots to do as I'm covering for Charlotte's absence."

Gallagher saw Luka step out of the marquee and give a quick thumbs-up

"I see how busy you are. It can wait." Gallagher gave him a little wave and let both men walk away. He followed behind a moment later, to see what was happening in the marquee.

Luka appeared at his side. "Good effort," he whispered, "but we need to get rid of these losers."

Gallagher went inside and saw, to his horror, that Santa Raymond had not been moved at all. Instead a tarpaulin had been hastily thrown over Santa's throne.

"What's that?" asked Daffyd, pointing.

"Raymond asked for a privacy screen," said Anika. "He has some medication that he has to apply privately every couple of hours. It's of an intimate nature. We'll remove it in time for the next group."

"You alright in there Raymond?" called Tom.

There was a brief rustling of the tarp. "Mm-hmh." Someone was in there with the body. Was that Gillespie?

"Can we leave him be?" asked Anika, shooing them away. "I feel very bad for him."

"Yes. Yes, of course," said Tom. "Do you have everything you need over here?"

"We definitely do," said Anika.

Gallagher watched Tom and Daffyd retreat down the path, still bickering about which important aspect of Charlotte's job they should go and check up on next.

"Righto Raymond, we can probably move that tarp for you now," said Gallagher loudly, conscious that Sophie was still present.

"Thanks," came Gillespie's muffled voice from underneath.

Like the world's worst magicians, Gallagher and Luka grabbed a corner each of the tarpaulin and walked it away from Santa's throne. Gillespie walked along behind it, shielded from view, and emerged from one end, walking naturally as if he'd just strolled in through the door.

Gallagher thought their amazing sleight of hand was lost on Sophie as she was scrolling through her phone, ignoring everyone.

Anika looked over at Gallagher. "I think we might need to delay that little project we talked about until the lunchtime break, don't you?"

Gallagher nodded. Santa Raymond would need to sit on his throne for a bit longer, but he didn't seem to mind.

30

CHARLOTTE

C harlotte stared out of the window of the train. At some point, they would cross the border into Germany. Perhaps they had already done so. The next stop was Arnhem. Charlotte wouldn't admit to Jack that she had no idea if Arnhem was in the Netherlands or Germany. She might look it up, if she could be bothered.

Right now her thoughts were on Santa Raymond and wondering if firing him was enough to extricate herself and Hedgelord from this unpleasant situation. There wasn't much to wonder about. It was patently obvious that a porn movie featuring Santa Raymond and a roast turkey with Hedgelord signage in the background was still very bad news.

Attempts to find out who Alejandro was selling the video to were not initially successful. Business Development Executive was the acronym that first came up. There were companies called BDE in Belgium, in Texas, and Basingstoke back in England. None looked like they were in the market for Santa-themed porn.

"Three trains, via Hamburg," said Jack. He was sitting across the little table from her, consulting his phone again. "It's going to take a while. Maybe we should have bought some Sudoku books or something."

"Hadn't pictured you as the Sudoku type," said Charlotte.

"What type is that?"

She thought for a moment. "Someone with time on their hands. That's what's weird about this job. When do you and I ever get any spare time?"

Jack looked up at the carriage ceiling as he considered the question. "There's a quiet time somewhere around early Feb, but yeah, point taken. You need to carve out time for a little quiet in your life, don't you?"

"I don't know. Not sure if I like quiet."

"No?"

"I think I'm just a people person."

Jack snorted, immediately holding up his hand in apology. "I'm sorry. I didn't mean to laugh there."

"You don't think I'm a people person?"

Jack hesitated.

"Fuck!" she said. "I'm absolutely a people person!"

"Said the woman who swears as much as she breathes."

She wrinkled her nose in annoyance. "I'm aware that I have a problem and I'm working on it. I have a bit of a temper, I know."

"And restraining orders from seven local churches."

"That's a lie!"

He waved his hand as though he could swat away the

words he'd just said. "No, sorry. I get it. Your temper gets the better of you. It's a funny situation for a so-called Christian to be in."

"No so-called about it. I'm just a passionate woman of faith. Even Jesus got angry at times."

"Really? I don't recall any 'blessed are the motherfucking peacemakers' bits in the Bible."

"You clearly don't remember the bit where Jesus drove the moneychangers out of the temple. He fucking whipped them, Jack. Like, Jesus unleashed! Jesus has no problem with me swearing. He knows I'm good in my heart."

Jack jiggled his head, like he was happy to accept that for now.

"I live for people and community work," she said. "It's all I ever want to do. I want to make the world a better place and make the people in it happier."

"I can buy that," said Jack. "I like to see the positive impact of my work. It's..." He looked away.

"What?" said Charlotte.

"Is it cheesy to say I like to see the smiles on children's faces?"

"No. Not at all."

"And I don't mean the smiles of children spoiled rotten by over-indulgent parents, although I don't mind those really. Happiness is happiness, right? I guess I mean, I like to see people – children or adults – lifted up from the grind of their everyday lives. I mean, that's why I love Christmas."

"Yeah?"

"And I know – God, I know – Christmas can be the worst time of year for lots of people. This drive to spend money we don't have on things we don't need. But that's not Christmas's fault. That's just the way people treat it. Christmas is an opportunity for all of us to find some extra happiness and to give it out to others."

Charlotte narrowed her eyes at him. "And you're not a Christian?"

He smiled. "Not unless you count being Christened by two very non-Christian parents and me attending maybe three carol concerts. No. I'm not. I'm one of those big ol' evil atheists you Christians hate."

"We don't hate anyone," said Charlotte. "That's kind of our USP. Hate the sin, love the sinner. But you still celebrate Christmas."

He shrugged. "It's older than Christianity – you know that. Christians just jumped on the bandwagon two thousand years ago. The trees, the gifts, the lights. Frankly all the weird pagan mythical creatures. That doesn't belong to any faith. Christmas is love and light in the middle of winter. Anyone can love that."

She couldn't disagree.

"So, are your lot coping without you?" Jack asked.

"My lot?"

"Back at Hedgelord."

"Oh. I don't know for sure, but I think there might be some sort of power struggle going on between Tom, who's at my level, and Daffyd, who runs the grotto. I've had messages from both of them, each moaning about the other."

"Who would you want running things?" asked Jack.

Charlotte's hesitation gave the game away.

"Ah, I see. Neither of them's really up to the job, eh?" Jack grinned. "I can probably guess what your thinking is. Tom gets a long way by being a grey man in a grey suit. He has no real authority, and if he's caught up in any kind of conflict he will automatically back down." He glanced at Charlotte for confirmation.

She concentrated on keeping her mouth very tightly closed, and tried to make her face as neutral as she could.

"Your poker face takes a lot out of you, doesn't it?" said Jack. "Anyway, I will press on. Daffyd. I know him. He's an oddball, but I think you need a certain amount of oddball in you to run a grotto, don't you? Can I picture him being effective outside of that very specialised environment? Absolutely not. He would be the first to spook any normal businesspeople he'd have to deal with."

"Uh huh." Charlotte wanted to acknowledge he had spoken rather than overtly agree to his assessment.

"Of course, maybe between the two of them you'd have the clay to form an entire, functioning human who could do what's needed," mused Jack, smushing the imaginary clay between his hands. "But they won't work together, will they?"

"No," sighed Charlotte. His summary was so very accurate that she had nowhere to go. How on earth did he know so much about what went on behind the closed doors of Hedgelord?

He sat back in his seat, satisfied he was correct.

"So what cover will you have?" she asked. "How can you be sure things are being taken care of to your satisfaction?" She wanted to needle him.

"Because at Bloomers we have well-documented and clearly understood business continuity processes. If I'm unavailable then my understudy will switch seamlessly into my role."

"Well," she said dismissively. "We value spontaneity and creativity at Hedgelord. Who wants to be hidebound by processes, eh? I like to give my team the freedom and support to fix things themselves."

31

ANIKA

Bloody hell! So much for a replacement Santa! thought Anika.

Anika ended her call to Hedgelord's backup Santa, the improbably named Mudge. It was such an unlikely name she was curious to meet him, but that wasn't going to happen because apparently Mudge was in a full body cast after what his wife called 'an unfortunate chimney accident'.

Chimney suggested more Santa-style activities. Was the role of Santa really so hazardous? It had always seemed like a job that required just sitting in a chair and smiling nicely. Santas had to be a certain age, it was true, but surely they weren't that much more fragile? She tried to picture her own dad in the role. It was non-traditional to have an Asian man as Santa, and she didn't think Hedgelord's customers were ready for that kind of departure, but she was pretty sure he could sit on a throne and hand out presents to kids without either electrocuting himself or ending up in a full body cast.

She paced the floor of the marquee, grateful at least that Sophie seemed to be absorbed by her phone.

"There are so many things to decide when it comes to a funeral," said Sophie, her voice cracking. "I mean, how am I supposed to know what kind of urn to choose?"

"Oh." Anika floundered. "What are the choices?"

"Metal, ceramic or biodegradable. I can even have Douglas made into a diamond."

"Which one of those things feels the most *Douglas*?" asked Anika, aware that it was an idiotic question.

"Hmm." Sophie sighed long and hard. "You're right. He would probably choose something biodegradable. Thank you for being so wise."

"Oi oi!" came a shout from the entrance to the marquee.

"Karen?"

Karen came in, clipboard in hand.

This was not good. Anika wondered how on earth she could get rid of the very person she was trying to keep away from this situation. Here was the most enormous Health and Safety fail possible, and the last person she wanted to see was the Health and Safety officer.

Karen gave a brief smile, but it fell quickly away. "Here on business I'm afraid. Tom's sent me over. He says that Raymond's got some sort of issue of an intimate nature. He wants to make sure that we accommodate him correctly."

"Is that a Health and Safety issue?" asked Anika.

"Tom thinks it is," said Karen. "Sounds more like occupational health to me, but I said I would take a look."

"Did he do his sad face?" asked Anika.

"Pack it in, you. That's my boss you're talking about." Karen's smile made Anika certain she'd been correct. "Now I need you lot to scarper for a few minutes so that Raymond and I can have some privacy."

"We'll have customers through in a minute," said Anika.

"They can wait, this is important."

Anika ushered Sophie and Gillespie out of the marquee. "I'll fetch you when Karen's done, Sophie!" she said. She turned to Gillespie and whispered urgently. "How do I stop this happening?"

Gillespie peered around the entrance. "I hate to say this, but it's already happening."

"I think I might listen in. Make yourself scarce for a few minutes," said Anika.

She stood near to the entrance, listening through the canvas. She could hear Karen dragging a chair across the floor so that she could sit opposite Raymond.

Anika peered round to see how close she was. Their knees were almost touching! She was certain to notice his lack of movement at any time.

"You alright with me sitting here, Raymond, eh?" Karen said.

Raymond, very understandably, said nothing. If he had, Anika would probably have vomited up her entire skeleton in shock.

Karen nodded as though his silence spoken volumes.

"Truth is, it's really nice to sit down for five minutes. The tills are absolutely mental at the moment. There's a special on icicle lights for the pensioners today, they can get them for a fiver. I think every pensioner for a hundred miles has come to get a set of icicle lights."

Karen paused for a long moment, looked at Raymond and then grimaced.

"Sorry, I hope you don't think I was being rude about pensioners, Raymond. You know me better than that." She looked at her feet. "In fact, I'll put a set of those icicle lights on one side for you, how would that be?"

She nodded again and looked about the marquee. "Nice place this. Quiet. Now listen, I'm supposed to make sure you're all right over here, and that Hedgelord's making it easy for you to apply your haemorrhoid cream or whatever it is. Is it haemorrhoids? Sorry. None of my business. Personal information. I know you're a proud man though, Raymond, and you want your privacy an' all. You don't have to say anything to me that makes you uncomfortable, but I just want you to know that you've only got to say the word if you need anything, yeah?"

There was the sound of Karen shifting in her seat.

"It's you and me that keeps them all going, love, isn't it? We prop up the rest of the world. You with your sprinkling of the old Christmas magic, and me with my Health and Safety duties. Different jobs but same end result I reckon. Who cares for the carers though Raymond, eh? Know what I mean? Tom's great and everything, but he doesn't seem to notice a woman struggling with all the crap that life's throwing at her, even when she's right under his nose. Just as long as I keep that till going then I must be fine, mustn't I? Don't they train managers in that sort of thing? Do you mind me...?" There was a long and hearty sigh. "It's M&M. That's the kids grandparents. On my ex's side. He's not on the scene, thank God, but they're ... they're relentless. I'm up to here with them, I really am. Ever had someone that you're obliged to spend time with, but you know they're doing you harm? It's like they're sucking up all of my oxygen. God knows what effect they're having on my kids. Worst case scenario? My actual nightmare scenario is that they're right and I'm wrong. That would make me the monster, bringing up my kids with my bad, sloppy ways. I literally couldn't bear that."

Karen coughed with embarrassment.

"Anyway, listen to me prattling away at you about my personal problems. I can see why you're a top Santa, you've got those amazing listening skills."

Anika risked another peek. Karen was hardly looking at Raymond now, she was completely wrapped up in her monologue and glancing up at him only occasionally.

"I best get back to those tills and you've got more kids to see, eh? Now don't forget what I said, will you?"

Karen got up from her chair, and Anika quickly ducked back outside the entrance and down the path. She doubled back and sauntered towards the marquee as Karen was leaving.

"You're all right to go back in there now, love," said Karen. "I've sorted Raymond out."

"You have?"

"Oh, yes. He's going to be fine."

Anika held her breath until Karen had definitely gone back into the shop, then she went back to the marquee.

"Shit," she whispered.

Gillespie appeared. "I just saw Karen," he said. "She told

me that Raymond's going to be fine." There was a ridiculously hopeful note to his voice.

Anika gave him a strained nod. "It seems like she came and had a chat with him without noticing he was dead."

Gillespie's face went through a complex set of expressions that probably mirrored Anika's own reactions.

"And he's definitely dead?"

"Yes," she said. "Sorry, Gillespie. He's still dead."

"Oh."

"Anyway, I have an update on a replacement Santa," said Anika.

"Oh, that's great news," said Gillespie.

"Not necessarily," said Anika, "because the update is – there isn't one. Santa Mudge has had an unfortunate chimney accident."

"How?"

"No idea. Didn't ask. Anyway, we're going to have to keep Raymond in the role for a little while yet."

"What? No! We can't just keep a dead guy around because there's no replacement Santa available," said Gillespie. "There must be something else we can do?"

Anika looked at him. "Like what?"

Gillespie looked around for inspiration, flapping his arms at his sides. He glanced at Raymond, who still looked very much as if he was snoozing. "Oh, I don't know. Maybe we just need to put some sunglasses on him. At least then we don't have to explain why his eyes are closed."

Anika grinned. "Great idea. Go and get some out of the shop when you fetch Sophie back over, will you?"

32

GALLAGHER

By three o'clock, as the midwinter sky was beginning to darken, Gallagher and Luka were finally about to sit down for a well-earned cup of tea.

"Should we put up a tree in here?" Gallagher asked Luka, waving an arm across the interior of the tea shed. It was a small space, which was mostly occupied by their chairs, a table on which stood the tea things, and a small fridge. "There's space for a small one up the corner."

"Why not?" said Luka. "Will be something to look at that isn't a poster of giant fucking hornet."

Gallagher warmed slightly at the prospect. He knew he was just trying to divert his mind away from the matter of bloodthirsty gangsters and dead Santas, but he was prepared to go along with the ruse.

The door opened. Snømann stood there, on the threshold of their inner sanctum.

"Fuck," said Gallagher. He always felt safe in here, which

was nonsense, because it was just a wooden shed in a garden centre, but still, this felt like a violation.

"Come. You will need to assist with unloading." Was that a gun he had raised inside his jacket? Something was pointed towards with an unmistakable threat of violence. Or was it just a finger?

Snømann turned away, expecting the two of them to follow. Gallagher exited the shed first.

"You have trolley?" asked Snømann.

Gallagher nodded and went to fetch the trolley and tarpaulin they had set aside for transporting Raymond to his car. "I'll take this out through the staff gate to the car park and see you out there, yeah? You need to walk out through the shop, otherwise someone's going to ask what you're doing."

Snømann nodded agreement, and waved to Luka to accompany him.

The three of them met outside, next to a Toyota pickup. It was a nondescript truck with regular British number plates. Gallagher wondered who it was registered to, then consciously pushed away the question, worried he might have accidentally memorised the numberplate. The less he knew or remembered about this the better.

Snømann unfastened the tailgate and pulled a crate towards them. "These are the crates that you will be looking after. They are heavy. Take care not to drop them."

Gallagher tested the weight of the first crate, and waved to Luka to help him lift it down onto the trolley. The crates were all the same: sizeable, but manoeuvrable. They were made from the same tough plastic as house-moving crates, with heavy duty rope handles on each end. There were no markings on them. Each one had a metal strap that went all the way round, like a festive ribbon. There was a heavy duty padlock and what looked like a customs seal applied to the bands where they met on top. The crates were unexpectedly heavy, and it took two of them to move each one. Gallagher was struck by the bizarre thought that if he put two or three of these together, he could put a mattress on top and make a nice supportive bed. Was that a sign of stress, daydreaming about getting some rest even while being forced at gunpoint to unload whatever sinister contraband was in these crates?

They loaded the crates onto the trolley, five of them in total. Nobody spoke while they were working.

"You will take them round through your staff gate and then I want to see where they are to be hidden," said Snømann.

"You sure?" Gallagher said. "If you don't know, then nobody can make you tell, can they?"

Snømann scrutinised Gallagher's face. "Is that a joke? Your British humour is..." He made a sour expression. "Your humour is inscrutable and is the enemy of clear communication. Please do not do it again."

"Come on," said Luka. "Let us get this inside."

It took Gallagher and Luka a good few minutes to manoeuvre the heavy trolley through to the plant area. Each time a wheel caught on any unlevel ground it took lots of shoving and heaving to get back on track.

"Fucking crates of rocks or what?" Gallagher huffed. It felt wrong to be sweating in December.

"Don't even joke about guessing what's inside while our friend is still here," warned Luka.

When they arrived at the tea shed, Snømann was inside, sniffing Luka's bottle of *slivovitz*. "Show me where you will put them."

By unspoken agreement, Gallagher led Snømann into the shed while Luka stood watch on the path.

Gallagher rolled up the bottom of the hornet poster and exposed the hidden door. If he expected Snømann to gasp with surprise and admiration, he was disappointed. He fished out the key to the padlock on the door and opened it inwards to reveal the annex they had built.

Snømann stepped through into the hidden space and walked around the inside of the *Tunbridge Slimline*.

"You will cover window with a board," he said to Gallagher.

Gallagher was about to protest that nobody could possibly get round to look through the window, but he managed to stop himself. "Yes."

"Good. This will work. Bring in the crates."

Gallagher nodded. Then he realised that Snømann intended to stand and wait while he did it.

"Luka's standing watch. Are you going to help me with them?" he asked.

"I am not. You will manage."

Gallagher hefted and dragged the first of the crates in through the tea shed. For a moment, he was worried that he would have to tilt it in order to get it through the doorway into the other shed, and he had no idea how he'd do that on his own, but by some small miracle it fit through the door, with no more than a few millimetres' clearance.

It took him about fifteen minutes to get all of the crates into place, and he had to ignore every piece of training ever given about safely handling heavy objects, but he managed it. Snømann offered nothing other than a nod that acknowledged that the task was done.

Gallagher locked the padlock on the secret door and rolled the hornet poster back into place.

"I will take a key," said Snømann, holding out his hand.

Again, there seemed little point in arguing or even asking why. Gallagher handed over the key.

Snømann did a little tour of the shed, inspecting the items that sat on the tables and even looking inside their tea caddy next to the kettle. "Your British obsession with tea," he said. "It is a strange thing."

"Is that right?" said Gallagher.

"You take a thing that is not native to your country and you make it an integral part of your national identity."

"I don't suppose I've ever thought about it."

"But what is strange is this..." Snømann dipped a hand in the caddy and pulled out a tea bag. "The Italians are passionate about coffee. It is part of who they are, even though the coffee bean is not native to their country and cannot even grow there. But they have taken coffee and made it part of who they are and – this part is key – they improved it. Italian coffee is arguably the best in the world. That is why the famous styles of coffee have Italian names."

"Yeah?"

"But you..." He waggled the tea bag in his hand. "You

have this passion for tea and yet your tea is the shittiest tea in the world."

"Whoa," said Gallagher. He was frightened of this man but felt he had to draw the line at someone besmirching the great British cup of tea. Gallagher was not a well-travelled man but, aside from the Brits and the Irish, he'd not known any nation capable of brewing a decent cuppa.

"You take the filthiest and cheapest black tea and you pour milk into it and you make out it is a good thing," said Snømann.

"That wounds me deeply."

The old man tossed the teabag onto the floor and ground it under the toe of his polished shoes. "When we bring something new into our culture or place ourselves in a new culture, we should always seek to elevate it."

Gallagher had no idea what he was talking about really so just nodded.

Snømann wagged a finger at the horrid poster of the Asian hornet. "People fear things because they are bigger, stronger and better able to exploit a new environment. But such things are inevitable."

"We talking about tea or hornets?" asked Gallagher.

"Those crates. That is my arrival. That is a first step."

A first step? thought Gallagher. He didn't like the sound of that.

"I like this place," said Snømann. "Apart from your vile tea and your strange humour. This environment suits me."

"The garden centre?"

"Everything. I like it here. I have come to exploit an opportunity but, just as importantly, I have come to elevate

you. I bring improvements and you can be a part of that or
—" he pointed at the hornet "—you can be the victim. You
understand?"

"Barely," said Gallagher.

Snømann sniffed as though he felt Gallagher understood
enough, then walked slowly out of the tea shed. A few
moments later Luka appeared.

"He's definitely gone?" Gallagher asked.

Luka nodded.

"Thank fuck for that."

"I think he is impressed with our secret shed," said Luka,
picking up his tea and discovering that it had gone cold.

"Oh?" said Gallagher. "Is that a good thing or a bad
thing?"

Luka tipped the tea into the gravel outside of the shed
and paused before he turned back to answer. "I have no
fucking idea, but he says there will be more crates tomorrow.
Ten more like these."

Gallagher reeled at the idea. Their task had now
increased considerably.

33

CHARLOTTE

The concourse of Hamburg's central train station was a huge space with white tiled floors and a high curved ceiling from which hung great columns of sparkling lights, making the place look like a vast cavern filled with glowing icicles. Shops, bars and restaurants ran along walkways at two levels inside the space. The place was filled with people going to and fro, many with colourful gift bags in their hands. There was less than a week to Christmas and it struck Charlotte that the good people of Germany were as shopping-crazy as the Brits in the run up to Christmas.

An octagonal analogue clock hung from the ceiling. It was half past four.

"Shall we grab something to eat?" said Jack, as they had nearly an hour to wait.

Charlotte pointed towards a bar across the way.

"Or something to drink?" he said.

Charlotte shrugged. "Just a small one. I want to pop somewhere first."

She'd spotted a gift shop on the upper level of shops. She had no plan, just a vague notion that if she had to spend the next umpteen hours with Jack Hartigan, she should maybe try and make him feel better. He'd been dumped by his beloved Kathryn and was in pain. Personally, Charlotte thought Kathryn sounded like a bit of a nightmare and he was better off without her, but still.

She found the gift shop to be filled with the usual kind of awfulness. If he craved a neck pillow, a Hummel figurine, or a model of a local landmark then there were plentiful options, but there was nothing that really fitted the bill for cheering up the recently-dumped.

A shop assistant sidled up to her while she was floundering.

"You are English," she said, which Charlotte thought was just plain impressive since she hadn't spoken a word since entering.

"How do you know?"

"I don't know," said the woman lightly. "Different people have different ways of behaving. It is always easy to spot the British."

Charlotte didn't question her further on that matter. She feared the behaviours that separated the British from the rest of Europe were not going to be flattering ones.

The woman picked up a resin model of a tall, jagged tower. "You are looking for a souvenir of Hamburg?"

"Er, not really. What is that?"

"It's the *Mahnmal St-Nikolai*. The memorial or church to Saint Nicholas."

"Oh, *the* Saint Nicholas?"

"Apt for this time of year, no? He's also the patron saint of sailors, which is why his church is in Hamburg. But most of the church is destroyed now. It was bombed in the Second World War."

Charlotte had a very strong urge to apologise, but considered it would be both embarrassing and inappropriate. "No. I don't think that's what I want."

She had no real clue what she was looking for until she saw the shop's selection of children's toys. There were some glove puppets that drew her eye.

"These are characters from children's fairy tales," said the shop assistant.

It didn't matter. One of them definitely resembled Jack, and Charlotte thought another resembled Kathryn. As she carried them to the cash register, she realised with a start that the one resembling Kathryn probably resembled her too – given that she'd been able to travel on the other woman's passport. She filed that weird thought away.

Five minutes later, she found Jack in the bar with a bottle of wine and two glasses. "What happened to just a small one?" she asked.

He grimaced. "All the stuff sold by the glass is awful. We can take the bottle with us when we go. It will be fine."

He poured her a glass and she placed her bag on the table. "I got something for you. Your post-breakup therapy starts here." She pulled out the two glove puppets and put them onto her hands. "Here we have our live action role-playing puppets: Jack and Kathryn."

"Oh dear," he said with some feeling.

"Time to lay those demons to rest. You can unleash some of those pent-up thoughts."

He laughed and leaned back. "Oh really? I don't know what pent-up thoughts you think I might have. We're not all bundles of rage like you, Charlotte."

"You're telling me you have no hard feelings about just being dumped?" Charlotte pulled a face. "Don't believe you."

"You want tears or screaming, is that it? Are you one of those people who insist that all feelings must be shared with the world? I would much rather keep mine inside."

"Aha, so you do at least have feelings? Come on then. Let's make a pantomime. You be Jack and I'll be Kathryn." She handed him the puppet, and they held them face to face.

"And this is supposed to make me feel better, is it? Fine." He took an enormous swig of wine and patted his puppet on the head. "Where shall we start, Tiny Jack?"

"Shall we get Tiny Kathryn to dump him and then you can respond in a more satisfying way than you did before? How did you respond by the way?"

He sighed. "I think I just said 'righto'. It didn't feel like it was a matter for negotiation."

"Fuck's sake. You can do better than that. I can coach you in satisfying swearing techniques if you like. Here we go then." She animated Tiny Kathryn. "I'm sorry Tiny Jack, but it's over between us."

Jack looked up at her. "This is where you tell me you'll

need me to pay off my instalments on the new rug in the lounge, even though you intend to keep it."

"You fucking what? She actually said that in the same breath as dumping you?"

"It was an expensive rug. I guess she was worried about the expense of shouldering the bill on her own."

"No fucking way!" Charlotte slammed a hand down on the table, making Jack jump. "Oh my god, this is what I'm talking about. Did you say 'righto' to that as well?"

He nodded.

"Right, well, consider this a do-over. Let's take it from the top. Are you ready Tiny Kathryn?" She held the puppet to her ear. "She says she's ready to fucking destroy you all over again. This time you give her both barrels, right?"

Jack nodded.

"I'm sorry, Tiny Jack, but it's over between us. And by the way, you need to keep paying for that rug I will be enjoying on my own."

Jack made his puppet nod slowly. "I will be sorry to see you go, Tiny Kathryn, but that rug was your idea from the beginning. I never really liked it, so you can either take on the repayments or sell it." He gave a small smile.

"Tell her to sell the fucking, bastarding thing! Go in for the kill! Maximum sweary emphasis!"

"Kathryn doesn't think that swearing is very clever."

"Then that's all the more reason to fucking do it. In fact, let's see how far we can take this. I'm going to re-write your speech."

She pulled a pen and paper from her bag and scribbled

for a few minutes while Jack topped up their glasses. "Here you go. Read this out."

"Oh, we're really going for this, are we?" he said as he scanned the page.

She nodded. "Want me to demonstrate?"

"Yeah! Let's record this, it should be peak Charlotte," he said with a grin as he fished out his phone,

She held up his puppet next to her face so that Jack could get a close-up shot, and she snarled the words that she'd written. "Kiss my fucking hairy ass, you cunt. It was all your twatting idea anyway, so you can either pay up or just fucking *zzcccchh*." The sound at the end was accompanied by a finger-across-the-throat gesture of savage finality.

"Ooh, that was good. I'll try it now." He seemed excited to say his line.

"Quickly! One run-through and then we need to go and get on our train."

They re-framed Jack's dumping and he was grinning with satisfaction by the end. "I honestly did not expect to enjoy that."

"You're very welcome. Let's go to Stockholm, shall we?"

34

ANIKA

nika sat in the marquee while Sophie and Gillespie handled the next grotto group. She briefly wondered whether they had normalised having a dead body in the room, because with his sunglasses on, Raymond looked a lot less freaky and threatening. He exuded a cheery, carefree vibe, like someone whose life was so very rock'n'roll that wearing sunglasses in December was part of his regular look.

She was trying to get a proper grip on Friday's events. The carriage rides had no paperwork at all, so she decided to take a walk over to the paddock. As far as she knew there was nothing there, but as she didn't drive a car, she'd never actually been beyond the hedge.

It took her a few minutes to cross the car park and nip through the gap, which was currently coned off. There was a sign that said the overflow car park was closed for the winter as it was unpaved.

As she emerged on the other side of the hedge, Anika saw that the field beyond was much larger than she had imagined, based on what she could see from the road. She walked on, seeing some buildings on the other side of a gate. As she approached she tried to decide what kind of place it was. There were a number of single storey buildings that might have been stables. There was also a house with a garden. Anika walked through into a yard which was pock-marked with muddy puddles.

"Hello!" she called.

After a couple of minutes, a woman appeared from around a corner. "Can I help you?"

"Oh, hi! It's Amy, isn't it?" Anika asked.

Amy nodded, clearly not recognising her.

"I work at Hedgelord. You delivered the reindeer on my first day there."

"Ah right. Cool," said Amy. "Are the reindeer all right?"

"Oh yes. Gallagher's looking after them. I was following up on an event that's booked for Friday. Carriage rides in the paddock. Do you know anything about it?"

"I do!" said Amy. "Cameron's idea I believe. There's a carriage in one of the barns behind the house. Want to see it?"

Anika nodded.

Amy unlocked a huge wooden door and they walked into a chilly barn. There was an old-fashioned horse-drawn carriage in there, and a couple of other smaller contraptions.

"Oh, it's all sorted then?" Anika said. "On Friday someone will get this onto the paddock, hook up the horses, and lead the couples around?"

"Yeah, about that." Amy patted the door. "I've been waiting for Charlotte to get back to me about where she's getting horses from."

"Wait, what? Don't you have horses here?"

"We do, but they're all booked out. Bloomers are doing their Festive Pony Experience."

"So the carriage is available but no horses to pull it?" Anika knew she was just repeating what Amy had said, but the gravity of the situation was only just sinking in.

Amy nodded. "I suggested that Charlotte might call Abbotts and Dalrymples, but I've an idea their horses are at Bloomers too."

"Oh. Are there any other horse ... places I can try?"

"Where's Charlotte? She'd normally be doing this."

"Yeah, she isn't available. What exactly am I asking for, if I find someone with horses? Do they need to be like a certain size or something?"

"If I'm completely honest with you, I think you're out of luck. I reckon you're looking at cancelling the event," said Amy.

Anika thought hard. Cancelling seemed like a coward's way out. There had to be a solution. "You know the reindeer?" she asked slowly.

"Absolutely not!" said Amy. "They are not suited to pulling humans round on a joyride."

"Sorry! Just trying to think outside the box," said Anika.

"Yes, well, if I hear of any thinking outside the box that results in animal cruelty, I will come down on Hedgelord like an avenging angel!"

Anika held up her hands to placate the avenging angel,

although she couldn't help thinking that Gallagher might enjoy the spectacle. "Absolutely no animal cruelty will be permitted. I promise."

Amy calmed a little. "I suppose you might see whether Cameron can bring in his ride-on mower to pull the dog sled perhaps?"

"Dog sled?"

Amy pointed to one of the other contraptions. It was a much skinnier thing than the carriage.

Anika tried to picture Cameron on a ride-on mower pulling startled couples along. "Now that is definitely thinking outside of the box," she said. "What would the body count look like, though?"

Amy laughed. "Yeah, maybe it does sound a bit risky. Not sure I have any other ideas."

"I'll make some calls," said Anika with a heavy sigh, "but I don't really know horse people."

"Best of luck!" called Amy as Anika walked back towards the garden centre.

35

GALLAGHER

"Ah, Gallagher, glad I bumped into you!"

It was Cameron. Gallagher knew that he definitely hadn't simply bumped into him because he was in one of the quietest corners of the whole place. What's more, Cameron's office overlooked the area, so he'd come down especially to see him, which was worrying.

Gallagher had been trying to put all thoughts of Snømann and his sinister crates out of his mind. He'd decided to do this by throwing himself into some physical tasks. He'd re-arranged the display of stoneware statues, making sure that they were all facing forward, which seemed important. He was even contemplating moving those pallets of compost from outside the landscaping office, although he hoped his mood might have improved before then.

The appearance of Cameron Crisp, the boss, was a surprise and a distraction, but not necessarily a welcome one. Gallagher hadn't even been aware that Cameron knew his name. Being known to the boss was surely not a great thing.

"How you doing?" he mumbled.

"I'm working on making sure that our Christmas party goes with a bang," said Cameron.

"Er, right. I heard about that."

"A proper blowout where everyone of us lets rip. That's the sort of thing we want."

"Yeah?" Gallagher was trying to understand where Cameron was going. In his mind the phrase 'let rip' very much applied to farting, but he didn't think Cameron had come to him to organise a farting contest at the staff party.

"This time of year it's just what the doctor ordered – like those special pills he doesn't put through the books, eh? See, Gallagher, the thing is I need to buy some gifts for people. It's been pointed out to me that I should try harder than I might have done in previous years and get something a bit more personalised."

"Oh, but I quite liked the matching tie and golf tee gift set that I got last year," lied Gallagher.

"Hm. Nevertheless I want to do better. Take a look at my list, will you? See if you might have some ideas for filling in the blanks."

He handed Gallagher a piece of paper with staff names down the left hand side. On the right were a few sparse comments. He hadn't got very far.

"Right," said Gallagher. He had to say something, but it was scrambling for time as he tried to engage his brain. "So you don't have all that many ideas yet then?"

"It's very much a work in progress," said Cameron. "I've

jotted down a couple of thoughts. Charlotte for instance, she's very keen on that religion stuff, so I thought maybe a little pope on a rope or something."

"Yeah. Pope on a rope, I saw you wrote that, but I'm not sure what it means."

"Used to be all the rage, didn't they? Pope on a rope. It's a pun version of soap on a rope, but the soap is in the shape of his Holiness. Hilarious, practical and thoughtful. Boom! Surely that's going to be a hit?"

"I can see you've put some thought into that," said Gallagher. "But there's a couple of things you might want to think about."

"Oh yes?"

"Well for one, soap on a rope was men's soap wasn't it? And wouldn't it be more like a gift for a Catholic?"

Cameron stared at Gallagher as if he was waiting for him to make his point.

"What I mean," Gallagher continued, "is that Charlotte is Church of England. I think. Or something."

"Ohh – you mean she's not such a pope-fancier as we might suppose?" Cameron said.

"Yeah, that."

Cameron slapped him on the back. "I knew I'd come to the right person. Very insightful! Well then, the million dollar question is what should I get her, then? What ideas do you have?"

Gallagher was frozen to the spot. The idea that he might carry any kind of responsibility for choosing the appropriate gift for a colleague, especially a senior one, was just too much. "I don't know if I have any ideas really."

"Oh come along! These people are all colleagues. What do you think of when Charlotte's name is mentioned?"

Gallagher stopped himself saying anything that equated to 'Out of control nutcase' and wondered how he might phrase it politely. "She is ... she doesn't hold back when it comes to expressing strong feelings."

"Oh, you mean whacking the ruddy fuck out of inanimate objects? Yes, it's a peculiar habit. Hm, I might have a think about that. You can get those squeezy balls, can't you?"

Gallagher said nothing. He privately thought that giving Charlotte one of those dinky little stress balls to manage her anger would be like trying to put out a burning building with a damp cloth.

"Good, let's move on then," said Cameron. "Do you have any ideas about your buddy Luka?"

Gallagher sighed. As if he actually knew anything about that mysterious bastard. "Fuck, mate, I don't even know what country he actually comes from."

Cameron waved a hand as if that was a very minor point.

"A dictionary!" said Cameron. "Damned if he doesn't miss words out of his sentences all the time. I think a dictionary would be just the thing."

"Ohhh ... I'm not sure about that," said Gallagher. "The words he misses out tend to be the ones that don't really matter. I'm pretty sure he knows more words than I do. A dictionary would be a bit insulting."

"Hmph. I don't see him as the sensitive type, but fair enough. How about a nice cut glass tumbler for his favourite tipple, perhaps? Never yet met a man of a certain age who doesn't need one of those."

Gallagher thought about the cracked mug that was Luka's usual tippling vessel – when he wasn't swigging directly from the bottle. He wasn't about to tell Cameron that drinking of any sort took place on Hedgelord premises. He just nodded in an attempt to be helpful. "Yep. Maybe."

36

ANIKA

Anika met Sophie and Karen in the café after they'd closed to customers for the evening. She was more than ready for the kind of energy boost which came with extra cream and chocolate sprinkles. Cream and sprinkles might not erase thoughts of a dead Santa wrapped in tarpaulin from her brain, but she was prepared to give it a go.

Karen tapped the table for attention. "Soph and I have been chatting."

"About what?" said Anika.

"About how important it is to get back in the saddle. Haven't we, love?"

Sophie gave a small and slightly nervous smile. It was a smile clearly meant to placate rather than one of actual agreement. "Back in the saddle. I'm not sure I was ever really in the saddle if I'm completely honest."

"What saddle?" said Anika. "Dog saddle?"

"The dating saddle," said Karen.

"Is that the saddle we need to focus on?"

"I think it got mentioned earlier, among other saddles."

"I think the dating saddle was something that happened to other people, not me," said Karen.

"Do we not need to address the dog saddle?" said Anika.

"I think it's related," said Karen. "There are many saddles, and the sad loss of Douglas has brough the saddles into sharp relief."

"And I do think the dating saddle might be a welcome distraction," said Sophie.

"I think we've used the word 'saddle' too many times now," said Anika. "I feel like I no longer know what it means. But we want to do whatever will help you, Sophie."

"Right, that's sorted then," said Karen. She held up her phone and took a picture of Sophie. "We might as well strike while the iron's hot. We'll get you set up for online dating."

Anika thought Karen was moving rather swiftly, but Sophie just gave a watery smile and watched while Karen typed into the boxes on her phone.

"How would you describe yourself in a single sentence, Sophie?" Karen asked.

"I just got the word 'saddle' in my head now."

"Probably doesn't belong on your dating profile."

"Friendly hard worker?" suggested Sophie.

"Flipping heck! We can do better than that. You're looking for love, not someone with jobs that need doing. What do you reckon, Anika? You're smart, come up with some words."

Anika felt the weight of expectation on her. Sophie's eyes

were even wider than usual. "Right. Let me think. We could use phrases like 'fragile beauty'."

"Fragile beauty?" said Sophie.

"Or 'delicate features'. You know, to describe your appearance – but they'll see that from your pictures. What we really need to talk about is what's at the heart and soul of Sophie." She wanted to find a way in which to describe Sophie's gentle naïveté that wouldn't just be a siren call to predators. "Warm-hearted, generous and loving are all words that would suit you well I think."

"How lovely. You're a sweetheart," said Sophie, her eyes crinkling with a smile.

"These are great, Anika," said Karen, typing them in. "Now, we need a bit of detail about what qualities you value in a partner, Sophie. Give us some ideas, will you, love?"

Sophie leaned back in her chair and stared dreamily into the middle distance. "I am a sucker for a soulful pair of eyes. You know – the ones you could just melt into. I want to spend hours just gazing into a gorgeous pair of eyes and enjoying them gazing back at me."

"Soulful eyes, got it."

"And loyalty is so important. You know – when you feel as if you could face anything when you're side by side? That thing. I don't think I function so well when it's just me. I love having a partner in crime who I know will always be there for me."

"Oh Sophie, love," said Karen. "I knew I was doing the right thing. We'll have you fixed up in no time. What other qualities? It's your chance to be super specific about your wants and needs. How often do we get that chance in life, eh?"

"I do enjoy snuggling. On the sofa, in the bed, just that warm, comforting presence that keeps me warm and safe. Oh yes, that's a point, I think size is important."

"Bigger the better eh?" cackled Karen. "Say no more!"

"We're talking general body shape though, not actual genitals?" Anika asked. She felt she needed to put the brakes on whatever Karen might have been about to write.

"Of course! Wash your mouth out, missy!" said Sophie with a giggle.

Karen gave a disappointed sigh and hit the delete key a few times. "I think we've got enough to get you going. You'll soon have those luscious big boys with their soft melty eyes lining up for your inspection."

"Aww," said Sophie, as if Karen had said she was going to buy her a plushie unicorn.

They all sipped their drinks, each confident that something had been achieved.

37

ANIKA

"I've seen you zipping about, Anika," said Sophie. "How's it going sorting out the events area?"

Anika gave a careful nod. A summary that omitted the dead Santa took some mental reshuffling. "Yeah, good. I've mostly got the grotto staffed up how I need it. There's a bit of a Santa scheduling, um, thing I need to get to."

"That Raymond's so lovely, isn't he?" said Karen, slurping some of the excess cream from the cup.

"Er..."

"I had a wonderful chat with him earlier. He's much more of a listener than I ever realised. Heart of gold. I hope Mrs Raymond knows what a lucky woman she is."

Anika froze in place. "A wife? Does he have a wife?"

"Dunno," said Karen. "Just saying that a husband like that would be quite the catch. I always assume that someone who properly knows how to have a decent conversation must be in a stable relationship. It's like training, isn't it?"

Anika thought about that. Karen's needs in her current, overworked and highly-stressed state probably meant her ideal partner in conversation was completely silent. It wasn't Anika's place to suggest that normal conversation didn't work like that. She made a light, non-committal grunting noise.

It hadn't crossed her mind that Santa Raymond might have someone else at home. It would complicate the plan to take him home, but maybe it still wasn't impossible.

"Oh yeah, horses are a problem too," said Anika when she realised the other two women were still waiting for her to finish. "There's a carriage ride booked for Friday, but no horses are available to pull it. Would you believe that Bloomers have got them all booked out?"

"I would definitely believe that," said Karen. "Can we use the reindeer?"

"Apparently not," said Anika.

"I know," said Sophie. "You can do it like the grotto, where the carriage stays still but you move the background so it looks as if the landscape's changing."

Anika gaped. Sophie's surreal suggestion was definitely one that hadn't occurred to her. The grotto had some sort of trick film projection that made it look as though the stationary seating was a sleigh travelling towards the North Pole. "How would you do that out in a field?" she asked.

Sophie shrugged as if it was very straightforward. "Really long pieces of paper that you paint the scenery on, one for each side, and then you get some elves to jog past holding it."

Anika could imagine the mental picture Sophie was

conjuring. What she couldn't imagine was producing it within the space of a day. She also wondered whether people would buy into the idea of a cartoon carriage ride. "Sophie, that is a genuinely cool idea. If we had a bit more time I reckon we could totally make it work. What worries me is the way we've sold it. The posters definitely make it look as though people will be snuggling up with their loved ones as they go somewhere, even if it's just round the corner.

"Another way you could do it," said Sophie, who was on a roll now, "is you could get Gallagher and Luka to sort out a load of Christmas trees. You'd probably need like ten or fifteen for each side, and then you'd need an elf to carry each one. They trot along, carrying their trees in a line past the carriage, so it looks as if it's dashing through a forest!"

"Oh yeah!" said Karen, all enthusiastic. "Then when each elf gets to the end of the line they run round, join the start, and do it again. You could have a carriage ride that lasted for as long as you like then."

Anika tried to imagine how she would conjure up thirty elves and persuade them to spend several hours running around with a Christmas tree each. It just didn't sound like something she could easily do.

"You know what? That is currently the second best idea I have. It just needs more elves than we currently have on the books."

"Second best?" asked Sophie.

"Behind asking Cameron to use his ride-on lawnmower to pull a lighter carriage."

The two women pulled different versions of the same face.

"God no, Anika!" said Karen. "Have you seen how he pulls out of the car park in his Jag. It would be utter carnage. The risk assessment would be unmanageable." She gave Anika a shrewd look. "You have checked that there are risk assessments in place for these events, haven't you?"

"Risk assessments?" said Anika. This was the first she'd heard of such a thing, but she nodded, a pretty good idea of what it might entail. "So that's a document that says we've looked at risk, yeah?"

Karen nodded. "You file them with me, as Health and Safety officer. I don't think Charlotte has given me any for the special events. You might want to check and see if she prepared anything, otherwise you'll need to get on with that, pronto."

Anika had already started a search on her phone to see what risk assessments looked like. They looked straightforward enough. One simply had to imagine what might go wrong and take steps to prevent it. "I'll do that, yes." She thought for a moment. "Just as a matter of interest, how is a risk assessment used when something bad happens?"

"We might have to produce the risk assessment to demonstrate that we considered the risk," said Karen. "It's not the only thing that gets looked at, but it's an important one when it comes to accountability. Nobody wants to be liable for injury or death because they ignored best practice, do they?"

Anika swallowed hard and nodded. "No of course not, right. Got it."

She left Karen and Sophie in the café and went to the office. She walked straight to Charlotte's desk and flicked through folders, looking for risk assessments. She told herself that she was looking to see whether Charlotte might have done something for Friday's events, but really she wanted to see if there was a risk assessment covering the Festive Farm children's grotto experience. She located it after a few minutes. It was a copy, signed by Charlotte and Karen. She flicked through the risks and found that electrocution was there – identified as a potential hazard! She bit down on her knuckle as she read the actions that had been taken to mitigate the risk.

- *All relevant staff briefed on appropriate use of extension leads*
- *dangers of overloading a lead*
- *'daisychaining' of multiple leads not permitted*
- *all portable equipment must have a current PAT test sticker*

SHE HAD BEEN WARNED by Karen, but had failed to pass that warning on to Santa Raymond. He might be alive now if she'd done that. Did that make her accountable for his death?

One thing was certain, she needed to keep the dead Santa under wraps.

38

CHARLOTTE

Charlotte eyed the sleeping couchettes on the train to Stockholm. "This is actually not terrible."

"I know, right?" said Jack cheerily. He had ordered more wine and put the glasses down on the weird yet functional table that magically contained a washbasin under its lid.

Charlotte was grateful for the idea of some decent rest. The previous night on the ferry had not been conducive to a good night's sleep, but these bunk beds looked very inviting. Any concerns about Jack snoring or farting were soon forgotten because she was pretty certain she'd be asleep the moment she settled down.

"Have you been in touch with work at all?" she asked Jack. They both sat on the lower bunk to sip wine.

"No. I was thinking about popping a few pictures up on social media. Nothing that speaks of what we're doing, obviously, but some of the pictures I've taken today are adorable and very Christmassy. I thought I might make an album and call it something like 'Where Am I?'

"So very mysterious," said Charlotte making woo-woo gestures with her hands. "Someone might feed those pictures into a search engine and actually guess correctly."

"So what if they do? For everyone that does, there will be two who get it all wrong. It's engagement, isn't it?"

"Fine!" said Charlotte. "Share your album and I'll pop my pictures on there too. If you're getting engagement, then I want some."

They spent a few minutes uploading the contents of their picture albums. Rotterdam's waterside streets and the clusters of sailing boats against a crisp autumn sky. The lights and decorations in Hamburg central station. Charlotte had a few blurry shots of forests and fields along their train route too. Now, it was dark outside. Their next stop would be Stockholm – across the Baltic Sea and in Scandinavia.

This was an unplanned little holiday – not a holiday at all really – but Charlotte couldn't help but find it all quite exciting.

"Next stop, Stockholm," breathed Jack.

"And we're supposed to find Alejandro there somehow?"

"Yes," said Jack.

"Do you know where he's going to be?"

Jack glanced at his phone, but in such a way that it was obviously a reflex, indicating he'd been looking it up already.

"His Santa, Irakli Egadze, has gone quiet on the social media front. I assume they're a few hours ahead of us and have already arrived there, but no, nothing. There's this *tomteparaden* on in Stockholm at the moment. That's Santa parade, right? And an event tomorrow night called *Santarchy* – like Santa Anarchy, I guess? – but Egadze has not said he'll be at either."

"So, no idea where he'll be." Charlotte sighed heavily. "And what will we do when we find him?"

"We'll talk to him," said Jack.

"We talked to him before," she pointed out. "I suspect he has absolutely no intention of selling videos of the filthy antics of my Santa Raymond and your Santa Seamus back to us."

"Then what? We take the video from him by force?"

That idea didn't seem right, either.

"I'm not sure we're cut out for that kind of thing," she said. "You might give off glimpses of alpha male big dick energy but really— Oh my God!"

"What is it?" he said.

A thought had just slapped into her brain. She looked at her phone and the most recent messages from Alejandro.

BDE are gonna pay ten times that. Couldn't be bothered to wait around.

"Big Dick Energy!" she said.

"Pardon?" said Jack.

She went to the internet and searched. It took a few questions, then a few more rephrased ones, but she could feel the shape of what she was looking for. When she found it, she gave a crow of victory and thrust her phone into Jack's face. He had to pull back to focus on it.

"Big Dick Energy Adult Film Productions?" he read.

"Alejandro sent me a message and—"

"You've been messaging Alejandro?"

"Really not important right now. He messaged me and told me he was selling the videos to BDE."

Jack's face twitched between annoyance at her keeping things secret and excitement that she might be onto something. "Great, well that's the buyer. Does that help us find him?"

"No. Not necessarily but—" she looked at her phone again "—they're based in Los Angeles."

"Are we going to take an emergency flight there next?"

Charlotte laughed at the thought. It was insane, but weirdly attractive. Here they were on a night train across Europe, like a couple from a James Bond film or old fashioned thriller. Despite the money this was costing them, it was proving a more than exciting way to spend a few days.

Jack was on his phone. "The CEO of Big Dick Energy is a woman called Comfort Dewvalley."

"That can't be her real name," she said.

Jack laughed, not at what she'd said, but at something on his screen. A deep, self-satisfied chuckle.

"What?" she said.

"I love people who constantly update their social media."

He showed her his phone. On her Instagram feed, there were – among several images showing acres of bare human flesh – pictures of travel, landmarks and, at the top, one of Comfort herself: an elegant middle aged woman, dressed up in a fur coat and a round fur hat, next to a sparkling Christmas tree.

"She's in Stockholm," he said.

"No fucking way!" whispered Charlotte.

"Yes way," said Jack. "Our Alejandro is meeting the buyer

in Stockholm. We find them and..." He fiddled with his phone and put it to his ear.

"What are you doing?" she said.

"Calling BDE Productions."

"But it's nearly eleven at night."

"So, like four p.m. in LA, right?" He held up a finger and stiffened. "Oh, hello! Is that BDE Productions?" He'd put on an absolutely terrible accent, possibly meant to be Spanish, full of grating phlegmy 'haitches' randomly slung onto the front of words. "I'm calling on behalf of my friend, Alejandro, who is due to meet with Comfort in Stockholm. Yes! Yes! Tomorrow evening, yes." He gave Charlotte a big thumbs up. "I wanted to drop something off to her. A little preview. Could you tell me—?" He had to pause while the other person spoke. "Amazing! You are such a darling. No, *you* have a nice day. Goodbye!" He ended the call, grinning like a delirious idiot.

"What the fuck was that?" said Charlotte.

"My superficial charm."

"I meant the accent."

"A spur of the moment thing. Acting. More importantly, we know where the buyer is and we know they're not doing the deal until tomorrow night."

She couldn't help herself. She gripped his hands in hers and did an excited jiggle dance.

"Oh, you are clever sometimes."

"Can I get that in writing?"

"Absolutely not."

39

ANIKA

At a quarter to midnight, Anika Chowdhry was sitting with her parents in their lounge.

A number of presents had appeared under the Christmas tree. Anika's mum had said she had no idea who they were from and tittered. She couldn't resist a little bit of Christmas mystery in their family life. A box of Ferrero Rocher was open on the little coffee table, paper casings scattered about as evidence of how many of them had been eaten.

The film *Die Hard 2* was on the television, although it was not yet cemented as a Christmas tradition in their house. It was a sequel to the very Chrismassy original *Die Hard* and also set at Christmas. Anika's dad did like the action, even if some of it was very silly. However, there was no Alan Rickman for Anika's mum to take a shine to, and neither the villainous William Sadler or heroic Bruce Willis (still just about clinging to his original hair) hit the mark for her.

Bruce Willis had been blown up, shot at, ejected from a plane, and generally beaten up for a good hour and a half now and only just realised that the blokes he thought were good guys were in on the evil plot. His response to this was to jump from a helicopter onto the jumbo jet containing the escaping villains.

None of this action nonsense was helping Anika with her big problems. She'd written a list of things to be resolved over the next couple of days. She'd written it in ascending order of concern, as though she could somehow build herself up to tackle the big ones by contemplating the small ones first.

- Santa Paws on Friday (sorted?)
- Children's Tea Party in the café on Friday (sorted?)
- Dog funeral for Douglas (Thursday)
- Carriage rides, but no horses!
- Getting a new Santa to replace Raymond
- Raymond

THE LAST ONE, the big one, was just the word 'Raymond'. She didn't need to write 'There's a dead Santa Raymond in the marquee who I might have killed by not following Health and Safety guidelines and I need to dispose of his body appropriately or perhaps go to prison for his murder.' For as long as she lived, the name 'Raymond' would be synonymous with the big Santa corpse she had left overnight at the garden centre.

Anika's dad paused the TV. "How did your manager respond to your request for a letter of commendation, Anika?" he asked.

"Huh?"

"You said you were going to ask for a letter of commendation."

"I ... did," she said. "Actually, my manager – the proper one, Charlotte – is away at the moment."

"Away?" said her mum. "She doesn't have the Covid, does she?"

"No, I think it's a work thing. She was in... I think she was in Holland on some training."

"That could be you, going on high-powered training days in Holland."

"Leaving you in the lurch in charge of everything in her absence," scoffed her dad.

Anika wanted to protest and point out that notionally there were any number of other people, above, below and alongside Charlotte who should be taking over, but she stopped herself. Being in charge was what she had wanted and, oddly, without seeking permission or treading on any toes it was what she was actually doing.

"She's given me quite a few responsibilities," she said.

"Has she?"

"She has. I asked and she gave me the responsibility."

Anika's mum gave a slow nod and seemed actually impressed. Which was an absolute rarity. "Well, it's good to see you making something of yourself. Make sure you make a note of all the things you've done, Anika."

"Take photos as evidence," said her dad. "Put them on your Link Me In profile on the internet."

Anika looked at her list. "Er, maybe," she said.

Her dad unpaused the TV. Bruce Willis was fighting the evil Major Grant on the wing of the taxiing jumbo jet, being battered with blows from all sides and in danger of being blown off entirely at any moment. Anika could empathise with that situation.

40

ANIKA

Anika spent a disturbed night trying to sleep while her brain juggled all of the problems at Hedgelord, including the fact that Santa Raymond was sitting all alone on his throne in the marquee. She and Gillespie had covered him over with a tarpaulin, in case someone came in to clean.

At some point during the night she must have drifted off to sleep, because she woke with a start from a dream where rodents were nibbling Raymond's corpse as it sat unattended. Was that likely to happen? She had to admit that it was a possibility, no matter how remote, and from that point on, sleep was completely unattainable.

She got up as early as she could reasonably manage without her parents fretting, and tried to slip out of the house before they were up. Of course that was impossible. Her mum had some sort of maternal radar that alerted her to Anika being up and about, and she traipsed into the kitchen with her dressing gown wrapped around her. "This is pretty early for you."

"Yep. Lots to do at work," said Anika. "I'm trying to make something of myself, like you said." She omitted the part where that 'something' might involve criminal negligence and the death of a well-loved senior.

"It's nice that you can do that," smiled her mum.

"Yes it is," said Anika, forcing herself to grin widely, as if she was having the time of her life. What did worry her, ever-so-slightly, was that she definitely *was* having the time of her life, in spite of all the things that had gone wrong. She felt as if she was a problem-solving weapon that was locked and loaded and pointing at a massive, impossible target. She could definitely do this, she just needed enough time, mental space, and confidence to work through all of the issues.

She walked to work, sifting mentally through the tasks that needed to be addressed and how she might go about them. She arrived at Hedgelord well before everyone else, so she went straight through to see Santa Raymond as a priority.

The poor dead man looked exactly the same as when she'd left him the night before, although he was now properly stiff and rigid. She went into the shop to find some mouse traps, because the haunting images from her dream wouldn't leave her. Once she had set up some small protection for Raymond's corpse she went up to the office to sort out the staff rotas for the day. She started firing off messages to all the grotto staff who'd be needed during the day, which was mostly straightforward, although she still needed a Santa. Then she needed to look at tomorrow's special events, which were much more of a headache. The most immediate and obvious problem was the lack of horses to pull the carriage. She sat in Charlotte's chair and leaned back, wondering what possible approaches might work. She stared at the ceiling, over which was Cameron's office.

Because she was confident nobody else would be around for at least another hour, she went upstairs and sat in Cameron's seat. It stood to reason that the view from the boss's chair must offer a different perspective, and it definitely did.

Her gaze drifted to the window, through which Cameron had a view that went right across the car park and over towards Bloomers. There was a small cardboard frame taped onto the window, positioned so that it made Bloomers into a tiny artwork. The cardboard frame was captioned *Twats*, which presumably kept Cameron's mind focused on important matters of strategy.

Anika leaned across the desk to stare at Bloomers. It had some of the answers she was looking for. Over there were Santas galore, and they had also booked all of the local horses. She checked in with herself to properly understand the thought she was currently nurturing. Was she seriously contemplating going to Bloomers and seeing if she might poach their Santas and their horses?

Her eyes drifted across to a little plaque on Cameron's desk that read *Doing Whatever it Takes to Be No.1*. She was fairly certain that it related to golf, as it had a cartoon picture of a smiling figure swinging a club, but it cemented the thought firmly in her head.

She *was* going to Bloomers.

41

CHARLOTTE

Charlotte woke as the train rattled across the Swedish countryside. It was eight o'clock but still dark outside. The sun didn't rise until nearly nine a.m. this far north. She'd had several hours of truly restful sleep, rocked by the motion of the train.

In the dark on the top bunk, she climbed into her trousers and tried to put on her bra and top. There was very little ceiling space and her elbows constantly got in the way.

It had been marginally easier to undress with dignity and privacy the night before. Jack had stepped outside the carriage while she got into bed and she rolled with her back to him while he got into bed himself.

She smiled at their prudish British manners. They were in Sweden now where, if cultural stereotypes were to be believed, men and women paraded around naked in front of each other without batting an eyelid.

With a series of grunts, she managed to get her clothes

on. She'd have to brush her teeth and splash water on her face at the tiny sink below. Train travel might be romantic, but it wasn't exactly the same level of comfort as staying in hotels.

"Morning," said Jack from below, clearing his throat.

"Welcome to Sweden," she replied.

"Indeed." Jack shifted and got up. He pulled on his jeans as he stood and then turned, bare-chested, to find his shirt.

Charlotte got a second's glimpse of his torso and was wondering where it belonged on the spectrum of six-pack gym obsessive to floppy-and-casual dad-bod, when he glanced up and caught her looking.

He didn't look away, embarrassed, so neither did she.

"Ready for the big climax?" he said.

"Er, what?" she said.

"Us. Getting the videos back. Succeeding in our mission."

"Oh. Oh, that. Absolutely. A hundred percent."

He grinned.

"I'm going to find us some coffee," he said, slipping on his shoes and stepping out.

He not only found coffee, but also located some not wholly unpleasant pastries. They drank and munched, watching through the window as dark forests gave way to apartment blocks and snow-covered streets.

The snow, rarely a part of Christmases back in the UK, looked pretty. Charlotte's opinion of it changed the moment they stepped outside of Stockholm Central Station.

"Oh, my fucking God! It's freezing!" she said, literally stammering with the sudden cold. A clock display outside the station handily told them it was minus one Celsius.

"We are not dressed for this weather," agreed Jack wrapping his arms about himself.

A frozen ten minute walk got them to the Gallerian. Inside the heated shops they could browse at leisure. They needed winter wear – thick coats, gloves, maybe even boots.

"You know," said Jack as he considered a Fjällräven parka coat, "if we can't bargain with Alejandro, and we're not going to just mug him for the video, then we need to be subtle."

"Not sure if you and I are masters of subtle," said Charlotte.

"A bit of subterfuge. You know, Mission Impossible the shizzle out of this thing."

"Like with fake faces?"

Jack grabbed a scarf and draped it in front of his face. "Or maybe just approach Alejandro in a way that means he won't recognise us."

"We wear scarves over our faces?"

"Or we do this thing somewhere where it will be okay if we have our faces mostly covered."

She frowned at him. "It sounds like you've already got a plan."

"Not at all, but I think we can work something out."

Suitably dressed, though the biting sub-zero chill of Swedish winter stung their faces, they made their way across the city centre.

"Stockholm is at the same latitude as Glasgow and Edinburgh, you know," said Jack.

"Scotland is never this cold," she said.

"The Scots are just hardier and don't notice?" he suggested.

It was only a further ten minute walk from the shopping mall to the Grand Hôtel and much of that was alongside an open park area called Kungsträdgården. Here, the Swedes had made an absolute virtue out of the Swedish weather and laid it out as a snowy wonderland. Down the length of the long open plaza there were conical tree-like lighting arrangements, and bright strings of colourful illuminations hung between lampposts. Much of the centre of the plaza was dominated by an open air ice rink that stretched around the statues of Swedish monarchs dotted about the place.

It was mid-morning, yet there were already families out on the ice, skating.

The Grand Hôtel was a large building of white stone that both outside and in matched its name in grandeur. Charlotte hung back while Jack went to the desk and secured a room. She looked about, oddly fearful she'd see Alejandro, or the improbably named Comfort Dewvalley, wandering through reception.

"Come on, we can do some planning while we have time," said Jack, waggling a key card.

As they walked into their hotel room, Charlotte frowned. "You booked a double! Getting a bit over-familiar now?"

"Easy, tiger," said Jack. "I don't think we're actually going to be staying here. If the operation tonight goes well, we're out of here, on the way back home, yeah? If it doesn't go well – to be honest, I don't know what that looks like – but I can't imagine our sleeping arrangements will be our top concern."

"Fair enough," she said. "We just need to make sure that it works then, don't we?"

Jack spread out several pieces of hotel stationery on the little desk. "Pull up a chair. We need to organise ourselves."

Charlotte grabbed the other chair and pushed it across the carpet. They were futuristic, tubular steel designs, presumably made to look good rather than be useful or comfortable. Each was semi-circular, with flared arms, so that as they both leaned over and steered their chairs, attempting to position them side by side, they repeatedly bashed them together like Morris dancers with walking frames.

"These chairs are really bad!" said Charlotte.

"Oh Charlotte, I'm so proud of you," said Jack. "You said that whole sentence without any swears!"

"Bollocks," growled Charlotte to make a point.

"Let's just sit on the bed," said Jack. He pulled the desk towards them as they sat side by side.

"So we know that Alejandro is meeting Comfort the distributor this evening."

"Stop jigging," said Charlotte.

"What?"

"If we're sitting on the bed then you need to stop that jigging thing you do with your leg. The whole bed's vibrating."

Jack put a hand on the offending leg to still it. "Sorry. It's a habit of mine when I get excited about something."

"What are you excited about?" Charlotte asked, warily.

"You and me, working together! About to pull off an amazing... You know, some sort of an amazing plan that we haven't yet thought of to stop this awful deal going ahead."

"And that's exciting? You buying into this whole Mission Impossible vibe, Mr Cruise?"

He grinned. "I am convinced we'll make an amazing team."

Charlotte tipped her head to look at him. "Oh, yeah. Your insanely blind optimism coupled with my anger management issues? All we really need to complete that heady cocktail would be some sort of extra stress caused by a recent relationship breakdown."

He recoiled. "Ouch."

She immediately cursed herself for her insensitivity. "I'm sorry. That was a shitty thing to say. I will now reverse time and answer your question without being a bitch. Do I think we'll make an awesome team? Yeah. I think we probably will. My brains, your superficial charm, yadda yadda."

He dabbed a finger onto her nose. "You think I have superficial charm, oh you tease!"

Ignoring his silliness, she dragged a piece of paper across the desk. "I'm making us a task list. I assume you're going to tell me the plan now, yeah?"

"Right. You know that Mission Impossible film?" he said.

"Oh, we're still on that? Which one?"

"The one with Tom Cruise."

"They've all got Tom Cruise."

"I don't know which one," said Jack. "It's the one in the hotel. They want to interrupt a deal between a seller and a buyer, just like us."

"Tom Cruise wanted to stop someone buying Santa porn?"

"I think it was nuclear bombs or something. What they

did was they stopped the meeting by making two fake meetings, one with the seller, one with the buyer. And at each meeting they pretended to be the other one."

Jack's explanation was rubbish, but Charlotte vaguely understood. "We go meet Comfort and pretend to be Alejandro, and we go meet Alejandro pretending to be Comfort."

"Exactly," he grinned. "We get the SD card off him and the payment off her. Then we give him the payment and we give her a fake SD card. Everyone thinks they're happy but we get the real video footage."

Charlotte wrote down *SD card* on the paper.

"But she's not going to take a blank SD card. She needs to see the video."

"Some video," he said. "We copy some of the videos across."

Charlotte tried to picture the scene. "If Alejandro lets us put his SD card in one of our phones then we could send some of the files to the other person who is with Comfort."

"We don't want to be fiddling with getting SD cards in and out of our phones."

She wrote down *SD card reader thing*, then added *earpieces*.

"Earpieces?" he said.

"Yeah. You know..." She put her finger to her ear like a secret service agent. "*Code Red. The otter has left the nest. The otter has left the nest.* We need to hear exactly what the other is doing."

"Okay. But we need better code phrases than that."

"Fine. We just need to decide who is going to deal with who."

"Well, Alejandro knows both of us," she said.

"Scarves remember," said Jack. "And I'm thinking that ice rink outside could be a lovely place for a rendezvous this evening. I think I should be the one to approach Comfort."

"Really? Why?"

"Because I'm a man and can pass myself off as Alejandro," he said, dropping into his atrocious Spanish accent.

"Assuming neither of them has seen photos of the other."

"Is it likely?"

"Which means I have to go and be Comfort Dewvalley in front of Alejandro," she said.

"Give us your best American accent."

"I'm not doing a silly accent."

"You can't go up to Alejandro using your regular voice. A British accent will automatically make him suspicious. Give us your best American accent."

"Fine!" she huffed. "On one condition."

"What's that?"

"That you stop jigging your fucking leg. It's going again."

42

ANIKA

Anika wondered whether Tom or Daffyd might offer any practical help for her problems with the upcoming events, so she waited until they were both in the office and asked them both for a chat.

Tom was first to arrive. He spent a few minutes grabbing himself a drink, then he stood and stared at the whiteboard containing the rota. Anika thought he still looked confused by it, even though it was bang up to date.

Daffyd came into the office with a noisy crash as the door opened too quickly and banged on the wall. Had he done that deliberately? "Oh?" he said as he turned to look at the whiteboard. "Oh."

Anika wasn't sure what message he was trying to convey. He seemed unhappy.

Daffyd turned to Tom. "I see that *someone* has taken control of the whiteboard."

Tom looked uncomfortable. "Have they?"

"Oh. My. God. Are you for real? Well, whoever that someone is, I hope they are very pleased with themselves for failing to loop in the person who merely operates the grotto." He held his hand to his heart, as if it ached with profound sorrow.

Anika felt this would probably be a bad moment to say she was the one who'd made the updates, so she kept her mouth shut.

Tom just kept looking between Daffyd and the whiteboard, as if the mystery might be solved if he stared at both of them long enough.

Anika gave a light cough. "It's great that you've sorted the grotto between you. There are special events coming up tomorrow that probably need some attention."

"I don't doubt it for a second," said Daffyd. "But I am confident that the same hand which has *interfered so profoundly* with my grotto will take care of things." He accompanied the sentence with an elaborate mime that looked as though he was milking a cow, or possibly tickling it, while pulling an oddly lascivious face. Then he turned and left the office, slamming the door behind him.

"I am very sorry you had to witness behaviour like that," said Tom.

Anika wasn't even sure what the behaviour was exactly, so she gave a small shrug.

"In fact, I think I might have to write that one up. It was highly inappropriate." Tom moved over to his desk and sat down. "Highly inappropriate." He pulled a pad and pen out of a drawer, the pen hovering over the page as he thought. He looked up. "Would you say that gesture of Daffyd's was merely offensive, or was it also sexually suggestive?" he asked.

Anika felt her face redden at the question. She had no idea what Daffyd had intended. In her experience of the weird little man, his offensiveness was just part of his DNA. He projected his own peculiar vibe of uncomfortable intensity wherever he went.

"I really don't know. Anyway, I'd best get on," she said. She would get no help from Daffyd and Tom while they were locked in this private battle. She would have to fly solo. "I need to go out and get something for the carriage ride event tomorrow, and for the grotto."

"Do you? That's lovely," said Tom. "Do you need any support with that?"

Anika was surprised by the kind offer before she recognised the tone of Tom's voice. He was offering help in the hope that he wasn't going to be asked for it.

"No, I'm fine, Tom," she said. "I'll be fine by myself." She left the office and Hedgelord's, walked along the road and across the roundabout to Bloomers.

She'd borrowed a coat from Karen to cover up her elf outfit. Her previous visits to Hedgelord's rival had been with Daffyd, who had dressed her up in a very revealing outfit to try and pull off a sting operation by seducing their most talented elf, Nathan. She hoped that by wearing a shapeless coat she might slip around the store unnoticed until she found a way to carry out her mission.

The store was busy, so she walked in without attracting any attention. She went over to the grotto to see if it was open yet. There was a sign up saying it would open in half an hour, but that there were no walk-in slots available. Anika could see that grotto staff were gathering and preparing to welcome customers. She hesitated for no more than a moment, then slipped off the bulky coat and tucked it under her arm, making her way into the grotto as if she belonged there.

She walked through the first couple of rooms, waving a greeting to anyone who noticed her, but mostly the people in there were elves carrying boxes of supplies and making sure the grotto was ready. A couple lounged on stools, and they glanced up guiltily as she walked past. They looked relieved when they saw she was just another elf.

She made for Santa's room, hoping that Santa would be there. It was quite normal for Santa to turn up late at Hedgelord's grotto, so she was mildly surprised to see this Santa was not only ready and suited-up in his room, but that he was helping Nathan the elf to arrange the furniture.

"If we make space at the side of the throne then it allows someone carrying a baby to get in closer," said Santa.

"I could just switch this seat for a wider one and push it right up to the throne. Parents of young babies need all the rest they can get," said Nathan.

The two of them noticed Anika at the same time.

"Can I help y—?" Nathan started, but then stopped himself. "It's you."

"Er yes. About that. I'm really sorry, it wasn't really my idea," said Anika.

"No, I see that," said Nathan with a kind smile. "It was a Hedgelord ruse to get in the paper. You were simply a pawn. I see that."

Anika was being drawn into the warmth of Nathan's

charisma. He made her believe in the magic of Christmas and the innate goodness of all humanity every time he smiled. It was part of what made him a champion elf, and what made Daffyd bitter about his loss to Bloomers. She wanted to smile back and return to Hedgelord, accepting that undercover missions to steal resources from Bloomers were a bad idea. However, Nathan had described her as a pawn, and she bridled at that. She was taking control of events at Hedgelord, and that made her much more than a pawn.

She smiled at Nathan and Santa. "I see now that it was very wrong. I am re-thinking my life choices. Who does the recruitment here at Bloomers?"

Nathan looked at her. "If you would like me to fetch someone I can do that. Just to be clear though, we would never poach staff. You're asking simply because you're interested?"

"Yep."

"I will be back in five minutes with the application form. Normally I'd ask Jack, our Christmas manager, but he's away on important work. The Netherlands I think, by the looks of the photos we've been sent."

"The Netherlands, huh?" said Anika. "Interesting. I think my manager Charlotte is there as well."

"Is that so?" said Nathan, intrigued. "Fancy that. Yes, let me go get that application form."

When Nathan had left the room, Anika rushed to the chair next to Santa's throne. "Hi Santa. Can I call you by your first name?"

"Seamus, you mean?"

"Thanks Santa Seamus. How much are they paying you here?"

"Eh? You what?"

"Whatever it is, Hedgelord will double it, if you can work a shift today. Tell Bloomers you've got a stomach upset. I promise we can make it worth your while."

Seamus's face went through a series of expressions. There was a brief flash of anger and then he grew contemplative. "Money, eh? Is that all that's on offer?"

Seamus's tone told Anika all she needed to know about where his mind was going. With horror she realised he was the same Santa who had been here when she'd attempted to seduce Nathan. From what she remembered, Seamus had been much more responsive to her wiles than Nathan.

"Whoa, Seamus. I'm not sure that's going to work out. Let's get back to the money, shall we?"

"Fine. Call me," said Seamus with a wink. He handed her a card.

She took Seamus's card and stomped out of the grotto, grabbing the paper that Nathan held out as she passed him standing outside the door.

She paused to think for a moment. She'd not quite managed to turn the Santa who was on active duty, but he was just one of several, presumably. She needed to find Bloomers' master list. With a bit of luck, it would be in the same place as some sort of master horse list. She needed to find the office.

43

GALLAGHER

Gallagher had tried to view the winter morning sun as a positive thing, but he feared he was slipping back into the darker days that were more familiar. The business with the criminal Snømann had put a dark spin on his week.

Gallagher recognised that his life had been a rollercoaster in and out of mental darkness for some time. His shitty apartment full of black mould and his piling personal debts were the background melody of his depression. It had all tumbled into a deeper darkness the other week, when he and Luka had found themselves in further debt to a psychotic drug dealer, Sonia Patterson. Fobbing her off with some stolen money (which had then ended up going to a noble charity cause) had lifted him out of his pit of despair.

Now this business with Snømann had plunged him back into the dark again. The blackness of the world felt more like home to him, because there was no escaping it for more than a short while.

"Beautiful morning," said Luka, coming along the path.

"Snow's forecast for later," said Gallagher. "Mad amounts of it. We'll probably all get stuck here and have to cannibalise each other."

Luka gave a casual shrug, as if he'd been there before. "Still. Sun is shining now."

Gallagher felt slightly jealous of Luka's chipper demeanour. Why was he able to smile at the weather when Snømann might come by at any moment and practise his ultra-violence on them?

"You know what we can do today?" said Luka. "We will pot up some Christmas trees and make them fancy. You know you like doing that. They sell for a lot, so Tom cannot argue is not good use of our time."

Gallagher smiled at Luka. "Aw, you're a good mate. You're right, if there's snow, they can put a few of those at the front of the store and they'll get bought straightaway. People don't want to faff if they think they might have trouble getting home."

"We are retail fucking gurus!" said Luka, his joint stuck out at a crazy angle as he smiled. "Come on, we will take trolley and get enormous pots so that customers can buy them at inflated prices."

They pushed one of their bigger trollies over to the racking where the giant pots were stacked up so that they remained above any frost which might damage them.

"What do you think? We start with three of each size?" Luka said. "Medium, large and massive."

"Yeah, let's not overload the trolley," said Gallagher.

They grabbed pots and started to load them up.

"What's that?" Luka pointed to something on the ground. Both of them bent to look.

"It's a fucking tenner!" said Gallagher, plucking at it swiftly. Despite pinching it firmly between his finger and thumb, the note stayed behind. "Oh. It's stuck."

There was a heavy grinding noise from overhead, and some part of Gallagher's brain realised this was a bad thing. He shoved Luka hard in the shoulders, sending both of them sprawling backwards, away from each other. As they landed on their backsides there was a devastating crash as some of the biggest pots crashed from the racking down to the floor, to the exact spot where they had both been standing a moment earlier.

"What the fuck just happened?" said Gallagher when he had recovered the power of speech.

"Did you knock the shelves?" asked Luka, levering himself to his feet.

"No I didn't. These are solid shelves, customer-proof."

"Yeah. True." Luka looked up to the top shelf where the pots had fallen from. "Maybe frost damage made them collapse."

"Really? Twice now we've nearly come a fucking cropper. First an exploding barbecue and now a pot avalanche."

"Pot-alanche."

"It's no joke, mate."

Luka gave one of his shrugs. "Is tenner still underneath? What do they say about every cloud has silver lining, eh?"

Gallagher pulled aside the smashed terracotta pieces. It was a good point.

"We gain a tenner and then we still get to make nice fucking trees," said Luka. "Can still be a good day."

Yet Gallagher remained unconvinced. Scumbag international crooks and a spate of nearly fatal accidents all in one week? Nah, something fishy was going on.

44

ANIKA

To seek out the Bloomers office, Anika thought about the layout of Hedgelord and applied the same logic. The entrance would be somewhere slightly quieter, so she made her way round to a part of the store where they sold comfortable footwear. Sure enough, there was a door for staff only. It had a keypad for security, so she hung around, looking at a pair of beige loafers with arch supports. It wasn't long before a woman went through the door, and Anika watched as she pressed the buttons. They were the clunky, difficult ones, so it was a laboured and obvious process. A few minutes later, after she'd seen the woman leave, Anika went through the door herself.

She found herself inside Bloomers' office. It wasn't so very different from Hedgelord's, but the furniture was a little newer, and it felt slightly less chaotic. The grotto rota was a similar mess of smudged and much-altered names in boxes, but there were no contact details on the wall.

There was another whiteboard which was headed
FESTIVE PONY EXPERIENCE. This was the event Amy had
mentioned, the one that had hoovered up every available
horse for miles around. It listed sessions, staff attendance,
equipment and extras. Were horses extras? It looked like it.
Kestrel Stables were listed against the afternoon's event, and
there was a phone number next to it.

Anika crossed to the desks, and scanned through the
folders stacked up on them, looking for events management.

She was pretty sure she'd found Jack Hartigan's desk
when she found folders neatly labelled GROTTO STAFF and
EVENTS OPERATIONAL PROCEDURES. She picked up the phone
on his desk and called the number for Kestrel Stables.

"Oh hi, this is Jack Hartigan's assistant, Emma, calling
from Bloomers. Just finalising the details for later today."

"Sure. I think everything's in hand."

"So, can you please confirm how many horses you'll be
sending?" she asked.

"It will be eight, as agreed."

"Perfect. Can I please just ask that you drop four of them
off in a different location? We'd like them to be delivered to
the paddock adjacent to Hedgel—"

The door opened and Anika ducked under the desk,
dropping the phone. She heard two people talking as they
walked in.

One of them was a softly spoken woman. Her voice was
smooth, and yet quietly assertive. "Do take care not to
automatically assume the worst, my darling."

"You know me, I am very much a creature of reason and
logic, yet I permit my intuitive side to speak to me. I can tell

that something is off about this whole situation." It was a man's voice. The sort of man who spoke with such a deep, loud voice he sounded like a Shakespearean actor trying to project to the back of a theatre.

"What's our best approach? If Jack's just taking a mental health break, we could make things worse by jumping to wild conclusions," said the woman.

"As always my dear, you speak a good deal of sense, but here's the difficulty. If he is genuinely in danger then it's essential we act quickly."

"The police you mean? Please, just because a man says he's 'all tied up', it doesn't mean he's literally been kidnapped."

"No? But someone has whisked Jack away. All the signs are there. And if what Nathan says is true, and it's that Charlotte Mitchell from Hedgelord who's taken him..."

The man made a thoughtful clicking noise with his teeth. "If we think Hedgelord's involved, there might be something to be said for tackling Cameron head-on."

"I don't think he's in yet. I didn't see the reflection from his binoculars while I was doing my sun salutations."

"Give him an hour. And then we take action. If someone has kidnapped our Jack, we don't want to be seen sitting on our hands. We know he was in Rotterdam, but those other pictures were from Germany. His captors are on the move. Perhaps we need to call Interpol."

The woman made a noise, considering the possibilities. "We give Cameron Clasp an hour to reveal his hand, and then we act."

"Good," the man agreed. "Now, we were going to inspect the Festive Pony Experience set up."

There was the sound of a door being opened.

"Ah, hang on," said the woman. "I need to update the Ron and Hermione nutritional scores before we go out. Karen forgot to put fruit in their lunchboxes again." There was heavy emphasis on the word *forgot*.

As they left and the door shut, Anika realised with a lurch that those were Karen's in-laws: Maremba and Marcus. Yes, Karen on the tills at Hedgelord had the owners or managers of Bloomers as her in-laws.

Anika emerged from under the desk. The phone line had gone dead, so she put it back on the cradle. She couldn't summon the nerve to call back. She looked over to the wall and saw there was a board headed RON & HERMIONE.

It was divided into rows and columns. There was a row for each day, and the columns had headings for PARENTING MOMENTS, INDIVIDUALISTIC IDENTIFIERS, NURTURING NEEDS and NUTRITION.

Anika couldn't help snapping a picture on her phone, because even a quick glance suggested that this was seriously weird. A PARENTING MOMENT was listed from three days ago:

- *K was late in getting H to choir practice when it was her turn to pass out the music*
- *Potential: pattern of anxiety / disappointment*
- *Solution: time management coaching for K*

"FUCK ME," whispered Anika to herself.

She really needed to get out of there. She had her own dead Santa to deal with, but it seemed there were other incidents afoot. Had Charlotte really kidnapped Jack?

45

CHARLOTTE

Even in a city the size of Stockholm, it had taken Charlotte and Jack a while to find an electronic gadget shop that sold all the things they required. Several hundred Swedish krona later and they had what they needed.

Back at the hotel, reception were able to put a call through from Charlotte's room to Comfort's.

"Go for Comfort," said an American voice.

"Oh, hello," said Charlotte. "This is Fabia, Alejandro Aramburuzabala's assistant." She realised she'd copied Jack's abominable Spanish accent and silently cursed herself. "I wanted to confirm the meeting for tonight. He thought it would be nice to meet on the ice rink in Kungsträdgården. Outside the hotel."

"Not the restaurant."

"When in Stockholm..." she suggested lightly. "There is a Santa parade and all the Christmas things."

The American woman gave a deep and thoughtful *'hmmm'*. *"When in Stockholm. The same time?"*

Charlotte floundered. "Five o'clock?"

"Not four?" said Comfort

"Four is great. My brain is on Spanish time. Four o'clock on the ice rink. Have you met Alejandro before?"

Jack was throwing warning gestures at her. This was not the agreed script.

"I have not had that pleasure."

Charlotte nodded and cast about for Jack's coat. "He'll be wearing a red coat. He knows you."

"Good," said Comfort and hung up.

Charlotte grinned at Jack. "Now, your fucking turn, Jack. Use your phone to contact Alejandro to meet me – Comfort – on the rink at nine."

"I shall do my best American accent," said Jack, drawling like the cheesiest Hollywood cowboy.

"Or you could just message him," suggested Charlotte.

Still unsure if he was going to message or mangle an American accent, Charlotte decided to take herself to the bathroom and take a long, relaxing bath. What point was there in staying in a five star hotel if you didn't take advantage of all the amenities.

46

ANIKA

Anika would be back at Hedgelord just in time for Douglas's funeral. Sophie had sent them the timings in their messaging chat. As far as Anika could tell, she hadn't sought any kind of permission, but was simply planning to bury her dead dog in the paddock while her friends supported her. It seemed harmless enough. As she walked, she realised that a natural consequence of it all was likely to be a lack of organisation.

She rushed round to see the plant guys as soon as she had returned. "Has anyone asked you about digging a hole in the paddock?" she asked, somewhat out of breath.

"No," said Gallagher, looking at Luka. "I think we'd have remembered a thing like that. Do we *need* to go and dig one?"

Anika nodded. "Yes please. Quick as you can, we'll need it in a short while."

"Righto. We'll fetch some spades shall we?" said Gallagher. Luka looked unhappy, but he went along too.

Anika hurried inside to find Karen and Sophie. She found them just inside the café and pulled up short when she realised that both were dressed entirely in formal black clothes.

"Oh. Right. I'm sorry. I didn't realise," she said, looking down at her bright red elf dungarees.

Sophie reached out and put a hand on Anika's shoulder. "You're fine love. Thank you for coming. Would you mind if we took a little walk around the pet section? I want to get a toy for Douglas, so he's got something to play with. You know, something old, something new, something borrowed and something blue. I've got everything except the something new."

Anika opened her mouth to say surely that was weddings, but she closed it again. Who was she to decide how Sophie should mourn Douglas?

They browsed the dog toys.

"This one's nice," said Karen, holding up a soft bone made from tweed fabric. "Tasteful, don't you think?"

"Oh no. Douglas would chew through that in five minutes. We need something sturdier," said Sophie.

Anika picked up a hard plastic toy, shaped like a rugby ball and pebbled with texture. "How about this?"

"Ooh, yes he'd enjoy that one," said Sophie. "The gnawing would keep him busy for hours."

"I'll take the tag off and run it through the till when we get back," said Karen. "My treat, eh?"

The three of them made their way out of the garden centre and across the car park, towards the paddock. Anika and Karen stood either side of Sophie, each holding one of her hands in support.

When they were through the gap and into the main paddock area, Anika saw that Gillespie was there, and Daffyd as well. Gallagher and Luka had put their spades aside and stood in respectful silence as the women approached. They had dug a hole, a few feet away from the ragged circle of mourners that had formed. The circle opened up, and Sophie stood at its head to address the others.

"Thank you all so much for coming today. It means a lot to me to see you all here, supporting me in remembering Douglas. I want to say a few words about him, if that's all right with everyone?"

There were encouraging smiles from around the group as Sophie unfolded a piece of paper from her bag and started to read.

"My boy Douglas came to me from the rescue centre at Hollerton. He'd been a long term resident there because people found his size intimidating." Sophie's face started to crumple as she mimed patting a head. It did suggest a large dog.

"I took him out for a little walk and we bonded immediately. It was like coming home." Sophie started to sob. "I don't think I can—"

Karen embraced Sophie and gave Anika a sharp nod.

"Oh right," said Anika. "Let me read the rest, Sophie." She took the piece of paper and stood straight, shoulders back, as she addressed the crowd. "Some people said that he was too much dog for me to handle, but I firmly believe you control a dog by forming a strong bond with him. Douglas and I did everything together. I've brought a photo album for you all to flick through if you'd like to see some pictures of us when we were happiest together."

Anika looked up as Sophie rummaged in her carrier bag and passed a faux-leather album down the line. As Gillespie opened it, she could see pictures of Sophie and a giant dog on the beach together, and pretending to pull a Christmas cracker.

She read on.

"He was a loving, faithful companion, and I will miss him more than anyone can ever know. I hope that wherever he is, over that rainbow bridge, there are ducks and squirrels that are just a bit too quick for him to catch, as that was his favourite game. If he'd ever caught one, I don't know what he'd do. Run free my sweet Douglas, and to everyone here, may you all find someone who looks at you the way that Douglas used to look at me."

As Anika finished reading, there was a low, collective 'aww' at the sentiment.

A brief silence followed where nobody seemed to know what was next.

"I believe we have some more tributes," said Karen, who still held Sophie in a supportive embrace. "But perhaps we should perform the committal?"

Nobody moved.

"Do you mean the actual burial?" asked Anika in a whisper.

Karen nodded.

"Can someone fetch the body?" Anika asked the group. She realised she had no idea where it was. Had Sophie brought it in her car?

There were some whispered interchanges and Gillespie went off, followed by Luka and Gallagher.

Anika felt awkward waiting, and thought she needed to say something. The photo album had come back round to her. "What sort of dog was Douglas, Sophie?" she asked.

"A Rottweiler," said Sophie. "A gentle giant. See how he smiled? It shows up well in some of these photos, doesn't it?"

Anika studied a photo showing Sophie and Douglas on a picnic blanket in summer, vivid green grass and blue sky framing them. Douglas sat to attention, while the unseen photographer captured Sophie's warm smile, her arm casually thrown around the huge dog.

"He looks adorable." Anika really meant it. Then she glanced behind and time froze.

She could see two wheelbarrows being pushed towards the paddock. Both had a tarpaulin hiding the contents, but the bulk suggested both contained a dead body. Gillespie pushed one, Luka and Gallagher pushed the other.

She turned back to Sophie and Karen. "Excuse me for just one moment, will you?"

She ran to intercept the wheelbarrows. "What are you doing?" she hissed. "Which one is the dog?"

Gillespie pointed to his barrow.

Anika turned to Luka and Gallagher. "Is that Raymond? Why have you brought him?"

"You said to," said Gallagher, a little defensively. "Well, we thought you did."

"No! This is a dog funeral. Put him back," hissed Anika.

"How about we park him by hedge and bury him after?" Luka said. "He's here now, may as well."

Anika fought to make calm words come out of her mouth. "No! We are going to take him home and make it look as though he died there. We're not just going to pop him in a dog grave!"

"Suit yourself," said Luka. He and Gallagher turned around and pushed the wheelbarrow back towards the marquee.

Anika accompanied the wheelbarrow pushed by Gillespie. She couldn't help lifting a corner of the tarpaulin, just to check that it was in fact a dog. It would be a terrible thing if the two had got mixed up. She saw dark brown fur and sighed with relief.

"How would you like to do the committal, Sophie?" she asked.

Sophie looked distraught at the question, so Karen chipped in. "I think we'll gently lift Douglas into the grave, then Sophie will add her small tokens, sprinkle on some soil, and we will continue with the service."

Anika could see a problem with that. The two best candidates for gently lifting a huge Rottweiler corpse were currently occupied manhandling a dead Santa back in the marquee. There wasn't anyone left behind who might reasonably take even half the weight.

"Would it be a good time for us all to close our eyes and say a small prayer?" she asked.

"Good idea," said Karen. She started to recite The Lord's Prayer, and when Anika was certain that everyone's eyes were closed, she made her way quietly to the wheelbarrow, slipped off the tarpaulin, and angled the wheelbarrow so she could tip the dead dog into the hole.

She thrust the handles up into the air, assuming that would do the job.

"...*Give us this day our daily bread...*"

The dog had died with its legs outstretched, and somehow it had become wedged at the top of the hole. She lowered the barrow, backed it away and went round to try and encourage it properly into the hole. She grabbed a stiff paw and tried to lift it up, but the other three were stuck fast. She had to prevent herself falling in, which wasn't the easiest thing. She tried to grab two paws in each hand, but she was unable to pull them free without toppling over.

"...*But deliver us from evil...*"

She saw the spade at the side of the hole and picked it up. If she used it as a lever, maybe she could release those troublesome paws and send the dog down into the hole. She slid the spade underneath the front paws and leaned back on the handle. Something shifted. She repeated the process on the back paws, and Douglas finally slid down into the hole with a soft *whump*.

"...*For thine is the kingdom, the power and the glory...*"

She returned to the place where she'd been standing and waited for everyone to finish the prayer. She saw Gallagher and Luka return, giving them a questioning thumbs up. They nodded, and Anika dared to breathe again.

Sophie rootled in her carrier bag and fetched out the things she wanted to bury with Douglas. She walked to his graveside. "Something old. This is his oldest blanket. It's just a scrap really, but he loved it very much." She dropped a small piece of ragged fabric into the hole. "Something new. We chose him a chew toy just now. Something borrowed, it's a pair of my socks. He liked these, and would hide them around the house. And something blue. It's his favourite dog biscuits. They come in a blue box." Sophie threw in each of the offerings, then gave a tiny wave. "Now we can bury you, my sweet boy." She grabbed a handful of earth and threw it into the grave.

"Now Daffyd will perform his tribute," said Karen.

Everyone stepped back and waited while Daffyd composed himself.

"I would like to perform *Because You Loved Me*, a beautiful song made famous by Celine Dion." He looked around the group. "It would help with Sophie's grieving process if you could all manage to shed a tear while I perform. Can you please do that?"

Anika looked over at Gallagher and Luka who both pulled a face that said they very definitely would not be doing that.

"I realise this is perhaps outside of some people's comfort zone," said Daffyd. "Let me help you with that. A gift, if you will, from a seasoned actor. It can help if you reflect on a time when you had to process your own loss, or if that's never happened, imagine you've lost someone or something very precious to you."

"Like fucking dignity maybe?" said Luka, very quietly.

Daffyd began the song. It was accompanied by much hand-wringing and vocal warbling. Anika decided she could circumvent the required crying by doing a few fake dabs at her eyes. She glanced around and saw most of the others were doing the same. Gallagher was openly sobbing however, and she was secretly grateful that he was taking one for the team.

As Daffyd finished he bowed once to Sophie and once to the grave of Douglas.

"Do you want a rose, Soph?" asked Karen. She held out a single stem rose from a bunch she held in her hand.

Sophie took the rose and cast it into the grave. She paused for a long moment, then moved to the side, allowing for the next person. Karen handed out roses to everyone present, but when she got to Luka he did not reach for a rose. Instead he threw up his hands.

"You know this is a fucking dog, don't you? Just a fucking dog? I can go to shelter now and get you another! I can get two so you have a fucking spare. Why are you all doing this?"

There was a long, shocked silence, then Karen moved towards Sophie. "It's all right love. We all process grief in our own way, he's upset, isn't he?"

47

CHARLOTTE

Mid-afternoon, Charlotte and Jack dressed for their planned interception of the video files.

"I'm very excited about this," said Jack.

"We need to stay focused," she warned him.

"You're saying you're not excited?

She was going to deny it, then thought why the hell would she? She gave a twirl in her new thick coat and stepped lightly over to the window overlooking Kungsträdgården. The city was already dark again and a web of coloured lights spread out beneath them.

"Literally on a covert fucking espionage mission in a European capital at Christmas," she said. "I mean this must fucking beat Paris."

Jack frowned and opened his mouth to argue, then he raised his eyebrows in surprise. "You know, it actually does. As far as Euro city breaks goes, this has been one of the best. I mean I don't know if my fantasy spy weekend involves hanging out with the sweariest leading lady on the planet, but..."

She grinned and pulled her woollen scarf across her lower face. "I can pass for Kathryn in a certain, light if you prefer."

"Oh, no," he said with deep sincerity. "I know who I'd rather spend my time with right now."

His gaze lingered on her a moment and she felt a warmth flush her cheeks. She looked away. "Yeah, and to be clear," she stammered, "you are, like, not as nearly as irritating out of the office as you are in it."

"Not irritating." He nodded. "That's like a five star review from you."

"You're like ninety percent irritating here," she added.

"Compared with...?"

"A hundred percent irritating in your natural environment."

"Oh, then we should stay away from Hedgelord and Bloomers as long as possible."

He was joking. Of course he was joking. But that wishful thought, that they could hide away from the rest of the world here in Sweden was weirdly compelling. It was also disturbing in that it implied a warmth between them and a—

She looked at Jack, and forced herself to be honest in the act of looking. "Fuck!" she said with feeling.

"What's the matter?" he said.

No way was she giving him the true answer: that she had started to find him attractive, like properly attractive. Like she could imagine that this man, who she'd already spent two nights alongside – one on a ferry and one on a train – was a man she wanted to spend another night alongside, but in this double bed with nothing between them.

She scowled furiously and pulled at her coat zip. "Just realised I need the loo before we go, and I'm going to have to fight my way out of this coat again."

"Oh, okay."

Five minutes later, after pretending to go to the toilet to cover up her embarrassment, she was ready to go. She passed a communication earpiece to Jack as they approached the lift. "You head out to find Comfort, codename 'Fabric Softener' and I'll go for Alejandro, codename 'Twatface'." she said.

"We're not using that codename for him," said Jack.

"Okay. Elfbollocks."

"No. It should be something we can feel comfortable saying in public while being watched."

"I'm happy with Elfbollocks."

"Jingle Bells, for example."

She sighed. "Fine."

She slotted the earpiece into her right ear and wiggled it into a comfortable position. "Okay, you go for 'Fabric Conditioner', I'll keep my eyes open for 'Elfbollocks'—"

"'Jingle Bells'."

"Yeah. Whatever."

Whether she'd grown acclimatised or the weather had genuinely warmed, but the winter wind blowing through the Kungsträdgården that evening felt merely bitingly cold and not bone-marrowly freezing. With collars up, hoods up, and a scarf over Charlotte's face, they walked side by side to the ice rink beneath the web of Christmas lights.

Charlotte pulled at his arm as he started towards the skating counter. "Er, are we going on the ice?"

"We're meeting people at an ice rink. I assumed we were going on the ice." He grinned, his breath steaming between his teeth. "Don't tell me you can't skate."

"I can bloody skate," she said. "I'm a fucking demon on the ice." Her smartwatch buzzed at the profanity. Frankly, it needed to cut her some slack. There had been far fewer temper outbursts over the last couple of days than usual.

"If you can skate there's no problem," he said.

They sat in a narrow marquee and swapped shoes for skates before heading out onto the ice. There were many people there, large groups of families and friends. Charlotte and Jack naturally split up and made casual circuits of the rink.

Jack's voice came through her earpiece. *"Ice Demon, this is Superficial Charm. Come in, over."*

"This is Ice Demon," she replied. "I can hear you, Smug Git, over."

"These walkie-talkie earpiece things are cool, aren't they? Over."

Charlotte smiled and held back on automatically agreeing. They were cool, but they had a job to do. "Keep an eye out of Fabric Conditioner."

"Will do. You look out for Jingle Bells."

"Wilko. Roger." She was starting to enjoy herself and was about to give an 'over and out' when she spotted a figure at the side of the rink. It was Comfort Dewvalley, the American porn distributor.

The woman was unmistakeable. She was tall and

statuesque, the kind of stunning austere beauty some women just seemed to nail in middle age. In a long furry coat and a round fur hat, Comfort looked like a screen goddess of an earlier era. She appeared to be unaccompanied as she stepped onto the ice.

"Smug Git," said Charlotte. "I see Comfort, I mean Fabric Conditioner, over by the entrance near the hot drink stand."

"*Got her,*" he said. "*Heading in.*"

Comfort skated in the manner of a person who was perfectly competent on the ice but wasn't going to get involved with this silly pastime more than was strictly necessary. Jack approached her from the side and fell in beside her.

"Hello," he said. Charlotte could hear him clearly through her earpiece and – God! – he was using that awful Spanish accent again. "*Miss Dewvalley.*"

"*Ah, Mr Aramburuzabala,*" she said.

"*Very good,*" he said. "*Most people do not even attempt it. But call me Alejandro.*"

"*Alejandro.*"

48

GALLAGHER

Gallagher moved away from the weird dog funeral, wondering what the hell had just happened. He knew his brain ought to be occupied by the near miss that he and Luka had just had, mistakenly wheeling the body of Santa Raymond to the wrong funeral, but that took a back seat to the strange emotional moment he'd just experienced.

He wasn't someone who cried frequently, but when Daffyd had urged them all to shed a tear he had found there were quite a lot of them stored up somewhere inside him. It had felt good to be given permission to let them out. There was the general background misery of his day-to-day life, and the much more distressing situation of being bullied and threatened by Snømann. On top of all that, the two unsettling accidents which had nearly killed both him and Luka had him on a knife edge of stress. Sobbing his heart out for a few minutes at the graveside of a dog had provided some sort of temporary release.

"Good performance my friend," said Luka, slapping him on the back. "Now we will go and deal with those trees, eh?"

"Weren't you a bit harsh back there? I don't think there's any such thing as 'just a dog' in Sophie's eyes."

"Some people need sense of fucking perspective. Now go into shop and get decorations. See if there are split packages or returns we can use."

Gallagher went inside. Decorating trees was a special treat. Those trees would go out to the homes of local families, and just for a little while Gallagher could indulge in the fantasy that he was a part of that. He was taking great care to decorate a tree that would bring joy, and it was a beautiful thing.

He stopped by the tills to see if there were any spoiled packages or returns, then he swung by the office on a similar mission.

"Ah Gallagher! So glad I caught you!" said Cameron. "I have an update!"

Gallagher's heart sank. This was going to be more of Cameron being clueless about the people who worked for him. "Oh yes? Well, I'm in a bit of a hurry actually, we've got a rush on Christmas trees."

"I'm sure you can spare a few minutes to talk about something as important as this. We're still over a week away from the big day!"

"Yeah."

"So, would you believe a niece of mine has set up a new

business that is an absolute godsend. Take a look at what she's been able to do."

Cameron beckoned for Gallagher to follow him up to his office. Gallagher sighed and trailed behind, up the stairs to the eagle's nest office that occupied the entire first floor on the roof of the Hedgelord building. Cameron trotted eagerly to a corner where a large cardboard box stood. He reached inside with both hands and put them behind his back.

"I'll show you two of these to give you the idea. It's an absolute belter, I can tell you. Look!"

He brought his hands round and each held a mug. They had photographs printed on them. Gallagher took the first one and angled it so that he could properly see the photo.

It was of Luka, and Gallagher was fairly sure it was the one from his staff ID card. The photo had been wildly distorted in order to fit the available space on the mug.

"Oh right. I see what you've done there," he said to Cameron. Which was take a photo the size and shape of a portrait and stretch it sideways to wrap it around a mug. Luka looked like some sort of chubby-faced Cheshire cat, with his wide, whiskery cheeks and the oddly-extended smile. He couldn't suppress a smile at the image.

"You approve! I'm so glad," said Cameron. "Here's another." He handed over another mug, which turned out to be Charlotte Mitchell.

Gallagher shook his head at the unflattering hamster cheeks she'd been given. "Well they're going to create a talking point, that's for sure," he said, trying to keep his face straight. "You've got a whole box of these? What a treat!"

Cameron slapped Gallagher on the back. "Good man. I'm

pretty excited for the party to be honest." The phone in Cameron's pocket started to ring, playing Dire Straits' *Money for Nothing*. He whipped it out as though Gallagher was suddenly not there anymore.

"Hit me," he said as a greeting, and almost immediately frowned. "Ah, yes. What? Missing employee?" He pulled a confused face at Gallagher. "I don't know anything about that. I'm sure she's not done anything. Listen, Maremba—"

He was cut off by whatever it was this Maremba was insisting on telling him.

"I can assure you we're not burying anyone in the paddock. I've no idea what you saw. And what kinds of lenses are you using to take photos at that distance?"

He walked to the window and looked out. "Can you see me now? Uh-huh." He gave the finger to the Bloomers building some distance away. "And can you see that? Wow. Impressive."

He turned around and sniffed, a decision made. "Fine. Come over. Mi garden centre es su garden centre, Maremba. You know that. Not literally, obviously."

He hung up, then seemed to remember Gallagher was there. "Must get going, young man. I have some visitors popping over shortly. Head honchos from Bloomers. We're having a pow-wow in the café."

"I thought we were mortal enemies with them," said Gallagher. "How come they're making a social call?"

"Mortal enemies is a good way to describe our relationship with Bloomers," said Cameron, nodding in agreement, "Have you ever met Marcus and Maremba? No? He thinks he's God's gift, even though his hair is clearly a wig. Bald as a coot underneath, he is. Tiresome fellow, quite honestly. She, on the other hand – she's like a luscious little fondant fancy, dainty and sweet. I can picture myself licking her all over before I take a bite, know what I mean?"

Gallagher blew out his cheeks, unsure of what to say. "Right. Fondant fancy, eh?"

"Apparently they have something urgent they want to discuss with me." Cameron licked his lips and Gallagher wondered if he was being distracted by his cake-based fantasies.

It was a relief when Gallagher was able to slip away and return to the shop. He quickly went in search of Anika. She was outside, not far from the Festive Farm marquee.

"They know!" he said.

"Know what?" she said.

"About the body. They said there's a missing employee and they think someone is trying to bury a body."

She paled and looked fearful; although not nearly fearful enough, Gallagher reckoned.

"Who?" she said. "Who said this?"

"The people over at Bloomers. Mungo and Maracas."

"Marcus and Maremba?"

"That's them."

"How could they possibly know what we're up to?"

"By spying on us through a photo zoom camera lens or something."

Anika frowned in deep thought. "I overheard a strange conversation earlier," said Anika. "Marcus and Maremba were thinking of calling the police, but they wanted to talk to Cameron first."

"Oh, fuck."

"Do you think they might have got wind of what's going on?"

Gallagher shook his head. "Who would have told them? There's not that many of us who know about it."

"They are grandparents to Karen's kids."

"Karen on the tills? Health and Safety Karen?"

"But she wouldn't tell them anything. She hates them."

"Maybe they're blackmailing her."

Anika considered this and dismissed it. "She's many things, but she's not a snitch. And she doesn't know about the body."

"Well, whatever, Cameron's off to meet this Mackie and Miranda in the café now."

"Here? Now?"

"Sounds as if he's got a bit of a thing for the woman."

"Shit. I've got to get into that meeting!"

She ran off.

49

CHARLOTTE

As Charlotte wove between people on the rink, trying to blend into the crowd, she saw Comfort thread her arm through Jack's.

"*This is a most unusual way to meet,*" came Comfort's voice. Her accent was one stretched syllable away from a drawl, but it had a controlled formality to it as well.

"*It's so rare to do any business deals face to face,*" said Jack.

Charlotte saw Comfort shrug. "*You are in Stockholm. I am in Stockholm. You have a plane to catch later, right? The Snooze Express, no?*"

"*I do,*" said Jack, just rolling with it.

While the two of them talked, Charlotte tried to see if she could spot the real Alejandro anywhere.

To the north side of the plaza there was an increasing number of Santas around a brightly painted red bus. That would be one of the Santa events in the city Jack had mentioned. It was possible that Iralki Egadze would be part of it, and therefore Alejandro might be close by. The man did appear to be a 24/7 elf.

The plan was to get the files off Alejandro, send at least one over to Jack via the phone and SD card reader in Charlotte's pocket, enabling him to get the payment, in whatever form it took, off her. Her mind kept viewing that as a big wad of cash, but she was pretty sure the adult entertainment industry would have embraced cashless transactions, even those bits featuring a Santa Claus defiling fake reindeer or debasing himself with a roast turkey.

"No, it can be lonely, but yes, I do have a special someone," Jack was saying to Comfort.

"Tell me more," said Comfort.

"Oh, what can I tell you? She – yes, it is a she – is a wonderful woman. We've known each other for years and years, but we've been taking things slowly."

"Oh?"

"She's not sure what she wants in life. I'm not sure she realises that me and her are meant for each other."

Comfort laughed. *"I don't think people are meant for each other, Alejandro. We are all just ships in the night, passing each other, looking for a little human warmth in the cold. You want my advice?"*

"Obviously," said Jack.

"Seize the moment. Carpe the fucking diem out that woman. Get some human warmth while you can. It's never gonna last."

Charlotte found it hard to not keep her eyes and overall attention on Jack and Comfort but, as she made another circuit, she saw a tall floppy hat at the side of the rink.

Alejandro. And he was in his full elf gear – including the hugely rouged cheeks.

"Fuck me," she whispered. The man really was a 24/7 elf. "Smug Git, this is Ice Demon. I've seen Jingle Bells and I'm going in. Ask her about the payment method."

Charlotte tugged her scarf up high, onto the bridge of her nose, and skated over to Alejandro. He was on the outside of the rink and wasn't wearing skates. Did that make a difference? She didn't know.

"Keep Fabric Conditioner to the middle of rink," she said, waving as she approached.

"Alejandro!" she called, slowing as she neared the side. She didn't care if her American accent sounded like a yee-haw cowboy, it was an accent far from her own and that's what mattered.

Alejandro gave her a half-smile and held out a gloved hand.

"Comfort, it is very nice to meet you," he said. Was that a note of nervousness in his voice? Was he nervous about this big deal moment? That could be a good thing, right?

"Mr Aramburuzabala," she said, shaking his hand. "I love your outfit."

"I know!" he said, tugging at his elf tunic gleefully. "It is work, but I love it."

"It is a busy time for you, I guess. But you're in Stockholm, I'm in Stockholm. Let's do some business."

He nodded. "You liked the showreel, I sent you?" he said. "A taster."

She nodded. "I did but I would like to have another look. See the actual files."

"And I would like to see the actual money," he said with a nervous grin.

Shit. Was he expecting actual cash? Like euros or krona or US dollars?

Through her earpiece she could hear Comfort say, like the most fortuitously timed prompter ever, *"I will arrange a bank transfer to your account. I'd do PayPal but they tend to take notice of payments of twenty grand."*

Charlotte repeated it back to Alejandro, word for word, even adding the bit about PayPal.

"Twenty grand," said Alejandro and actually licked his lips. The elf pornographer was hungry for this deal, so hungry it was embarrassingly palpable.

"Give me your bank details and let me look at the videos," said Charlotte.

He brought out his phone, used his teeth to tear off his glove so he could use it, and found his bank details. She read them out for Jack's benefit, but also tapped them into the messenger app on her phone to DM him, so he could relay them to Comfort. Fuck! This was going well.

He then opened up the video app on his phone to show her the videos just like he had done at the expo in Hull.

"No," she said. "Let *me* look at them." She held up the card reader. "I need to check, er, file quality."

Alejandro hesitated, but not for long. Keenness was overcoming caution. He fiddled with the side of his phone to eject the SD card. It was there, right in front of her, less than an arm's length away. It was tempting to just reach out and snatch the phone from him. Take the files, skate away and the mission was done. But she held back. What if she went for the snatch and missed? No, she had to wait until he gave it to her. They could go through the pretence of finishing the deal, everyone walk away happy. She just had to be patient.

He winkled out the tricky SD card from his phone. It was such a tiny thing. The cause of such woe.

She took off her own glove so she could take it and insert the fiddly card into her card reader.

"Lovely nails," he said as he held it out to her.

"Thank you," she said.

"Plum pudding," he said and drew his hand back.

For a moment, she didn't understand.

He stared her in the eyes. "Charlotte?"

She was going to deny it, but that was stupid. He'd seen her for who she was. What kind of man looked at your nails *and* remembered what colour you'd painted them?

"*Mi tesoro*," he gasped. There was fear and wonder, and a weird dream-like joy on his face, like this was the maddest and most astounding thing that could happen to him.

She yanked down her scarf. "I need that video!"

Alejandro stepped back. "I knew this was too good to be true."

"You can still make the deal. You can still have your twenty grand."

"*Is everything okay?*" said Jack through her earpiece.

"*Why wouldn't everything be okay?*" said Comfort, not understanding who he was talking to.

"We have Comfort Dewvalley," said Charlotte. "She's ready to pay you. She has your bank details. We just need to delete those videos."

Alejandro, unconvinced, backed away further. Charlotte,

imbued with an energetic zeal, grabbed the top of the barrier fence and vaulted over it. She had never vaulted over a fence in her life but – fuck! – she did it now. She landed on the snowy paving slabs with a hard clatter of her skates.

"You gonna run after me with those on?" said Alejandro.

She reached down and flipped the catches on her boots. "Quick release clips, motherfucker!" she snarked and stepped out in thick socks onto the snow.

Alejandro turned to run. Charlotte hefted one of the boots and flung it at him like an over-arm boomerang. It collided with the small of his back and sent him stumbling. She ran forward, but Alejandro was still on his feet and running away.

"Elf-fucker on the move!" she shouted. "I need your help, Jack!"

50

ANIKA

Anika headed over to the café and soon spotted Cameron, who looked as if he'd just arrived with his two guests. They were a tall and slender couple in late middle age. Marcus possessed a striking beak-like nose and a thick head of unnaturally dark hair – either a freak of genetics or a very expensive wig. He had the bearing of a Roman emperor in a smart casual suit. The woman by him had a cat-like beauty to her face, framed by perfectly curled black ringlets. Cameron, in his little sailboat captain's suit, looking like a dirty little oik next to these regal creatures.

Anika walked over to their table and smiled up at Cameron. "I've come to take minutes for you." She held up a pad and pencil.

"Have you?" Cameron asked, surprised.

"It's part of the mentoring scheme we talked about," said Anika.

"Did we?" Cameron started to question her on the

fictitious scheme, but she saw him glance over at Maremba and instead he smiled. "Yes of course we did. It's so important to nurture young talent. Take a seat, Anita."

She sat down, and put the date at the top of the page. "Who shall I say is present? Cameron Clasp and...?"

"Marcus and Maremba Stone of Bloomers," said the tall man, his voice deep and resonant.

Anika nodded her thanks.

"Welcome to Hedgelord," said Cameron. "A colleague will shortly be bringing us some refreshments."

Maremba raised her hand. "I have some very specific dietary requirements, based on both health and ethical concerns."

"We can deal with questions when it arrives," said Cameron with a dismissive wave of his hand.

"These are not questions, they are requirements," said Maremba. She was a tiny, precise woman who conducted herself as if she expected to be both admired and listened to. "I don't expect to see any animal products on this table."

"I'll go," said Anika, getting up from the table. "If you'd all just hold on for one moment

She found Sophie, who had returned to her canteen duties, although she was still wearing her funereal black. "Listen," said Anika, "Cameron has some VIPs with him and he's arranged snacks. Please make sure there are no animal products in them, will you?"

"No meat, of course lovely," said Sophie.

"Not just meat," said Anika. "That includes other animal products like cheese or honey."

Sophie laughed as if Anika was joking, then saw she wasn't. "What, really?"

Anika nodded. "How about I take a tea tray over with me and you can double check the rest?" She returned to the table with a selection of teas and milk alternatives, then picked up her pen and smiled brightly at everyone.

"Let's begin, shall we?" said Marcus. "It's a serious situation so I think we need to dive straight in."

"Whilst being mindful and empathetic," added Maremba. "So perhaps we could all take a moment to clear our minds and set our intentions."

"What are our intentions, exactly?" asked Cameron.

Marcus gave him a stony look. "To listen with compassion and to solve problems in a collaborative manner."

"Oh, yes. Yes, of course. Compassion. I'm all about bloody compassion."

Anika was no expert at reading body language, but she'd never seen someone's words so obviously at conflict with their thoughts. Marcus did not look ready to collaborate: he looked as if he'd rather slam Cameron's face with the jug of oat milk sitting between them.

Maremba held up a hand. "Nicely put, my lover, thank you. Now the issue at hand is the kidnapping of a key Bloomers employee."

"Bloomers employee?" said Anika, surprised. She remembered herself and pretended to take some notes. "Sorry. Do go on."

Maremba cleared her throat. "We believe that Jack Hartigan is being held captive by Charlotte Mitchell and we wanted to meet with you before we took it to the authorities."

There was a long pause. Anika held her breath. This was very bad and extremely unexpected, but at least it wasn't about the dead Santa in the marquee. As she turned the idea over in her mind, she didn't find it all that difficult to imagine Charlotte kidnapping someone. She glanced at Cameron, wondering what he made of the accusation.

Cameron burst out laughing. "Charlotte? Our Charlotte, kidnapping someone? Oh that's hilarious!"

He chuckled for a long moment, failing to notice the hostility that was radiating from Maremba and Marcus.

"You think this is funny?" Maremba asked. Her voice was calm but icy.

"Funny? God yes – she's a slip of a thing! How on earth do you think she overcame your man? We are talking about that events manager of yours, yes? Granted, he's not very tall, but I assume he's a man in possession of a pair of fists? He's not going to let a woman pop a sack over his head and push him into the back of a van, is he?"

"There is more than one way of incapacitating someone," said Maremba, placing a calming hand over her husband's. "And women are perhaps more capable than you clearly like to give them credit for. Can I ask what Charlotte has said to you about her absence?"

"Personal improvement," said Cameron with a triumphant grin. "My people are all proper go-getters, like to work on their skills."

"Cameron, I can tell you are an experienced people manager," said Maremba. "But doesn't it strike you as peculiar that a senior colleague would take unplanned absence on one of the busiest days in the annual calendar?"

"It speaks only of the absolute trust she has in her colleagues to pick up any slack," said Cameron.

Anika glanced out of the window of the café over Cameron's shoulder. She could see Daffyd and Tom engaged in some sort of tug of war with a large banner for the following day's events. Daffyd was trying to pull it towards the front of the store, while Tom was heading towards the grotto. Luckily it was a thick vinyl banner; if it had been made from paper it would have been torn in half by now.

"I'm sure your team is extremely flexible and competent," said Maremba, whose attention had also been caught by the events outside. "But perhaps we should show you the video evidence we've been sent."

"Video evidence?" Cameron asked. "Like a ransom demand?"

Maremba inclined her head. "It's not yet clear what Charlotte is asking for. Marcus, would you like to pull up the video?"

Marcus placed his phone on the table, found the video and pressed play. It showed Charlotte, with her hair back off her face, which wasn't her usual look. She also looked as if she might be slightly drunk as she spoke directly to the camera.

"Jack, you twat! Don't you dare be happy, I forbid it. I am gonna make you wish you'd never been born. Sparkles? There will be no sparkles on my watch!"

"Is that it?" asked Cameron. "What does it even mean?"

"I think the meaning is clear," said Maremba. "It's a threat from Charlotte to Jack. You can hear that she addresses him directly."

"Yes, but what's that business about sparkles?" asked Cameron. "Makes no sense."

Marcus held up a hand and spoke with the air of someone delivering a lecture. "As you may or may not know, I have spent many years studying various fields relating to human behaviour. I would suggest that the word 'sparkles' is being used to codify the world of Christmas events management, which is where Charlotte and Jack have previously come into conflict. I have it on good authority both have been in an escalating cycle of unhealthy competition for some time now. I imagine you are a part of that, Cameron. Charlotte is presumably acting with your blessing?"

Cameron held out his hands. "When is competition *ever* unhealthy, eh? Look at us now, sitting round a table and talking like adults! And yet afterwards we'll go straight back to the job and try to shaft each other in every way that's ruddy well possible. Even if we had our own codewords—" he paused to wink at Maremba "—we'd still all be trying to win this game we're all playing. I'm not at all sure I see kidnapping potential in what you've just shown me."

"There's another video," said Maremba. "Have you got that one, darling?"

Marcus found another video and held up his phone again. This one showed Charlotte holding up a glove puppet. Anika had only met Jack Hartigan a couple of times, but the puppet did look like him. Charlotte was crouched low, talking to the puppet, her delivery an angry snarl.

"Kiss my fucking hairy ass, you cunt. It was all your twatting idea anyway, so you can either pay up or just fucking zzcccchh." The threat was unmistakeable, as Charlotte mimed cutting her own throat as she stared at the puppet, naked malevolence on her face. Anika swallowed uncomfortably.

Cameron's face had fallen. Gone was the previous assured swagger, and in its place was thoughtful concern. "Well that one packs a punch, doesn't it?"

Maremba nodded. "I'm glad you understand the gravity of the situation."

"Has Jack been in touch with you?" asked Cameron. "What was the last thing you heard from him?"

"The very last message he sent said he was tied up and unable to get away," said Maremba. "I imagine perhaps he used dictation to send one last desperate message before his phone was taken from him." Her lip trembled slightly, before her poker face reasserted itself.

"Good grief," said Cameron. "I should try to call Charlotte." He pulled out his phone.

Maremba put out a hand in gentle warning. "Can I ask that you don't, given the circumstances?"

Cameron made a small blustering noise. "I think I know how to talk to my own staff."

"Even when they might be in the grip of a psychotic episode?" asked Maremba. "It's a job best left to the professionals. It requires specialist knowledge and a very light touch. Besides, you still haven't answered the question of whether Charlotte is acting with your blessing in all of this."

"Are you seriously asking whether I've asked Charlotte to kidnap your Poundland Ryan Reynolds?"

Cameron's outrage was punctured somewhat by Anika's small bark of laughter at the imagery. She quickly turned it into a cough and bent over her notepad.

"You think that Jack looks like Ryan Reynolds?" Marcus said, incredulous.

"No! That's my point. He's too short for one thing and—"

"Jack is not a piece of meat, Cameron," Maremba seethed. "Tell me honestly, are you denying you have told Charlotte to do whatever it takes to grind Bloomers into the dirt?"

"Oh that? Well yes, I definitely said *that*. Not kidnapping though. I mean, I didn't specifically say 'no kidnapping', but I think we had an understanding."

Maremba sat back, arms folded and said nothing.

"What?" Cameron demanded. "I suppose you're going to show me Bloomers' beautifully written and framed 'no kidnapping' policy are you?"

Maremba turned to Anika. "Let the record show that Mr Clasp is now getting agitated and defensive."

"Um, you do know I'm just writing minutes, don't you?" said Anika.

"How do you know about me saying that to Charlotte, anyway?" asked Cameron. "It was a remark I made in the privacy of my own office."

Maremba smiled at Cameron. "I will obviously not be sharing how I came by that information. Now, Marcus darling, I think it's time we went back to run our business."

Marcus nodded and stood.

"What do you plan to do about this alleged kidnapping?" asked Cameron.

"We will take that question away for further discussion," said Maremba. "I trust you will let us know if you hear from Charlotte?"

Cameron shrugged. "Yes, of course. I fully expect her to be here for tomorrow night's staff Christmas party. It's an event nobody will want to miss."

"I'm sure you're right," said Maremba with a broad smile as she and Marcus stood up to leave.

51

CHARLOTTE

Charlotte ran on nothing but socks across the snow-covered Kungsträdgården.

"Excuse me, Comfort," Jack was saying in her earpiece. *"My assistant is having technical difficulties."*

Alejandro was a wiry bastard and had a fair turn of speed. He ran north, past the Santas and their red bus, who were also heading in the same direction. The streets were well-lit but night covered all and made shadows everywhere. It wouldn't be hard to lose him, even if he was dressed as a bright and cheery elf.

People shouted at Charlotte as she ran past in her socks. Alejandro cast a fearful glance back and, in doing so, nearly ran straight into a tram that was moving along the road. He yelped, ducked sideway and ran on.

He might be wiry and he might be fast, but he was no long-distance runner. He was flagging as turned into the next street over. Charlotte wasn't much fitter and her socks had poor grip, but she had fury and desperation on her side. She ran on, turned the corner, and skidded to a halt.

"Father fucking Christmas!" she yelled.

This shopping street, lit brightly by hundreds of dangling yellow lights, was filled side to side with Santas and elves. A great cavalcade of Santas: marching and partying through the street.

"What's going on?" said Jack in her ear.

"I'm on..." She cast about for a street sign and couldn't find one. "I don't fucking know where I am. It's the shitting *tomteparaden* or whatever." She looked about madly, trying to spot Alejandro among the crowd. "It's like trying to find Wally at a Where's Wally convention!"

But even as she said it, she saw a perky tall hat weaving through the crowd.

"Spotted him!" she said. "Going into the parade." She barged forward through the gangs of festive figures. "Move it, Santa!"

She elbowed aside a jolly Saint Nick, squeezed between two Kris Kringles, and had to shake off a Père Noël who thought she wanted to dance. At the far end of the dense gang of Santas she saw Alejandro climb onto the rear of a little Christmassy fire truck with a Santa and gaggle of other elves.

Alejandro saw her approaching and spoke urgently to the Santa. It was Irakli Egadze, world-ranking Santa. The man's silver-blond beard and his powerful but cuddly physique was unmistakeable. Irakli stared at Charlotte and slapped the side of the fire engine, shouting something Charlotte didn't understand.

Charlotte wailed as the fire truck began to pull away, moving at little more than a jog towards the edge of the crowd. Even at that speed, it would soon be beyond her. She thrust herself forward with the last of her energy and leapt up on the rear of the truck, almost entirely into the arms of Irakli.

"Get off, you mad bitch!" Alejandro shrieked.

"I just need the video!" she shouted.

Irakli, huge and implacable, started to peel her away from himself, to push her off the back of the truck. "Lady, there is no room," he said.

"Just go!" squealed Alejandro and punched her. He actually punched her: a sharp little jab below her eye.

In shock, she stumbled back and stepped onto nothing. She tumbled from the fire truck, managing to grab hold of Irakli Igadze's pocket as she fell. It ripped away and she tumbled and rolled onto the hard cold road, little white packets landing around her.

She was too surprised and hurt to breathe at first, and when she could it came in tiny, painful gasps. She pushed herself to her hands and knees. A crowd of concerned people was gathering round her.

Her eyes focused on the little packets that had fallen from Irakli's pocket. They were like little tea bags. No – they were like the little tobacco pouch she had seen Alejandro sucking on at the expo. It was another strange additional detail to an already strange day.

She picked several up, like she couldn't believe they were there.

Jack pushed through the crowd and crouched beside her, holding her. He was saying her name over and over again.

The crowd were vocal in their opinions of what had happened. Jack tried to reassure the people around them. "It's fine. It's fine. I don't think she's hurt."

But it wasn't fine. Alejandro still had the bastard video and had escaped again.

52

ANIKA

Anika drew a line under the minutes she had scribbled during the meeting. Nobody wanted or needed her notes, but she felt compelled to make it tidy. And she needed to have a big think about what all of it meant. Anika felt like a woman with too many plates spinning over her head.

She had a dead Santa to deal with. There was a children's party, a doggy Santa event (currently with no Santa) and a Christmas carriage ride (with no horses). On top of that, it appeared that Charlotte had kidnapped Jack Hartigan somewhere in Europe or, if not exactly that, something equally odd.

Sophie and Karen clattered into view and sat down heavily at the table. Anika turned over the page so that the notes were hidden from casual view.

"They left before we could bring out the plant-based chicken drumsticks!" said Sophie. "I had to defrost them."

Anika thought that was probably a good thing. "They finished their meeting. They didn't look hungry, so I think we're fine."

"Listen to Sophie's news!" said Karen. "She's only gone and got herself a date!"

"Wow Sophie, that's great work," said Anika.

"I'm not sure about that. I don't think I really did anything," said Sophie. "I just clicked swipe on the app, and bing, it happened. I'm not sure I'm ready for this."

"It's great news though. Keep up the momentum," said Karen. "Now, there's no time to lose, you've got tons to do."

"Have I?"

"Tell her, Anika!"

"Huh?"

"There's a whole list of things, I reckon. I mean, I'm way out of touch with how these things are now. You're young Anika, what's the current vogue for lady gardens?"

Anika nearly swallowed her pen in surprise.

"Karen!" said Sophie. "You are too much." But she still turned her gaze onto Anika.

Both of them stared at her, as if she was some sort of expert on the etiquette of how pubic hair should be presented. "Are you both seriously expecting me to know what's fashionable with ... fanny styles?"

"Yes!" they said together.

"But how would that even work? It's not like all the girls at uni get together and have vajazzling sessions where we sip wine and swap tips!" She frowned at how that sounded once it had escaped her lips.

"Well, no. It usually comes from fashion magazines, doesn't it?" said Karen. "Stuff like that."

"Fashion magazines? Do people still read those things?" asked Anika. "No. I can safely say that none of my friends read them. It would be more likely to come from a TikTok video. And before you ask, I have never consulted TikTok to see whether I need to style my fucking minge!"

"Language, Anika!" said Sophie. "You're starting sound like Gallagher."

"Well, listen to yourselves! Why don't you go and ask Gallagher what he likes to see in a lady's pants?" She saw their eyes meet. "No! No! Definitely don't do that." She sighed. "Sophie, I think you should let your lady garden be in whatever state you think best. Surely we can do better with dating tips than body shaming?"

"Fine. You start," said Karen. She looked a little put out.

"What do you know about this man?" Anika asked Sophie.

"He is tall. Very nice eyes in his profile picture," she said.

"Yes – but what do you know about *him*? He must have a profile. What does it say his interests are?"

"He's in business. Corporate re-engineering. He has interests that include skiing and various target sports. It sounds as if he's quite a high-flyer," said Sophie, smiling like a giddy schoolgirl.

"So it sounds like he has a fairly serious personality?" asked Anika. "You could reflect a version of yourself to match that. Maybe choose an outfit that brings out your more thoughtful, serious side?"

"Oh gosh that's clever," said Sophie, chewing her lip.

Karen pulled a face. Anika guessed she hadn't moved on past the idea of vajazzling.

"Do you have any particular concerns, Sophie?" asked Anika. "Maybe that's where we should focus our efforts."

Sophie looked thoughtful. "It's all a question of getting used to each other, isn't it? In the beginning there's that wariness with each other, then finally everyone..." She shook herself out and made a wobbly noise.

"What's that?" said Anika.

"I don't know," said Sophie. "Eventually everyone decompresses a little bit. After that we get on with the business of training out any bad habits so that everyone can get along."

"Training, Soph?" said Karen, placing a hand over hers. "Are you talking about dogs again? We were talking about men, weren't we?"

Sophie's eyes were wide. "Are they really that different? I've never especially thought so."

Anika shrugged. It was a good point.

"Clothes then," said Sophie. "I mean, serious clothes. I guess that means no frills or dots or twiddly bits."

"Right," said Anika. It wasn't the definition she'd have started with, but Sophie was working up to something.

"It's just that all my clothes have frills or dots or twiddly bits. I don't think I have anything serious."

"You need to be yourself Sophie, just maybe err on the side of slightly more serious," said Anika.

"I've got an idea," said Karen. "Come round mine this evening. Both of you."

"Really?" said Anika, who had a whole evening planned of fretting about the mountain of problems she was facing.

"Absolutely. Sophie, bring some of your clothes and I'll grab some stuff from my wardrobe. We're about the same size. We can try a few things, look at make-up options while we're at it. How would that be?"

"Sounds nice," said Sophie. "You'll come too, Anika?"

"Do you want me to? I mean..." She didn't want to point that there were at least two decades between her and Karen, and maybe another two between Karen and Sophie, and the idea of watching two old women try out clothes was far from enticing.

But the only other option was sitting at home worrying, and possibly watching *Die Hard 3* with her parents. And *Die Hard 3* wasn't even a Christmas film.

"Sure, I'll come," she sighed.

53

CHARLOTTE

After managing to get Charlotte's shoes back, which included paying for damage to a lobbed skating boot, Charlotte and Jack limped together back to their Stockholm hotel.

"So, we didn't manage to Mission Impossible the shit out of this thing like you promised," she grunted.

"I think I used the word 'shizzle'," said Jack. "But we gave it a bloody good try."

Her feet hurt. Her hips hurt. Her cheekbone where Alejandro had punched her definitely hurt. She leaned against Jack. He was a comforting rock at the moment.

She still had hold of the packets of chewing tobacco that had fallen from Irakli's pocket. She didn't know why she was still holding onto them really.

Her phone buzzed. It was a message, from Alejandro. The bastard had taken a selfie of himself alongside a small plane, clearly at an airport. He was giving a big thumbs up to the camera and the cheesiest and most evil grin.

"*Snooze, you lose, motherfucker,*" she read.

Jack grunted and led her to the lift back up to their room.

"You seem unworried," she said.

"He's getting on a plane. Comfort said he was getting on a plane."

"The Snooze Express did she say?"

"And we know where he's going next," said Jack.

"We do?"

"Irakli Egadze has a week-long engagement in Lapland, doesn't he?"

Charlotte let out a ragged, disbelieving laugh. "The chase continues? To fucking Finland?"

"Maybe," he said. "We stopped that meeting with Comfort."

"Who you were getting rather pally with."

"I was playing a role."

"Telling her all about your lovely Kathryn."

He held her so he could look her in the face. "I wasn't talking about... I was telling her a story. I..."

She found herself staring at his lips: they were suddenly the most fascinating sight. When they parted slightly she couldn't bear it anymore. She pulled him in and pressed her own lips to his. She felt the moment telescoping outside regular time and space, ripe with possibility – which was exhilarating, and more than a little scary.

A mild sound of muffled surprise gave way to a gasp of pleasure as his lips moved against hers. For a long moment they were locked in an embrace. No thought existed, only the pleasure unlocked by skin on skin contact, and a roaring insistence that rose up.

"Charlotte."

"I want you naked," she said.

He kissed her again.

She gasped as they parted. Both of them were flushed and panting, leaning in, ready to go again.

"Is that you want-me-naked?" he said. "Or you want me, comma, naked?"

"What?"

"I'm just asking."

"Stop it," she panted, "or I'll remember reasons not to want you."

"I'm surprised you do want me."

She didn't know what to tell him. That, away from the crazy pressures of running the Christmas sections of their respective garden centres, Charlotte found Jack's company more than tolerable, and that right now, the idea of hiding away from the rest of world in the dark cosiness of a Scandinavian Christmas city was the best thing she could imagine.

Charlotte kicked the door closed behind her and stood with her back to it.

"Oh my phone's—" Jack started.

"No." Charlotte wrenched the phone from his hand and tossed it onto the desk. "Siri, Jack is going to be deep in work mode. Properly deep."

There was some kind of tinny response from the phone, but both Charlotte and Jack ignored it, their eyes fixed on each other.

Jack grinned and kicked off his shoes and wriggled out of his clothes. She ran a hand down his bare chest.

He reached across and started to help Charlotte with her own clothes.

"How did we even get here?" he said in disbelief.

"I can assure you, I wasn't expecting it to happen like this. This isn't how I planned for this to go but I've got you now and I guess there's no going back."

54

ANIKA

By the close of day, Anika was back in the Hedgelord office, trying to solve some of the problems that remained for the events team. A large and very obvious gap was – where on earth they were going to find another Santa? She pulled out Seamus's card and gave him a call from the desk phone.

"Seamus, it's the events team at Hedgelord," she said, attempting a voice something like Charlotte's.

"Ay up it's that naughty elf, isn't it?" said Seamus. *"What can I do you for?"*

Anika rolled her eyes. "Would you be available to work some shifts for Hedgelord? We can make it worth your while."

"You can access my availability calendar and booking portal on my website. Details should be on that card I gave you."

Anika quickly looked up the website and consulted the

calendar. "Yeah, I'm going to need more shifts than this. What can we do about those where it says you're booked?"

"Well it's blooming obvious isn't it? I'm booked."

"How can we un-book what you're doing and make you available? I'm especially interested in tomorrow afternoon. What can we do about that?"

"Yeah, no can do I'm afraid. I might manage an hour, but then I'm offski. Important prior engagement."

"An hour? Yes! Please come. An hour is much better than nothing."

Anika wondered how she was going to make the rest of the event work, but that was a smaller problem than she'd started with, so she fist-pumped the air as she rang off. It felt like progress. All she had to do now was solve all the remaining problems with tomorrow's events, dispose of the Santa corpse, and try not to worry about one of Hedgelord's management team suffering some kind of catastrophic breakdown and kidnapping her rival from Bloomers.

She wondered what Cameron was doing about that particular problem. She strongly suspected he was simply ignoring it and hoping it would go away.

She was instantly proven wrong, as Cameron came bursting into the office. "Anita!"

Outside the office, Hedgelord was closed for the evening. It had been a long and weird day, and she apparently still had dress-up (and perhaps some light vajazzling) with two older women to look forward to that evening.

"There's been a development," he said. He grabbed an office chair and scooted over to her on it. "I've got Maremba and Marcus on the line. They've patched me into what they think might be a ransom call from Jack's phone."

"Oh, okay," said Anika.

"We think he's been kidnapped by Charlotte."

"Er, what?" she said.

"I know it's incredible. He's making these awful noises and she's saying something about having him completely at her mercy."

"I'll er, continue to make notes then shall I?" said Anika, pulling out her phone. She hit record, which seemed like the fastest way to do it.

Cameron put his phone on the desk and turned on the loudspeaker.

On the line, Jack gave a gasp. *"Got me – hnh! – right where you want me, haven't you? God! You're enjoying this, aren't you?"*

"Make as much noise as you like," Charlotte snapped back. *"No one's coming!"*

"That poor man!" said Cameron. "What can she be doing?"

"Hmm," said Anika.

LAID BACK on the screwed up sheets of their hotel bed, Jack grinned up at Charlotte.

"I can tell you've thought about this way too much. You've been wanting to do this for weeks, haven't you?" he said.

She sat astride him, leaning into his hands as they cupped her breasts.

"Don't flatter yourself," she grunted. He writhed beneath her. "And don't struggle. We're doing this my way or not at all."

She leaned further down and kissed him.

"I hate you, Jack Hartigan. I've hated you for years."

"Yeah," he said and kissed her back. "I kind of got that."

She tweaked his nipple at his sarcastic tone. He gave a yelp of pain and bucked beneath her.

"WHAT'S SHE DOING TO HIM?" Cameron whispered.

Anika was listening along with Cameron. They were listening to the same thing and yet she had the strangest and clearest notion that Charlotte wasn't torturing Jack, but Cameron kept getting messages from Marcus and Maremba and he was so busy answering them that he was paying less attention to the sounds.

"*And what are you going to tell people when we get out of here?*" said Jack.

"*You're not telling anyone anything,*" said Charlotte firmly. "*And, right now, you're not going anywhere. Not till I've got what I need.*"

Jack moaned.

"The poor man," said Cameron.

"Yeah, I'm not sure that's what's going on here," said Anika.

"Marcus and Maremba have called the police."

"Really?"

"It's a work phone and they've logged into a Find My Phone thingy. Can you believe she's doing all this in an actual hotel? In Stockholm!"

"Yeah, about that," said Anika. "Is it possible that this is something ... um ... different?"

"I mean, I never thought Charlotte was the torturing type..."

"Yes. No. Quite. Like, what else does it sound a little bit like to you?"

Cameron pulled a face. "I don't know. It's all very vocal, isn't it?"

"Exactly," she said, making slow encouraging motions with her hands. "And men and women can get very vocal when...?"

As Cameron listened to the speaker phone she could see the same idea forming in his mind. "No! Surely not?"

"Think so."

"But Charlotte hates that man. She said."

"Yeah," said Anika. "Hate and desire. They're kinda..." She twisted two fingers together.

It was at that moment that an enormous crashing sound was heard from the phone.

"Police broke down the door!" mouthed Cameron, pointing with glee.

The sounds of Charlotte and Jack shrieking in shock and surprise was followed by the sounds of confusion and eventually apology.

"My phone?" came Jack's voice. *"Oh fucking hell."*

The call was cut off and Anika and Cameron stared at the silent phone.

Cameron raised his eyes to a shelf overhead. "That looks like a half bottle of Talisker up there. Fetch it down here will you, Anita? I feel like I need a drink after that."

55

CHARLOTTE

Charlotte and Jack had been polite to the six policemen who had raided their room because it was generally a good idea to be polite to shouty Swedes waving guns around.

"Can I apologise again," said *Kriminalinspektör* Alicia Karlsson, although she sounded more amused than contrite.

"Oh, it's quite understandable," said Charlotte. Her mouth was on auto-pilot because she was still in shock. She had gone from being fully naked and riding Jack like a bucking bronco to standing in the corner and dressed in a sheet toga like a student at a fancy dress party. And she had absolutely no memory of the intervening moments between one and the other.

"Well, this is certainly uncharted territory for us," said Jack who, hastily wrapped in a bath robe, sounded like he was functioning on stunned auto-pilot too. "First time with a police raid mid-coitus. I have no idea of the protocol here."

"Again, apologies," said Karlsson. "We were acting on information from your concerned employers."

"Right," said Jack.

"They thought you had been kidnapped."

"Who would kidnap us?" said Charlotte.

"They thought one of you had kidnapped the other."

"Which?"

"You kidnapped me, surely," said Jack.

"Oh," she said. "Confident that someone would want to kidnap you, are you?"

"I'm just saying you're the one with the energy and the, er, moxie."

"Moxie, huh?" Charlotte shook her head. "I feel really lightheaded. I was just naked in front of seven people all at once, and now I feel a bit weird about being naked in front of lots of people."

"Yes," nodded Karlsson. "The British are like that, yes? The Swedish, less so."

Karlsson looked more than a little like a Swedish cliché. She had long blonde hair, tied back in a ponytail over the back of her stylish leather jacket. She moved over to the room desk and peered at the items on it. Being nosy was a detective's habit, Charlotte supposed.

"So, can I ask what you are doing here?" said Karlsson.

Charlotte's mind veered between refusing to tell her and making up some outlandish story, then realised there was no harm in telling the truth.

"A Christmas elf has made a pornographic movie of the Santa who works at my garden centre and is going to distribute it on the internet if we don't stop him."

"Mine too," said Jack. "My garden centre. My Santa. A different Santa. The same elf."

"It is a blackmail plot?" said Karlsson, unfazed by their story.

Jack sighed. "No. He just likes making and selling porn. The Santas consented. We just don't want our places of business appearing front and centre in widely distributed porno movies."

Karlsson pulled a face. "So no law has been broken?"

"No. Sadly not. We're now going to have to book ourselves onto a direct flight to Lapland if we're to catch up with him."

Karlsson shook her head. "There are no direct commercial flights from Stockholm to Rovaniemi. You will have to transfer at Helsinki."

Charlotte tutted. "We're going to run out of money at this rate."

"And you will have to leave these here," said Karlsson. She had picked up some of the white tobacco pouches Charlotte had brought back to the hotel with her.

"Why? What are those?" said Jack.

"They were in Iralki Egadze's pocket," said Charlotte. "It's these tobacco pouch things. Alejandro had some in Hull."

Karlsson fixed her with a glare. "Hull. This is an English city? Like London or Oxford?"

"Well, not like London or Oxford..." Jack admitted.

Karlsson tutted. "*Snus*. It's a tobacco product that is legal in Sweden, and in America where everything seems to be legal. But it's a criminal offence to export it to EU countries and the UK. Some people still smuggle it across the borders."

"Oh," said Charlotte. "Naughty Alejandro."

"Hang on," said Jack. "What's it called?"

"*Snus*," said Karlsson.

"*Snus*. Snooze. The Snooze Express."

Charlotte looked at him. "The Snooze Express? That's what Comfort said."

"The plane," said Jack.

"The plane to Finland."

Charlotte's mind was suddenly awhirl with ideas. "Irakli and Alejandro travelling from country to country—"

"—Private planes and helicopters most of the way—"

"Excuse me," said Karlsson, holding her hands up. "What are you talking about?"

Jack and Charlotte exchanged glances. She hoped the same ideas were forming in his mind as in hers.

"What if we told you that we know this porno elf and his Santa were smuggling *snus* – *snus*? – across borders right now?" she said. "That they're flying to Rovaniemi right now."

"This is a serious matter," said Karlsson. "This is the business of big crime gangs."

"That's what they're doing," said Jack.

Karlsson laughed bitterly. "I don't suppose you know what flight they're on."

"Sadly, not—" began Charlotte, then fell silent. She found her phone dropped among her discarded clothes on the floor. She flung aside her trousers and opened up her messenger app. She found the last message from Alejandro. "You fucking beauty," she said and laughed.

She showed the picture to Karlsson. Alejandro had taken his selfie alongside the small passenger plane and there, slightly blurred but quite legible, was a string of letters.

"The serial number or call-sign or whatever you call it," she said. "That identifies a plane, right? And they all have those..." She waved her hand, unable to remember the word.

"Transponder," said Jack. "You can find a plane by its transponder."

"*Jävlar!*" exclaimed Karlsson. "We can! We can do that." She held Charlotte's phone in her hand while she made a note of the plane's number.

"And you can arrest them?" said Charlotte.

"Of course," said Karlsson, beginning to make a phone call on her own phone.

"And you could seize Alejandro's phone and the SD card inside it?" Charlotte added hopefully.

Karlsson grinned. "If this is successful and we bust a *snus* smuggling gang, I will make sure the Finnish police destroy it utterly." She turned her attention to her phone. "*Hei*, can I speak to *Överkommissarie* Koskinen? This is *Kriminalinspektör* Alicia Karlsson in Stockholm." She put her hand over her phone to talk to Jack and Charlotte. "I will keep you informed," she said, backing out of the room. She waved a finger at the discarded clothes and rumpled bed. "And my apologies again."

With that, she was gone and the door closed.

In the silence, Jack and Charlotte looked at each other.

"Is that it?" he said. "Did we do it?"

She wasn't sure. She raised an eyebrow. "Are the Finnish police going to sort it for us?"

"And we're...?"

"We're done?"

She analysed it in her mind and couldn't come up with an answer that wasn't "Yes". She looked at him, loosely wrapped in his bathrobe.

"We're not *quite* done," she said.

He laughed. "I completely forgot where we'd got up to."

"Oh, no," she said in a small silly voice. "We'll have to start all over from the beginning again!"

She loosened the sheet where it was tied under her arm and let it drop to the floor.

"Ah," said Jack, untying his robe. "It's all coming back to me."

56

ANIKA

Anika headed round to Karen's after she'd had tea with her parents. The house was on a modern housing estate, with a wide drive on which was parked three cars when Anika arrived on foot.

"Come in, come in!" said Karen when she opened the door. "Sophie's inside. My parents-in-law are still here, mind. They brought the kids back from clarinet and dodgeball."

Anika was ushered into a large lounge with an L-shaped sectional settee across two sides. Maremba, Marcus and Sophie sat sipping tea. Two children sprawled on the floor amongst a mess of toys. As Karen walked across the floor she scooped up toys automatically.

"Maremba, Marcus, this is Anika. Anika, these are my parents-in-law: Maremba and Marcus."

"I believe we've met," said Maremba, staring curiously at Anika.

"Huh." Karen seemed to be briefly thrown off her stride

by the idea. "Drink, Anika?" She went to fetch a cup of tea when Anika nodded.

Anika sat on a large footstool and smiled around at everyone.

"Now, Hermione," said Maremba. "Before Marcus and I leave, I would like us to make an entry in your variety journal. Would you fetch it please? Ron, that goes for you too."

Anika thought it was strange for the children to call their grandparents by their first names. Karen hadn't painted a particularly kind picture of Marcus and Maremba, though.

The two children went to a bookcase and each fetched an A4 pad.

"Can you think of an example from today where you expressed your free will and it felt good?" Maremba asked Hermione.

"I chose not to look left and right before I crossed the road coming out of school," said Hermione. "As an experiment. It's possible I was seeking attention."

Sophie choked on her tea and watched, her eyes wide.

"And what did you conclude from your experiment?" asked Maremba.

"That I should be mindful of the safety dimension on the variety cuboid," said Hermione. "Because I made a cyclist come off their bike. I did enjoy the attention, though."

Anika couldn't remember how old Hermione was. Eight maybe? And what on earth was the variety cuboid?

"How about you, Ron?" Maremba asked.

Ron glanced sideways at Hermione, envy in his eyes. "I told mummy to go fuck herself."

Anika was fairly certain Ron had made that up on the spot to try and beat his sister.

Maremba exchanged an indulgent smile with Marcus. "And how did that make you feel, Ron?"

"Good?" Ron said.

"Why don't you both go and write that up in your journals? You've been very brave, both of you, exercising your right to free expression and uncovering some of the challenges we all face when we do that."

The children went over to a tiny, child-sized table next to Anika and knelt down with pens to update their books.

Karen returned with Anika's tea. "Here you are, love."

"We'll be leaving in a moment or two," said Marcus, smoothing his trousers over his knees. "Did you give any thought to the idea of involving the children in the winter solstice celebration?"

"Um yeah. If it involves getting naked then it's not happening," said Karen firmly.

"You'd be with them the whole time, if it's a safeguarding concern," said Marcus.

"Yes, you said. And it's still a firm pass from me. I'm not getting naked, the children are not getting naked. It's not happening. I'm sure your forest yoga people are all lovely, but we're not doing it."

"It's a shame for them to miss out on such a *freeing* experience," said Maremba. "But perhaps when they are older they will choose to involve themselves."

"Perhaps they will," said Karen. She wore a smile that looked as if it might collapse into a snarl at any moment.

Marcus and Maremba stood to leave, and the children

embraced them one by one, showing them their journal entries.

"Lovely to see you," said Maremba as they left. "Ron, Hermione: Marcus and I will collect you to see the Santa charity drive tomorrow."

"That sounds nice," said Anika.

Maremba gave Anika the briefest of glances before looking back at the children. "Remember to bring your notebooks. If we are to make an anthropological study of the people engaging in these crude rituals, we must make proper notes."

"We will, Maremba," said Hermione.

When the door closed behind them, Karen rolled her eyes and sank into the settee. "I'm fetching the wine as soon as I've necked this cup of tea. Kids! Off you go and get ready for bed. You can watch telly in your rooms for an hour – give me a bit of peace and quiet."

"But Maremba says that the golden hour is for quality family time," said Hermione.

"You're supposed to read us a story," said Ron. "Marcus brought us an anthology of folk tales from New Guinea."

"And tomorrow we can have a look at them, but tonight I'm busy. Now scoot!"

"Is it always like this?" asked Sophie after the children had left. "Your in-laws are a bit strange, aren't they?"

"A bit strange doesn't begin to cover it."

"I have to ask," said Sophie. "I'm not one to judge, but is Marcus's hair real?"

"It's very thick, isn't it?" said Anika.

"Is it a wig?"

Karen shook her head, smiling. "I don't know. You think I haven't wondered? If it's a toupee then it's stuck on with superglue, I swear. Now wine! And then we'll take a look at your outfit choices, Soph."

Sophie had a carrier bag filled with an unfeasible number of garments that featured frills, dots and bows.

"God help us Soph, it's like you've spent your whole life cosplaying Minnie Mouse," said Karen as she pawed through the choices. "Do you never go to the shops and think 'Oh, maybe today I'll get myself a plain blouse'?"

"No," said Sophie. "It's not really who I am. I'm not even sure I have a serious side to be honest."

"Course you do. You passed your food hygiene, didn't you?" said Karen. "Sophie the exam passer is serious. We just need to build on that."

Anika had been looking through Sophie's blouses, and she pulled one out. "You know these ones that tie at the neck? Surely there's different ways of doing that?"

"Is there?" Sophie asked.

"Ohh ... I see where you're going with this!" said Karen. "I get why they call you Smartypants. Soph, you normally make a big bow that sits under your chin, don't you? Well, I reckon Anika's suggesting we do it more like a man's tie, or something."

"But I don't want to look like a man," said Sophie.

"Go and put it on, let's have a play," said Karen.

They eventually compromised by tying a very loose bow that would hang down in loose folds.

"Perfect," said Karen.

Anika nodded.

Karen poured more wine. "Now that we've got that sorted, have we definitely taken vajazzling off the table?"

There was a chorus of protest from Sophie and Anika, until Karen held up her hands in defeat. "Fine."

Ron tottered into the room wearing pyjamas and looking sleepy. "Mummy, what's vajazzling?"

57

CHARLOTTE

The buzzing of Charlotte's phone woke her.

It was still dark beyond the windows of their hotel room. In the cosy cocoon of their bedsheets, Jack lay against her, spooning her from behind, an arm draped across her waist. By the soft sounds he was making, he was still asleep.

The phone kept buzzing.

Charlotte shuffled as gently as possible towards the nightstand on her side of the bed to reach the phone.

Jack mumbled something in his sleep and tried to pull her closer.

"It might be work," she said.

"Tell 'em to sod off," he murmured.

"I will."

She grabbed the phone. It was an unknown number, and not a UK one either. She answered.

"Hello?"

"Good morning, Miss Mitchell. It is Alicia Karlsson."

It took Charlotte half a second to place her. "Detective…"

"Yes. I hope I have not disturbed you."

"Um…"

*"I have just had word from my Finnish counterpart,
Överkommissarie Koskinen. I have sad news."*

Charlotte sat up at once, Jack made to pull her tighter.
She lifted his arm away. "What news?"

*"That cargo plane did indeed fly to Rovaniemi as you said, but
by the time local police got to the airport, the plane had been
unloaded and the passengers were gone."*

Charlotte felt a cold plummeting thing in her chest. The
passengers were gone, which also meant Alejandro and the
SD card with the reputation-destroying videos on it.

"No. You said you would find them."

*"I did. And we will. Gangs involved in snus smuggling are
involved in other forms of illegal cross border activity. If we know
these people are in Lapland now, then this might be a chance to
apprehend them, still with the goods on them. It will be tricky, but
I will be going out there this morning to assist. The Finnish
Customs and Border Guards will be helping."*

"Wait – you're going to Lapland this morning."

*"A government charter plane is waiting at Stockholm
Arlanda."*

Charlotte slapped Jack on the thighs to wake him up.
"You'd have space on that plane for two more people,
wouldn't you?"

"I would … but I cannot take you to Lapland, Miss Mitchell."

Her mind raced. "We have key information about
Alejandro, one of the men you're after. He worked for me for

several years. And ... and I know a great deal about Irakli Egadze." She didn't add that most of what she knew about Irakli was linked to his successes in the Clausing business.

Jack was sitting up beside her, his hair a mess, a tired frown of confusion on his face.

"*A plane is a plane,*" said Karlsson eventually. "*We have seats. If you can get to Arlanda Airport in ... fifty minutes, then you can come. You will brief us on the plane and that will be your final involvement in the matter until we have arrested the gang and retrieved your pornographic videos.*"

"We will be there," said Charlotte, ending the call and jumping out of bed to look for her scattered clothes.

"*Where* will we be?" said Jack.

"We've got ten minutes to get dressed and get out of here," she said. "We're on a plane to Lapland."

58

ANIKA

Anika woke up with a mild headache from all of the wine she'd drunk at Karen's. It seemed as though both Karen and Sophie had relished the opportunity to let their hair down and made the most of it.

Anika couldn't afford to indulge her hangover though, she had a corpse that needed to be disposed of. She had micro-managed all activities in the marquee to minimise the chances of anyone stumbling across Raymond in his temporary wheelbarrow resting place, but she knew she was pushing her luck. The drop in temperature was a good thing, because at least that meant he'd be preserved while he waited.

There was so much to do – and then there was the mandatory staff party at Hedgelord that evening. Nothing wrong with parties, but Anika did not currently feel in a party mood.

At work that morning she found Gallagher, who was also

in early, making tea and staring at the weird new hornet poster he'd put up.

"Listen, can you help me get Raymond out of here today?" she asked.

Gallagher gave a reckless shrug, as if he had nothing left to lose. "Sure."

"Let's get this done, then we can all look forward to the office party tonight."

"Yay," he said with zero enthusiasm.

"I sneaked a look at Raymond's personnel file to see if he had a partner as his next of kin. It only mentioned a brother, I reckon he lives alone. "

"*Lived* alone. So what's the plan?"

"His car's in the car park. We drive him to his house, put him in his bed, then maybe tip off the emergency services to do a welfare check on him."

"We're driving him home in his own car? We'll leave a massive trail of fingerprints and whatnot won't we? We could pop him in the van, wheelbarrow and all. Be a lot easier."

"We can wear gloves. If his death doesn't look suspicious, why would they even look at his car? Being caught outside his house with his corpse in a wheelbarrow would be a lot worse. And his car would be in the wrong place."

He gave her a mock salute. "You're the Smartypants, I trust in your plan."

Anika could clearly see how it ought to work. Which wasn't quite the same as being confident that it *would* work, but it came close.

As they made their way to the marquee, the appearance of Daffyd made them both freeze in their tracks.

"Busy day for the events team today," said Daffyd.

"It is," said Anika. "I think everything's in hand though."

Daffyd made a grand gesture that encompassed his entire body. "I hereby donate my services to this grotto for the day. I can help in this small corner at least.

"Ohh, surely you'd be much more effective in the office?" said Anika. "I think we can manage here."

"All hands on deck, as we often say in the world of elfing. Expertise of the highest calibre is needed at the coal face on a day like today."

"Which particular deck, or coal face, did you plan to help with?" asked Anika.

"Whichever one is happening in the marquee," said Daffyd. "I believe Tom is managing things globally. I am a mere underling."

And there it was. Anika realised Daffyd wanted a front row seat to witness the car crash that he expected to result from Tom's mismanagement.

"It will be Santa Paws in here," said Anika. At least it was supposed to be. She only had a Santa booked for an hour, but she couldn't let Daffyd see there were problems.

"Lovely. I will get ready with my squeaker toy."

Anika smiled and turned away. She bundled Gallagher back into the tea shed. "Change of plan. We'll need to do it at the end of the events, when Daffyd's out of the way."

Gallagher nodded. The sound of Daffyd aggressively testing squeaker toys could clearly be heard from this distance. It was likely to be a trying day in the marquee. Anika slumped into a seat in the tea shed.

"I have a Santa problem," she said to Gallagher. "Santa

Seamus has promised to do the first hour, but I haven't yet worked out what to do after that."

Gallagher nodded. "You've got some ideas though." It was a statement, not a question.

"Yes. Some are better than others." Thoughtfully, she tapped both forefingers against her chin. "I could hold Santa Seamus by somehow tying him to the throne..."

Gallagher pulled a face. "Hardly likely to be the best Santa if he's tied down, eh?"

Anika nodded in agreement. "I already offered him more money, and that didn't work. I could offer him sexual favours, but I don't want to. So far, my best idea is to get Santa Seamus to train up another Santa."

"A trainee Santa? Yeah, you're a bit limited."

"Luka would be ideal, but he's made it very clear that he won't do it. Daffyd would probably be willing, but can you imagine a more sinister Santa?"

"No. I actually can't."

"Gillespie is much too young. Sophie wearing a beard is possibly the most realistic option – which says something about the quality of the options available."

"How long have you got to come up with something?"

"A couple of hours."

Gallagher grinned. "Easy. Plenty of time for a Smartypants solution." He pottered outside with his mug of tea and his morning joint.

Anika wished she shared his confidence. She turned her attention to the other events. There was a children's party booked in the café, and everything seemed fine with the preparation for that. There was a live entertainer booked, and Sophie had confirmed the catering was all lined up.

That left only the carriage rides in the paddock. She'd had no luck at all in finding a horse that might come and pull the carriage. She wondered whether she might be able to go over to Bloomers once their event was underway and somehow persuade one of the horse owners to bring one over to Hedgelord. She had no compelling leverage, so she pushed that idea away ... but then she had another thought. Was there anything to be gained from the fact that Bloomers' events manager was missing? All of the pain that Hedgelord was currently experiencing was probably reflected over the road at Bloomers. If there was confusion and miscommunication over here, then it was likely to exist over there, too.

Anika wandered outside to find Gallagher again. "Hey – how easy would it be to make a fake sign? You know the sort of thing, where it says something like 'Horses for Bloomers event, entrance this way' and have them pointing over here so we can steal their horses?"

Gallagher grinned. "It would be fairly easy, I reckon. Are we taking inspiration from Road Runner cartoons now? I can probably paint a fake tunnel for them to go into while I'm at it."

Anika scowled at him. "Fine. There's probably a better idea. It's just that I have so many problems to deal with. How is it possible that everything is so messed up?"

Gallagher fixed her with a wry look. "Just because it's messed up doesn't mean you're the one who has to sort it out. You do know that, don't you?"

Her scowl deepened. "I know that. It's just that I really *like* making messed up things better."

"Keep reminding yourself that you're doing this because you like it," said Gallagher. "Just in case you suddenly don't."

Anika smiled. Gallagher made these pronouncements as if he had made every mistake that was humanly possible and wanted to save her from doing the same. "Thanks, Gallagher."

59

GALLAGHER

Gallagher and Luka spent the early morning rounding up the big customer trollies. They were in the habit of migrating out to the car park, because customers wheeled the heavier items (which were mostly Christmas trees at this time of the year) out to their cars. Gallagher and Luka brought them back to the plant area, so that they were in the correct place for next time.

It was an endless task. Luka had called it Sisyphean, which Gallagher assumed meant 'bloody annoying'.

They filled the air with gentle arguing over whether there would be a free bar at the staff party that evening. Luka was adamant that an office party without free booze was no party at all. Gallagher refused to view things so optimistically.

"Look over there, my friend," said Luka as they pushed trollies across the snowy car park. "Is your Christmas gift from the universe." He nodded to a taxi that had pulled up.

Three women piled out, all of them dressed in the most

striking outfits. They wore huge, billowing dresses in different shades of iridescent blues and greens. Each's hair was piled up in elaborate styles, topped with a tiara. One had blonde hair, another was a brunette, and the third had rich auburn hair.

Cameron appeared at the front door of the shop a few moments later, straightening his tie as he made a beeline for them. "Welcome, my princesses!" he roared. "Welcome to Hedgelord. This way!"

"Fucking hell," said Gallagher to Luka. "What's he got planned with that little lot? Orgy or tea party?"

As Cameron swept the group of princesses inside the shop, he rubbed his hands together. "You will be so good in our carriage. Who wouldn't want a ride with a pretty princess, eh?"

"Ah. That mad old twat has booked them for the carriage rides. I'm pretty sure Anika's not expecting this."

"They are for customer event? No. Surely they are hookers?" Luka said. "Riding them is what he just said. You heard him."

"I think we're supposed to say sex workers," said Gallagher. "But I don't think that's what they are. I'm going to tell Anika."

"Because Anika is now running hookers as well? Fucking elf is getting to be a proper boss."

As he turned to go inside, Gallagher's attention was drawn to a white Mercedes car parked across in the car park. A woman sat at the wheel. She wore sunglasses and a headscarf, like she was one of those old time film stars or something. But what drew Gallagher's attention was the way she tightly gripped the steering wheel in gloved hands as she stared out, seemingly straight at him.

"Luka," he said, softly.

"What is it?" said Luka.

"That woman."

"What woman?"

The Mercedes suddenly shot out of its parking bay and turned towards the exit.

"What about it?" said Luka.

"She was looking at me."

"You are handsome man."

Gallagher shook his head. "No, I think she was watching us."

Luka sniffed contemplatively. "You think the police are spying on us?"

The thought had never crossed Gallagher's mind until that very moment. In fact, his mind had been drifting in other directions. "You know what," he said. "It actually looked a bit like that Sonia Patterson."

"Drug dealer Sonia Patterson?"

"How many Sonia Pattersons do we know?"

Luka's frown deepened. "Sonia Patterson is no longer our concern. We did job for her and then owed her money. We paid her back the money. Job done."

"Then she was forced to give her money to charity in front of Mickey Bubbles and now Snømann has severed her from his business."

"So, she's hanging round like an angry ex-girlfriend?" said Luka, unconvinced. "No."

"And maybe sees us as engineers of her bad fortune."

Luka barked with laughter and slapped him on the shoulder. "You worry too much, my friend."

"I'm not sure I worry enough."

There was nothing to be done about in now. The white Mercedes had gone. Gallagher went to find Anika. She was in the marquee, where Daffyd was doing some sort of warm-up for a group of elves.

"And hup and hup and knees high!" he yelled, like a nightmare aerobics instructor. "Cutesy look to camera everyone!"

Anika was part of the group, but she looked very grateful for the chance to leave when Gallagher beckoned her over.

"Is he high?" asked Gallagher, with a nod to Daffyd.

"No. It's like he's on some sort of manic mission to get everyone hyped up. I think it's part of the weird competition he's got going on with Tom," said Anika.

"So what's Tom doing?"

"Oh, I don't even know if he's aware of the competition," said Anika. "I think it's entirely in Daffyd's head."

"Events people. All fucking mad," said Gallagher with feeling.

"Oi! That's me you're talking about. What did you want me for, anyway?"

"Oh yeah. Were you expecting a trio of models dressed up as princesses for the carriage ride thing?" Gallagher asked.

Anika shook her head. "No, it's not that sort of event. We're expecting smoochy couples wanting nice pictures for Insta."

"Well it looks like Cameron thinks it *is* that sort of event.

He's taken them up to his office." He looked away for a long moment. "I mean, it could be that Luka's right about them being sex workers..."

"Shit. I'd better go and see."

"No problem," said Gallagher. "By the way, where's, erm, you-know-who at the moment?"

Anika raised a finger to discreetly point. "Still in the wheelbarrow, ready to go. You see that wall over there, behind Santa's throne? The one built of straw bales? He's encased in the middle of that. Should be safe from prying eyes for the rest of the day."

Gallagher nodded. It was a good solid hiding place, but easy enough for them to get him out as soon as the coast was clear. He watched Anika as she went off to find the princesses. He hoped for her sake that it was a tea party rather than an orgy Cameron had planned. Then again, Cameron had been to public school, and Gallagher wouldn't be at all surprised if those two things were routinely combined. He didn't trust the upper classes.

60

CHARLOTTE

Detective Karlsson had promised that the plane taking them to Finland was not large and she had not been lying. Throughout the flight, Charlotte was squashed down in her passenger seat next to Jack, pressed even more tightly together by their thick coats. Outside there was no cloud cover, and she could see a stippled pattern of snow-covered forests and icy rocks below the plane.

There might have been a knot of tension in her stomach, which flared every time she thought about Alejandro and the porn videos of Santa Raymond and Santa Seamus, but that aside, she couldn't think of anywhere else she'd rather be.

Yes, it was true that once they were back in England, back on home ground, maybe the magic of this ... this thing with Jack would be hard to maintain, and maybe they would find themselves falling into old patterns. But for now, forcing herself to live in the moment with this solid, dependable man beside her and the glory of a winter snowscape below her, she could not think of anywhere else she would rather be at all.

At some point, some messages had appeared on her phone. Her mum had sent a gentle, querying reminder that she hadn't heard from her in a couple of days. Messages like this were normal. Charlotte would send back one of her bland platitudes. There was also a message from Cameron at work wanting to know, with some sense of urgency it seemed, if she would be attending the office Christmas party that night. His message included the actual words '*It's going to be a magical once in a lifetime experience.*' She didn't bother replying, but showed the message to Jack.

He grunted in amusement. "Office Christmas party. You could take me as your plus one." He dug out his phone to show her a message from one of his bosses, Maremba Stone. Charlotte read it out to see if she could understand it.

"*Hope you're enjoying this unauthorised time off, Jack. I admire your newfound autonomy but do not forget the spiritual and social contract with the Bloomers community. Will be incommunicado later. Taking the grandchildren to see the Rotary Club Santa this evening. The binding of charity collections and the commercial representation of the winter spirit is crass and vulgar but it is important that the children witness naïve local customs.*"

She frowned at him. "What kind of human being writes sentences like that?"

"My bosses. Marcus and Maremba. They are ... unusual people, but they are, for want of a better word, good people."

"So," said Detective Karlsson, raising her voice slightly

over the sound of the engines, "you both do 'Christmas' work."

Charlotte laughed. Jack nodded.

"If you'd like to call it that. Yeah, management of the seasonal merchandise events. But at different garden centres."

"You must like Christmas very much."

"Yes, we do," said Charlotte. "I mean, who doesn't? It's a special time of year."

"Too commercial maybe?" suggested Karlsson.

"Despite working in retail, I don't think either of us disagree with that," said Jack. "We like what Christmas represents, how it brings out the best in people." He tilted his head. "Charlotte's the one with true faith."

She wasn't sure what he meant by his tone, but she nodded. "I do happen to be a Christian," she said. "And that's important to me. But the festive season has many facets, enough for everyone."

"It must be a very happy time of year for you both," said Karlsson. "So much joy."

Charlotte looked at Jack and she could see in his face that he was also thinking about the stress and chaos and occasional conflicts the Christmas season caused for them both.

"Oh, yeah," she said. "Joy's the right word."

61

ANIKA

Anika went to Cameron's office and knocked on the door.

"Enter!" bellowed Cameron.

Anika went inside and saw the princesses – all not quite modelled on characters from Disney's *Frozen*. They sat on wheeled chairs, their huge skirts billowing out. She nodded to them as they sipped daintily on cups of tea.

"Ah, glad you're here Anita," said Cameron. "You can take the pretty princesses over to the carriage rides, show them what's what, eh?"

"I'm sure I can help, yes. So what exactly is the plan with the, er, pretty princesses?" Anika glanced over at the women, wanting to apologise for the awful name, but none of them looked at all bothered.

"Plan? I'd have thought it was obvious to a bright young thing like you, Anita. People sit in the princess carriage and get to meet a pretty princess. It's what Christmas is all about, isn't it?"

"Uh huh?" Anika turned to the women. "You've done a lot of these then?"

They all shook their heads.

"Hah! Just goes to show that we're ahead of the competition! I know Charlotte was sceptical about this idea, but we're going to show everyone a clean pair of heels, aren't we?"

Anika was struck by another thought. There were a number of events on today and now she was wondering in what other ways Cameron could, to be blunt, fuck them up. There was the Santa Paws throughout the day for people to bring their dogs to meet Santa. And there was the children's Christmas tea party in the café. Coupled with the carriage rides, which currently had zero horses and three more princesses than expected, the recipes for disaster were all very much present.

"Are there any other bookings you made that we might want to know about?" she asked.

"Yes of course. Children's party entertainer. Dicky Dong should go down a treat, eh?"

Anika wasn't sure what she'd been expecting, but it wasn't that. Some optimistic part of her had hoped for a spare Santa, but if she'd been given a thousand guesses, she still wouldn't have come up with a children's entertainer called Dicky Dong.

"Dicky Dong? Are you totally sure he's a children's entertainer?" she asked.

He laughed. "Well, with a name like Dicky Dong he's

hardly likely to be anything else is he? Ding dong, the witch is dead, sort of thing."

"Or, you know, like *dong* is slang for...?" Anika said.

Cameron gave her a blank look.

"Penis," she said.

Cameron looked at her. "Dong? No! Never heard of a man's todger being called a dong. Plenty of fruity names for the old boy, but dong? Absurd." He cradled his groin as he spoke, as if it might be insulted by the conversation.

Anika looked over to the pretty princesses, in case they wanted to back her up, but they were all looking away, keen to avoid conflict.

"And maybe someone with that name isn't a children's entertainer, but does something a bit more ... adult?" she said.

"Blue stuff?" said Cameron. "Ha! God, that would not be appropriate would it?"

"No, it wouldn't."

"You'd best get onto that," said Cameron. He waved his hand at the princesses. "I've done my bit. Got an office party to organise. It's going to be monumental."

"Right, I'll look out for Dicky when he arrives," said Anika. She turned to address the women. "I'll give you ten minutes to finish your tea and then I will show you what needs doing."

Her phone buzzed. It was a message from Gillespie. The new Santa had arrived.

She did a little fist pump. At least something was going her way.

Anika rushed over to the marquee to find Santa Seamus

on the scene, ready to do Santa Paws. Poaching Santas from Bloomers was somewhat underhand, but having a genuinely alive and definitely not dead Santa was a good result.

"Santa Seamus! Is there any possibility I can persuade you to stay longer than an hour?" she asked.

"Ooh you're a live one, aren't you?" he said, patting her on the back. "If I wasn't otherwise engaged I'd do it just for the cheek of you keeping on and on at me. I can give you an hour and no more. I've got the Round Table Santa charity drive this evening and need to rest up beforehand."

"Santa charity drive?"

"Oh, you know, flower. I sit on the back of a pretend sleigh on a trailer and wave to the kiddiwinks as the charity goes collecting door to door."

"Oh, yeah. The Rotary Club thing."

Seamus sucked in through his teeth. "No, no. I'm definitely Round Table. Raymond has sometimes done the Rotary Club, and that's all well and good – except their Santa trailer is a deathtrap and that Glen Lightfoot can't drive for toffee." He took a deep breath and patted his barrel chest with both hands. "But listen, dear, I've enjoyed today and I'm happy to come do some Clausing for you, say from next week onwards."

"That's brilliant," said Anika and waved him off as she went to check on the Santa Paws line outside.

Dogs were starting to queue at the entrance, so Anika had them open the grotto early. This was for two reasons. The unexpected snow was falling quite heavily on the visitors and their dogs, and it was a general principle that a queue of dogs was likely to cause disruption, bringing all of the doggy sizes, shapes and personalities together, yanking their owners along for the ride.

While she wondered how she'd fill the Santa gig for the rest of the day, a man and a woman came down the path with six huskies between them.

"Wow, what gorgeous dogs!" said Anika.

The man issued a brief 'sit' command and all of the huskies sat in an obedient line.

The round-faced woman grinned at Anika, her frizzy hair escaping from underneath a woolly hat. "We've come up from Suffolk to get some family pictures at Santa Paws. It's so exciting! Marcin loves his dogs. I've made them all little Santa hats for the occasion." She pulled a number of what Anika guessed were crocheted Christmas hats.

"Izzy loves to make things," said the man.

Anika scritched one of the huskies under its chin and looked up at the couple. "Izzy, Marcin, it's lovely to meet you. Tell me... These huskies, have they ever done sledding?"

62

CHARLOTTE

Night had fallen by the time the plane landed in Finland. A big jeep thing came across the tarmac to meet them at Rovaniemi airport. The runways were cleared of snow, but the flat landscape beyond was covered in it. A thin faced man with a fluffy parka hood encircling his face came over with another man to meet Charlotte, Jack and the Swedish officers.

"I am *Komissarie* Eskola," he said, with a wave rather than a handshake. "This is Customs Officer Mäkinen. Welcome to Lapland. We are going to go straight to Santa Claus's village. You can brief us on the way."

"He did just say Santa Claus's village, didn't he?" Jack whispered to Charlotte as they walked to the vehicle.

"I think he did," she whispered back.

There was room for all of them in the jeep, which was good because there was already a driver and another police officer in there. They set off towards an access road and through the fencing surrounding the airfield.

"Rovaniemi is the official hometown of Santa Claus and the gateway to the Arctic," said Officer Eskola. "Rovaniemi is a busy town, especially during the winter months. Each year, we welcome over half a million visitors from around the world."

"Half a million?" said Charlotte.

Eskola nodded. "Americans, English, all across Europe. They come here to experience the magic of Christmas, witness the Northern Lights, and enjoy the unique Arctic activities we offer. Our Santa Claus Village is located right on the Arctic Circle. It's three p.m. Sunset was two hours ago. It's just up ahead here." He pointed along the tree-lined road, then swivelled to address the visitors. "We have two main priorities here. We have an opportunity to bust a major smuggling ring."

"This is just tobacco smuggling, right?" said Jack.

The customs officer gave a disgusted snort. "Tobacco, drugs, people smuggling. It is often the same gangs. We believe a Finnish crime syndicate might be using Rovaniemi as a staging point for smuggling operations from Sweden and into Russia, via the Raate border crossing. Their boss is a man with the name of Snowman. Cute, huh? If we can disrupt that, even arrest some of the major guys..." Eskola made a whistling sound and fanned himself as though he was too hot.

"You said two priorities," said Detective Karlsson.

"There are hundreds of tourists at the Santa Claus Village right now. We do not want their lasting memories of

Lapland to be Finnish police officers and noisy foreigners ruining their wonderful Christmas experience."

Charlotte thought that comment sounded a little snarky, but Karlsson simply gave a grim little nod.

The big jeep turned onto a larger highway, went straight past a large wooden sign for "Santa Claus Village", and turned off onto a rough track and into what appeared to be either a car park or a dumping ground for unwanted vehicles. The space was currently filled with Finnish police officers. At least, Charlotte assumed they were Finnish police officers. They had an unmistakeably militaristic air to them: booted feet, masked faces, all armed with guns, many with the kinds of rifles Charlotte had only ever seen in the movies.

"So we're going for the subtle softly-softly approach, huh?" she said as they got out.

Officer Eskola grinned at her. "You think we capture criminals with stern voices and wagging fingers?"

"They are British," said Karlsson.

"Oh, yes," said Eskola. "You do capture criminals with stern voices and the wagging fingers. I have seen."

"And maybe a taser or two," admitted Jack.

Another officer had a map of the area on a tablet device. Eskola conferred with his colleagues in Finnish, occasionally shooting questions to Karlsson in English. There were very few questions for Jack and Charlotte. She'd been worried that, having got themselves on the flight with offers of inside knowledge, they'd be asked to produce some stunning insights. But it became clear that Detective Karlsson understood the situation perfectly, and they were just minor window-dressing in a cross-border policing operation.

"So we start on these buildings here," said Eskola, pointing out a place on the map. "Those are the likely storage facilities. Local intel tells us there have been crates freighted out of there in recent days. From there we move in, building by building. Your Santa guy – Egagli?"

"Egadze," said Charlotte. "Irakli Egadze. He's not our Santa."

"He's the number two Santa in the world," said Jack.

"Right," said Eskola. "He and your elf friend might be here at Santa's house. We have circulated your pictures."

He spoke to the police officers in Finnish, did a circling motion with his finger in the air, and they moved off towards the trees in groups, quiet and stealthy.

"They seem very intense," Charlotte said to Jack.

"The Finns are the best people," said Karlsson. "But never cross them." She gestured up through the trees. "The operation will be focussed on the storage buildings that way. You are not coming."

"Naturally," said Jack.

"So, go into the Santa Claus Village. I hear the Santamus restaurant is good. Try the meatballs."

"Will they be reindeer meatballs?" said Charlotte.

"Of course," said Karlsson and jogged off to catch up with the Finnish police officers. Jack and Charlotte were suddenly alone in a chilly car park.

Charlotte watched the wind tug at the treetops. "This has been quite a strange trip, hasn't it?" she said.

"Yes, it has," he agreed slowly. "But fun."

"Oh. Definitely fun. Yes. What's been your favourite bit?"

"The sex, obviously."

"Obviously," she agreed. "Besides that?"

He gave a little frown, then took her gloved hand in his. "Am I right in thinking we've been given a free pass to go visit Santa's Lapland village and possibly meet the real Santa Claus?"

"That's what I heard."

They turned, orientated themselves, and made for a path that cut through the trees back towards the highway and the entrance to Santa's village.

63

ANIKA

Anika fetched the pretty princesses from Cameron's office. As soon as they'd reached the bottom of the stairs, one of them broke character and started to laugh like a drain. "Dicky Dong? Seriously, that boss of yours thinks he's a children's entertainer?"

"I dread to think," said Anika.

"I want to meet him now," said another princess.

Anika held up her hands. "You will meet him, but can I suggest something? You won't be doing carriage ride – the event is not what Cameron seems to think it is. How do you feel about helping out with a children's party?"

The princesses looked at each other.

"Children are the worst," said one.

"Yeah, but horses are worse than children," said another.

"Do you do a lot of work with both?" said Anika.

"Nursery nurse during term time," said the third princess, holding up her hand.

"They stink and they bite," said the blonde princess.

"Children or horses?" said Anika.

The auburn-haired one shrugged. "We get paid whatever we do. Don't know about you, guys, but we know where we are with a children's party."

"That's great," said Anika. "Let's get you over to the café. You can be the party entertainment, and I'll work out what to do with Mr Dicky Dong."

As Anika was shepherding the pretty princesses through to the café, Karen waved from the customer service desk. "Got a Mr Dong for the events team, Anika."

The name set the princesses sniggering again, but Anika ignored them. "Please follow us, will you?" she called to Mr Dong.

Dicky Dong looked like a portly older man. He wore a thick coat, buttoned up so high that it covered most of his face. His flat cap was pulled low.

"Hello there," said Anika as they walked. "You're the comedian, yes?"

"I am that, yes sirree bob," said Dicky Dong.

"What's your material like? Is it suitable for children?"

He pulled off his hat so that he could fix her with a penetrating gaze. "Is that some sort of joke?"

"Er, no."

"Dicky Dong is synonymous with the highest levels of smut, innuendo and crudity."

"Yes, I see. The person who booked you somehow didn't join the dots. This event is a children's party."

Dicky Dong made loud huffing noises as they walked into the café. "Well, I don't know what I'm supposed to do about rank stupidity – do you?" He unzipped the top part of his coat, revealing a lush white beard. "Then I'm about as much use to you as Viagra in a monastery."

Anika grinned. "As a matter of fact, you could be more useful than you imagine."

She left the pretty princesses with Sophie in the café, so they could all get their heads together to work out how they'd handle the guests at the children's party. She took Dicky Dong with her to the marquee, where the couple with the huskies were just emerging.

"Hello again!" said Anika. "Get some good pictures?"

"Yes!" said the woman, Izzy. "We're thrilled. It's brilliant here!"

"That's wonderful to hear," said Anika. "Would you all come with me and look at something?"

The couple glanced at each other and shrugged. "Sure," said the man.

64

GALLAGHER

Luka found Gallagher and beckoned for him to follow to the front of the store.

"What is it?" said Gallagher.

"He has called again," said Luka.

"Who?"

"Who do you think? Snømann."

"Shit. What now? This is never-ending. And not in a good, *Neverending Story* kind of way."

"More crates."

Gallagher sighed. "Fuck. We don't owe this man anything. We're just doing this because ... well..."

"Because he is big and scary and is horrible criminal and threatened to burn your face with hot trowel?"

"Yes, that." As the automatic doors slid open, Gallagher pondered something. "Do you think he's the one who arranged for our barbecue to explode and for all those pots to fall on us?"

"Why would he do that?"

"I dunno." Gallagher shrugged hopelessly. "Mix up the pleasant chit-chat with some scary violence. A kind of good cop, bad cop thing."

"Makes no sense. Only people who would want to kill us are our enemies. Do you have any enemies, Gallagher?"

"I don't think so."

"No? No vengeful ex-girlfriends?"

Gallagher blew out his lips. "I've not had enough girlfriends to build up a supply of vengeful ones. I'd happily face a vengeful ex if I'd actually had a girlfriend beforehand."

"Handsome man like you? No girls? It is a mystery."

Gallagher scratched his scrawny neck and sniffed noisily. "A bloody misery more like."

Outside, they stood by the congregation of large trolleys near the doors.

"What about you?" said Gallagher.

"What about me? I've had girlfriends, sure."

"Enemies. Do you have any enemies?"

Luka nodded sincerely. "Dead or alive?"

"Um, alive, for the purposes of this question."

Luka counted on his fingers. "Seven. Not currently in prison, five. Currently in this country, only two."

"Wow," said Gallagher, impressed. "You've got enemies *and* you can count them—" He fell abruptly silent as he recognised Snømann's truck pulling into the car park. "We're going to be spotted taking that stuff in," he said.

"We are men who carry goods," said Luka, probably not sounding as confident as he wished. "We can carry crates through and not be questioned."

"It is your lucky day," said Snømann with a grin as he unfastened the tailgate of his truck.

"You are in a jolly mood," noted Luka cautiously.

"It is Friday. Date night. Weekend celebrations start here."

"And why is it our lucky day?" asked Gallagher.

"You have been selected to store another fifteen crates."

"Fifteen? You said ten!" Gallagher protested.

"It is a sign of my accelerating faith in this current venture," said the crook.

They started to load crates onto the trolley.

It was back-breaking work. The crates were heavy, and they had to lift each one down from the truck, wheel the trolley round to the plant area, then carry each one individually from the path, through the tea shed, and into the secret shed. Every step of the way brought with it the risk of discovery or questions.

"Last batch," said Luka as they wheeled the trolley away from the truck.

Gallagher glanced back and saw no indication that Snømann was leaving the car park. He would no doubt want to come and inspect their work to make sure he was satisfied.

"Ah Luka! Gallagher!" It was Tom.

"Fuck," said Gallagher quietly.

Without discussion, Gallagher and Luka both continued on their way, pretending not to hear. It wasn't a very effective strategy, because a few moments later Tom was there, blocking their way.

"What on earth's the matter with you? Didn't you hear me?"

"Was listening to music," said Luka.

Tom's face scrunched in confusion. "What music? I don't see any earphones."

Luka stepped away from the trolley, in an attempt to draw Tom back down the path. "You have heard of mindfulness, yes? Is a mindfulness technique practised where I come from. Music is summoned from within. Requires high levels of concentration."

Gallagher tried to heave the trolley out of the way while Luka distracted Tom with his elaborate bullshit, but it was simply too heavy for one person. All he could do was barge it a few inches along with each shove.

Tom wasn't giving up so easily. "I need the two of you back on Christmas trees. People want them at the front of the store, so they can pop in quickly and just take one. Can you please put twenty through the baling machine and put them in a container by the front door?"

Luka pulled out his tiny notepad and went through the pantomime of recording the task, while Tom watched him. Gallagher had almost got the trolley round the corner, out of sight.

"What's on that trolley?" Tom asked.

Gallagher froze.

"Hang on," said Luka. "Did you say twenty Christmas trees?"

"Yes I did," said Tom, turning back to Luka once more. Gallagher gave the trolley another shove.

Tom glanced over at Gallagher.

"Wait!" said Luka. "Which size trees should we choose? All average height and make big price label? Otherwise we must price each tree individually. Is important that we get this right, no?"

Tom turned away again to answer Luka's question, and Gallagher gave a mighty heave to get the trolley out of sight. Even when he was certain he was out of Tom's sight, he kept going, knowing he couldn't rest until every one of the crates was hidden away.

He drove himself into a frenzy, working up a sweat in spite of the snow that had been falling for most of the day. It felt as if it took him forever, but in reality it was probably no more than half an hour before he was able to put the Asian Hornet poster back in place over the secret door and collapse into a chair in the tea shed.

"Thank fuck for that!"

A few minutes later he dragged himself outside to find Luka baling Christmas trees, while talking with Snømann.

"Ah good. It is done?" asked Snømann.

Gallagher nodded.

"You will obviously take great care that nobody disturbs the merchandise. We will be back in touch," said Snømann.

Gallagher and Luka both nodded as Snømann walked away.

"Enjoy date night," said Luka.

"Well that's about done me in," said Gallagher, inclining his head towards the shed. "Although you might have had the shittier end of the stick."

"How come?" asked Luka.

"You had to do what Tom asked just for once. I bet that was painful."

65

ANIKA

Anika led Dicky Dong and the couple with the huskies through the paddock, ignoring the line of people who were waiting for the carriage rides that currently had no viable carriage and took them over to the stables.

"In here," she said and took them inside the barn. She pointed to the dog sled Amy had shown her. "This is a dog sled, yes? Is there any chance your huskies could pull this and offer rides for a couple of hours?"

The woman eyed it. "What do you think, Marcin?"

He pulled a face. "Is a little old-fashioned, but it looks in good condition. We can do this. It will be good exercise for the dogs."

Anika's face broke into a huge grin. "Really? It would save the day for us, honestly!"

"Sure," said Marcin. "Let us pull it out of there and see what we can do."

Anika stood back with Dicky Dong and held some of the dogs' leads, although they were so well-behaved they didn't really need to be restrained. Marcin, and the woman, Izzy, checked over the sled and declared it to be workable. A few minutes later they had harnessed up the dogs and Marcin stood at the rear of the sled, urging them along on a brief test run. They ran joyfully in a tight circle. Anika wasn't sure how Marcin was controlling the dogs, but he definitely knew what he was doing.

"So you stand on the back to control the dogs while two people sit in that little seat in front of you?" Anika asked.

"Yes," said Izzy. "It's a couples thing, yeah? They'll love it."

"I think they will!" grinned Anika. "Let's go, shall we?"

Anika assigned some elves to administer the husky rides and took Dicky Dong back to the marquee. "Dicky Dong, I want to introduce you to Santa Seamus," she said as they entered the grotto in between time slots.

The two men shook hands.

"I've got to be honest with you, your name's a bit racy for the Santa role," said Santa Seamus.

"Ah, I'm not a Santa. I'm a comedian," said Dicky.

"Different skillset all together," said Seamus.

"Yes," said Anika. "But today we don't need a comedian. We need a Santa. Any chance you'd like to learn the ropes from a seasoned pro like Seamus here? It would be another string to your bow."

Dicky looked between Anika and Seamus, stroking his white beard. "Santa, eh? I guess I could give it a go."

"Squeeze up, squeezebox!" said Seamus, standing up and

patting the throne. "Let's start with some of your basic Santa postures. You'll need to sit with your feet planted firmly on the floor and your knees wide. From there you can assume any of the regular Santa positions. We'll run through those in a minute, but if Santa Paws is your focus for today, you'll need to practise sitting with an upright spine while holding the lead of a feisty dog in the gap you've made here. You're basically going to make it sit and look at the camera by nudging it gently into place with your knees."

"I'll find you an outfit," mouthed Anika, as Dicky sat and tried to absorb the steady flow of Santa lore from Seamus. "Are we calling you Santa Dicky for the day?"

Dicky nodded. "Yep. Sure."

Anika stepped away and organised some clothing for Santa Dicky. Santas very often had their own robes, and she thought they had some sort of weird contest about who had the deepest plush fabric, or the most massive hood, but Dicky would be fine in one of the standard issue suits.

She found Karen on the tills. She looked up from a customer and smiled. "All right Anika, love?"

"I am!" grinned Anika. "I can't believe it, but I actually am! All of the events are sorted. I took the Pretty Princesses from the carriage rides and put them onto the children's party. I took the totally inappropriate comedian from the children's party and made him Santa for the Santa Paws. I took some visiting huskies from Santa Paws and they are now pulling the carriage rides. It's like a beautiful circle of life."

"Na, that's a circle of pure Anika cleverness that is!" said Karen. "Well done love, that's an amazing job."

Cameron appeared at the tills. "You'll never guess what I've just seen!" he declared.

"No. We won't," said Karen.

"I went down to the paddock to make sure the pretty princesses are all right—"

"That was very noble of you," said Karen, scanning a packet of shortbread for a customer.

"I take the welfare of employees very seriously," he said, straightening his tie. "Anyway, the princesses were not out in the paddock. I expect they were taking a break. There was a team of huskies giving people rides. What a hoot! We should try and book them."

"Yes," said Anika weakly. "They would be popular." Occasionally, she'd wondered how much of Charlotte's time was spent managing the slightly insane expectations of their boss; she was beginning to realise it was probably a lot.

As Cameron wandered back to his office, Karen leaned back in her chair. "You did make a risk assessment for the husky rides, didn't you?"

"I ... did," said Anika. By which she meant she would do in the next few minutes. "You will find it in the folder."

Anika hurried to the office to fill out the risk assessment. She'd started to capture some ideas as she walked, typing them into a laptop. Slips, trips and bites seemed to be the main risks, so she'd need to talk to Izzy and Marcin about how those might be addressed. She was sending it to the printer when Karen burst in.

"I've got it! I've got it!" said Anika. "The risk assessment's here."

"Bugger the risk assessment!" said Karen, panicked. "I've just heard someone's found a dead body!"

Anika froze, suddenly awash with a petrifying and sickening horror.

And it had all been going so well!

66

CHARLOTTE

Despite Detective Karlsson's suggestion that they go try Finnish reindeer meatballs, there was simply too much to see at the Santa Claus Village.

Charlotte realised that, yes, this was a pretend town at some arbitrary point in the Arctic region of Lapland, built in order to capitalise on a facet of the Father Christmas mythos with no basis in history, mythology or religion; that this was, in essence, no different to the painted plywood grotto or Festive Farm marquee at Hedgelord. But that was sort of the point. The magic of Christmas could be found anywhere – should be found anywhere – and it could equally be found – should be found – at a pretend Santa's village in the frozen north.

There were log cabin shops filled with pottery, carvings, toys and kitsch models of Santa and his reindeer. There were workshops (manned by elves dressed appropriately for the weather). There were reindeer (actually in their natural habitat). There were snowmobile tours where groups of adults and children could go off into the snowy fields to look at yet more snow and, perhaps, get a glimpse of the Northern Lights (which signs dotted around assured them were a common sight).

Charlotte and Jack stepped out of a shop, arm in arm. She had a pair of tree ornaments in her pocket, wrapped in a stripy paper bag; Jack had a bag of traditional *salmiakki* sweets in his. *Salmiakki* was salty liquorice and not a taste sensation Charlotte was in any hurry to try.

Jack was consulting his phone and tutting.

"The real world getting in the way of us enjoying the here and now?" she asked.

He tutted again and apologised. "If I could get a signal. Was just thinking about how we get home again."

She held him close. "Do we have to go home again?"

Jack wrinkled his nose. "Kind of have to. If I want to keep my job and pay the mortgage."

"At least you won't have to pay for that rug anymore," she said. "Is it your mortgage, or a joint one?" she added.

"My mortgage, her rug. She's still got a flat over in Ransom Butterby." He pulled a face. "Untangling two lives is a tricky thing."

"Having second thoughts?" said Charlotte, immediately wishing she hadn't.

"She's the one who wants to be untangled," he said and looked at Charlotte. "And ... and I'm glad. Definitely for the untangling now. I'm a fully on-board untangler."

She patted his chest. "We fucked in a Swedish hotel room, Jack. Which was great—"

"It *was* great."

"—but this thing between us doesn't have to be anything yet."

He pulled back. "Are *you* having second thoughts?"

"No! No, not at all. I'm just saying, I'm big enough to recognise there might be some untangling to be done before – if we want to – we get entangled ourselves. I'm happy with that."

He waggled his bag of *salmiakki* in her face. "Want to suck on some salty liquorice?"

"Yeah, you're all right, mate," she said, waving him away.

From a distance came the sound of sharp, cracking pops. There were two, then three, then maybe half a dozen in reply. It sounded far away, but people in the lit-up village street turned to look round.

Charlotte immediately thought of the Finnish police officers and their guns.

"Could be fireworks," suggested Jack without confidence.

"Could be..."

There were two more shots and then silence.

"It's all done now," said Jack, but it was more of a question than a statement. "They'll get the phone, we can have the videos or they can be locked away in police evidence. Whatever. Job's done."

"Sure," she said.

Jack put a piece of black liquorice in his mouth. He appeared to be pretending to enjoy it. His sounds of pleasure were too vocal and forced.

A walking figure coming down through the village caught Charlotte's eye. It wasn't the elf costume that first caught her eye. It wasn't the fur-trimmed hat or the jutty spike of hair sticking out of it that first caught her attention either. It was the way in which the man walked. He was walking in a very casual manner. Not just an offhand, casual manner, but an emphatically, deliberately casual manner. The man was aiming for such high levels of nonchalance, he might as well have been swinging his arms like a merry Cockney and whistling a jaunty tune as he kicked through the snow in his elf boots.

It was Alejandro Aramburuzabala, doing a very bad job of looking innocent. And it was obvious he was walking away, at the highest speed one could employ while being ever-so-very-much a casual man just about his daily business. Alejandro was fleeing. Whatever had happened with the police raid and Irakli Egadze and the *snus* smugglers, Alejandro was attempting to get away as fast as he could.

Charlotte nudged Jack in the ribs. Jack looked.

At the same moment, Alejandro saw them too. He literally froze in surprise.

"Oi, we want a word with you!" said Charlottle.

Alejandro remained frozen for another second, then leapt into a run. Jack spat out his salty liquorice and gave chase. Charlotte was after them a split second later. Once again, Charlotte could see that the wiry Spaniard could really sprint over short distances, but he would tire soon.

"You've got nowhere to go, mate!" Jack shouted after him.

Alejandro didn't seem inclined to agree. He stumbled through an extended family, knocking neatly-wrapped Christmas presents from a man's hand. He skidded on the snow as he took a corner. A woman yelled after him in Finnish.

Charlotte caught up with Jack, was even beginning to overtake him. Running in thick winter coats was exhausting, but by God, she would have him.

Alejandro ran into the fenced off sort of corral area where half a dozen snowmobiles were lined up. A man in a padded jumpsuit and helmet was just bringing the lead snowmobile round for the next group due to head out.

"We just want the phone!" Jack shouted.

Alejandro barged through the queue, pushed the snowmobile guide off his vehicle, and jumped on it.

"Fucking kidding me!" Charlotte panted. Beneath her coat and gloves her smartwatch's profanity app buzzed. It was no respecter of context or understanding of when swearing was exactly the right thing.

It seemed to take Alejandro only a moment to work out the controls on the still-running snowmobile and he set off with a high-pitched engine whine across the field.

Charlotte didn't hesitate. Her course of action seemed logical, inevitable – even if it was unwise and ridiculous. She climbed onto the next snowmobile and turned the ignition. She'd owned a moped many years ago and the functionality seemed almost identical. As she disengaged the clutch and opened the throttle, Jack slid on behind her. She looked round questioningly.

"Come on!" he said. "Let's fucking get him!"

She accelerated away. The snowmobile bounced on the uneven terrain. She held onto the handlebars and gripped the body with her knees. Jack's arms squeezed round her waist and put his head on her shoulder.

67

ANIKA

Anika, filled with fear, found herself tugged across the grounds of Hedgelord: first by Karen, then by Jill the elf, who had apparently found the body. Anika's mind (which felt like it had floated away from her body in some horrible delirium) was weighing up whether to pretend to be surprised at the sight of Santa Raymond's body, or just admit everything. She wondered which would get her a lighter prison sentence.

But Jill wasn't taking her to the marquee. She was pulling Anika over to the fields next to Hedgelord. Whatever she had anticipated in those moments of horror, it wasn't there being another body on the Hedgelord site.

It suddenly clicked. "Body?" she said as they entered the paddock.

"That's right," panted Jill.

"Human?"

"Oh. Oh, I see," said Karen, whose brain had obviously caught up.

What Anika hadn't anticipated was that the body in question might be canine. She certainly hadn't anticipated huskies to be busy digging up Douglas's grave in the paddock.

Which was not good – or nice – at all.

But it was much better than Jill somehow discovering the dead Santa Raymond.

"Hi!" called Izzy, the huskie-owner, walking over. "The dogs are just taking a five minute break."

The dogs pranced excitedly away from the grave, and zoomed in a wide circuit around the big field.

Anika walked over to Douglas's grave. It was now an enormous empty hole. She bit down on her lip. "Oh your lovely dogs should definitely get some rest, yeah. Have they been digging for long?"

"No, just a few minutes. I've been over there, talking to some of the couples. This whole event is so very wholesome. I love that these cuties are making themselves some precious memories!"

"They are, aren't they?" said Anika. She wondered what sort of memories they would be if the corpse of a dead dog being worried at by a pack of huskies was a backdrop for the photos. She looked to see if Douglas was anywhere obvious, but couldn't see him.

"I'm just filling out a risk assessment, and I need your input," said Anika. "Take a look at what I have so far. I'll be back in a moment."

Anika handed the laptop to Izzy and walked round to the

stables. As she rounded the corner she saw two of the huskies fighting over the body of doggy Douglas.

"No! Drop it!" hissed Anika. She waded in, knowing she had to rescue the poor dead dog. She wrestled the corpse from them and dragged it to the side, then realised she had no idea what to do next. She looked around and saw a wheelie bin.

"Oh Douglas, I am so sorry to do this to you, but it's better than the alternative." She dragged him over to the bin and tried to lift him in.

"Oh my god Douglas," she huffed. "Why could you not have been a chihuahua?"

It took her a few minutes, with lots of huffing and straining, before she got Douglas into the bin.

She went to find Izzy again. The dog's owner handed back the laptop.

"Hi Anika, I added some ideas into your document. Hope that's okay? The dogs seem to be a bit calmer now as well. Whatever had them all excited just now has worn off. What are they like, eh?"

68

GALLAGHER

Gallagher and Luka had watched Anika as she flitted back and forth all afternoon between the various special Christmas events.

Luka had borrowed a flipchart from the office and erected it inside the shed, running a book on possible outcomes for the day. As night settled over the garden centre and all events, festive and shopping-related, drew to a close Gillespie the elf came over from the marquee. He was panting with exertion as he'd sprinted across all the way.

"I want to place a bet," he gasped.

"Too late, you cannot bet on an outcome that is already known," said Luka. "I know you're not the brightest, but that is like rule number one of placing bet."

"I was stuck in the grotto, wasn't I?" complained Gillespie. "Anyway, I don't know what's happened. Can I still put on a bet if I don't know?"

"No. Don't be fucking imbecile."

Gallagher leaned forward, "What were you going to bet on?" he asked out of polite interest. "If you'd been able to?

Gillespie looked at the list. "You've got 'grotto fire' on here, haven't you? I was going to put a tenner on that."

Gallagher gave him a look and shook his head. "Seriously? You'd have seen the flames or heard the sirens, wouldn't you?"

"I suppose," said Gillespie. "I just liked the sound of that one."

"Hey everyone, what's up?" Anika appeared at the entrance to the shed.

Gallagher moved to stand in front of the flipchart. "Nothing. It's all quiet in here." Luka shuffled up to stand at his side, so that the two of them completely blocked Anika's view.

"Why are you two being weird?" she asked and pushed through to take a look. "Well fuck me. This I did not expect. 'How the events afternoon will end'. You've been running a book on how I'll fail."

Luke gave a shameless shrug. "It has generated lot of interest. You should be pleased."

"I should be pleased?" Anika yelled. "You have odds of three to one on me being sacked by the end of the day! How is that supposed to make me pleased?"

"I am merely offering a service here," said Luka. "Besides, that one was not the lowest odds out of all choices."

"Yeah? What was, then? Oh ... Cameron caught shagging a princess at two to one. Yeah, that figures."

"He placed a bet on that one himself," said Gallagher. "I wish I had that man's confidence."

"You've even got fifteen to one on me having an epic angry meltdown like Charlotte," said Anika, pointing at another entry that had caught her eye.

"Very popular, that one," said Luka with a nod.

"You're all—!" Anika clamped her mouth shut on whatever it was she thought they were. "You know what? Never mind. Because you're all coming to help me with Santa Raymond."

"The stiff?" said Gillespie, nervously.

"Our dear departed friend, Santa Raymond. We can finally sort him out."

There were relieved mumblings of "finally" from Gallagher, Luka and Gillespie.

She paused and smiled at them all. "I do appreciate this, really."

"Come on, let's get on with it," said Gallagher. "Luka's promised to buy me a drink with some of his ill-gotten gains."

"How much *did* you make running that book?" asked Anika.

"It would not be prudent for me to say," said Luka.

Anika raised her eyebrows. "That much huh?"

They went into the marquee, which was now completely silent. It took them a few minutes to dismantle the straw bale wall and expose Raymond in his wheelbarrow.

They all stood round in a respectful silence.

"He looks as if he could just be sleeping," said Gillespie.

"And that's very much what we want him to look like, said Anika. "Tucked up in his own bed. Like he just slipped away in the night. Right, has anyone been through his pockets to get his keys?"

They all looked at each other. Nobody wanted to be the one to say anything in case they got lumbered with the job.

"Fine," Gallagher sighed. He approached the body, hands hovering high, as if they had minds of their own and did not want to get involved with rifling through the pockets of a dead man. He plunged them down and forced himself to rummage underneath the folds of the Santa gown. Gallagher wasn't even sure that Raymond had pockets, now he came to think about it. With no small amount of relief he discovered Raymond was wearing trousers with pockets. Gallagher located the left hand one and slid his hand in. He could feel Raymond's leg through the pocket liner, like a slab of chilled meat. The pocket was empty.

He had to work harder to get to the right-hand pocket because of the way Raymond lay in the barrow. Gallagher tugged at the Santa gown to shift him over. Raymond's head turned, and Gallagher couldn't help looking at his face, which was extremely pale. He was extremely glad Raymond was still wearing his sunglasses.

Gallagher's fingers found their way into the pocket and he touched metal. He grabbed it and tried to drag it out. It met resistance, and he was horrified at the thought that he might inadvertently tear a hole in Santa Raymond's leg. Was that a thing? Would he bleed?

He tried to calm his breathing and forced himself to slow down. He rearranged Raymond's position again using the red gown, and the keys slid out of the pocket. Gallagher held them up in triumph.

"Well done," said Gillespie. He looked as if he wanted to throw up.

"Let's get him round to the car park," said Anika.

"Hold on," said Gallagher, not believing what he was about to suggest. Hadn't frisking a dead man been bad enough? "We going to wheel him all the way to his car in the barrow? I know it's quieter now, but it's still unmistakeably a body in a barrow. There's CCTV overlooking the car park and enough lights for someone to be able to see what we're doing."

They all looked at each other. They knew he had a point.

"What if—" Gallagher looked around at them, wondering if any of them had the stomach for this "—what if we wheeled him part of the way, and when we get to the car park we have him propped up between two of us, as if he's a bit drunk or something?"

They all looked at each other again. Gallagher could tell they were evaluating who was the strongest. It inevitably ended with him and Luka pulling a face at each other, knowing it would be them.

"Gillespie on barrow, Luka and me on propping up, Anika on getaway vehicle," said Gallagher finally. "And a stiff drink will definitely be needed afterwards."

"Good!" Anika clapped her hands. "I can't drive, but I can definitely unlock the doors of the getaway vehicle."

Gillespie picked up the barrow and the small party went through the staff gate out to the car park. It was dark, but Gallagher couldn't decide whether that made things better or worse.

"You want me to tip the barrow a bit?" asked Gillespie, as

Luka and Gallagher positioned themselves on either side of Raymond, ready to try and pick him up.

"Yeah, just a bit. Hold it steady," said Gallagher.

The two plant men grunted as they each picked up an arm and slung it over their shoulder.

"Oh fuck man, this is so gross!" moaned Gallagher. He'd wondered if there could anything worse than going through a dead man's pockets, now he knew.

"Imagine is side of beef," said Luka. "Just moving a side of beef."

"You trying to make me a vegetarian or what?"

"Hey everybody!" said Anika, as they were halfway across the carpark. "I can hear a car coming."

They did their best to form a tight cluster around the corpse as Luka and Gallagher carried it in the most natural-looking way they could manage.

A brightly-lit vehicle turned the corner and illuminated them all in its headlights. They couldn't help stopping, momentarily blinded.

"Here he is!" came a voice from the vehicle as a door slammed shut. "You've not been picking up your phone, Raymond!"

"Shit," murmured Gallagher. "What the fuck do we do here?"

Anika stepped forward. "Sorry, your lights are so bright."

"Is it Snømann?" Gallagher whispered to Luka.

"Sorry, love," said a man's voice. There was a pause while someone dipped the headlights. Gallagher could now see the trailer on the back of the vehicle: a construction of red-painted plywood. It was a sleigh. The man slapped it proudly. "Glen Lightfoot from the Rotary Club, love."

"Huh?" said Anika.

"We're doing the rounds tonight."

Gallagher couldn't recall seeing one in years, but now he understood. The Rotary Club, the Lions, and other bunches of do-gooders would parade a Father Christmas around the streets, dispensing sweets and collecting money for charity.

"Raymond's supposed to be coming with us, but we've had the devil's own job trying to get hold of him today."

"I thought it was the Round Table sleigh thing tonight," said Anika.

"Bastards decided to do it on the same night as us," muttered Glen darkly. "But we'll outshine them. I'll crank the speakers up to ten."

"Oh, right. Well, you've found him now." Anika coughed lightly. "The thing is, Raymond's had quite a bit to drink today. A leaving do got out of hand."

"It wouldn't be the first time we've had a half-cut Santa on the sleigh," laughed the man, Glen. "Get him on board, we're late as it is."

"Be right with you!" called Anika. She stepped back into a huddle with Gallagher, Luka and Gillespie. "What do we do?"

"What else can we do?" said Luka. "Looks like he's going on the fucking sleigh."

"But he's dead!" said Gallagher in a muted squawk. Dead, but clearly not about to lie down.

"Here's what we'll do," said Anika. "Luka and Gallagher will lift him into place on the sleigh. Gillespie and I will sit either side of him. We're dressed as elves so we can blend in. All of us go round with the sleigh, then we get them to drop us back here when we're finished."

"How long this will take?" asked Luka.

Anika shrugged. "Couple of hours?"

"What the fuck are we doing?" squeaked Gallagher. Everyone else seemed to be acting so very matter-of-factly about the whole thing. Why was no one else terrified that they were handling a dead man very publicly in front of absolute bloody strangers.

Luka rolled his eyes. "Fucking Rotary club."

Anika frowned. "I think it's a good thing. It's what Raymond would have wanted. Like a farewell tour."

"Would have fucking *wanted*?" said Gallagher.

"No, is true," said Luka.

"You're all fucking mad."

69

CHARLOTTE

I t turned out that the big open area around the Santa Claus Village went on for some distance. The Finnish countryside around was, apart from the lines of trees, mostly flat, and thick snow covered it all.

Alejandro – fugitive, elf, pornographer, smuggler – rode in a straight line across the snow, turning only when forced to by lone trees or folds in the landscape. Charlotte merely had to follow his trail. His tracks threw up snowy spray and she squinted against it as she closed in on him.

"We've got company," yelled Jack over the thrumming roar of the engine.

"What?"

He brought a hand forward into her vision and then jerked it back.

Charlotte risked a backward glimpse. There were two snowmobiles coming after them. One seemed to be the snowmobile safari guide. She didn't look long enough to hazard a guess who the other one was.

It didn't matter. Their target was in sight.

Charlotte nudged closer. Alejandro's speed was erratic. Maybe he was blinded by the snow. Maybe he was unfamiliar with motorbike controls and wasn't keeping the throttle steady. Charlotte pulled to the side and started edging round him.

"Nowhere to run, Alejandro!" Jack hollered.

Alejandro glanced their way and gave an honest-to-God wordless yelp of alarm, like some cartoon character. Desperately he tried to steer away from them, but that reckless action, coupled with a slight rise in the terrain, was enough to tip him straight off. Charlotte throttled down and circled back to him.

Alejandro came to his feet. He was calf deep in snow, and fat clumps of it stuck to the fluffier parts of his elf outfit.

Charlotte braked to a halt, stalling her snowmobile.

"Back off!" yelled the evil elf. "I'll post it! I'll post it all to the internet!" He had his mobile phone held high.

"You have no distributor, no deal!" said Charlotte.

"Free porn for everyone then!" snarled Alejandro. There was a wild and unhinged look about him now, equal parts angry and afraid. He fiddled with his phone.

A snowball struck him in the chest, distracting him. Jack was off the snowmobile and already patting another snowball together. Charlotte didn't need asking twice. She jumped off, scooping up a mound of snow, and lobbed it at Alejandro. It caught his hip.

"Stop it!" he shouted.

Jack's follow up snowball knocked his beautiful elf hat off his head.

Charlotte ran forward, keeping low. Alejandro tried to step away but he was too slow. Charlotte came at him, arms wide for a rugby tackle.

"Motherfucking elf's going down, bitch!" she yelled and threw herself against his waist.

Alejandro, a skinny runt of a man, was taken back by her attack. He crumpled over her and the two of them went down into the snow. He kicked and wriggled, but she held on. There was snow in her eyes, and all she could sense were the clothes held in her grip. She kneed at him and tried to pull him closer.

Alejandro gargled and yelled. They tumbled together. Her foot slipped in the snow and they went down again. She lost her grip. When she'd righted herself, Alejandro was staggering drunkenly away.

Red-faced and covered in snow, he gave a sudden strangled gasp and looked at his hands. They were empty. He'd dropped his phone. As the other snowmobiles drew up, Alejandro pawed at the snow at his feet.

"Looking for something?" said Jack.

Charlotte looked over at him. Jack Hartigan had found Alejandro's phone in the snow.

"Mate," he said, grinning wearily. "You haven't even got any signal out here."

"*Fuck!*" the elf man screamed.

The snowmobiles came to a stop on either side of them. The snowmobile guide was swearing in Finnish. Or at least, language that passionate had to be swearing.

The other rider was the Finnish police officer, *Komissarie* Eskola. He walked towards Alejandro unhurriedly. There was nowhere for the man to run.

"I thought I told you two to stay out of harm's way," he said.

"Couldn't help ourselves," said Jack, grinning.

Eskola grunted. "Do you know what our Norwegian friends say about the British?"

"No," said Charlotte. "What?"

"They say British people aren't foreigners. They're just crazy Norwegians."

Charlotte gave this some thought and decided there were worse insults.

Eskola spun Alejandro around to handcuff him and read the elf his rights.

Charlotte approached Jack. He held the phone in his hand and, inside it, the SD card that could have caused them so much misery. He suddenly tutted.

"Problem?" said Charlotte.

He tugged at his coat pockets. "I've managed to lose all my salty liquorice."

She brushed snow off him, then put her hand to his cheek. "Such are the casualties of war," she said and pulled him down to kiss him.

70

GALLAGHER

The plan to put a dead Santa on the Rotary Club sleigh was insane. It was clearly bonkers. And yet, Gallagher couldn't help but notice, they were definitely doing it.

Anika called to Glen, the driver of the vehicle. "We're bringing him round. We'll need to sit with him, mind. And we'll need to keep the kids at arm's length."

"Yeah yeah, all good. Hop on board," said Glen.

The trailer had been transformed with a painted plywood canopy and fairy lights, and it had tiny bench seats facing both forwards and backwards.

Luka and Gallagher wrestled Raymond into place in the centre position.

"Is this safe?" asked Gillespie, squeezing in to sit on Santa Raymond's left side.

"Actually or legally?"

"It does not look very safe." said Luka. He and Gallagher

sat facing backwards, Anika wedged herself on Raymond's right.

The SUV pulled out of the car park. As it did so, Gallagher glanced back and, for a moment, thought he saw a white Mercedes coming out of the car park after them. Hedges got in the way before he could take a proper look. The SUV and trailer trundled into town.

"He'll need to wave and stuff, won't he?" said Gillespie, inclining his head towards Raymond.

Luka gave a grunt and dipped his hand into a pocket. He handed something to Gallagher.

"What?" Gallagher asked as he looked at the tiny piece of metal in his hand. "What am I doing with a screw-in hook?"

Luka rummaged through the rest of his pockets and eventually pulled out a length of string.

"Oh, I see," Gallagher said with numb fatalism. He reached overhead and screwed the hook into the canopy above Raymond's arm. Luka handed him the string and he threaded it over the hook, tied one end to the sleeve of Raymond's robe, and handed the other end to Anika. "Try that."

Anika wrapped the string around her hand and pulled. Raymond's arm rose in a limp facsimile of a wave. "Oh, that's not bad. Let me practise a bit more." She adjusted the length of the string by running another loop around her hand and tried a smoother, more natural wave.

"It's mad how good that looks," whispered Gillespie.

"So the way I see this working," said Anika, "when we get into town, Luka and Gallagher will get down and walk. You might need to go and rattle tins, collect some donations or whatever, but stay close in case we need you. Gillespie, you and I will interact with the kids. We mustn't let them get inside the sleigh. Tell them any lie you need to, just keep them out. Understand?"

Gillespie nodded. "Any lie I need to tell them. Got it."

The SUV pulled up near to the first of the residential streets. Several people in Rotary Club hi-vis jackets were waiting for them. The driver, Glen Lightfoot, came round to the trailer.

"Everyone all right back here?"

"Yep," said Gallagher, climbing down to block the line of sight between Glen and the deceased Santa on the back. "Want to give us some tins for collecting money?"

"Er, yeah. Sure." Gallagher and Luka were issued with tins and hi-vis vests.

"I'm turning on the music now," said Glen, "then we hit the first of the streets. Ready to go, Raymond?"

Anika gave the string a small pull and Raymond waved his arm.

"Great stuff," said Glen loudly. Then, as an aside to Gallagher and Luka, murmured, "The glazed look on his face! How much has he been drinking?"

"After today he'll probably not touch another drop," said Luka.

"Yeah?" said Glen. "We'll keep moving so the kids leave him be, shall we?"

After he climbed back into the driver's seat, a speaker on top of the sleigh started to honk out distorted versions of Christmas classics. It took Anika a moment or two to recognise John Lennon's *Merry Christmas, War is Over* played at full volume.

As soon as the music started, people began to line the street as the SUV trundled slowly forward. Luka and Gallagher walked on either side of the sleigh alongside other charity collectors, collecting coins in their tin and offering sweets from tins they'd also been given.

Anika waved Raymond's arm slowly from time to time, while she and Gillespie grinned widely and waved their own hands like lively elves.

The streets on the new estates were easy for the sleigh to navigate. The driver kept to the crescents and through roads, so that he could drive slowly and keep going.

71

ANIKA

Despite the gut-clenching horror of doing a charity Santa ride with a deceased Saint Nick, Anika started to relax into the routine. There were the occasional parents who really wanted their children to approach Santa, but Anika helped fend them off with gentle words. After Gillespie told a family that Santa had tuberculosis, Anika sighed and retracted her former statement.

"Gillespie, I was wrong. You may not tell *any* lie. If we get some sort of medical SWAT team descending on us, what will we do then?"

"Dunno."

Anika pointed at a man and woman on the corner of a street. "Newspaper reporters," she said.

"Are you sure?" said Gillespie.

"Joe and Kitty from the Three Counties Echo. Trust me, I know."

Only last week the Three Counties Echo had published a picture of Anika handing a charity cheque to a local church minister, with seemingly little concern for the fact that the giant novelty cheque covered up so much of the skimpy outfit Anika was wearing at the time she appeared to be using it to cover her nakedness.

"We only want them to be writing a good story about this event. Or even better, no story at all."

Gillespie nodded in understanding.

One of the charity collectors approached the trailer.

"We've got London Road next," she said. "Best keep weight on the trailer to a minimum."

As the SUV turned the corner, Anika understood. In a town with very few steep hills, London Road was perhaps the steepest of them all. From the park by the town's tiny and sluggish river, it ran up to the edge of town and out, presumably in the general direction of the nation's capital.

Gillespie seemed to have the Raymond watching duties under control, so Anika decided to check on Gallagher and Luka, and generally keep the public at a respectful distance.

"Gillespie, don't let him fall, eh?"

Gillespie nodded. "I've got this." He put his arm around Raymond's shoulders.

Anika jumped off the sleigh. Numerous families were gathered at the bottom of the hill by the park railings. Anika recognised Marcus and Maremba Stone and, in front of them, dressed in warm scarves, were Karen's kids, Ron and Hermione.

"Hello again," she said to Karen's parents-in-law (or ex-parents-in-law or whatever the correct terminology was). "I thought I would come and say hi to Ron and Hermione. Is Karen around?"

"I expect she'll be along very soon," said Marcus. "We do like to try and be as flexible as we can with Karen and her time management."

Anika frowned slightly at his tone, but turned to Ron and Hermione. "Santa on his sleigh gave you a special wave, did you see?"

Hermione looked up from her notepad on which she'd made copious notes.

"I saw him wave," she said. "It looked like the same wave he gave everyone else, so I'm not certain I'd say it was special."

"It was," said Anika. "I pointed you out to him and said you needed a special one and he agreed."

Maremba gave her a sceptical glance.

"I don't have many special powers as an elf, but that's one of them. I can also distribute sweets." She held out her hand, and both Ron and Hermione were suddenly much more interested.

"Belief in mystical powers," said Maremba. "You should write that down, Ron. Animistic practices among urban people."

"Someone is handing out sweets," said Ron, hopefully.

"Yes," noted Marcus. "Maremba and I will collect some for your photographic study of the event while you finish noting your first impressions."

"Or they could just eat the sweets," suggested Anika.

Marcus and Maremba looked at her like she was quite mad, then apparently went to get some sweeties for research purposes, leaving the children there. Anika shook herself. What could she do? There were no quick fixes for some families, and she had to catch up with the Santa sleigh trailer as it laboured up the London Road hill.

72

GALLAGHER

Despite the insanity of the situation, Gallagher found he was starting to enjoy his role with the Santa sleigh. As he strode the streets collecting coins from people, he found it genuinely uplifting to see how excited the children were when they piled out into the street, often wearing a coat over their pyjamas, to see Santa go past on his magical sleigh.

"Mate, this is a beautiful thing!" he said to Luka.

"What is?" Luka called back to him.

Gallagher spread his arms wide to indicate absolutely everything, collecting tin in one hand, sweetie tin in the other. "This! How come I never knew?"

"Is pretty nice, yeah," agreed Luka.

Gallagher rattled his tin. He'd seen some people slip folded-up paper money in there, while others came armed with a giant tin of low denomination coins they'd saved – then took forever trying to coax them through the small slot.

It was all good, although the amount of money definitely didn't always match the apparent prosperity of the houses they passed. He was certain the best donations were coming from the smaller terraced houses as they approached the centre of the town.

The SUV, already moving at little more than a crawl, slowed to a stop. There was a vehicle coming down London Road, effectively blocking their path. For an instant, Gallagher though he was staring into a mirror, but no, it was another SUV towing another makeshift Santa sleigh trailer.

"It's the bloody Round Table," muttered one of the collecting women.

"They know this is our route," said another.

Glen in the SUV noisily put on the handbrake and got out to remonstrate with the Santa sleigh blocking his path. On the back of the other trailer, the Santa stood. Gallagher peered hard into the dark. It was Santa Seamus. Seamus was waving merrily to all and sundry, taking this pause to get up close and friendly with the locals.

Gallagher glanced back at their own trailer. Gillespie, a smile frozen unconvincingly on his face, operated Santa Raymond's waving hand, more than likely praying no one came too close. Gallagher and Luka were on opposite sides of the trailer with the towbar between them.

"We'd best go defend Santa—" Luka began, then pointed past Gallagher, eyes wide.

Gallagher turned. On this hill, between every five or six houses, were entryways that went round to the back. These led to an access road which ran between the properties' backyards. The kind of place where people left their wheelie bins and such. But in the entryway of the one directly behind Gallagher it was not bins, but a white Mercedes car, its headlights on full beam. And it was accelerating hard, coming straight at Gallagher.

And he'd been having such a lovely evening.

From somewhere, he found the gumption to move. He half stumbled, half jumped over the towbar and the front end of the trailer, just as the Mercedes rammed into it. The trailer jolted violently. With a yelp, Gillespie toppled from his position beside dead Santa Raymond and off the trailer.

The SUV had barely moved, though the barrelling Mercedes had crumpled against the rear end of the bigger vehicle.

Heart pounding, Gallagher stumbled to his feet. Luka reached out to help him. There were shouts and gasps from the local on-lookers. The spectacle of a slightly tacky Santa sleigh touring the town had just taken a turn for the dramatic.

The Mercedes' driver door opened and a woman pulled herself out.

"Sonia Patterson!" said Gallagher. "I fucking knew it!"

"Sonia Patterson who put our heads in torture vice?" said Luka.

"Yes!" said Gallagher. "Whenever I say Sonia Patterson, assume that's the woman I'm talking about!"

Sonia shook herself, leaning on the door, and glared at Gallagher. "Why won't you fucking die?" she snarled.

"This?" said Luka, confused. "This was assassination attempt?"

Gallagher patted his friend. "And the other stuff, mate.

The barbecue, the pot-alanche. It was..." He screwed up his face. "Why? Sonia? We don't owe you anything anymore."

"There's what you took from me!" she spat.

"Us?"

"Snømann won't return my calls. I can't keep up the mortgage payments. My boy – my beautiful boy—! William is applying for sole custody. Can you imagine?!"

Luka shrugged. "We do not know this William."

The towbar of the trailer, bent out of true by the Mercedes stood between them. Sonia climbed up onto the very front end of the trailer to get at them.

"And you two!" she hissed. "Grinning like happy idiots."

"I am far from happy," said Gallagher honestly.

"I saw you! Saw you! Just now!"

"Oh, well, caught up in the moment..."

Sonia stood on the trailer towbar, looming over them like a crazed avenger. "You don't deserve happiness when I have none!"

"Listen, lady," said Luka, holding out two calming hands. "Life must seem terrible for you right now. It can be tough. And this William character – he sounds like a complete douche-bag. But I have had similar experiences in my own life which I think you will find most relevant. I was in Gdansk at the time and—"

What had happened in Gdansk was never revealed, for at that moment, the buckled towbar shifted beneath Sonia's feet, the front end of the Mercedes gave a groan, and the trailer came loose from the SUV.

It started to roll backwards. Sonia stumbled and fell onto the trailer, gripping tight as it accelerated down London

Road. Santa Raymond still sat in the rear of the plywood sleigh, unsupported and lolling about.

"Oh God!" yelled a member of the public.

"Runaway sleigh," yelled another.

Gallagher watched Sonia Patterson's expression of wide-eyed shock as she was carried away.

73

ANIKA

Anika had switched into elf mode as she walked up the hill to catch up with the sleigh. She had capered and sung along with the tunes from the loudspeaker, while high-fiving any children that she passed. She'd just started to join in with *Last Christmas* when there was a collision up the road. Anika couldn't see exactly what had happened, but it was clear from the loud bang some catastrophe had occurred. That and the loudspeaker going silent. Her singing petered out as she tried to make sense of what was going on.

There were some horrible, metallic scraping noises, then the sleigh-trailer slid past her at speed, rebounding and scraping off parked cars as it went. Santa Raymond bounced around on the rear. His arms flapped wildly from side to side, like one of those giant air-powered floppy characters outside carpet shops and car dealerships. There was also a woman clinging onto the trailing front end for dear life.

People screamed in panic and pulled their loved ones away from the side of the road. Luka, Gallagher and Gillespie were running down the slope with no hope of catching the escaped trailer.

Anika looked to the bottom of the hill.

"Oh, shit!"

As the sleigh had driven on up the hill, the crowds had either moved with it or dispersed, but down at the bottom, by the railings in front of the park, were two children. Ron and Hermione stood together and alone in the path of a half-ton of metal and painted plywood.

She shouted at them, but they were only staring in dumbfounded surprise.

The sleigh should have just run into and obliterated them, but a pothole made it bounce and swerve into a parked car. It tilted and spun. As Anika watched, the body of Santa Raymond was flung clear and he whirled, legs and arms out like a Santa-sized street sweeper. With unholy accuracy he flew at the children. Raymond swept Ron and Hermione across the pavement, rolling around them like a big red cushion. A split second later, the wrecked trailer cartwheeled across the space where the children had just stood, powered straight on through the railings and into the park.

Anika, heart in mouth, ran down to the children.

There was a high scream. Maremba and Marcus Stone were rushing over to their grandchildren. Before they reached them, Ron was sitting up in a daze. With a groan, young Hermione pushed herself up too, and stepped away from dead Santa Raymond.

Maremba swept the children into her arms. "I'm so sorry, babies. I'm so sorry. Are you hurt? Are you hurt?"

Anika spotted Karen forcing her way through the crowd. "Oh, God! Kids!"

"Over here!" Anika yelled.

Marcus was feeling the children over as though he could somehow detect bone fractures through touch alone. "Tell us where it hurts," he was saying.

Hermione and Ron were breathing hard, still stunned, but as they shared a look it seemed to confirm that, despite the immediate carnage around them, they were actually fine.

Karen swept them up into her arms and hugged them.

They looked round at Santa Raymond. Anika's mouth leapt into action.

"Oh, no. I think Santa might be hurt," she said in a wooden voice. "He's a hero though. Did you see how he saved those kids?" She waved Luka and Gallagher over. "Guys! Guys! Please come and check on Santa! See if he's hurt."

Luka threw out a hand. "He is dead."

"Or—" said Anika with laboured emphasis "—you could check on this injured man and see if he is dead or not. I do hope he isn't. He saved these children."

Gallagher was the first to get on board with her thinking. "I saw it! I saw everything! He jumped clear so he could get those kids out of the way. Man's a hero."

"Santa saved us," said Hermione, breathless.

Karen looked over towards Santa Raymond sprawled on the floor. Anika saw her hopeful expression and shook her head.

"Let's go home, eh, kids?" said Karen, steering them away.

74

CHARLOTTE

"Final call for passengers on Ryanair flight FR452 to London Stansted," said the announcement at Helsinki airport.

Charlotte showed the boarding pass on her phone to the gate attendant, then followed Jack down the sloping corridor to the tarmac and their waiting plane. For the umpteenth time, she went to her pocket and checked the little SD card was still there.

"Still got that?" said Jack, speaking above the engine whine as they walked to the plane.

"What should I do with it?" she said.

"You should have thrown it into a bin at any point in the last three hours."

"And have someone find it?"

He chuckled. "Snap it in half then, and flush it out of the airplane toilet at fifteen thousand feet."

"This is more than just our two videos," she said. "This is a whole series of movies."

"Ah," he nodded. "You feel Alejandro's cinematic endeavours are generally worth preservation?"

"Hey, I'm not judging people who like to watch a bit of Santa on Santa action. Everyone's got their kinks. I just don't want people watching *my* Santa doing unspeakable things in *my* grotto."

They climbed the ladder and entered the plane. They moved between the yellow and blue rows to find their own seats.

"Do you remember when we met Alejandro—" he counted on his fingers "—three days ago? When we met him – when you literally dragged me over to him – you thought he just had a video of my Santa, Seamus, and you were delighted. You would have pressed 'send' right then and posted it to the internet."

She thought about arguing, but it would be an obvious lie. "I think I would have, yes. I think I would have been delighted by the mere possibility.

"Why?" he said. "Why would we do that to each other?"

She sat back in her narrow chair and thought, making noisy thoughtful sounds as she did so. "I don't think I liked you," she said honestly. "I'm not sure I've got more than that."

He nodded slowly. "Why? Why didn't you like me?"

She shrugged. "You're the enemy, the competition. It seems that everything we try to do at Hedgelord, you try and beat or undermine with your efforts at Bloomers."

"We work in retail. Competition is kind of the key."

"Yes," she agreed, "but you also come across as—" she screwed up her face "—smug and unbearably chipper, too."

He smiled. "By unbearably chipper, do you mean happy and friendly?"

"Yes, but don't forget the smug bit."

"You mean confident?"

"I mean arrogant."

"You mean I know what I'm doing."

"I mean you *know* you know what you're doing. You would lord it over us mere struggling humans at every opportunity."

"Huh." He seemed genuinely surprised by that. "I will work on that. And yet..." He adjusted his hand to take hold of hers on the narrow armrest between them. "...something happened between us."

"Let's not over-analyse," she said. And she meant it. She feared that if they looked too closely at what had suddenly blossomed between them in the last few days, especially in the hotel room in Stockholm, then that lovely magical thing might explode into nothingness under the scrutiny.

"Do you still think I'm smug and arrogant and overbearing."

"I didn't say overbearing." She turned in her seat to look at him. Fuck he was good looking, she thought, and in thinking that recognised, as much as her cynical soul was capable of falling in love with someone, right now she was halfway down the path to falling hard for one Jack Hartigan. "I think you are a very confident man, with a very positive outlook and I, Charlotte Mitchell, absolutely felt threatened by your upbeat, confident and hard-working manner."

"Oh," he said, nodding. "If it helps, I've always felt I've had to play catch-up with your tireless, intelligent and passionate attitude to your work."

She too nodded. "Intelligent."

"And passionate."

"Which is code for angry and sweary?"

"On occasion."

She squeezed his hand. "I think we've seen each other at our most vulnerable this week."

He smiled. "Ah, catch a man just after his girlfriend dumped him..."

"In Paris."

"In Paris, no less."

"Any messages from Kathryn?"

He started to reach for his phone, then stopped. "What would it matter if there were? That's over."

She wrinkled her nose, uncertain. "We're going back to the real world now. Let's not pretend this – *this* thing – is the new normal."

He leaned over and kissed her. "We can make it the new normal."

"Uh-huh?" she said.

"You don't think?"

"I mean, when you said that it sounded super cheesy, but yes, okay." She put her hand to her pocket where her phone was and thought about her own messages. "You know ... it's the Hedgelord staff Christmas party tonight. In about ... three hours' time."

"Ah, you'll just miss that."

"Miss the start," she said. "Plenty of time to catch the tail end." She leaned over and kissed him back. "We could publicly road-test this new normal of ours."

For once, Jack Hartigan looked actually scared. "You and me ... walking into the lion's den? Like, hand in hand?"

"Embarrassed to be with me?" she joked.

"More worried I'll be torn limb from limb. Or that Cameron Clasp will go get his hunting rifle."

"Oh, I'll protect you," she said, putting her head on his shoulder as the cabin crew began their announcements.

"Be sure that you do," he replied and laid his head on top of hers.

75

ANIKA

Clearing up the mess from the Santa trailer disaster was not a quick process. Although Karen had spirited her children away swiftly, and Gallagher, Luka and Gillespie were only too happy to melt into the shadows now that their Santa-watching duties were definitely concluded, Anika could not bring herself to leave the scene just yet.

Ambulances had arrived and taken away the two casualties. Santa Raymond was swiftly covered up and taken away in one ambulance, the woman who had driven into the trailer and then unwisely clung to it as it careened down the hill in another. It was a miracle that no further people had been hurt.

Nonetheless, with the dead Santa being a Hedgelord employee, and the local newspaper reporters hovering close – with an actual news story in front of them! – Anika felt her newfound sense of managerial responsibility meant she should help put the most positive, pro-Hedgelord spin on matters.

The crashed Mercedes and Glen Lightfoot's SUV were going to require some brute force to separate. The Round Table Santa sleigh at the top of the hill was therefore unable to continue with its chosen route. That didn't stop the amiable and attention-seeking Santa Seamus, who simply hopped off his trailer and wandered down London Road, giving out waves, hugs and selfies to any who wanted them.

In a sane world, the children and families crowded along London Road might have been too traumatised by the trailer accident to give another Santa the time of day. But the truth was almost everyone recognised they had just witnessed an astonishing event – a terrible one, but astonishing nonetheless – which meant this would most likely be one of the most memorable Christmases of their lives. In short, an extra Santa on top of the carnage was just cementing it in many minds as possibly the best Christmas ever.

Anika heard one astute child ask Santa Seamus how it was possible that Santa died saving those children, yet here he was again, live and in the flesh.

"No one can kill Santa!" exclaimed Seamus, clutching his big belly in mirth. "If Santa ever dies, he just pops back to life like that – you know the one – Obi Wan Kenobi. Or is it Gandalf?"

Anika wasn't sure how strong Seamus's grasp was on notions of resurrection, Santa mythology, or indeed popular film franchises, but the answer seemed to appease the children, and Seamus continued to do a good job of generally holding people's attention while emergency workers dealt with trashed trailers, ruined railings, and the unfortunate human debris of the incident.

Anika abruptly found Joe, the Three Counties Echo reporter at her side.

"You're Anika Chowdhry, aren't you?" he said. "You were in the paper last week."

"Fully clothed now, you notice," said Anika quickly, indicating her normal elf attire.

Joe gestured round as photographer Kitty snapped pictures with her camera. "Ah, so this is a Hedgelord charity drive and a Hedgelord trailer at the centre of the accident?"

"Not at all, Joe," said Anika. "It is conceivable that Hedgelord employees such as myself might want to devote our time to charity events outside the workplace. We're a caring bunch like that. This charity event, the trailer and the vehicle towing it, are all from the local Rotary Club, and I think we all saw the accident was caused by a third party driving into the side of the trailer."

"But the Santa on the trailer, possibly killed in the accident, he was a Hedgelord employee?"

"Ex-employee," said Anika, mindful of Charlotte's instructions. "He no longer works – worked? – no longer *had worked* for Hedgelord at the time of the accident."

"I see. So, going forward, who is the Santa at Hedgelord?"

Just then, sweeping in with an arm around Anika's shoulder, as though he'd been waiting for his cue, Santa Seamus beamed at the journalist. "I am glad to say that Anika here has asked me to step in and take on the Santa Claus position at Hedgelord."

"Er, I have," said Anika. "We have done that."

"Santa Raymond," continued Seamus, "dear departed Ray-Ray, was a wonderful Santa. His body of work speaks for itself. He had something inside him, a need to care, a hole which he filled with love and smiles. A remarkable capacity for entertainment. It's a legacy I hope to continue."

"Can we quote you on that?" said Joe.

"Please do," said Seamus before Anika could agree. "As the most famous Santa for some miles around," he went on, "I think it's a challenge that I must accept. Those who've seen me at work know the joy I take in my work. I give a hundred and ten percent. And I am going to bring some of that same unique magic and charm to the grotto at Hedgelord. Watch out, Seamus is about!"

Kitty had come in with camera already raised. Seamus squeezed Anika's shoulder. Anika put on a grin and a silly elf pose as Kitty took photos of her and their new Santa.

Seamus waved his hand as though painting out a news headline. "Amidst trailer tragedy Super Santa Seamus vows to keep Christmas magic alive! How's that for you?"

"We'll come up with our headlines," said Joe, then consulted with Kitty. "Yeah, we'll run with that."

There was a whoop-whoop of sirens as a fire engine turned up. Anika wasn't sure why a fire engine was needed, unless they were here to cut the two crashed vehicles apart. Whatever the case, the local residents clapped and cheered as their Christmas evening just got better and better.

76

GALLAGHER

Gallagher had concluded that after the day he'd had – after the *whole damned week* he'd had – tonight was a night for drinking. And if there was one element of the Hedgelord staff party that Cameron Clasp had got right, it was the free bar set up in the Pagoda Café for the partying staff members.

Gallagher finished off his fourth can of imported lager and tossed it into the bin.

Around him, the whole workforce of cashiers, shelf-stackers, warehouse men, caterers, cleaners, pet shop attendants and office staff enjoyed free booze, a hired karaoke system, and generally managed to ignore the fact that they were spending even more time in their workplace than they normally would.

Luka had also sunk several pints and looked like he was in a good mood. He caught Gallagher's eye and mimed smoking a joint.

Gallagher nodded firmly.

Luka pointed questioningly towards the door leading to the outside and their beloved sheds.

Another nod from Gallagher and they made separately for the café exit.

"Man, I need to get wasted," Gallagher said as they teamed up.

Luka nodded. "Dead guys, bad guys. I tell you, friend, I have worked harder this week than I am used to."

"Amen, brother."

At the threshold of the café exit, Cameron appeared and flung an arm around each of them. "Guys! My favourite buddies!"

"Hey boss," said Luka.

"Tsk, not tonight," Cameron said with a withering face. "Tonight I am not your boss."

"Oh?"

"I am just like you. Please accept me as a plantyman." He accompanied the word 'plantyman' with a strange wiggle of a dance.

"Plantyman?" Gallagher asked, imitating the moves.

"You've got it!" hollered Cameron, coming in for a hug. As he was locked in the embrace, Gallagher gestured to Luka over his shoulder. "I think he's very drunk!" he mouthed.

Luka nodded.

"We gonna do karaoke?" Cameron asked. "We got the dance routine down already like the ... that band." He did a fresh wiggle.

"Bananarama?" said Luka.

"Spice Girls?" said Gallagher.

"Yes! Them!" agreed Cameron. "Karaoke boys doing their best rendition of *Sound of the Underground*."

Gallagher looked at Luka in horror. It sounded like a bit of a stretch for someone who normally did Blur's *Song 2* because it was a very short song where the words were nearly all shouting.

"Sure thing, Cameron," said Luka. He leaned over to whisper to Gallagher. "Will be fine. He will pass out first. Then we smoke."

It turned out that Cameron's enthusiasm for karaoke helped him to power through his inebriation. The three of them took their places at the front of the crowd as the music started. Gallagher had only a vague recollection of the Girls Aloud song. It turned out Luka had none. If Gallagher had hoped Cameron might actually know the words then he was sadly mistaken.

Daffyd, self-appointed master of ceremonies waved a hand as the song drew to a close. "Ladies and gentlemen, let's hear it for Cameron, Luka and Gallagher. If you don't want to hear them sing again then please come sign up."

Apparently Cameron had not endured enough public embarrassment on stage. "Do ya think I'm Sexy?" he yelled.

"You're not bad," replied Luka into his microphone, without missing a beat.

The Rod Stewart song started and the three of them engaged in as much drunken smouldering and hip swivelling as they could muster while staying upright. At least Gallagher was happy he knew the words to this one.

77

ANIKA

Anika jogged into Hedgelord. From the Santa sleigh crash scene, back home for a quick change into some actually sensible clothes, then to Hedgelord (her dad for once insisting on giving his 'manager daughter' a lift to the 'work event), Anika had been moving non-stop. Only as she entered the shop and saw the disco lights and heard the throbbing music coming from the café, did she actually slow down and catch her breath.

She went into the Pagoda Café, gave a cursory nod to Luka and Gallagher who were singing at the top of their lungs on the little karaoke stage, and sought out a glass of fizzy plonk from the free bar.

"Thought Muslims didn't drink," said Jill the elf.

"A) not a Muslim," said Anika, "but thanks for showing an interest. And b) the day I've just had would be enough to make anyone drink."

She downed the glass, picked up another, and wandered round the café until she came across Sophie and Karen.

"Those poor children!" whispered Sophie, eyes wide. "What a thing to happen. Amazing that Santa Raymond was able to save them like that."

"I know. The man died a hero," said Karen.

Anika slotted straight into the conversation. "That he did," she said firmly. "He died at that point, saving the children. Very noble." She frowned. "What are you two doing here?"

"Charming," said Karen. "Can't we enjoy a night out?"

"I meant, aren't you at home with the kids? After that shock?"

Karen smiled. "My mum's looking after them. The kids are bouncing already. Seriously, I've never known them get excited by those 'what I did during the holidays' homework assignment. And I've certainly never seen them make a start before the holidays actually begin."

"Really? 'The day I was snatched from the jaws of death by a flying Santa'?"

Karen considered it, nodding. "Pretty much. But I'm sure Hermione's already thinking ahead to the book deal and Netflix adaptation."

"And you," Anika said to Sophie. "I thought tonight was the big date night."

"It is," said Sophie.

"Well?"

"He's coming here," she said.

Anika looked at Karen. Karen seemed unfussed.

"This the big date with tall handsome businessman?" said Anika. "And you thought you'd bringing him to this—" She couldn't quite find the words to describe the party scene around them, in which noise and alcohol and sheer energy were trying hard to compensate for anything resembling style or class. "—this event?"

"Well," said Sophie, "he's here to look at me, not the surroundings."

Karen grinned. "Is that a bit of sassy attitude there, Soph?"

"I may have had a couple of fortifying gin and tonics already," she said.

"Well now we're all going to let our hair down on the company's dime," said Karen. "Let no drink go undrunk. We'll look out for your man when he arrives, eh?"

Sophie's phone gave a loud beep and she dug it out of her handbag. "He's already here."

"Excellent," said Karen.

However, when Karen and Anika began to follow Sophie to the main entrance, the older woman put a hand up to stop them.

"I will go meet him and then bring him in," she said. "Don't want you two gooseberries frightening him off." She headed out.

"So, what do you reckon he looks like?" said Karen, passing Anika a fresh glass of fizz.

"You mean, do I think he'll have a surprising resemblance to her dead dog Douglas."

Karen snorted and jiggled her head in amused

agreement. "Dead dog Douglas. Try saying that three times fast while drunk."

"I'd need to be drunk first," said Anika.

Karen lifted a finger under the base of Anika's glass to indicate such things could be easily remedied.

78

CHARLOTTE

The taxi had driven them straight from the airport. Charlotte made sure she kept the receipt. It might have been a considerable drive, but it wasn't the biggest expense she was going to try and get Cameron to sign off from this week.

Jack shut the taxi door and looked across the dark car park at the Hedgelord building. "Enemy territory," he said.

Charlotte grunted with laughter. "Hedgelord, Bloomers. I think we can agree that it's all the same really."

He stuck out his elbow to offer her his arm. "A bold statement."

"You know it's true."

They walked slowly towards the entrance.

There was a man and a woman outside, standing close together talking. Charlotte recognised Sophie who worked in the garden centre café.

"Evening, Sophie," she said.

Sophie turned. "Oh – Charlotte. Back from your training?"

"Training, yes," said Charlotte. "Exactly that." She felt compelled to say something about the man on her arm. "This is Jack, my date for the evening."

Sophie gave Jack a brief moment of scrutiny. "Have we met before?"

"Almost certainly," he said.

Sophie nodded, then gestured at the tall, older gentleman with her. "And this is Marti, my date for the evening."

"Welcome to Hedgelord," said Charlotte.

Marti gave a casual wave. "I like it here very much," he said.

Charlotte steered Jack inside. "That's how we do it," she said.

"Do what?" said Jack.

"Introduce you to everyone, one person at a time."

"You are nervous about this?" said Jack, apparently surprised.

"A little. Yes."

The interior of the garden centre shop was mostly unlit, but there was a powerful disco vibe and the most godawful singing coming from the Pagoda Café. Charlotte saw there were two women looking their way: Karen Woodbine and Anika Chowdhry, both wearing expressions of first disappointment and then confusion.

Anika scuttled over.

"Anika, hi," said Charlotte. "I hope everyone's been able to cope this week."

"You've brought Jack to the Christmas party," said Anika, like it was most unlikely thing imaginable.

"Yes, I have," said Charlotte. "Jack and I have been, um, working together for the past few days."

"Yes. Well, I don't know if you know, but I was sitting in on that phone call."

"What phone call?" said Jack.

"The, er, one from the hotel in Sweden," said Anika. "You know..." She looked like she was about to raise her hands to do a mime, then held them deliberately down to her sides.

"Oh, fuck," said Charlotte.

"Well, quite," said Anika. "Listen, Cameron heard it all too, and I don't know what he'll think if—"

She was cut off by a loud voice coming over the karaoke PA system. "Oh hello! Do you see what I see?" shouted Cameron drunkenly. "It's only the happy couple back from their Scandi sex tour!"

Dozens of eyes turned to them.

"Three cheers for the shaggy couple, Charlotte and Jack!"

Someone wrestled the microphone from Cameron. He tried to fight back, but alcohol had robbed him of co-ordination and strength.

Still the eyes stared.

Charlotte swallowed noisily.

"Just smile and wave," said Jack out of the corner of his mouth and did just that.

Charlotte woodenly joined in. "Was this a horrible idea?" she whispered back out of the corner of her own mouth.

"It's not the most embarrassing thing to happen to either of us this week," he replied.

On the little karaoke stage, Daffyd had gained permanent control of the microphone. "Thanks for such an amazing performance from Cameron and his backing singers," he shouted.

"I'm no backing singer," complained Luka as the three of them stumbled from the stage.

"It will take a brave act to follow that, I'm sure you'll agree, ladies and gentlemen," said Daffyd. "So now I'd like to invite to the stage a man who claims that anything I can do, he can do better: Tom Eccles!"

Sales manager Tom nearly choked on the beer he was drinking. "What?"

"And together he and I will sing Whitney Houston's *I Will Always Love You*. Unless he's too much of a coward and can't."

Suddenly all of those eyes were now on Tom.

"And like that, attention moves onto the next thing," said Jack, sighing happily.

"Good, good," said Charlotte, realising she had been holding her breath. "Anika, thank you so much for all you've done this week. Tell me, Santa Raymond..."

"Yes?"

"...Is he gone?"

Anika seemed to take a moment to find the words. "Yes. Yes, he's definitely gone. Never coming back. Bit of a convoluted story there, and I think I've sourced a new Santa for the grotto."

"Good, good. We can sort out the details in the morning."

The video files were safely in Charlotte's pocket and Santa Raymond had been given his marching orders. Jack would need to decide what to do about Bloomers' Santa Seamus, but that was their problem.

"Right now, I'd say we need a drink," said Charlotte.

"A good idea," said Jack.

On stage, Tom and Daffyd began a wobbly duet.

Jack found them a table while Charlotte went to get drinks. She picked up two bottled beers and searched around for a bottle opener.

"It's good to have you back," said Karen, who was looking for a bottle of wine which still had some wine in the bottom.

"It's good to be back," said Charlotte.

"And you'll be pleased to hear we've had almost no accidents this week at Hedgelord."

"Almost none? That must be some kind of record."

"No one injured. No one died."

"That's the main goal of any garden centre, surely. Zero fatalities."

Karen leaned in closer to whisper in what she, somewhat tipsily, thought was a conspiratorial manner. "You with him now?" She was nodding unsubtly towards Jack.

"Let's see, shall we?" said Charlotte.

"But I thought he had a girlfriend."

"Kathryn."

"Right. Kathryn. So are you two having a secret, you know, fling?"

"Nothing like that, though it's none of your business. Jack isn't the cheating kind, is he?"

"Oh, oh, right." Karen resumed her search for wine.

Charlotte looked over to where Jack was waiting for her and wondered whether this might indeed be the start of something. The journey back from Lapland had been a much more pleasant experience than the outbound trip – mainly because she and Jack were enjoying the heady exhilaration of constantly thinking about what they would be doing when they were alone together.

They had both agreed to go home and get a good night's sleep, but she strongly suspected they might find an excuse to delay that for a couple of hours, after tonight's party.

How did she feel about him, bedroom antics aside? She had to admit that he had been good company over the last few days. He'd been thoughtful in all of the right ways, and he had a knack for defusing her blow-ups. She tried not to get carried away with herself, but she dared to imagine they might function well as a couple.

79

GALLAGHER

Gallagher found himself arm in arm with Cameron and Luka.

On the stage, Daffyd and Tom took deep breaths before launching into the walloping climactic chorus of *I Will Always Love You*. Neither hit the high notes properly, though neither seemed to care.

Cameron had somehow managed to steer them over to the table where Jack Hartigan was sitting. He slid, chuckling, into the seat opposite Jack.

"Here he is! The dirty, dirty dog!"

"Hello, Cameron," said Jack. "Gentlemen," he nodded to Luka and Gallagher.

"I didn't know the pair of you had it in you!"

"What?" said Jack. "Oh, the sex. Yes. Yes, both Charlotte and I are physically capable of having sex. Thank you for noticing and bringing it to everyone's attention."

Cameron nudged Luka. "I was on the phone with

Maremba and Marcus when you'd butt-dialled us from your bed. A real booty call."

"You were listening to them having sex?" said Luka.

"Not in a creepy way," said Cameron. "Very much a fun way. The noises they were making ... Marcus and Maremba seriously thought Charlotte had kidnapped their young buck here. Instead there they were, banging each other's ruddy brains out!"

"Lovely," said Gallagher faintly, not sure he needed to hear about other people's sex lives, especially when he didn't really have one to speak of.

Cameron leaned across the table. "Tell me something. I have to know."

"We don't have to interrogate the man," said Gallagher.

"Is it a wig?" said Cameron.

"Pardon?" said Jack.

"Marcus Stone. His hair. It's a rug, right?"

"Oh!" said Jack, apparently understanding. "Yes, I think so."

Cameron thumped the table. "I knew it!"

"No man has hair like that naturally," said Jack. "I haven't seen it come off, but I reckon so."

"A bloody rug!" Cameron guffawed. He reached over and patted Jack's hands. "I won't tell them you told me. I'm the soul of discretion, you know."

Gallagher spotted Charlotte coming back with beers. "Come on, mate," he said to Cameron. "Time to dish out those quality presents you bought everyone, yeah?"

Cameron stared in happy surprise. "Presents! I almost forgot! Mugs for everyone!" He stumbled to his feet.

Charlotte gave the three men a querying look as Luka and Gallagher led Cameron away. Gallagher rolled his eyes in reply, realising he'd very much been lumbered with the Cameron-watching duty.

As Charlotte slid in next to Jack, Gallagher thought it was weird to see the two event managers sitting together. They did seem to have that weird love/hate vibe between them. They looked as if they were either preparing for a bare knuckle boxing match after the party, or a shagging marathon. He really couldn't tell which, but that probably said a lot about what he knew of people.

"Presents!" yelled Cameron.

He lurched onto the stage where Daffyd and Tom, buzzed up by their singing efforts, were discussing what they might try next.

"Everybody!" said Cameron into the mic. "I don't want to stop the fun, but it's time to offer a few small gifts to show you all how valued you are. I have my two glamorous assistants to help me. You've heard their voices, now please appreciate their nimble gift-finding skills!"

There was applause for Luka and Gallagher as they fetched the sacks Cameron was pointing to and pulled wrapped gifts out as he instructed.

Gallagher picked out some of the boxes, remembering the dreadful mugs Cameron had ordered, using those unnaturally stretched photos from the staff ID badges. He smiled to himself, wondering how they would be received.

Cameron called people over to receive their gifts. As Gallagher watched, they were all smiles as they took their boxes, but their expressions changed – from mild disappointment to utter horror – when they sat back down and unwrapped them, depending on how badly their face had fared. He wondered how many of the mugs would make it through to tomorrow morning.

"Oh, now here's Karen's gift," said Cameron.

Karen came up and smiled warily at Cameron. Gallagher thought maybe she'd seen some of the other mugs.

"Karen, I heard about your experience earlier," said Cameron, giving her an awkward embrace. "I do hope that you and your young 'uns are all well?"

"We are, thanks," said Karen. "What a thing to happen, eh?"

"Were Marcus and Maremba shaken by it too?" asked Cameron. Gallagher thought he looked a little too hopeful.

"Yeah, they were." She tilted her head towards where Jack and Charlotte sat. "You were talking to Jack a while. What's the deal there?"

Cameron paused for a long moment. "Well, I was asking about the old, you know..." He pointed vaguely at his own head. "The rug thing. But that's all cleared up. And, yeah, as I understand it, he's on a promise tonight." He leered and winked.

"With his girlfriend, you mean?"

Cameron looked at the couple. "Really?"

"He's a one-woman guy. Charlotte said."

"Well, whatever, I think they're clearly in love."

Karen took her gift from Cameron. "Thank you for the present."

While Cameron felt around in his sack for the next gift, Luka unwrapped his mug.

"What the fuck is this?" he said to Gallagher. "I look like fucking Gruffalo."

"You do," Gallagher agreed. "And the mug looks good too."

"CAMERON HAD a lot to say to you," said Charlotte after taking a much-needed swig from her bottled beer.

"He did," Jack agreed. "Not much of it made sense."

"Oh, that's normal."

His phone buzzed. He looked at it. "I have to take this," he said.

"Really?"

He squeezed her hand. "Back in Blighty and back to the old responsibilities. The holiday fun never lasts."

Leaving his beer on the table, he slid out and made for the door. He put the phone to his ear as he went.

Anika slid in across from her.

"Here, this one's yours." She pushed a box across the table to Charlotte. Charlotte opened it. It was a mug with a horrifically widened version of her staff ID picture printed onto it. Anika laughed at it. "They are terrible."

"They are," said Charlotte. "These are just the funniest things ever!"

"Cameron has a knack for putting his foot right in it."

"He has no idea these are so bad, does he?"

Anika showed Charlotte her own mug. "Makes me look like my mum, which is more than a bit disturbing."

"A glimpse into your future, huh?"

"I've actually done well this week," said Anika. "I think I might have a future in retail or events or something."

"I can believe that," said Charlotte. She held up her mug as though making a toast. Anika chinked hers against it. "Bright futures for you at Hedgelord, Anika."

Karen hurried over to the table and shook Anika. "She's finally brought her date inside. Come! Come!"

Charlotte frowned as Anika stood. "What is it?"

"Sophie's brought her internet date to the party," said Karen.

GALLAGHER GAVE Jack Hartigan a cursory nod as the man made for the exit, phone to his ear. But Cameron, unable to pick on social cues even when he wasn't drunk, grabbed Jack as he went past.

"Mate, mate. I am so sorry I didn't get you a mug."

"It's okay," said Jack. "I didn't expect a mug."

"Oh, no. You're upset, aren't you?"

"No," said Jack tugging away and pointing at his phone. "Just got to do this. Marcus and Maremba finally realise I'm back in the country, so it's back to the old routine. Just need to sort out this one thing." He put his phone to his ear. "No, Maremba, I'd rather not come and explain things personally right now but—"

The sound he made as he was interrupted indicated that perhaps Jack wasn't going to get his own way.

Jack pulled away from Cameron and nearly walked into Sophie from the café, who was walking in with a tall gentleman on her arm. Her date. Gallagher did a double take. It was Snømann. It was the crate-delivering, threat-making, drug-dealing criminal Snømann.

"What the fuck is he doing here?" whispered Luka.

Sophie stepped forward, looking as pleased as punch to have this fucking monster on her arm. Gallagher found he couldn't even breathe.

"Well, hello you!" said Karen, bustling through to greet them. "Finally, you're here. And you've brought your fella. Welcome!"

Sophie made introductions. "Marti, this is my friend and colleague, Karen. Karen, this is Marti."

Snømann took Karen's hand and shook it gently. "I am delighted to be here," he said.

"That accent. It's delightful," said Karen.

"My English is clumsy," said Snømann and managed a sincere looking smile.

"And this..." said Sophie with a sweeping gesture to the rest of the nearby people. "These are my colleagues."

Marti Snømann inhaled deeply, as though breathing them all in. "I feel much warmth and friendship here. I look forward to being around and seeing very much more of you all. Much, much more." His sparkling eyes latched onto Cameron. "This is the big boss man. Perhaps he and I should discuss business sometime."

Luka and Gallagher exchanged a numb glance.

80

CHARLOTTE

By the time Charlotte finished her beer, Jack had not come back. She peeled off the bottle label and shredded it on the tabletop. Jack still didn't return.

She took out her phone to message him and saw there was a message from Jack already waiting.

I've had to go. Sorry. Just a momentary thing.

This was not the message she wanted or expected.

Karen and Anika were sitting at a table together, watching Sophie and her date try to slow dance to Daffyd and Tom's rendition of East 17's *Stay Another Day*. Gallagher and Luka were sitting next to them, seemingly on a mission to down as much alcohol in one night as possible.

Charlotte approached their table. "Hello ladies," she said.

Anika looked at her and smiled. "Hi."

"Jack who I came in with..."

"Jack from Bloomers?" said Anika.

"That Jack, yes. Did you see when he left?"

Karen blew out her lips. "Dunno. About ten minutes ago."

"He had to go," said Gallagher.

"Yeah. Cameron reckoned he was hoping to hook up with girlfriend or something," said Karen.

"What? Kathryn?"

"Yeah, that's her. He's, you know, a one-woman man. You and him weren't...?" She made a vague gesture which didn't mean anything, but which Charlotte understood perfectly. "You didn't think he and you would...?"

Charlotte's hurt look must have been blatantly obvious.

"Oh, hun. As you said, he's not the cheating type," said Karen.

Charlotte felt something horrid welling inside her. "Are you sure that he's gone to Kathryn? Are you absolutely sure that's what Cameron said?"

Karen made a deliberately concentrated frown as she tried to remember.

"Cameron said he'd spoken to Jack. Jack had said the whole thing with the rug had been cleared up."

"The rug," said Charlotte.

"Though I don't know what that means. And he said that Jack was on a promise tonight."

Gallagher nodded. "Jack said he was back in the country so it's back to the old routine."

"The holiday fun never lasts," said Charlotte hollowly, recalling Jack's words.

She looked at the message on her phone again.

I've had to go. Sorry. Just a momentary thing.

That's what she had been to him. A momentary thing.

Oh, God. How could she have been so stupid?

"Excuse me," she said in a small voice and, with her ugly mug in hand, walked out into the car park.

The night was dark and bitterly cold. A scattering of snow, some melted and refrozen again covered the ground. The world beyond the car park was dark and silent, but for the distant lights of the supermarket near the roundabout and the faint glow of the town beyond.

She clenched her hands around the stupid, stupid gift Cameron had given her.

"You fucking mug!" she yelled and hurled it into the night.

It hit the roof of a car by chance rather than by design and smashed into pieces. It wasn't enough.

She made fists and yelled at the sky.

"*Fuuuuuuuuuuck*! Fucking fucking fuck *fuck*! You goat-brained, shit-spewing, cum-juggling *fuckmonger*! Fucking rat-bastard cockweasel dingleberry *assclowns*!"

Her profanity-detecting app was buzzing like a coked-up bee with all the words coming out of her mouth.

And even that was not enough. She took a deep breath and just screamed at the sky. And if the angels in Heaven were shocked by the violence of her outburst, they could just come down and have words with her about it.

Jack fucking Hartigan! He'd taken advantage of her ferry tickets and used her to achieve his own aims while they bumbled and raced their way across Europe! He'd fucked her in a Stockholm hotel room like she was some cheap one night stand! And then! And then when they'd completed their mission, he'd what? Patched things up with stupid

Kathryn, given in to whatever the argument was over their expensive rug and run back to the old girlfriend? The bastard!

But then a thought struck her. She plunged her hand in her coat pocket. She fumbled around for a second, for a thing so tiny it was possible to completely miss it. But she found it and dug it out.

The SD card taken from Alejandro was such a small thing, but Jack had forgotten it. Now, she had the power to strike back at that conniving and manipulative user in the worst way imaginable!

81

ANIKA

On Saturday morning, Anika strolled at a relaxed pace into Hedgelord.

She had had a few drinks at the Hedgelord staff party and enjoyed it for what it was but, tired after a week of running around after everyone else, she had decided to go home at a sensible time. At midnight her parents had still been up, her dad watching *Die Hard 4.0*. Anika was unfamiliar with it, knowing only it was the one where Bruce Willis finally went bald for the role. The villain appeared very angry that his underlings weren't doing what he wanted them to. After the week she'd had, Anika could empathise.

She'd gone to bed and slept deeply.

In the Hedgelord shop she found a number of café staff still cleaning up the mess from the night before. Anika noticed that quite a number of gift mugs had been left behind after the party: a mass of hideous stretched faces.

Sophie was merrily tidying them up and putting them with the cups they handed out to café customers.

The Saturday rota had Anika down as just doing some bog standard elfing in the grotto. With Charlotte back she should be able to focus on pure elfing, even if it was only for the weekend. Thinking on such things reminded her that if Santa Seamus was as good as his word then he should be coming in at some point to take over the Santa Claus duties.

She swerved, turning in the direction of the main office. She'd need to make Charlotte aware of that change, and maybe ask what the problem had been with Santa Raymond to make his removal so urgent. Thinking on Seamus, she was also reminded of the reporter from the Echo and the possibility of some good press for Hedgelord to come out of the terrible accident the day before.

By the time she reached the office door, she'd found the Echo's website and was chuffed to see the Santa Seamus story as the number two story on the page, below the accident itself. The story came with a big picture of a cheery Santa Seamus standing with a smiling Anika the elf.

Santa Seamus vows to keep Christmas magic alive.

They had actually gone with Seamus's headline.

"As the most famous Santa around people know the joy I take in my work," said Seamus (65). "I give a hundred and ten percent. I am going to bring some of that same magic to the grotto at Hedgelord."

Anika was grinning as she entered the office.

Charlotte, wearing a thick winter coat, was slumped on her desk, asleep. Her face half rested on her coat sleeve and half on her computer keyboard.

"You been asleep here all night?" said Anika.

Charlotte mumbled something but did not wake. Anika approached, and saw what was on Charlotte's screen.

"Oh. My. God," she whispered.

Charlotte came awake with a start, snorted, and looked up at Anika. "Ugh. I didn't mean to fall asleep..."

Anika pointed at the images on the screen. "Oh, God, where did you find that?"

Blearily, Charlotte sat up. There was the imprint of several keyboard keys across her cheek. She wiped away a little drool and looked at the screen. "Find it? I put it there."

"What?"

Anika didn't consider herself to have had a wholly sheltered life, but she did not spend any of her time looking at porn sites. The sheer quantity of colourful *jiggling* videos on display in the space of single computer screen was both eye-catching and mind-blowing. Acres of pink and brown flesh, visible from all angles, offered tantalising promises of what might be viewed if one clicked on that particular thumbnail. But Anika's attention was almost entirely held by a looping video in the centre of the screen in which Santa Seamus was doing something vigorous and unholy to what appeared to be a fake, life-size reindeer.

"W-w-why?" she whispered. "Why would you do that? Why would *anyone* do that?"

Charlotte's voice was husky, bitter and vengeful. "I've uploaded that video to LubeTube, TitTok, InstaCum and Porn4U dot com. It's Santa Seamus."

"I can see that," said Anika, stunned. "And my mind

circles around again to 'why'? Why, Charlotte? Why would you do that?"

"Because Jack Hartigan betrayed me. He took advantage of me when I was at a low point and just used me to get what he wanted. I was his ... his holiday fling before he went back to that stuck up slag, Kathryn."

"Okay," said Anika, her mind frantically trying to swim back to the calm waters of normality. "First up, let's have less of the female-shaming language, Charlotte."

"Are you lecturing me, elf?"

"Yes, I bloody well am," said Anika, finding a nugget of anger for herself. "I don't know if Jack betrayed you. Frankly, I don't care. But I have spent this last week holding the fort. I have stopped one disaster after another, and I come back to find you trying to ruin everything."

"No – you see Seamus works for Bloomers. I deleted the one of Santa Raymond. It's gone. All gone. We're in the clear. But those fuckers over at Bloomers are going to get what they deserve."

"No!" Anika snapped. "It's us! We're going to get whatever you think Bloomers deserves!"

"What? No. I—"

She was interrupted from speaking further by Daffyd and Tom rushing into the office, both trying to squeeze through the door at the same time. They each had a mobile phone held out in their hands.

"Have you seen this?" said Tom, panicked.

"I was telling her!" said Daffyd.

"No. You told me and now I'm telling her," snapped Tom.

He waved his phone. "Daffyd sent me a link to this ... this horrible video."

"People are finding it already?" said Charlotte.

"I found it when ... I was also sent a link," said Daffyd. "By, er, a concerned friend who accidentally went onto a porn site when searching for, um, tractors."

"Our Santa is in a porn video!" said Tom.

"No," said Charlotte. "There's not a video of Raymond, is there?"

"I'm talking about Seamus!" said Tom. "He's doing something ... something... I don't think I'll ever be able to watch Bambi again."

Charlotte's mouth was open. "Seamus isn't our..." She saw the look on Anika's face and finally got it. "But..."

"We hired Seamus yesterday," said Anika.

"Then we unhire him!"

Daffyd was reading from his phone. Anika recognised the words immediately.

"Santa Seamus is pleased to join the team at Hedgelord and continue Raymond's good work... Er... I give a hundred and ten percent. I am going to bring some of that same magic to the grotto at Hedgelord..."

"It's in the papers," said Anika.

"He's going to bring the same magic to our grotto," said Tom, his voice cold and dead.

"A hundred and ten percent," said Daffyd. "Oh, heck."

Charlotte, panting in alarm, looked from one person to the next to the next. "I didn't mean to..." she whispered.

The door opened and Jack Hartigan stepped in. Unlike

Charlotte he looked fresh and well-rested. As fresh as the big bouquet of winter flowers he carried in his hand.

"I came by to apologise for running out last night," he said. "The bosses needed to catch me up on some work stuff, but I'm here for you now."

He realised no one was moving. He looked at the stunned faces around him and smiled nervously.

"Okay, what did I miss?"

ABOUT THE AUTHOR

Heide Goody lives in North Warwickshire with her family and pets.

Iain Grant lives in South Birmingham with his family and pets.

They are both married, but not to each other,

ALSO BY HEIDE GOODY AND IAIN GRANT

Rise of the Elves

The explosive finale to The Festive and the Furious Christmas comedy trilogy.

It's nearly Christmas, and Hedgelord Garden Centre is under new ownership — but something isn't right. Sinister figures in black have taken over the shop floor, efficiency is at an all-time high, and nobody seems to know exactly who's in charge or what they're building in the warehouse.

Charlotte Mitchell would love to get to the bottom of it, but she's got bigger problems. Thanks to a spectacularly bad decision, she and her longtime rival Jack Hartigan have just destroyed the town's famous nativity scene — and promptly been sacked.

Now jobless, aimless, and deeply unaccustomed to being on the outside, Charlotte is struggling to accept her new reality. But when one last reckless plan drags her and Jack into a high-stakes undercover mission, they uncover something far worse than corporate restructuring.

With gun-toting gangsters, tooled-up Santas, and wildly inappropriate cracker gifts, Christmas is heading for a disaster of biblical proportions.

Can Charlotte put the pieces back together, uncover the truth, and save Christmas once and for all?

Rise of the Elves

Clovenhoof

Getting fired can ruin a day...

...especially when you were the Prince of Hell.

Will Satan survive in English suburbia?

Corporate life can be a soul draining experience, especially when the industry is Hell, and you're Lucifer. It isn't all torture and brimstone, though, for the Prince of Darkness, he's got an unhappy Board of Directors.

The numbers look bad.

They want him out.

Then came the corporate coup.

Banished to mortal earth as Jeremy Clovenhoof, Lucifer is going through a mid-immortality crisis of biblical proportion. Maybe if he just tries to blend in, it won't be so bad.

He's wrong.

If it isn't the murder, cannibalism, and armed robbery of everyday life in Birmingham, it's the fact that his heavy metal band isn't getting the respect it deserves, that's dampening his mood.

And the archangel Michael constantly snooping on him, doesn't help.

If you enjoy clever writing, then you'll adore this satirical tour de force, because a good laugh can make you have sympathy for the devil.

Get it now.

Clovenhoof

Sealfinger

Meet Sam Applewhite, security consultant for DefCon4's east coast office. .

She's clever, inventive and adaptable. In her job she has to be.

Now, she's facing an impossible mystery.

A client has gone missing and no one else seems to care.

Who would want to kill an old and lonely woman whose only sins are having a sharp tongue and a belief in ghosts? Could her death be linked to the new building project out on the dunes?

Can Sam find out the truth, even if it puts her friends' and family's lives at risk?

Sealfinger

Printed in Dunstable, United Kingdom